FIC
NEUHARTH

ALSO BY
Jan Neuharth

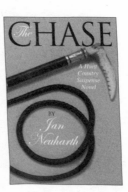

K*The*ILL

A NOVEL BY
Jan Neuharth

PAPER CHASE FARMS PUBLISHING GROUP
MIDDLEBURG, VIRGINIA

Published by

Paper Chase Farms Publishing Group

a division of Paper Chase Farms, Inc.

Post Office Box 448

Middleburg, Virginia 20118

www.paperchasefarms.com

www.huntcountrysuspense.com

This novel is a work of fiction. Names, characters, places, organizations, business estab-lishments, events, and incidents are either products of the author's imagination or are used fictitiously. Any resemblance to actual events, locales, or persons, living or dead, is entirely coincidental and not intended by the author. The author's use of names of actual places and streets does not alter the purely fictional character of the work.

Library of Congress Control Number: 2010923108

ISBN: 978-0-9841898-2-3

PRINTED IN THE UNITED STATES OF AMERICA

First Edition

Book and cover design by Judy Walker

www.JudyWalkerDesign.com

For

Dr. Dan

My deepest appreciation and respect go to the talented professionals who worked with me on this book: my editors, Mike Sirota, Nancy Butler-Ross, Lisa Wolff, and Melaina Phipps; photographers, Ruthi David and Susan Whitfield; and my book designer, Judy Walker. You worked with tight deadlines, turned stumbling blocks into solutions, and made the journey fun.

I am indebted to the following folks for lending their expertise to my research efforts and for patiently answering my pesky questions—no matter *how* many times I asked: Ann Heacock, Michael Hoffman, Dave Mazzarella, Keith Meurlin, Will O'Keefe, and Gary Shook; and Janell Hoffman, RN and Dr. Edward Puccio from INOVA Loudoun Hospital Center. Your guidance was invaluable—the fault for any errors or inaccuracies in translating fact to fiction lies solely with me.

Heartfelt thanks to my friends who kept my feet on the ground and kindly gave their time, support, good humor, and sound advice: Janell Hoffman, Fern Kucinski, and Michelle Martinson. I owe you more than dinner for this one.

John Anderson, you went above and beyond the call of friendship, and your keen eye helped smooth out the bumps. Thank you.

Special recognition goes to Michelle Hostler, whose generous contribution to The Fairfax Hunt won her the right to name a character in this novel. Michelle, I hope you enjoy Michelle de Becque as much as I enjoyed brainstorming with you to create her.

Thanks to Al and Dan for their honest feedback and wise counsel, and my mom, Loretta, for her gentle support.

Love, gratitude, and hugs to Joseph, Dani, and A.J., for enduring late nights and long weekends, for tolerating those "absent" moments when my thoughts drifted to the characters living in my head, and for tirelessly helping sort out plot scenarios—especially the rescue scene. You helped in more ways than you can know.

A GLOSSARY OF EQUESTRIAN TERMS
CAN BE FOUND AT THE BACK OF THIS BOOK.

CHAPTER

1

A shot exploded in the hushed twilight and grumbled through fog in the hollows. The report cracked back through soggy crimson leaves, then faded into a stillness that swaddled the rambling Virginia countryside. On a nearby knoll, a lone buck darted for cover in the surrounding woods. The bite of gunpowder hugged the raw air.

The shooter lowered the rifle and leaned it against the rail. Adrenaline pumped hard, but the shooter curbed the swell of triumph, sucked in a deep breath, and exhaled a cloud that oozed into the dusk.

Focus. Wipe off the prints.

The stock tie around the shooter's neck was fixed in a square knot, fastened with a gold safety pin. The shooter flicked the pin open and tugged the tie loose. The white cotton, crisp from the dry cleaner, softened as the gun was wiped clean, extra care taken in rubbing the walnut-burl stock. Squinting at the gun in the dwindling light, the shooter admired how the tiny imperfections added to the beauty of the swirls in the wood. It was custom-made, of course. What a pity to have to leave it behind.

Riding boots clunked hollowly against the gray wood planks of the elevated deck, but no effort was made to tread quietly. The closest farm was half a mile away. The only person within earshot was dead, or would be soon.

Sidestepping a dark puddle, the shooter squatted next to the body, extended two fingers, and checked for a pulse. Wide blue eyes stared vacantly, ghostlike in the shadowy dusk.

Satisfied, the shooter grasped the rifle with both ends of the stock tie and placed it on the deck, tipping the body just enough to wiggle a wallet out of the dead man's back pocket. Letting the body fall back down, the shooter slid the sleeve on the dead man's left wrist to expose a gold Rolex watch. The temperature had plummeted with the setting sun, causing the shooter's fingers to move stiffly as they worked to release the catch on the band and slide the timepiece over the dead man's hand.

A fox screamed somewhere in the woods and a shiver tingled down the shooter's spine. Smiling, the shooter rose and fingered a salute at the dead man.

Good night, Master.

*A*bigale Portmann resisted the urge to guide the mare and avoided looking down at the sheer cliff to her right. She let the sure-footed Arab choose her own way along the craggy path.

"Jesus Christ, Portmann." Fear raised the pitch of the reporter's voice in front of her. "Of all the stupid things I've ever done to get a story, this is by far the stupidest. Why the hell didn't you talk me out of it?"

Abigale tugged the scarf away from her frozen mouth. "Don't try to ride him, Joe," she called, unsure whether he could hear her or if the driving wind swallowed up her words. "Just give him his head. He doesn't want to fall any more than you do."

"Fuck."

The horse's head shot straight up in the air. Abigale could tell it was getting increasingly irritated with Joe's death grip. Joe yanked on the left rein, trying to steer the horse around a sharp turn that skirted the precipitous drop. The horse fought to escape Joe's heavy hand, danced to the right, and teetered on the edge of the pass. Abigale gasped as its right hind hoof punched air, searched for a foothold, then found firm footing back on the trail.

One of the Afghan trackers on foot slipped back and grabbed the horse's bridle, scolding Joe in Dari. Even though Joe didn't understand the Afghan language, Abigale was pretty certain he'd get the drift of what the tracker was saying.

Their ten-horse team had been climbing the mountain since daybreak, in blinding sleet and snow for the last couple of hours. Icicles hung from the horses' manes and the eyebrows of the tracker leading Joe's horse. Abigale eyed the packhorse carrying their laptops, satellite phones, and her camera equipment. The Reuters name on their gear was obliterated by snow and ice.

Joe and she had huddled in the hotel bar in Kabul deep into the night, bouncing back and forth two questions: How big is the story? How grave are the risks? In the end, they'd both agreed gaining access to the remote encampment justified the trek through the mountain pass to the Panjshir Valley. Yet both knew their quest for the elusive story might be a death sentence.

Abigale shifted against the blankets that served as a saddle, trying to keep her circulation moving. Despite Joe's fear that his horse would plunge off the trail, she knew their greater danger was freezing to death in the sudden blizzard. Horses were survivors, most of them. Even the rogue ones that didn't care if they unseated their riders didn't want to hurt themselves. But, accidents happened. The snapshot of a beautiful chestnut mare flashed through Abigale's mind. No surprise. This was the first time she'd sat on a horse since that night in Virginia. She shoved the thought away.

Still, the feel of the horse between Abigale's legs unlocked dusty childhood memories: foxhunting, showing, lazy summer hacks. Maybe Uncle Richard was right, she should go back. Enough time had passed. Perhaps this year—if her mother was well enough to travel from Switzerland—they'd accept her uncle's invitation to spend Christmas with him at Dartmoor Glebe.

Abigale's belly clenched at the mere thought of it. Who was she kidding? It would take much more than that to persuade her to return to the Virginia hunt country.

3

*S*wollen clouds hugged the spine of the Blue Ridge, spilling tendrils of fog over the patchwork of horse farms sprawled lazily across the Shenandoah Valley. Margaret Southwell eyed the drab morning sky and flicked the wiper lever up a notch as her pickup truck clunked through a pothole on St. Louis Road.

"Looks like the *Farmer's Almanac* let us down, Duchess. So much for an October with below-normal rainfall and record warmth." The yellow Lab beside Margaret opened her eyes and thumped her tail leisurely against the worn leather seat. Margaret scratched the dog behind the ear. "Aw, I know, it makes no difference to you. You'll head straight for the pond and end up wet anyway."

She eased the truck around the blind curve that hid the entrance to the steeplechase racecourse at Longmeadow Park, moaning as her back absorbed the jolt of another pothole. Thank God the repaving project was due to be completed before race day.

Margaret swerved around an abandoned car perched on the shoulder, allowing herself a smile as the chained black iron gates came into view. She was the first to arrive. If she didn't delay, she might have time to unload the snow fence before the rest of the work crew started rolling in. Maybe that would put an end to the recent talk about how she should start taking it easy at her age. Her father had hunted hounds into his late eighties, retired as master at the age of ninety-one, and her mother had hunted—sidesaddle, mind you—until she was seventy-nine. With that gene pool she didn't plan on slowing down anytime soon. Besides, they said seventy was the new sixty.

Margaret parked the truck in front of the gates and tugged a waxed rain hat over her tightly permed gray curls. "Stay put, Duchess. I'll be right back." She grabbed her Barbour coat off the seat back and opened the door, shrugging into the olive-green jacket as she stepped down from the cab.

The ornamental gates squawked in protest as Margaret swung them inward, one at a time, fastening each side with an iron hook to the sturdy white wooden fencing that bordered the 250-acre estate. She drove through the entrance and followed the gravel road, which dipped and swelled with the terrain as it wound around the perimeter of the steeplechase course. The blazing hues of crimson and gold foliage provided a brilliant backdrop to the foggy, faded green of the racecourse. Margaret inhaled deeply, capturing the serenity. On Sunday, white tents and catering trucks would top the berm and five thousand or so partying race fans would dot the landscape: the locals in tweeds and sensible shoes; the women from Washington fashionably dressed, teetering around the rugged landscape on spiky heels.

Margaret topped a rise and the parking area by the stewards' stand came into view, revealing Richard Evan Clarke's silver Lexus SUV parked in the lot. Her mouth puckered into a frown. That was peculiar. If Richard had arrived before her, why hadn't he left the front gates open?

She pulled her truck up next to the SUV with the shiny new foxhunting license plate: SLVRFOX. The personalized plate was Richard's comeback to the countless old-fart jokes he'd had to stomach on his seventieth birthday. Of course, the moniker was nothing new. It was common knowledge that several ladies in the hunt had referred to Richard as the "silver fox" for years—a blatant reference to his movie-star looks, not his age.

Margaret leaned over and peered through the rain-streaked passenger window into the Lexus. Empty. She scanned the grassy panorama. No sign of Richard. That meant he must be working on the far side of the course. The timber on several fences needed to be repaired, and with all the rain the drainage ditch on the far turn would need to be opened. Still, Richard should have waited for Smitty to come with the Gator rather than traipsing that far on foot. Stubborn old workhorse! Just last week, she'd had a heart-to-heart with Richard, pointed out now that he was in his twentieth season as master of the Middleburg Foxhounds, it was due time others helped shoulder more of the burden. But, from the look of things, her advice had just gone in one ear and out the other.

Margaret killed her pickup's engine and opened the door. She should be able to spot him from the upper deck of the stewards' stand. "Come on, Duchess. Let's go find Richard."

The Lab slid stiffly from the cab, sniffed at the blowing mist that blasted her face, and stretched into a walk, nose to the ground, heading in the direction of the pond.

Margaret tugged a box of race programs from behind her seat and shouldered the truck door closed. "Hold on, girl. I have a delivery to make first. Then you can have your swim."

Duchess circled back and they set off toward the stewards' stand, Margaret's Wellies crunching on the bluestone path. She noted the way the two-story green and gray wooden tower glistened through the drizzle and gave a grunt of satisfaction. What a difference the fresh coat of paint made! She had raised hell when Richard had suggested they could get by another year without a paint job. What kind of an impression would that make on the race announcer and judges? Not to mention the horde of VIPs. It would be like inviting guests for dinner and using mismatched everyday dishes just because you were too lazy to hand-wash the good china.

A pair of crows circled the weathered cedar-shingle roof, cawing as they landed on the railing of the under deck. *Damn birds.* She and Richard had spent the better part of a morning scraping droppings off the railing before the paint job. Now the crows were back, mucking it up again. Margaret pursed her lips at the sight of the plastic owl perched on the center of the rail. She had told Richard it wouldn't do a lick of good, that he was just throwing good money away, but he had insisted on buying the damn thing anyway. She figured it could only be pride that prevented him from removing the useless deterrent, given the fact that the crows used it as a roosting place.

Margaret waved her hand toward the stand. "Go on, Duchess. Go get 'em, girl."

Duchess cocked her head and looked at Margaret, her tail swaying in a low wag.

One of the crows let out a loud caw and Margaret gestured toward the stand again. "Go on. Shoo them out of there!"

Duchess barked and bounded toward the stewards' stand.

"Good girl. Go get them."

The Lab disappeared up the stairs and Margaret chuckled as she watched the crows take flight. "That's a girl, Duchess. You found yourself a new job."

As she shifted the box of programs to her left arm and reached for the stair railing, Duchess's bark deepened to a growl.

Margaret grasped the handrail. "It's okay, girl. That's enough. You scared them away."

Duchess responded with a shrill bark and Margaret tilted her head toward the top level of the stewards' stand, attempting to see the Lab through the slats in the gray stairs. What on earth had gotten into her? Had the crows flown back? She reached the mid-deck landing and as she rounded the corner she saw Duchess backed against the rear railing of the top deck, a growl rumbling in her throat.

"All right, Duchess. That's enough."

Duchess's brown eyes flitted toward Margaret, then back across the stewards' stand.

Margaret neared the top of the stairs and stretched up on her tiptoes to peer at the outside rail. The crows were gone. So what was Duchess raising such a ruckus about? The knee-wall blocked Margaret's view of the deck flooring, but from what she could see the top level was completely empty except—

She cackled as her eyes settled on the plastic owl. "Duchess, you silly dog. That bird won't be flying anywhere, no matter how hard you try to scare it off. Come on over here and I'll show you. It's just a useless blob of plastic."

She patted her thigh as she rounded the corner. "Come on—"

A moan swelled in Margaret's chest. The box of programs thudded to the deck and spilled down the steps.

She stumbled forward and dropped to her knees beside Richard.

Winfield Smith braked at the sight of the string of taillights, easing the truck and utility trailer to a crawl. He spotted a road crew about twenty cars ahead and saw a worker clad in a yellow rain poncho twirl a sign, switching the display from a red STOP to an orange SLOW.

The line of vehicles crept forward, but when Smitty was one car from the work crew, the worker twirled the sign to STOP again. *Didn't that just figure?* Margaret and Richard were probably already at Longmeadow, cooling their heels, waiting for him to arrive with the Gator so they could get to work. The paving project had been under way for almost two weeks and the traffic snarl had delayed him on his way to Longmeadow more than once. He knew if he blamed his tardiness today on the paving Richard would commiserate with him, but Margaret would probably just give him that look of hers and tell him he should have left earlier. And she was right. There was no excuse for it. He was the huntsman, and the huntsman shouldn't keep the master waiting.

Smitty blew out a sigh. He drummed his fingers on the steering wheel as he eyed a handful of workers shooting the breeze next to a nearby asphalt truck. Taxpayer dollars hard at work.

There was a lull in the flow after a dozen or so cars snaked through the work zone and the worker spun the sign back around, waving the first car forward. Smitty nosed his truck into the oncoming lane, but as he hit the gas a hefty man clutching a two-way radio shot into the lane and jerked a hand up to stop him. The man's face reddened as he shouted something at the worker directing traffic flow.

Smitty hunched his shoulders and raised his hands at the man. *Now what?*

The man wagged his head, muttering, as he strode over to Smitty's truck.

Smitty lowered the window, blinking as the mist coated his eyelashes.

"Sorry about that," the man said, eyeing Smitty from beneath his rain hood. "Dumb kid saw a lull in the traffic so he went ahead and waved you on without waiting for the go-ahead from the other end." He yanked a shoulder at the work site and Smitty saw two approaching vehicles. The car that had been in front of him in line eased onto the shoulder to allow them to pass.

"Looks like you got yourself a long day ahead of you," Smitty said.

The man snorted. "You got that right. The worker who normally mans the sign didn't show up today so this kid's filling in. He doesn't know what the fuck he's doing."

The two cars rolled by and he patted Smitty's door. "Okay, you're good to go."

"Have yourself a good one," Smitty said, raising the window. Loose bits of fresh asphalt pinged beneath the truck as he eased through the work area. On the other side, he waved at a second flagman and punched the accelerator. He was no longer tardy now, he was downright late.

He rounded the bend just before the entrance to Longmeadow and sped past a rusted blue sedan parked on the shoulder with a white rag hanging off its gas cap. As he cleared the gates to the racecourse and began to bounce along the gravel road, someone tooted a horn behind him. Smitty shot a glance at the rearview mirror and saw Thompson James's Ford Explorer. He braked to a stop and lowered his window as Thompson swerved onto the grass and pulled even with him.

"Morning, Thompson. Glad to see you made it. Margaret told me you weren't going to be able to join the work party today."

"I wasn't. I was on my way to the office when I got an emergency dispatch for this location, so I turned around."

In addition to being treasurer of the hunt, Thompson was a member of the volunteer rescue squad. Smitty saw the whirl of flashing blue lights on the windshield of the SUV. He frowned. "Here? What's the emergency?"

"There's a gunshot victim. That's all I know from the dispatch." Thompson jerked his head toward the rise to his left. "In the stewards' stand."

"Good God almighty."

CHAPTER
5

*A*bigale was photographing troops near the encampment when an incoming artillery shell shrieked through the afternoon sky. Before she could dive for cover, the shell blasted into the ridge to her right. The concussion slammed her to the ground. She hugged the craggy terrain for a moment, unsure whether another round from the Taliban would follow, then gingerly pushed herself up and checked to make sure she wasn't bleeding. Her body ached as if she'd been sucker-punched by a giant fist, but nothing seemed broken. She searched for Joe, saw him writhing on the ground twenty feet away, clutching his calf through blood-soaked khakis. She scrambled over, reaching him just as a medic did.

The medic peeled back Joe's pant leg. "You've got a shrapnel wound!" He shouted to be heard as the Allied troops fired back with their own artillery.

"Bloody hell!" Joe screamed. "It feels like it blew off half my fucking leg."

"You'll be okay," the medic said.

Someone yelled for the medic, pointing to a soldier who was down.

"Go on. That soldier looks worse off. I can bandage his leg," Abigale said.

"Thanks." The medic threw a handful of supplies at her. "I'll send someone over to help move him."

Joe moaned as Abigale pressed a wad of surgical pads to the angry wound. His bearded face twisted into a grimace, narrow lips stretched tight with pain. "Jesus fucking Christ, Portmann. Take it easy."

She grabbed his hand and jammed it against the dressing. "Hold this. Tight. You need to put pressure on it to stop the bleeding."

"I hope the hell you know what you're doing."

"Don't worry, I've wrapped horses' legs a hundred times."

"That's supposed to make me feel better? I'm not a fucking horse!"

She smiled, hurriedly wound gauze around Joe's leg, and tied it off as two soldiers hauled him away to the medical tent.

Another shell whistled toward the ridge and Abigale ran for the nearby trench, where she huddled with several of her colleagues to wait out the artillery fight. They joked, trying to make light of the situation.

"Joe's probably happier than hell he took some shrapnel so he'll get a chopper ride out of here," Alex, an AP photographer, said. "He's been working to come up with an exit strategy since the minute he jumped off that goddamned horse. He told me he'd stay here until the spring thaw if he had to."

"The horse saved Joe's bacon more than once," Abigale said. "He's lucky the horse didn't send him sailing over the cliff, the way he was jerking on its mouth."

Alex reached over and gave Abigale's ponytail a playful tug. "Isn't that just like our girl, standing up for the underdog."

"Trust me, Joe was the underdog, not the horse."

A crusty veteran from *The Daily Telegraph* plucked a flask from his pocket and sucked down a swallow. "Neither wind nor rain nor dark of night—nor a bloody horse—shall keep us from a story," he said, raising the flask in a toast.

Abigale smiled absently, cradling her camera in her hands. The recent blasts of outgoing fire had gone unanswered. She eyed the faded sky. Was it safe to leave the trench?

"Look at Abigale . . ." The Brit's eyes watered as he choked his way through a raspy smoker's cough. "She's just itching to get back out there and risk having her lovely arse blown off."

"Maybe you should take a page from her playbook, old chap," Alex said, grinning. "Abigale didn't win herself a Pulitzer by hunkering down in a trench."

CHAPTER

6

*M*argaret shifted against the wooden bench on the mid-level deck of the stewards' stand and pulled the blanket tighter around her, vaguely aware of the disagreeable smell of wet wool, the scratch of the fabric against the back of her neck. Duchess stirred at her feet, stood, circled, then lay down again, snorting a sigh as she rested her head on Margaret's boots.

The stench of blood hung in Margaret's nostrils. Her eyes stole back to the floorboards of the deck above her and her stomach heaved. She took slow breaths, determined not to vomit again. Nausea rose, then settled back down with a shudder.

Footsteps clopped up the stairs toward her. It was Thompson James and the balding, round-faced deputy who'd been so kind when he'd questioned her earlier. She stood to meet them, a blast of wind coating her face with a chilly mist. Duchess scrambled to her feet and settled protectively against Margaret's leg.

Thompson's eyes darted anxiously beneath the brim of a baseball cap, snaking from Margaret to the deck above. "God, Margaret, I can't believe this. What happened? Are you okay?"

She let the blanket slide from her shoulders and held it out toward the deputy. "I'm okay, but I need to get out of here."

"Of course," Thompson said, nodding. "We can sit in the ambulance. It will be warm in there."

Margaret saw Thompson's gaze drift to her outstretched hand, no doubt taking in the noticeable tremble. She shoved the blanket at the deputy. "Nonsense. I don't need an ambulance, Thompson. I just can't sit here any longer."

"Sure. I understand."

"Come on, Duchess." Margaret nudged the dog with her knee as she slipped between Thompson and the deputy and grabbed the stair railing, concentrating on sidestepping race programs as she picked her way down the stairs.

A small group was swarming around the ambulance and sheriff's cars. Several brown-uniformed sheriff deputies. A handful of rescue workers. A Virginia state trooper, his rain poncho gusting in the breeze. A two-way radio crackled from one of the cars.

Rain plastered Margaret's hair as she stepped out from the stewards' stand and she realized she'd lost her rain hat somewhere. She turned her collar up against the bone-chilling trickles dribbling down her neck.

Through the blur of activity she spotted Smitty. He faced away from her, huddled in conversation with Carol Simpson, the head of the rescue squad, and one of the deputies, his hands flying here and there as he spoke.

She weaved her way through the group to Smitty and put a hand on his shoulder. He spun around, his distress visible in the twist of his mouth, the stubborn thrust of his jaw. "What in God's name is going on, Margaret? They're telling me Richard got shot, but won't tell me a goddamned thing beyond that." He pawed at the tweed cap on his head, wagged a hand toward Carol. "Carol here let Thompson up in the stand, I guess because he's an EMT, but won't let me get within ten yards of there. Never mind that I've known Richard for north of twenty-five years. That—"

"Smitty." Margaret looked him in the eye. "Richard's dead."

Smitty sagged as if someone had let the air out of him. The tip of his nose reddened and he sucked the inside of one cheek, making a popping noise with his lips as he blew out a breath. "What in God's name happened?"

She glanced at Thompson and the deputy as they approached, feeling fat raindrops mix with tears on her cheeks. "I don't know. Richard was dead when I found him."

"But Carol said Richard got shot. Who shot him? Was it an accident?"

The round-faced deputy stepped forward. "We're treating it as a criminal homicide."

"A homicide!"

"Richard's wallet is missing," Margaret said. "So is his watch."

Smitty frowned. "Are you thinking a robbery gone bad or something?"

"We haven't ruled that out," the deputy replied.

"Here at Longmeadow?"

The deputy raised a shoulder in response.

"But it's in the middle of goddamn nowhere. Ain't no one going to just happen by here, find Richard in the stewards' stand, and decide to rob him."

"We're exploring all possible scenarios," the deputy replied. "Given the fact that Mr. Clarke had no wallet or watch on him, robbery is a strong possibility."

Smitty blew out a breath and his gaze flickered between Margaret and Thompson. "Richard always carried his wallet with him. Even foxhunting."

Margaret nodded.

"But not his watch," Thompson said. "We all know how Richard felt about not letting the clock dictate the duration of a hunt."

"He'd already changed after hunting yesterday," Margaret replied. "He'd have put his watch back on."

"You're right," Thompson said. "He probably was wearing it. Still, he did have a way of forgetting it sometimes. But given that his wallet is missing, it's probably prudent to assume that his watch was stolen as well. Either way, we're still talking robbery." He thought for a moment. "What about his cell phone? Did they take it?"

"No, but it wasn't on him. We found his cell phone in his Lexus," the deputy said.

"I hear what y'all are saying," Smitty said. "But . . . a robbery, here? Who would do that?"

Thompson said, "There's a road crew paving near here on St. Louis Road. I just drove through there and saw a couple of rough-looking characters. It probably bears checking out."

The deputy tilted his head as if weighing the possibility, nodding slowly as he wrote something on his notepad. "Could be. Mr. Clarke might have tried to resist and they grabbed his hunting rifle and shot him."

Thompson's jaw dropped. "*What?* Richard was shot with his own rifle?"

*M*argaret saw the ache in Smitty's eyes as the deputy explained that Richard's rifle was found beside his body in the stewards' stand. She knew Smitty was thinking the same thing she had been when she'd first seen Richard's gun lying next to him: *suicide.*

The deputy said, "The chest wound is consistent with having been shot from several feet away."

"Then that rules out suicide," Smitty said, his face reddening slightly as if embarrassed for having had the thought.

The deputy nodded.

"But why would Richard have had his rifle with him?" Thompson asked.

"I'll bet I know why," Smitty said. He pulled a handkerchief out of his pant pocket and blew his nose. "Because of the damn coyote, the one's been killing Polly Fanning's sheep."

The deputy waved his pen at Smitty. "Tell me more about that, Mr. . . ."

"Smith. Winfield Smith. But folks call me Smitty."

"Okay, Smitty. Tell me about Mr. Clarke having his rifle here."

"There's been a coyote causing a nuisance at Possum Hollow, the farm just west of here, and Richard and I both spotted it at the racecourse, more than once. Richard mentioned it to Mrs. Fanning, the owner of Possum Hollow, and told her he'd take care of it if he saw it again. He's been bringing his hunting rifle along with him when he comes to work on the course. As far as I know, he kept it in his SUV, but he could've spotted the coyote and taken his rifle up in the stewards' stand to get a better shot at it."

"But why wouldn't they have stolen the rifle?" Thompson said. "As I recall, Richard had it custom-made. It must have had quite some value."

"You got that right," Smitty said. "It's a Savage Model 99. A real beauty. That's probably why they didn't take it. It's one-of-a-kind. Anyone who knows a lick about guns would know they'd have a hard time unloading a beauty like that one without getting caught."

A vibrating cell phone hummed. Thompson reached under his raincoat and dug his phone out of his back pocket. He looked at the display, then at Margaret. "It's Wendy Brooks."

"Answer it."

Thompson flipped it open. "Hi, Wendy."

Margaret heard Wendy say something about the gate.

"Hold on." Thompson lowered the phone from his ear and covered the mouthpiece with his hand. "Wendy's at the gate. She says they've got the whole entrance cordoned off. There are a couple of sheriff's deputies out there."

"Does she know about Richard?"

"No. She said the deputies won't tell her what's going on. She's just upset because they've blocked access and the crew can't get in to work on the racecourse. She called me because she couldn't reach you, Richard, or Smitty. She thinks I'm in Reston, at work."

Margaret heaved a sigh, a breathy cloud that seeped into the mist. "Once word of Richard's death gets out, it's going to spread like wildfire in the community. We owe it to Richard's friends to make sure they hear it from us first."

"I agree."

"Do you know who else is out there with Wendy?"

"I'm not sure."

"Is Manning there?"

Thompson raised his shoulders in an "I-don't-know" shrug.

"Find out."

He pressed the phone to his ear. "Who's there with you, Wendy?"

Thompson nodded slowly, as if counting off the names she mentioned. Margaret tapped her foot, arched an eyebrow, and he said, "Manning's not there?"

He covered the phone. "Manning hasn't shown up. In fact, Wendy said she tried to call Manning a couple of times this morning to remind him that he'd promised to help with the course, but wasn't able to reach him."

Margaret hugged her arms to her chest. "Tell Wendy we're calling off the course work for today. Have her send everyone home."

"Okay."

"And ask Wendy to come to my house. I want to break the news to her. Then we'll start calling folks. I'd like you there, too."

"Of course."

She glanced at Smitty. "And you."

"You bet."

Thompson took a step away as he resumed his conversation with Wendy, and Margaret glanced at the deputy. "Are you finished with me?"

"I believe I have everything I need for now."

Thompson snapped his phone shut and Margaret raised an eyebrow at him and Smitty. "Ready?"

Thompson jerked a thumb toward the ambulance. "Let me just check with Carol and make sure they don't need my help. Then I'll head over to your place."

"All right." Margaret put her arm around Smitty's shoulders. "Do me a favor, Thompson," she said, urging Smitty toward the kennel truck.

"Yes?"

"Find Manning."

he scent of frying bacon wafted over Manning Southwell and a pang of hunger gnawed momentarily at his gut before it somersaulted with nausea. He groaned and rolled over, sliding a pink-and-white striped pillow over his head. Somewhere in the distance a door squeaked, followed by the sound of bare feet padding across the wood floor. Manning squeezed his eyes shut, willing himself back to sleep. His fingers twitched and he started to drift off, only to be jerked awake again by a muffled cell phone belting out a tinny rendition of "Moonlight Serenade." He gritted his teeth, waiting for the tune to fade.

Finally, silence. And then, the nearby shuffling of footsteps on carpet. The creak of a floorboard. Manning lifted a corner of the pillow and raised an eyelid. Julia Farleigh approached slowly, a tray in her hands. Her silky blond hair hung loose and slightly mussed, flirting with the rhinestones that sprawled "Love" across the chest of her thigh-length pink T-shirt.

A smile lit Julia's face when she saw he was awake. "Hey, sleepyhead, I made you some breakfast." She set the tray on the nightstand and the mattress sagged as she perched on the edge of the bed, curling one slender leg beneath her. She lifted a glass off the tray and offered it to him. "Here's fresh-squeezed orange juice."

Manning tried to prop himself up on one elbow, flopped back on the mattress, and let out a moan. "Any chance you have some Tylenol to go with that?"

She held the glass to his lips and he raised his head enough to swallow a gulp, letting the cold juice swish the thickness from his dry mouth.

"You really shouldn't take Tylenol, Manning. Not with the amount of alcohol you consumed last night. Haven't you read the warnings?"

He winced as he let his head sink back and closed his eyes. "That would sound like swell advice if I didn't have a marching band banging in my head right now. Be a sport and get me a pain reliever, will you? And some vodka for the orange juice would be nice."

Julia let out a deliberate sigh and clunked the glass on the tray. "I have some Advil in the medicine cabinet. I'll be right back."

"Moonlight Serenade" blasted again and Julia called out from the bathroom, "You might want to see who that is. Your cell phone's been ringing all morning. Someone must really want to talk to you."

Forcing his eyes in the direction of the music, Manning saw his white riding breeches draped across a wingback chair next to the bed. He reached out and snagged them, fishing his cell out of the back pocket. The ringtone died as he flipped the phone open and squinted at the display: 7 MISSED CALLS. He scrolled down and saw that the first three calls were from Wendy Brooks, the hunt secretary. He glanced at his watch. Ten-thirty. *Shit.* He had promised to be at the racecourse by nine o'clock. Wendy had probably called to chew him out for not showing up.

The other missed calls were identified as PRIVATE. That was no help. Should he place a call back? His thumb hovered over the SEND button when Julia emerged from the bathroom waving a bottle of Advil at him. He palmed the phone shut and tossed it on the bed.

The instant the cell phone landed, it began to ring again. *Christ!* He snatched it up and glanced at the display on the front: PRIVATE. He flipped the phone open and held it to his ear as he extended his other arm to Julia, wiggling his fingers for the Advil.

"Hello."

"Thank God, I finally reached you. It's Thompson." Thompson James's voice bellowed from the receiver and Manning tilted the phone away from his ear.

He held his hand out and watched Julia shake two tablets from the bottle. "One more," he whispered. She gave him a look, but rattled the bottle until another pill dropped into his hand. He tossed the tablets into his mouth and took a gulp of juice.

"Now's not a good time, Thompson," Manning said, wiping his mouth with the back of his hand.

"Well, make it be a good time." Thompson's voice cracked. "I've been trying to track you down for over an hour."

Manning smiled at Julia as she rolled her eyes at the phone. He reached up and toyed with the ends of her hair.

"Manning."

"Yeah, I'm here. So, what's up?"

"It's Richard."

Manning scooted up against the pillow. "What about him?"

"He was shot. He's dead."

"What!" Manning struggled to a sitting position and swung his legs over the side of the bed. "When? What happened?"

"I don't have time to go into details. Just get yourself over to your mother's house. She wants you there, Manning. Now."

"At least give me the headlines. Who shot him?"

Silence.

"Thompson."

Manning jerked the phone away from his ear and looked at the display. DISCONNECTED.

"Damn it." He dropped the phone onto the bed and cradled his head in both hands, doubling over as nausea cramped his stomach.

"What's the matter?" Julia caressed the back of his neck with her long nails.

He glanced at her over his shoulder. "It's Richard Evan Clarke. He's been killed."

"Oh, my God. What happened?"

Manning snatched his briefs from the floor beside the bed and thrust his feet into them. "I don't know, but I've got to get over to Mother's." He stuffed his cell phone into the pocket of his breeches and pulled them on, zipping up as he looked around for his shirt.

"Your shirt's right there," Julia said, pointing a well-manicured finger toward a bench at the foot of the bed.

Manning slipped the shirt on and grabbed his tweed jacket and riding boots off the floor next to the bench. "I'll call you," he said, fumbling with the shirt buttons as he headed toward the door.

"Manning, wait."

He turned around.

"Where are you going? You can't drive anywhere."

"Why not?"

"Your car's still at the Blackthorne. Remember? You were in no condition to drive last night so I brought you home with me."

Manning stared at her, trying to recall some of what had happened the night before.

Julia's plump lips parted in a pouty glare. "You do remember, don't you?"

"Not exactly," he murmured.

"Oh, boy. You were in worse shape than I thought. I guess you've learned to hide it well." Julia slipped out of bed and opened the door to her closet. "Give me a sec. I'll throw on some clothes and give you a lift to your car."

bigale's eyes burned. A fine dusting of Afghan sand coated her lashes and hair. She ran her tongue over parched lips and felt grit crunch between her teeth. She was back at camp, eager to get to her laptop computer so she could view the photos she'd shot on the ridge. But first she needed to check on Joe.

She and Alex wove their way through the medical tent, where they found Joe on a cot hunched over his laptop, pounding away on the keyboard. His leg was bandaged, but other than that he appeared to be okay.

"Don't go getting any ideas about embellishing your account of what happened," Abigale said. "I've got pictures that tell the real story."

Joe spun to face them but didn't crack a smile at Abigale's teasing.

"You lucky son of a bitch, no doubt you earned yourself a first-class ticket out of here," Alex said.

"Yeah, they're putting me on the next chopper. Abigale too."

"*Me?* Why?" Abigale asked.

Joe's eyes flickered to Alex, then back to her. "London's been trying to reach you. There's been a family emergency."

Abigale's heart lurched in her chest. "My mother."

"No," Joe said. "Your mother's okay. She's the one who called the bureau. It's your uncle in Virginia. He's been shot."

"Uncle Richard? *Shot?* What happened? Was he deer hunting? How badly is he hurt?"

Joe regarded her somberly as he handed her the satellite phone. "Call Max."

Abigale couldn't stop her hand from shaking as she punched in the number for her editor. She clutched the phone to her ear, waiting what seemed like an eternity for the call to go through. Joe scooted over and patted a spot next to him on the cot. She dropped down on the edge facing away from him as a hollow *ring-ring* trilled in her ear.

"Max Chapman."

"It's Abigale."

"Jesus. Abigale, I got a call from your mother. I guess Joe told you. Your uncle in Virginia—Richard—he's been shot. We've got you on the next chopper out of there."

"How badly is he injured?"

There was a long suffering pause. "He's dead, Abigale. Your uncle was murdered."

10

*M*anning parked his BMW in front of his mother's house behind Wendy Brooks's Jeep. Thompson's Explorer and the hunt's kennel truck were parked farther up the drive.

He killed the engine, leaned over, and rummaged through the glove box for a tin of breath mints. As he straightened back into the driver's seat, he glanced at his reflection in the rearview mirror. He popped a mint in his mouth and shoved his fingers through his hair, forcing the blond waves into some sense of order. God, he looked like shit. He had skipped shaving before hunting yesterday and now the two-day-old growth of beard made him look like some Hollywood bad boy. Nothing he could do about that now. Nothing he could do about his bloodshot eyes, either.

Manning grabbed his tweed jacket off the passenger seat and climbed out of the car, slipping the jacket on and turning the collar up against the drizzle as he hurried along the stone walk toward the house. He saw lights on in the kitchen and veered off the walk, cutting across the lawn to the back. Through the glass in the mudroom door he saw his mother standing by the kitchen counter, talking on the telephone. Her back was to him. He stomped his feet on the doormat and opened the door.

She glanced over her shoulder as he entered and he saw her eyes travel down to his boots. He smothered a sigh. *Don't worry, Mother. I remembered my manners and wiped my feet.*

Manning shook the rain off his jacket and hung it on a hook in the mudroom. As he walked into the kitchen, Margaret banged the receiver back on the base. He spotted a tremble in her hand.

"If one more person tells me that Richard is in a better place, I think I'll scream," she said, turning to face him.

Manning wrapped his arms around her and she gave him a quick squeeze before backing out of his embrace. "We've been looking for you all morning," she said, settling against the counter, her arms clamped across her chest.

"I came as soon as I heard."

"Um-hmm." Her lips puckered into a crooked line and her blue eyes blazed as she gave him a good once-over. "Where were you? You look like you just climbed out from under a rock. Still dressed in yesterday's hunt attire."

Manning glanced away.

"Never mind. I already know the answer." Margaret drew in an exaggerated sniff. "You reek of some woman's perfume. That and day-old whisky."

God, Mother. He released a slow breath, refusing to be baited into an argument. "Tell me what happened to Richard."

Margaret turned and grabbed a coffee mug off the counter by the phone, wrinkling her nose as she took a sip. "This is cold." She flung the contents in the sink and reached for the glass carafe in the drip coffeemaker, glancing at him as she poured steaming coffee into her mug. "I just brewed a fresh pot of coffee. Would you like a cup?"

"No. Thanks."

Her disapproving eyes roved over him. "Are you sure? You look like you could use one."

Before he could respond there was a knock, and the door that led to the hall creaked partially open. Smitty poked his head into the kitchen. "Can I come in?"

"Of course," Margaret replied, lifting the mug to her mouth and eyeing Manning over the rim as she took a sip.

Smitty's gaze shifted back and forth between Margaret and Manning as the door swung closed behind him. "Wasn't sure if I was interrupting something."

Manning looked away and perched on the edge of the kitchen table, rubbing the back of his neck as he stretched it from side to side.

"What do you need, Smitty?" Margaret asked.

"Percy Fletcher just showed up at the front door, all full of questions. I told him you were on the phone, but he's made himself at home in the library with Thompson and Wendy. Seems to think that being your neighbor gives him the right to intrude."

"That's all right. I'll go talk to him." Margaret glanced at Manning as she pulled open the door. "Are you coming?"

He sighed and shifted to his feet. "Yeah, I'll be right there."

*A*burn shot through Manning's gut as he watched the door swing closed behind his mother.

Smitty arched a bushy eyebrow. "You all right?"

He took a breath. "I just don't get it, Smitty. Richard's dead and she can't get beyond the fact that I didn't show up to work at Longmeadow this morning, that it took her a while to locate me."

"You're her son. She needed you this morning. It's her way of showing her disappointment that you weren't there."

"Mother needed me? I doubt that."

"It's the truth."

"You can't tell that from the way she's acting now."

"She's shed all her tears. At least publicly. You know how your mother is."

"Oh, yeah." Manning's fingers curled in the air like quotation marks. "Just get back on the damn horse and get on with it."

Smitty clamped his mouth into a pucker and slowly shook his head. There was an uncharacteristic hardness in his eyes. "She's not getting any younger, Manning."

Manning narrowed his eyes. "What are you saying?"

"You need to step up to the plate, son. Your mother just lost her oldest and dearest friend. She and Richard have had each other's backs since high school—that's more than fifty years. Margaret would kill me for saying it, but she can't go through this alone. She needs you by her side."

Shouldn't that work both ways? Manning thought. He was grieving Richard's death, too, but his mother wasn't there for him. He eased out a slow breath. "Yeah. All right."

Smitty gave him a tired smile and plucked a bottle of Virginia Gentleman from the liquor cabinet. "I think you and I might need a little something to help us get through today. What say I make us both a proper cup of coffee?"

They carried their steaming mugs to the library, and Manning dropped down in a barrel chair next to Percy in front of the fire. He took a healthy draw of the spiked coffee as he listened to his mother recount how she had found Richard in the stewards' stand at Longmeadow. She said it appeared Richard had been shot with his own hunting rifle during a robbery, and that the authorities were going to interrogate the members of the nearby road crew repaving St. Louis Road.

"Jesus Christ." Manning ran his hand along his jaw, his fingers rubbing noisily at the stubble of his beard. "It just doesn't add up. How would someone from the road crew have spotted Richard? You can't see the racecourse or the stewards' stand from the road."

Thompson looked at him as if he were dense. "No, of course not. But one of those characters could have seen Richard turn in the entrance to Longmeadow. Margaret said the gate was closed when she arrived, so if someone saw Richard drive through and close the gate they could make a pretty good assumption that he was alone and wasn't expecting anyone to join him."

"Someone might have seen Richard drive in, but I don't think Richard was the one who closed the gate," Margaret said. "It makes no sense for him to do so while he was at the course. You know we always open the gate when we arrive and fasten it when we leave. I think it's more likely the killer closed the gate to delay the possibility of someone driving in and finding Richard's body."

"When was Richard killed?" Percy asked.

"I don't know if the medical examiner has determined a time of death yet, but Richard had clearly been dead for some time before I arrived."

"So he might have been murdered last night," Percy murmured. He shot a look at Manning. "Was the gate open or closed when you left Longmeadow yesterday afternoon?"

"What are you talking about?" Manning asked.

"The *gate*. When you left Longmeadow yesterday afternoon, was the gate open or closed?"

A chill wrapped around Manning. "I wasn't at Longmeadow yesterday."

"Since when? After the hunt yesterday, that's where you said you were heading."

"Is that true, Manning, that you went to Longmeadow?" Margaret asked.
"No."

Margaret raised an eyebrow at Percy.

"Bull-*shit*!" Percy drawled. "When I left the tailgate, I asked if you wanted to grab a beer with me after you took your horse back to the barn and you said you were heading over to Longmeadow to help Richard work on the course."

Had he? Manning avoided his mother's accusatory glare and drained the last of his coffee. "I might have said that's where I was going, but that's not where I went."

"What do you mean, that's not where you went?" Margaret demanded. "Good God, Manning, are you saying Richard was at Longmeadow yesterday, *waiting for you*, and you never showed up?"

Jesus Christ. Had that happened? He shook his head. "No. I told Richard I wouldn't be able to make it after all."

Margaret lingered at the door with Smitty after the others had left. "What do you make of Manning saying he told Richard he couldn't meet him at Longmeadow?" Margaret asked.

"What do I *make* of it?"

"Yes. Do you believe him?"

"You want my honest-to-God opinion?"

"You know I do."

"I don't think he remembers."

Margaret sniffed. "You think he was too drunk."

"He was three sheets to the wind when he left the tailgate."

Margaret felt a sting in her nose, and her eyes filled with tears. "Good God, Smitty, what if Richard was waiting for Manning when the killer found him?"

"Might be that's what happened, but we can't change fate. Besides, if Manning had been at Longmeadow with Richard, what's to say he wouldn't have been shot as well?"

She shook off a shudder and clasped her arms to her chest. "I suppose you're right. But if Manning did stand Richard up and that led to Richard's murder, I'm not sure he'll be able to live with himself."

Smitty cocked an eyebrow. "What about you?"

"Will I be able to forgive Manning?"

He nodded.

"I honestly don't know."

"Oh, boy." Smitty squeezed her shoulder. "We've got a real mess on our hands."

"Don't we ever."

They eyed each other. Margaret knew they were both thinking the same thing: how in the hell were they going to get on without Richard?

"Should we cancel the races?" Smitty asked.

"Richard wouldn't want that. He'd want us to carry on."

Smitty grunted in agreement. "I don't know how we'll pull it off without him."

"No doubt some things will fall through the cracks, but we'll muddle through. First thing I have to do is light a fire under Sheriff Boling to get the crime scene investigation wrapped up and allow us back into Longmeadow. We have a good two days' worth of work to get the course ready."

He ran a palm across his shiny scalp. "What about the funeral?"

"I called Richard's sister, Caroline, and spoke with her assistant. The doctor says Caroline isn't well enough to make the trip from Switzerland. I assured her we'd handle all the funeral arrangements for the family."

"Missing her own brother's funeral?" His stooped shoulders sagged. "That don't seem right."

"The cancer's bad, Smitty. And the chemo has been very rough on her. She can't keep anything down. After Richard's visit to see her last month he told me she's wasting away to nothing."

Smitty frowned. "Richard never said anything."

"He didn't talk about it much, but after that last trip he confided that the doctor told him the outlook was bleak."

"Christ." He let out a low whistle. "She's all the family Richard had, except for Abigale."

Margaret nodded. "Caroline's assistant is trying to get word to Abigale now."

"Is she still in Afghanistan?"

"Yes."

"You think she'll come?"

"Of course."

"You sure?"

"Yes."

"I hope you're right."

A heavy silence was broken by the sound of rain splattering off the eaves.

"It was many years ago, Smitty. I don't think she's battling those demons anymore."

"Manning is."

Margaret felt color rise in her cheeks. "That's different. Manning has other issues."

"Okay." Smitty raised a shoulder. "I'm just saying."

*A*bigale saw Emilio waiting beyond the security fence as soon as she climbed out of the helicopter in Kabul. He wrapped her in a hug, then reached down and grabbed the handles of the large duffle at his feet. "I probably didn't pack it like you would have, but I managed to stuff everything in there."

"It doesn't matter. I'm sure it's perfect. Thank you."

"They've got you on a military transport all the way to the States?"

"From here to Ramstein, then I'll catch another to Andrews."

"Did you learn any more about what happened?"

"No. Just that my uncle was shot. Murdered." Tears swam in Abigale's eyes and she looked away. She'd sworn to herself on the chopper ride that she wouldn't do this, that she'd hold it together until she was alone.

Emilio ran his knuckles across her cheek. "*Cara mia.* I'm so sorry. Were you very close to him?"

"I spent every summer at his farm in Virginia from as far back as I can remember until I was seventeen."

"Virginia. I hear it's beautiful there. What kind of farm?"

"Horses. Foxhunters, mostly."

"Foxhunting? Not exactly for the faint of heart." He flashed a grin. "I can see you doing that."

She smiled through her tears. "It drove my father mad, the whole foxhunting scene. He always told Uncle Richard he hadn't spent thousands of Swiss francs teaching me to ride so I could risk breaking my neck dashing across the Virginia countryside."

"But you did it anyway?"

"Until my father put an end to my Virginia visits."

"Because of the danger of foxhunting?"

"No."

"What happened?"

"Nothing." Abigale reached for the duffle. "I'd better go."

"I'll walk with you."

"No. Let's say goodbye here. It'll be easier."

"Easier?" Emilio cocked his head. "How so?"

She took a deep breath. "I won't be coming back to Kabul."

"Why not?"

"My editor wants to reassign me."

"Reassign you? Why? Things are just starting to heat up here."

"Maybe so, but the war's unpopular in the States now. Max said no one wants to see photographs of it."

Emilio scowled. "Americans! They couldn't get enough of it when you won your Pulitzer."

"That was four years ago. Baghdad. Different environment. Americans were still reeling from 9/11. They supported Bush's war on terror then. They don't anymore."

"If Reuters is starting to yank guys, the rest of the media won't be far behind. God knows where we'll all end up. Any word from London where you'll be assigned?"

"Not yet."

Emilio caressed her shoulders. "So we'll find a way to make it work. I have a million frequent-flyer miles. I'll visit you. Or we can meet someplace. Perhaps my friend's villa in the French Riviera that I told you about—"

Abigale pressed her fingertips to his lips and shook her head. "Don't."

His chocolate eyes narrowed. "Why not?"

"When we started this, we both vowed that there would be no strings attached, remember? No heartbreak. No hurt feelings. That when the time came for one of us to move on, we'd move on."

Emilio sighed, then gave her a tight smile. "*Sí*, we did," he said softly. He reached for a long strand of hair that had worked its way loose from the clasp at the nape of her neck and twirled her auburn curls around his fingers. Leaning in, he touched his lips to her forehead. "I'll miss you."

Abigale closed her eyes and let herself melt into his embrace. Then she stepped back. "Stay safe, okay?"

14

$\mathcal{M}$anning punched Julia's number on his cell phone as he drove. He drummed his fingers on the steering wheel. *Come on, come on, answer.* Five long rings, then voicemail.

"Hi. It's Julia. I'm probably out riding. Leave a message."

He waited for the beep. "Julia. It's Manning. I need to talk to you. It's important. Call me on my cell as soon as you get this message." He thumbed the END key on his phone. Now what?

Who besides Julia could tell him how long he'd been at the Blackthorne Inn yesterday? He could always go to the pub, see who was around, ask who had been working the evening before. But then what? Tell them that last night—even yesterday afternoon—was a total blank? That he couldn't remember where he'd been or what he'd done for, what, sixteen, eighteen hours? No way was he going to do that.

He remembered leaving the hunt. And taking his horse back to the barn. And, once Percy had brought it up, he vaguely remembered talking to Richard at the hunt, agreeing to help repair the timber on one of the fences. But he'd never made it to Longmeadow. At least he didn't think he had. Had Richard really been waiting for him? Could *he* be the reason Richard had been alone at Longmeadow? The reason Richard was murdered? Or had he told Richard he couldn't make it, as he'd just told his mother he had? *Damn it!* He pounded a fist on the steering wheel.

Manning's cell rang and he snatched it off the passenger seat, muttering, "Please let it be Julia." He glanced at the caller ID, feeling a twinge of guilt at the fleeting urge not to answer his mother's call.

"Hello."

"It's your mother."

He stuck the cell between his shoulder and ear as he accelerated and shifted gears. "What's up?"

"I'm getting ready to pay Sheriff Boling a visit, but I wanted to let you know I spoke with Abigale. She's leaving Afghanistan now and will arrive tomorrow afternoon."

Manning's mind flashed to a moment in time he'd fought furiously to shove to the pit of his memory. The truck behind him flashed its lights and Manning realized his speed had dropped, creating a line of traffic that crawled behind him. He shook the thought away and stomped on the accelerator.

"How's Abby handling it?"

"As you'd expect. Caroline is too ill to make the trip, so Abigale will be coming alone," Margaret said. "I've invited her to stay with me. I thought it would be nice to have a little get-together for her tomorrow evening. Make her feel at home."

A dinner party? Jesus Christ. That was classic Mother. Throw Abigale into the mix as soon as she arrives.

"Manning?"

"Yeah."

"What do you think?"

"I think she'll be exhausted after flying all the way from Afghanistan, and the last thing she'll want to do is make small talk at some dinner party."

"Well, she has to eat. Besides, it's not a dinner party. I just want to surround her with friends."

"Okay," he said, not meaning it.

"Good. I'll invite Smitty, of course. Who else do you think we should include?"

"It's up to you."

"I know it's up to me. I'm not asking you for permission, I'm asking for advice. You better than anyone knows who Abigale's friends were. Who would help make her feel at home?"

Manning groaned. "God, Mother, I don't know. Most of the kids we hung out with went off to school and moved on after that. They don't live here anymore."

"Some of them must still be around. What about Percy? As I recall you, Abigale, and Percy were like the Three Stooges that last summer."

"For a while. Until the night Abby and Julia Farleigh went skinny-dipping in the Community Center pool and Percy stole their clothes."

"That sounds like Percy."

"Yeah. Julia got over it after a day or so, even thought it was kind of funny. But Abby wouldn't give it up. Finally, someone blabbed and outed Percy and she was pissed as hell."

"Well, I'm sure she's gotten over it by now. I'll invite him. Percy was her friend and Richard's as well. I think he should be here."

"Suit yourself."

"Um-hmm. Who else? What about Julia? Was the skinny-dipping a one-time thing or were they close friends?"

Manning eased out a sigh. *That's* all *he needed—to have Julia there the first time he saw Abigale again.* "They were friends, but that was a long time ago, Mother. It's not like they've kept in touch all these years."

"That doesn't matter. I'll invite Julia. Now, let's see, that makes six. The table holds eight, so we can invite two more. Any other suggestions?"

"Not really."

"Then I think I'll invite Wendy, since she'll be instrumental in assisting us with the funeral arrangements. Thompson would be a good one to round it out, don't you think?"

Manning didn't respond. His mother knew exactly how he felt about Thompson.

C H A P T E R

15

*M*argaret refused the offer to take a seat in the reception area at the sheriff's office. If she'd learned anything over the years, it was that sitting usually increased one's wait time.

"Sheriff Boling shouldn't be too much longer," the young woman at the front desk said. "Are you sure I can't get you a cup of coffee?"

"Nope. I'm just fine, thanks." Margaret gave her a smile, then glanced at her wristwatch. "Is the sheriff in a meeting?"

The woman's brown curls jiggled as she jerked her head toward a closed door at the back of the room. "Big hubbub going on in his office." She leaned forward and lowered her voice. "I think it's about that man they found shot dead at Longmeadow Park this morning. Couple of deputies came rushing in here about thirty minutes ago, been holed up back there with the sheriff ever since."

"And you think it's about the murder?"

"Well, when they went back there, before the sheriff closed the door, I heard one of them say, 'We have us a suspect, Sheriff. And, get this, he's a Hispanic.'" She rubbed her hands along the sleeves of the moss-green sweater that she'd probably purchased because of the way it accentuated her eyes. "That's Sheriff Boling's top priority, you know. Cracking down on gangs. They've been keeping the seriousness of the problem quiet, so as not to hurt tourism and all, but gangs have become a real problem in this county."

"Is that so?"

"Yes, ma'am. Most folks figure the gang activity is in the eastern part of the county, closer to Washington. But it's out here, too."

"Are you saying the shooting was gang-related?"

The woman held both hands out in a balancing motion, as if weighing the evidence. "Hispanic. Gangs. They go hand in hand."

Margaret grunted in response, but she stopped short of disagreeing with the woman. No sense getting on her bad side. Never know when she might be useful.

The door to the sheriff's office screeched open and the receptionist wheeled around in her chair. She rose as Sheriff Boling strode through the doorway, ushering two deputies ahead of him. "Great work, fellas," the sheriff said, clasping one of the men on the back as he wove his way around the receptionist's desk. "Keep me in the loop."

"You bet, Sheriff."

The front door clanged shut behind the deputies and Sheriff Boling glanced at the receptionist. "Any calls come in for me while I was tied up, Charlotte?"

Bright spots of color flushed the young woman's cheeks and she ran her palms down the sides of her gray wool skirt. "No, Sheriff Boling, but this lady, Mrs. Southwell, has been waiting to see you."

The lines around the sheriff's mouth drooped as his eyes settled on Margaret. "I'm so sorry. I didn't notice you standing there." He grabbed her hand in both of his and gave it a firm squeeze. "Please accept my condolences about Mr. Clarke."

"The wait was no problem," Margaret replied. "I'm sure you're busy, but I'd be most grateful if you could spare a few minutes to talk about the investigation into Richard's death."

The sheriff's head bobbed vigorously. "Of course. In fact, I just came out of a briefing about it." He spread his arm toward the back of the room. "Come on in my office."

The sheriff stood aside at the doorway and gestured for Margaret to precede him into the spacious office. "Have a seat on the sofa." He winced as he swung the door closed. "I keep forgetting to ask Charlotte to have someone oil that door."

Margaret managed a polite smile. She waited while he settled into one of the leather club chairs that flanked the couch.

"It looks like we may already have a break in the case," the sheriff said, hiking up his pant leg as he crossed one knee over the other.

"Oh?"

"Yes, ma'am. Seems there's a road crew, been working repaving St. Louis Road at a spot just due south of Longmeadow."

"I'm aware of that."

"Okay. Well, a couple of deputies went out there to question the workers. See if anyone had seen anything that might be helpful. Anyhow, it turns out one of the workers, a nineteen-year-old Hispanic boy by the name of Reyes— Dario Reyes—didn't show up for work this morning."

"Have they been able to locate him?"

"Nope, but they found his car abandoned by the side of the road—"

The leather sofa squeaked as Margaret leaned forward. "Near the entrance to Longmeadow."

Sheriff Boling arched an eyebrow. "How'd you know that?"

"I saw a car there. This morning. It was parked on the shoulder, but it still took up a fair share of the road. I remember swerving to drive around it."

"That was Reyes's car. The last any co-workers saw him was around four-thirty yesterday afternoon when he drove away after work."

"He had his car at the work site?" Margaret said.

"No. That's the whole point. He didn't. His car was parked in Leesburg. The VDOT road crew travels to the work site as a group. He'd have to have driven back to the area after he got off work."

"Does he live out near Longmeadow?"

"Nowhere near. He lives in Sterling."

"That's in the exact opposite direction."

The sheriff shot a finger at her. "Bingo."

"Oh, my," Margaret said, sinking back with a sigh. "What do you suppose brought him back there?"

"I'm figuring, Mr. Clarke might've caught Reyes's eye when he drove through the work site. You know, refined-looking older gentleman driving an expensive Lexus and all."

"Hmm, perhaps. But if he came back with the intent to harm Richard—if he's the one who shot Richard—why would he leave his car in a place that would implicate him in the crime?"

The sheriff broke into a broad smile. "The fool boy ran out of gas. Gas tank's dry as Goose Creek in August."

"Forcing him to abandon his car," Margaret murmured. "Has the medical examiner determined the time of Richard's death?"

"Not yet, but his initial estimate is that Mr. Clarke had been dead for quite a few hours. In other words, it is more likely he died last night than this morning."

"So you think Reyes saw Richard drive though the paving area yesterday afternoon and went back there after work with the intent to rob him?"

"That's my hunch."

"Could be." As much as Margaret wanted to believe that Richard's killer had been identified, a prickle of doubt nagged her. Everything seemed to point toward a robbery-related shooting, but still . . . Of course, she couldn't come up with a more plausible scenario. Richard didn't have any enemies. Sure, he was one to take a strong stand on an issue if it was something he felt passionate about, but people out here disagreed on matters all the time. The battle lines that had been drawn over the development of a resort hotel had soured more than one friendship. But folks didn't go around murdering each other over their differences. Robbery—plain old greed—was the only motive that seemed to fit.

"The entrance to Longmeadow is down the road from the paving area, around that blind curve," Margaret said. "Reyes couldn't have seen Richard turn in there."

"No, not from where they were paving. But Reyes might've figured he'd be able to cruise the area and catch a glimpse of the Lexus from the road. It's my understanding that Mr. Clarke had been frequenting Longmeadow on a regular basis the last few days, getting the place ready for the races. Is that right?"

"Yes."

"Well, then, it stands to reason that Reyes would assume that Mr. Clarke lived near there. A secluded rural location like that is a dream come true for someone contemplating a robbery."

"That's possible, I guess. But—"

"Or," the sheriff held up his finger and plowed ahead, "could be Reyes heard talk about the upcoming races. Knew there was work going on at Longmeadow. Hell, Mr. Clarke might've even told the kid himself. Reyes's job was traffic control, twirling the sign from STOP to SLOW. Maybe Reyes struck up a conversation with Mr. Clarke after seeing him drive through there a time or two. If so, Mr. Clarke might've told him he was working to get Longmeadow ready for the races."

Margaret couldn't deny that was a possibility. Richard would strike up a conversation with most anyone. If Richard had stopped his vehicle next to Reyes, it wasn't inconceivable that he might have exchanged pleasantries with the boy while waiting for traffic to move.

"Do any of the other workers remember seeing this boy, Reyes, talking to Richard?"

"Nah, not yet. But there's a whole lot of *yo no comprendo* going on right now. And those who do understand, they don't remember nothing." He snorted a laugh. "We'll shake them down a bit, threaten to have INS start sniffing around, and their comprehension and memories are bound to improve. In the meantime, we need to nail down the time Mr. Clarke arrived at Longmeadow. All the pieces of the puzzle fall together if Mr. Clarke drove through the paving area before they wrapped up work on the job site at four o'clock."

"Michael, Richard's barn manager, should know what time Richard left his farm to head in that direction. But I have to believe Richard would have driven past the work crew before four o'clock. It gets dark by six these days. I doubt Richard would have bothered going to Longmeadow if he didn't have enough daylight to put in at least an hour or two of work on the racecourse."

"And Mr. Clarke was working by himself yesterday afternoon?"

Either that, or waiting for Manning, Margaret thought. She said, "As far as I know."

Gathering her pocketbook, she rose from the couch. "I've already monopolized too much of your time, Sheriff, but before I go I'd like to know when we'll be allowed back onto the premises at Longmeadow. We have the point-to-point races on Sunday and final preparations have to be made. Several obstacles are in need of repair and we still have to put the snow fence in place. This rain has handed us some additional chores, but the clouds appear to be breaking up. If we could get back to work tomorrow, I think we can get the course in good shape."

The sheriff stood. "So you intend to hold the races as planned?"

"Yes, we do. We've discussed it and feel that's what Richard would have wanted. It won't be easy to pull off, but we'll manage."

Sheriff Boling's broad fingers pulled at his chin and he gave her a slow nod. "As a matter of fact, I think it'd be good for the whole community if the races go on, business as usual. We're still licking our wounds from the negative image dumped on this county when we had that Doug Cummings mess. Killing. Kidnapping. It gave folks the heebie-jeebies; tourism dropped drastically the following year. Our economy can't stomach that happening again. Having your races would be a good incentive for folks to get out into the community rather than hunkering down and locking their doors. I think it's in everyone's best interest to wrap this up as quickly as possible."

Margaret leveled a look at him. "Not at the expense of a thorough investigation into Richard's murder, I hope."

"No, no, of course not. I'm going to assign Lieutenant Mallory to head up the investigation. He's one of my best men."

"I know Lieutenant Mallory."

The sheriff touched his palm to his forehead. "Of course you do. Mallory was my go-to man when your busload of campers went missing."

Margaret nodded. "I was very pleased with how Lieutenant Mallory handled it."

"Well, good. And now that we have a suspect, I anticipate the pace of this investigation will escalate rapidly. At the very minimum, I'll tell Mallory to see that we conclude our crime scene search as quickly as possible and grant you and your hunt members access to Longmeadow Park."

*M*anning sat in his darkening kitchen, eyeing a bottle of Maker's Mark whisky that he'd plunked on the table beside an empty glass. He'd been there since Julia's call, playing cat-and-mouse with the itch to pour a drink. He'd gone so far as to remove the wax seal and screw cap, and now, even from across the table, the smoky vanilla aroma danced in his nostrils. Still, he resisted.

Last night's blackout had really scared him, and all afternoon he'd sworn to himself he'd lay off the booze for a while. Not that he hadn't had memory lapses before from drinking too much. Who hadn't? But he'd always been able to remember snippets of events. This time, he couldn't remember anything that happened from the time he'd left the barn after hunting until he'd awakened in Julia's bed.

According to Julia, he'd sailed into the pub at the Blackthorne Inn a little after three o'clock, obviously feeling no pain. He'd sat at the bar and downed a beer or two. Shot the breeze with the bartender. Then, Julia said, he'd received a call on his cell, had mumbled something about forgetting he had to be someplace, and dashed out, promising to be back later.

Julia had no idea where he'd gone and couldn't remember exactly what time he'd returned, just that it was after dark, and that his tweed jacket was wet, so she assumed he'd spent some time outside.

A low ray of fading sunlight slanted across the table, trapping Manning's cell in a dust-filled golden beam. His long fingers reached out and tapped the phone, twirling it back and forth on the pine tabletop. He'd viewed the recent call history so many times since speaking with Julia that he'd lost count, yet he picked it up again and thumbed down the list—as if the data might have changed.

"Shit." The word hissed through his lips as he stared at the highlighted display: an incoming call from Richard's cell at 3:42 yesterday afternoon.

Sweat beaded on Manning's forehead and he folded the phone, then tossed it on the table. Shoved it out of reach. He sank back in the chair and pounded his palms against his skull. *Think, dammit!* What the hell had happened? Could he really have driven from the Blackthorne to Longmeadow and back, and remembered nothing of it? It was hard to believe, but not entirely out of the question.

He knew the road to Longmeadow like the back of his hand, so making the trip when he was feeling a nice buzz wouldn't have been difficult. And helping Richard replace rails on the timber fences wasn't exactly rocket science. A couple of drinks wouldn't have impeded his ability to do that. He narrowed his eyes, trying to picture Richard and himself mending jumps. The scenario fit like a well-worn glove, but it didn't trigger the slightest recollection about the previous afternoon.

Of course, just because he couldn't remember, didn't mean he hadn't been there. And if he had been, the obvious question was whether he could have—*should* have—done anything to protect Richard. Or whether he'd seen anything that could provide a lead as to what had happened. A clue that was locked away in the deep recesses of his drunken haze.

Fear crashed over Manning in waves, biting at his gut. What if he hadn't made it to Longmeadow? The alternative scenario was no better. That meant he'd stood Richard up. Caused Richard to hang around waiting for him. Alone. A sitting duck.

Not that it would ever have entered his mind that Richard, or anyone else for that matter, might be in danger alone at Longmeadow. That was almost laughable. The kind of thing people who lived other places worried about. Not people in Middleburg. People out here worried about lame horses, droughts, storms, preserving open space.

Sure, the community had its fair share of scandal, even murder. Domestic disputes, revenge killings, crimes of passion. And there was the occasional tack theft, or, rarer still, horse theft. There had even been a time, years back, when a nutcase had slipped into barns in the still of night and sodomized horses. But city crimes—random robbery and the like—just didn't happen in Middleburg.

And yet it had happened.

Manning blew out a loud sigh. "To hell with it." He reached out and tilted the bottle, watching the golden liquid glug to the rim of the glass. He raised it to his lips and knocked back a mouthful, closing his eyes as the burn slid down his throat.

17

*A*bigale clutched the wool blanket tighter across her chest as she scooted lower in the hammock seat of the C-17 and leaned her head against the backrest. During her stint in the Middle East she'd become adept at catching shut-eye whenever—wherever—she could. But sleep eluded her. The drone of the plane's engines, normally hypnotic, did nothing to drown out the questions racing through her mind.

She knew only the headlines from a brief phone conversation she'd had with Margaret from Kabul: Margaret had found Uncle Richard at Longmeadow racecourse, shot dead with his own hunting rifle. His wallet and watch were missing, and the authorities were treating it like a botched robbery. Period. That's all she knew. She didn't know whether her uncle had died instantly or if he'd suffered. Had no idea if there was evidence of a struggle, or whether the sheriff had identified a suspect. When Abigale had pressed for more details, Margaret had told her she'd fill her in on everything when she arrived.

Abigale had called her mother during the stopover in Germany, and had thought she'd done a good job of playacting when she'd told her mother she would be okay returning to Virginia. But her mother had seen through it. She, better than anyone, knew why Abigale hadn't been back in seventeen years. The last thing her mother had said to her was, "Just remember, Manning's not the boy you once knew. He's a grown man now. He has made his own choices with his life. None of it is your fault." *What the hell did that mean?*

She opened her eyes and caught a glance from one of the soldiers strapped to a gurney in the aisle of the military transport, his face no more than a few feet from hers. He smiled tentatively, then shot his eyes toward the camera that hung against Abigale's chest. "Think I could ask you to take a photograph of me?" His drawl was Deep South, the clear voice of a boy, not yet weathered by age. She pegged him at around eighteen or nineteen years old.

"Of course," Abigale said, unsnapping her lens cap.

"I want it for my baby boy," the soldier said. "So when he grows up he'll be proud of his papa."

His arm snaked out from beneath the military-green blanket and Abigale peered at the photo clutched in his hand. "He's beautiful. What's his name?"

"Caden."

"Why don't you hold Caden's picture so I get it in the shot? Yes, just like that. Perfect."

"Make sure you get the flag in the background, okay?"

"You bet." Abigale angled the camera so it captured the American flag that hung from the plane's ceiling. She snapped several shots and wrote down the soldier's email address, promising to send the photos to him. "Good luck with your recovery. Are you going to Walter Reed?"

He nodded. "Wish I was going home straight away, but my wife and boy will be up to see me, so that's the next best thing. Home is where the heart is, right?"

Abigale sank back against the narrow seat, struck by the irony of the soldier's parting words. She'd lost her heart—maybe her soul—in Virginia seventeen years ago, so where did that leave her?

C H A P T E R

18

argaret tugged on her work gloves when she spotted the dark-green sports car speeding toward them along the perimeter of the racecourse. Manning was late, as usual, and he was driving far too fast across the soggy turf. But he'd arrived.

She turned to the small group that had gathered to work on the racecourse. "Okay, Manning's here, so let's divide up chores and get to work. As you can see, the snow fence is in my truck, so whoever wants to tackle that job should come with me. The rest of you can start with the timber fence repairs. Smitty knows which obstacles need work. Just remember, I gave Lieutenant Mallory my word we'd confine our activities to the perimeter of the course and not stray up the hill to the parking lot or the stewards' stand."

"Any idea when we'll be allowed up there?" Wendy asked, sheltering her eyes from the sun with her hand as she nodded in the direction of the hill.

Margaret glanced at the yellow crime-scene tape that surrounded the stewards' stand. "The sheriff is pushing to have the investigation wrapped up today. I hope we'll be able to get in tomorrow."

"The deck will need to be repainted," Thompson said. "We'd better be able to get that finished by tomorrow or it won't be dry by Sunday for the races. Especially if we get more wet weather."

"I thought you and Richard had finished all the painting," Wendy said to Margaret.

Margaret exchanged a look with Thompson.

"There's quite a bit of blood," Thompson said. "We'll need to repaint the planks on the top deck. A portion of the deck below as well."

Wendy's eyes widened and she clamped her palm over her mouth. "Oh, God."

Margaret put an arm around her. They watched in silence as Manning jogged toward them, his long stride gobbling up the distance with ease.

"Sorry I'm late," Manning said.

"You're in time to help put the snow fence around the horse van area," Margaret replied. She caught a whiff of cologne intermingled with a fresh, soapy smell, and noted that his hair was wet but neatly combed, his face cleanly shaved. "There's a thermos of coffee on the tailgate."

She turned away as Manning reached for the thermos. "Who else wants to help with the snow fence?"

"I will," Wendy said.

"Okay. The three of us ought to be able to handle that. Thompson and Percy, why don't you work with Smitty." Margaret glanced at Wendy. "Are you expecting anyone else to show up to help?"

"Charles Jenner said he and Tiffanie would try to be here."

Smitty groaned and rolled his eyes at Margaret. "Don't tell me. You're assigning them to my work group."

Margaret flashed a brief smile. "How perceptive of you."

"They're just what I need today," Smitty mumbled. "Charles will most likely show up hauling some brand-spanking-new chain saw that's too powerful for him to handle, and Tiffanie will probably bring a pair of garden pruners and be dressed like she's going to a hunt breakfast. I wouldn't be surprised if she wants to clip the boxwood on the brush fences."

A glint of sunlight caught the corner of Margaret's eye and she turned to see a shiny black Hummer growl toward them. "Speak of the devil, looks like the Jenners have arrived. See you all later."

"I'll figure out a way to pay you back for this," Smitty said, wagging his finger at her.

Margaret smiled. "Don't count on it." She scanned the racecourse. "Now if I can just find where Duchess has run off to, we can get on our way."

"She's probably in the pond," Manning said, sipping his coffee.

"No doubt." Margaret turned in the direction of the pond, calling, "Duchess! Come on, girl." She stared at the embankment that hid the pond, expecting to see the Lab bound into view, wet ears flopping as she ran toward them. But the only movement on the knoll was a swirl of orange leaves tossed about by the breeze. She called louder, "Duchess!"

Still no dog.

A germ of fear wormed its way down Margaret's spine and she cupped both hands around her mouth. "Duchess!"

"That's not like her," Manning said. "Let me try."

He set his coffee cup on the tailgate, placed two fingers on his tongue, and trumpeted a shrill whistle.

Nothing.

Manning shrugged a shoulder. "Wonder where she went off to?"

Margaret tramped down the slope toward the pond. "Duchess! Come on, girl. Duchess!"

"Hey, hold on," Manning said, following her. "What's the rush?"

Margaret lengthened her stride. "I'm worried something might have happened to Duchess. She always comes when I call her."

The toe of her boot caught on a clump of bottlebrush grass, and Manning grabbed her elbow as she pitched forward. "Whoa. Be careful you don't fall and break something."

She accepted Manning's steadying grip on her arm as they navigated the grassy dips and bumps. When they reached the rise that offered a clear view of the pond, Margaret stopped. A pair of Canada geese took flight and she scanned the grassy undergrowth at the pond's edge. There was no sign of Duchess. A few ripples radiated near the lily pads, but the rest of the pond's surface was smooth as glass.

Margaret shot a glance at Manning and saw he was chewing on the inside of his lip. That meant he was worried. "I don't like it," she said. "I don't like it one bit."

He puffed his cheeks and blew out a breath. "Let's not jump to conclusions. We're not near a road. What could happen to her here? There's no reason to suspect anything other than she ran off chasing a rabbit."

"There was no reason to suspect that anything would happen to Richard here either, but it did," she snapped.

Manning opened his mouth, then clamped it shut with a shake of his head. He turned away. "Duchess!" His low baritone rumbled in his throat. He tilted his head and listened for a moment, then blew a piercing whistle. "Come on, Duchess!"

Margaret held her hand to her ear and strained to listen. Had she heard a bark? A pair of crows glided overhead, their raucous caws drowning out all other sounds. "Goddamned birds," she muttered, eyeing them as they swept down to land on the railing of the stewards' stand.

Then she heard it again, clearer this time. It was a dog barking. "Did you hear that?" she asked.

"Yeah."

The barking grew louder, more insistent, and the pair of crows scattered from their perch.

Manning's arm shot forward. "There, look!" He pointed at the stewards' stand. "She's barking at the crows."

"Oh, thank God." Margaret clasped one hand to her chest. "Duchess, get over here!"

The Lab twirled around and looked at them.

"Come on."

Duchess lowered her head, grabbed something with her mouth, and ran toward them.

"That dog's just too smart." Margaret shook her head. "I encouraged her to chase the crows yesterday and she must have decided that's her new role."

Manning smiled. "Feel better?"

"I feel foolish, that's how I feel. I overreacted. I'm on edge because of what happened to Richard."

Manning nodded, then shoved his hands in the front pockets of his jeans, rocked back on his heels, and lowered his gaze. "It's haunting me, too. In fact, there's something I want to talk to you—"

Margaret cut him off. "What's that Duchess has in her mouth?" She squatted on one knee as the dog wiggled to a stop in front of her. "What do you have there, girl? Give it to me."

The Lab opened her jaw and dropped the article in Margaret's gloved hand.

"Dear God. It's Richard's wallet."

"Are you sure it's Richard's?" Manning asked, eyeing the buttery London-tan leather, now blemished with rust-colored mud and wet blotches from Duchess's mouth.

"Absolutely. I gave it to him for his birthday to replace that god-awful one he'd been carrying. It was so old the tan leather had turned brown. And I don't mean a nice, well-oiled saddle kind of brown. For a man who loved fast cars and well-bred horses, Richard could be downright miserly about spending money on himself," she said affectionately.

Manning knelt next to her and draped an arm around Duchess. "Wonder where Duchess found it."

"Based on the mud, I'd guess maybe it was dumped in the shrubbery surrounding the stewards' stand. I edged and weeded that area last week, so there's plenty of fresh soil exposed. I haven't gotten around to mulching yet." She turned the wallet over, holding it gingerly by the edges. "I can't imagine they'll be able to get much evidence off it."

"Everything all right?" a man's voice called from behind them.

Margaret looked over her shoulder and saw Thompson about twenty paces away, jogging toward them. "Duchess found Richard's wallet."

Thompson huffed to a stop beside her. "You're kidding."

She rose and held out her hand. "It's a little the worse for wear."

Thompson lifted it gingerly by the corner and examined it. "You never know. Forensics are pretty good these days. They might be able to get some prints off it."

"Yeah. Like yours, now that you've touched it," Manning said, rising to his feet. "Smart move."

Thompson arched an eyebrow. "Where does your expertise on criminal investigations come from, personal experience?"

"Fuck you, Thompson. The only criminal investigation I've been involved in was when I borrowed the hunt truck and *you* reported it stolen."

The incident with the hunt truck had happened months ago, but it was still a sore spot with Manning. He maintained that Thompson had known full well who had taken the truck, and that he'd reported it stolen just to cause trouble for Manning. Margaret didn't really believe Thompson had done it deliberately, but it had resulted in an embarrassing situation for Manning. He'd had horse customers from California in the truck with him when he'd been pulled over and hauled away in handcuffs to the sheriff's office. "All right, put your personal differences aside," Margaret said. "We don't have time for bickering."

Thompson pressed his lips together, yanked a handkerchief from his back pocket, and wrapped it around the wallet. "We should notify the sheriff's office right away. Would you like me to make the call, Margaret?"

"I suppose. Although they'll want to come out and interview me. Fill out a report." She eyed the racecourse. "Who knows, they might decide to extend the restricted area. Or ask us to leave the property altogether. We'll be in a real pickle if that happens. I don't see what difference it would make to delay calling for a couple of hours. Buy us some time to get some work done."

"I think the prudent thing to do is to report it right away," Thompson said. "What if there's evidence on the wallet linking Reyes to the shooting?"

"You're right." Margaret sighed and peeled off her gloves. She dug her cell out of her coat pocket. "I'll call Lieutenant Mallory."

Manning stared at Margaret, then Thompson. "Wait a minute, what are you two talking about? Who's Reyes?"

Thompson arched an eyebrow. "You haven't heard?"

"Heard what?"

"I tried calling last evening to tell you, but wasn't able to reach you," Margaret said. "They've identified a suspect. A boy by the name of Dario Reyes. He worked on the road crew."

"Are you shitting me? Why the hell am I just now finding out about that?"

"Watch your language, Manning," Margaret said. "If you had answered your phone last night, you would have learned about it from me at that time."

Anger flared in Manning's eyes. "Well I'm here now, Mother. Would you mind filling me in?"

She pressed the cell to her ear and held up a hand to silence him. "Good morning, Charlotte. This is Margaret Southwell. Is Lieutenant Mallory available? It's important."

anning raised the hammer and slammed two nails into the timber fence. "That should do it for this one." He swiped his sleeve across his sweaty forehead and pulled on the fence to make sure it felt secure.

Smitty tossed his toolbox into the bed of the Gator. "We made short work of that job, didn't we?"

Charles Jenner tugged on his belt and hiked his khakis higher across his generous belly. "I still think it would have gone quicker if we'd used my nail gun."

Manning exchanged a look with Smitty. Easy for Charles to say, considering he hadn't done more than stand by and offer advice. "What's next?" he asked Smitty.

"I think that wraps it up. Looks like Percy and Thompson are about finished shoveling open the drainage ditch on the far turn. You and Wendy got the snow fence put in place. That's it until we can set the national fences."

"When are they being delivered?"

"They were originally supposed to be delivered today, but with the sheriff's investigation and all Margaret had it rescheduled for Friday."

Manning raised an eyebrow. "That's cutting it close."

"You're telling me," Smitty said, flipping the lid on a six-pack-sized cooler and hooking the necks of two bottles of Budweiser. He held them out to Manning and Charles.

"It's about time. We've earned these," Charles said, grabbing a bottle.

Manning smiled at the face Smitty made behind Charles's back. "I think I'll pass."

Smitty waved the bottle at him. "You sure? It's cold."

"Nah. I'm good."

"Suit yourself." Smitty twisted the cap and took a long draw from the bottle. He ran the back of his hand across his mouth. "Ah, that hits the spot."

Manning eyed the open cooler. A film of moisture glistened invitingly on the brown glass bottles. Budweiser was Smitty's brand of choice, not his, but that had never stopped him before. He gnawed on his lower lip. What harm would it do to have one beer? Just one.

A car door slammed in the distance and Smitty tipped the neck of the beer bottle toward the stewards' stand, where a sheriff's car was pulling away. "Looks like they're finished up there. Margaret's heading back down the hill."

Manning glanced at his watch. "She's been up there with them for almost two hours."

Charles snorted. "Probably riding roughshod over the whole damn investigation."

They watched Margaret pick her way down the slope. "It look to you like she's moving awful slow?" Smitty asked.

Manning nodded. "She seemed a little unsteady on her feet this morning."

"Come on. Let's go pick her up with the Gator."

Charles opened the door to his Hummer. "I've got to head out. Glad I could help today. Don't forget to tell Margaret that Tiffanie was sorry she wasn't able to make it."

"Yeah, I'll be sure to tell her," Manning said, holding onto the seat as Smitty gunned the engine.

They rolled to a stop beside Margaret, and Manning hopped out and gestured for her to take the front seat. "I'll get in back."

Margaret plopped down beside Smitty, and Manning climbed into the utility bed. He banged down the lid on the cooler and shoved it aside.

"You were up there a long time," Smitty said.

She gave him a tired smile. "I thought my presence might speed things along."

"Did it?"

"They're opening the entire property back up starting tomorrow morning."

"Hey, that's great," Manning said. "Did they find anything?"

Margaret glanced at him over her shoulder. "No, but they do think Duchess found Richard's wallet in the boxwood by the stewards' stand. Her paw prints are visible in the mud around the shrubs."

"Any human footprints?"

She shook her head. "They're surmising the wallet was tossed in the bushes from the deck of the stewards' stand. There's no money or credit cards in it, by the way. Just Richard's driver's license and hunting license."

Manning's mouth tightened. "So that confirms it, then. It was a robbery."

"It sure looks that way." Margaret heaved a long sigh as she surveyed the racecourse. "It looks like you've accomplished a lot in my absence."

"We've finished all the course repairs," Smitty said.

"That's sensational. You should be in charge more often."

"Oh no, don't go getting any ideas along those lines. It's Manning who helped things get done so quick." Smitty twisted in the seat and clasped Manning's arm. "Felt just like I was working alongside Richard, that's how it felt."

"Well, I'm grateful to you." Margaret waved a hand at the key. "C'mon, let's get this thing fired up. Duchess is probably fit to be tied being locked up in my truck. And I need to get dinner started before Abigale arrives."

Smitty tipped the brim of his baseball cap and turned over the ignition. "Yes, ma'am."

Manning was jostled against the side rail as Smitty punched the accelerator. He grabbed onto the front seatback as the Gator bounced over the field, trying to ignore the clink of the beer bottles in the cooler.

$\mathscr{A}$bigale set her duffle on the floral chintz bench that stood at the foot of the double bed. "This room is lovely, Margaret. Thanks so much for inviting me to stay here."

"I'm happy to have the company. Besides, I couldn't tolerate the thought of you staying alone in some sterile hotel room."

Abigale worked up a smile. "I'm pretty used to it by now. In Afghanistan, and Iraq before that, I considered myself lucky to even get a hotel room."

"Well, I hope you'll feel at home while you're here, in spite of the circumstances." Margaret patted her arm. "I'll leave you alone to get unpacked. You have an hour until folks arrive, so you can even work in a quick catnap before you freshen up and dress for dinner."

Dress for dinner? That was a joke. Abigale looked down at her jeans. She couldn't remember the last time she'd dressed for anything. She drew her arms tight across her chest. "I'm afraid my wardrobe options are pretty limited: khaki or black slacks, white or black blouse."

Margaret waved a hand, as though batting away the notion. "Oh, don't you worry about that. You'll look lovely in whatever you wear. Just relax and settle in. I'll be in the kitchen if you need anything."

"Shouldn't we discuss the funeral arrangements? I've written down some thoughts, my mother's wishes. And I have so many more questions about what happened to Uncle Richard." Margaret had told Abigale the sheriff had identified a suspect—a "person of interest"—in her uncle's murder, but she still hadn't filled her in on many of the details.

"I know, dear. There will be plenty of time for all of that tomorrow. The funeral's not until Monday. Tonight is just about being together with family and friends. Why don't you try to get some rest before dinner."

As soon as the door closed behind Margaret, Abigale flopped on her back across the patchwork quilt tucked neatly on the four-poster bed. She kicked off her shoes, let them clunk to the floor, and bent her knees to ease her throbbing back. She inhaled deeply, let the air escape slowly. Was there a muscle in her body that didn't ache? She stretched, wincing at the muscle spasms in both calves, the sharp pang that shot from her neck across her right shoulder. Her eyes burned with a grit that reminded her of the hot-white Iraqi sands. She rubbed her closed lids, knowing that would only make it worse.

The knot that had hung like lead in Abigale's stomach since landing at Andrews Air Force Base flared into a fiery cramp that almost took her breath away. She massaged the tender spot just below her breastbone, trying to ease the burn that shot up her chest. It seemed surreal, being back here. Like a time warp. Margaret's farm, Fox Run, looked almost exactly the way she remembered it. Yet an ugly truth—murder—lurked beneath the serenity. It left a gaping hollow space where her uncle should be. She'd lived with death, witnessed it almost every day for the last five years, yet the fact that her uncle had been murdered—here—was almost beyond comprehension.

Abigale blew out a ragged breath. How was she going to make it through this? Laying Uncle Richard to rest. Handling his affairs. Performing the role her mother would play, if she weren't bedridden almost four thousand miles away.

And how was she going to face Manning?

Margaret heard the slam of the back door. "I'm in the dining room," she shouted in the direction of the kitchen.

She tucked in the final fold on the last of the white linen napkins she'd arranged at the top of each Pimpernel placemat, then stepped back and surveyed the table with a critical eye. The cherry wood was badly in need of refinishing, but the gleam of the Spode china and Waterford crystal drew attention away from the sad state of the table. She nodded her approval. It would do.

Margaret lugged the silver chest out of the bottom cabinet of the china hutch and rested it on a chair. The brass nameplate on top was tarnished and scratched, the elegantly engraved "Southwell" nearly indecipherable, but the Tiffany sterling inside was so well polished she could almost see her reflection. Margaret removed the carving knife with the hound handle and set it beside the place setting at the head of the table, then placed the fox-handled serving fork next to it.

"Something smells good. What're we having?"

She turned and saw Manning standing in the doorway to the kitchen. He held a bouquet of flowers in one hand and a folded necktie in the other. The collar of his white dress shirt was unbuttoned beneath his navy blazer.

"Pot roast." She ran her eyes over him. "You look nice."

Manning extended his hand that held the tie. "I wasn't sure about the dress code, so I brought this along in case."

"You're fine as you are. It's casual." Margaret inspected the bouquet in his hand. There were a half-dozen or so sunflowers, accompanied by stalks of lavender and willowy branches with shiny green leaves. "Sunflowers. What an unusual choice. They're beautiful."

Manning's face reddened. "They're Abby's favorite. Or were, anyway." His eyes darted toward the ceiling. "Is she upstairs?"

"Yes."

His expression tightened and he glanced away, waving the flowers. "What should I do with these?"

"There are some large vases in the cupboard in the pantry. Select one that you like. There's a cerulean Baccarat that would complement the china nicely."

"All right."

He turned toward the kitchen.

"Manning."

"Yeah?" he said, looking over his shoulder.

"Are you okay?"

"Why wouldn't I be?"

"Seeing Abigale, after all these years. Dredging up the past."

Manning turned away. "It's nothing I can't handle."

22

The mirror over the sink was clouded with steam from the shower. Abigale wiped a circle with her palm and frowned at the pale reflection that stared back at her. Bluish shadows hung like half-moons beneath her dark-brown eyes, making her look as exhausted as she felt. When had those tiny lines popped up? She rummaged through her cosmetic kit, found an old stick of concealer, and dabbed it around her eyes, then finger-combed her hair. She wrinkled her nose as she studied her reflection in the mirror. No matter how many hairdressers told her how lucky she was to have "natural body," she regarded her mane of curls as a curse. Sure, given proper time and a blow dryer she could tame it into soft waves, but more often than not she simply pulled it back. Tonight, her fingers moved swiftly as she wove it into a French braid. Abigale twisted around, looked over her shoulder at the mirror, and tucked in few wayward hairs. "Guess that's as good as it's going to get."

She dressed quickly in her black slacks and blouse. A dark, spicy aroma wafted up from downstairs and her stomach grumbled, reminding her that it had been over twenty-four hours since she'd last eaten a meal. In spite of her misgivings about the evening, she was suddenly grateful to Margaret for going to the trouble of cooking dinner.

Abigale paused at the top of the stairs. She heard voices below, coming from the library, and thought of the last time she'd been in that room. "That was then, this is now," she whispered as she gripped the stair railing and started down the steps. "You can do this."

As she stepped off the last stair, the front door swung inward and a man's voice called out, "Knock-knock. Anyone home?"

An attractive brown-haired man, probably in his mid-to-late thirties, breezed inside and quickly closed the door. He had on a gray wool overcoat, buttoned up the front, beneath which she caught a glimpse of a blue shirt and red-and-blue striped bow tie. He turned in her direction and his dark eyes lit up. "You must be Abigale."

"Yes."

He grasped her hand firmly between both of his. "I'm Thompson James. Your uncle was a close friend of mine. I'm so very sorry for your loss."

"Thank you."

Thompson gave her hand a quick squeeze before releasing it. "It's freezing out there," he said, exaggerating a shiver as he unbuttoned his overcoat and hung it on the coatrack by the front door. "When did you arrive?"

"Just a couple of hours ago."

He straightened his bow tie as he turned back to her, his mouth curved down in a sympathetic smile. "You must be exhausted. That's a grueling journey from Afghanistan."

"Have you been?"

"Not Afghanistan. But I've been to Iraq."

Margaret poked her head around the corner and waved her arm, gesturing them into the room. "Abigale, I thought I heard your voice. Hello, Thompson. Both of you, come on into the library. Everyone's gathered in front of the fire."

Thompson held out his hand. "After you."

Abigale was smothered by the scent of pipe tobacco as a stout, older gentleman grabbed her in a bear hug. After squeezing her so hard she let out a groan, he released her, a broad grin crinkling his face. "You're a sight for sore eyes. What a beautiful woman you turned out to be! Not that I'm at all surprised, mind you."

"Smitty?"

He winked. "You betcha. Still kickin' after all these years."

Abigale leaned forward and gave him a peck on the cheek. "It's wonderful to see you."

Margaret grabbed her elbow and tugged her over to the stone hearth. "Come closer to the fire, Abigale. It's colder than a you-know-what tonight. Now let's see, I think you know most of these folks, except Wendy Brooks." She nodded in the direction of a plump, pleasant-looking woman wearing wire-framed glasses, who was seated on the sofa.

The woman smiled and tucked a strand of short brown hair behind her ear. "Hi, Abigale. I'm the hunt secretary. I've had the pleasure of riding to hounds with your uncle since I moved here from Michigan about ten years ago."

"It's nice to meet you."

An attractive, slim blond seated next to Wendy waved her hand. "Hey, Abigale. It's me, Julia."

Abigale's eyes widened. "Julia Farleigh?"

"Yep."

"Oh, my God. I wouldn't have recognized you. You used to have brown hair."

Julia flashed a smile, revealing a perfect row of unnaturally white teeth. "And braces. Not to mention an extra thirty pounds. In *all* the wrong places." She ran a hand down her sweater and smoothed away the wrinkles, showing off her flat abdomen and voluptuous curves.

Abigale laughed. "Not anymore. You look fabulous."

"Thanks. You too."

A man leaning against the hearth straightened and held out his hand. "Percy Fletcher. Long time no see."

Abigale fought to hide her shock at Percy's appearance. His athletic build had turned soft, and a barrel chest strained against his shirt buttons. A receding hairline added years to his portly appearance.

"Wait, you're not still going to pay me back for that swimming pool incident, are you?" He raised an arm across his face in mock defense as Abigale reached for his hand.

She arched an eyebrow. "You know what they say: 'Revenge is a dish best served cold.'"

Percy pumped her hand and raised his glass. "Touché. Fair warning."

Laughter floated through the room and Abigale breathed out a sigh. Perhaps she'd get through this after all.

Margaret patted her arm. "Now let's see, that's everyone, except Manning, whom you know, of course."

Abigale's eyes followed Margaret's gaze to the man who stood beside a liquor cart in the far corner of the cozy room. There he was, a grown-up version of the boy she remembered. The years had hardened Manning's muscles and added bulk to his broad shoulders; no hint of a middle-aged pouch on him. His wavy hair, more sandy now than blond, was shorter, and his face harder, accentuating his high cheekbones and strong jaw. But there was a different air about him. His eyes, blue as a summer sky, showed no hint of the naughty-boy gleam she remembered. The gaze he leveled at her seemed clouded with weariness. Or was it wariness?

Manning stepped forward. "Hello, Abby."

She had expected the moment to be uncomfortable, but she wasn't prepared for the rush of sadness that seemed to suck the air out of the room. Her father's angry shouts whirled in her head, as vividly as the day seventeen years ago when he'd paced this same room, hurling hateful accusations at Manning.

Abigale knew she should cross to him, but she didn't move. She just stood there. She managed a smile. "You look great."

Manning snorted softly, giving her a look that seemed to say, *So that's how we're going to play it—just make small talk?*

His blue eyes hardened as he raised his glass to his mouth. "So do you."

*A*bigale pushed the remnants of her apple pie on her plate as she looked across the table at Thompson, trying to focus on the story he was telling about being ambushed on the drive from the airport to his hotel in Iraq. But Manning's presence at the end of the table trumped her ability to concentrate. With one ear, she listened to Manning and Smitty discuss the entries for the upcoming steeplechase races. The sound of Manning's deep drawl swaddled her like her favorite cashmere sweater. She had no doubt that if she closed her eyes she'd see the apple orchard, bathed in moonlight; picture Manning and herself sprawled on the grass, counting fireflies, searching for constellations in the velvet summer sky, talking about all the places in the world they wanted to visit one day.

She shook off the memory and forced her attention back to the conversation with Thompson. "What were you doing in Iraq?"

He raised his glass, swirled the red wine around the goblet and inhaled, then took a sip. "Spearheading an audit of several defense contractors."

"Oh, interesting. Do you work for the government?"

"Are you kidding? Do I look like I work for the government?" He leaned back and stared down his nose, but gave her a grin.

"I didn't mean that as an insult. In Switzerland, working for the government is considered prestigious."

"In America, it's a badge of mediocrity."

"Good to know."

He tilted his head and stared quizzically at her. "You don't have an accent."

"Pardon me?"

"You're Swiss, but you speak perfect English without the trace of an accent. Were you educated overseas?"

"I went to college here in America, but the lack of accent is owed to years of voice lessons."

He cocked an eyebrow. "Why voice lessons?"

She lifted a shoulder. "My father insisted. My family was in the hotel business and my father thought speaking English without an accent made the American guests feel more at home."

The conversation between Manning and Smitty stopped, and out of the corner of her eye she saw Manning look in her direction.

Abigale forced her attention back to Thompson. "So, if you don't work for the government, who do you work for?"

"I'm a partner with Knightly and Knightly."

"Is that an auditing firm?"

"We're the nation's oldest accounting firm. My specialty is auditing companies to determine if they're cooking the books. The U.S. government retained us to audit several defense contractors in Iraq after all the allegations arose about extravagant expenditures of taxpayers' money."

"What did you find?"

"We're not finished yet. It's an ongoing investigation."

"So you'll be going back over to Iraq?"

"Not if I can help it. My team is still there doing the grunt work. One of the perks of being in charge is that I don't have to spend any more time in cesspools like Iraq than I absolutely have to."

Manning snorted, but Thompson displayed no reaction. He flashed a smile at Abigale. "Your experience in Iraq was probably vastly different from mine. We should get together and compare war stories, so to speak."

"Sure, Thompson," Manning said. "I'll bet that's just what Abby would like to do."

Thompson gave him a cool smile. "Why don't we leave that up to Abigale to decide?"

"That's enough, boys. Abigale didn't travel all this way to listen to the two of you throw barbs at each other." Margaret folded her napkin and placed it on the table beside her plate. "If everyone has finished with dessert, I suggest we retire to the warmth of the fire in the library. I've set up the coffee service in there."

As Margaret rose, the shrill ring of the telephone drifted in from a distant room. "Oh, wouldn't you know it. Manning, would you answer that, please?"

Abigale followed the others into the library and had just settled onto the sofa beside Julia when Manning poked his head through the doorway, shrugging a barn jacket over his sport coat. "That was Javier. Dixie's gone down in her stall and he can't get her up. I'm going down to the barn to help."

Margaret looked up from pouring coffee. "Don't tell me she's colicking again."

"It looks that way. Javier said the bedding in her stall's all torn up. He's trying to get hold of Doc Paley." Manning backpedaled toward the door. "I'll call you as soon as I know something."

Margaret set the silver coffeepot on the tray with a clang. "I'm coming with you."

Manning's mouth tightened. "Javier and I can handle it, Mother."

"It's Dixie we're talking about!" Margaret's voice cracked like a whip, and her heels tapped a quick rat-a-tat-tat as she strode toward the door. "Do you actually think I would sit here sipping coffee while she's in distress?"

The front door banged closed and no one spoke for a moment. Then Julia shrugged and smiled at Abigale. "Welcome home."

"Margaret seems pretty upset," Abigale said. "Dixie must be a special horse."

"Yes, indeed," Smitty replied. "She's a homebred. Margaret raised her from a foal and did all the training herself. Showed her on the line. The whole nine yards. Dixie turned out to be Margaret's most-winning show hunter ever. Last year Margaret retired her from the show ring to breed her, and that's when all the problems started."

"What do you mean?"

"The mare didn't take much to being in foal. She went off her grain, picked at her alfalfa. Despite Margaret's best efforts to maintain her, by the time the foal was born last March, Dixie was a tired shadow of her former self.

"A while after the foal was born, Dixie started to perk back up. She was back to her old habits of kicking the stall and screaming come graining time, and she started to pick up weight. Then, about three months after Dixie delivered the foal, Margaret found her thrashing in the pasture one night, colicking something awful. Margaret rushed her to the Equine Medical Center and it turned out to be a large-colon torsion. Twisted gut. They performed emergency surgery and removed over seventy percent of the mare's large intestine. The surgery was a success, and Dixie should live a normal life as long as she's kept on a special diet, but the mare keeps colicking. You can almost set your clock by it when there's a change of weather."

Smitty reached up and rapped his knuckles on his head. "Nothing as serious as the colon torsion, knock on wood, but it scares the bejesus out of Margaret every time it happens."

Abigale said, "I'll bet. I hope this turns out to be another mild episode."

"Me too. I think I'll stop in on my way past the barn and see how she's doing." Smitty set his coffee cup on the end table. "I imagine you'd just as soon we get out of here and let you get some rest." He patted Abigale's knee as he rose from his chair. "It's nice to have you back here after all these years, even if it is under such tragic circumstances."

She stood and gave him a hug. "I'll see you tomorrow."

Thompson stretched out his hand. "It was a pleasure to meet you, Abigale. Or do you prefer to be called Abby?"

"Abigale's fine."

"Manning's the only one ever got away with calling her Abby," Percy said, winking at her.

Heat flared in Abigale's cheeks, but she ignored Percy's remark.

"Abigale, if you don't mind, I'd like to stay and tackle the kitchen," Wendy said. "The last thing Margaret needs is to come home from the barn to a sink full of dirty dishes."

"Of course. I'll help you."

"Make that three of us," Julia said.

*A*bigale felt someone's eyes on her and turned from the sink to see Duchess standing behind her, her brown eyes glued to the plate in Abigale's hand.

"Do you think Margaret would mind if I gave Duchess some scraps?"

"Aw, look at her." Julia smiled and scratched the Lab behind her ear.

Duchess sat, head cocked to one side, tail sweeping the floor. Abigale laughed. "You know a softie when you see one, don't you? Okay, I'll give you a little bit if you promise not to tell your mom when she gets home."

She scooped some leftover pot roast into the ceramic bowl that was next to a fluffy-looking dog bed, then helped Julia and Wendy finish washing the dishes.

"Well, we made quick work of that," Wendy said, draping the wet dish towel on the handle of the oven door.

"Thanks so much, both of you, for staying and helping." Abigale glanced at the clock on the wall and was surprised to see it was only nine o'clock. It felt like midnight. "It seems like Margaret's been gone a long time. That's probably not a good sign."

Wendy rummaged through her purse and retrieved a pen and a credit card slip. She wrote on the back of the receipt and handed it to Abigale. "Here's my phone number. If it's bad and there's anything I can do to help, please call me. No matter the hour."

Abigale nodded. "Thanks. I will."

A bitter blast of air gusted in when Wendy slipped out the door, and Julia rubbed her hands up her arms. "Brrrr, it feels more like February than October tonight. I'll bet you're dying to crawl under the warm covers and get some sleep."

"Actually, I think I'm beyond tired. I'll probably wait up until Margaret gets back."

"Do you want company?" Julia's eyes flickered, as if she feared Abigale would reject her offer.

"Sure, I'd like that."

Julia's face relaxed into a smile. "Great. Let's go sit by the fire in the library."

"Should I brew a warm pot of coffee?"

"You could." Julia arched a thinly plucked eyebrow. "Or . . . we could raid Margaret's bar."

Abigale laughed softly. "I vote for option number two."

"Courvoisier or Grand Marnier?"

"You choose."

Julia poured two generous tumblers of cognac and they flopped on the sofa.

"So, girlfriend, what have you been doing with yourself these last seventeen years? Besides being a famous photojournalist and winning yourself a Pulitzer prize." Julia tucked a long leg beneath her as she snuggled into the deep cushion.

"Oh no, that's not fair." Abigale shook her head. "You first."

"I'm waitressing at a pub outside Upperville. Showing in the summer, foxhunting in the winter. Looking for Mr. Right."

"How's the search going?"

Julia wrinkled her nose. "Still looking. There's a major shortage of eligible men in this town. All the good-looking ones are either already taken or they're gay."

"What about Thompson?"

"Thompson's an okay guy. I dated him for a while when he first moved here. But there's definitely no *there* there." Julia made a circle with her thumb and forefinger. "Zero sexual attraction. In fact, it made me wonder if I'm not his type, if you get my drift."

"You mean, he's gay?"

"I kind of got that impression. Either that, or he's saving himself for his wedding night."

Abigale sipped the cognac. "What's the story with Manning and him?"

"You think there's something *sexual* going on between Thompson and Manning?"

"That's not what I meant," Abigale said, smiling. "I was referring to the tension between them."

"Oh, that. They haven't gotten along from the get-go. Thompson looks down on Manning, thinks he's irresponsible. And Manning thinks Thompson is a brown-noser. Thompson moved here while Manning was living in California, and I think when Manning returned he didn't like how close Thompson was to Margaret and Richard, kind of like Thompson had invaded his territory, you know? Then there was an incident with the hunt truck— Manning took it without permission and Thompson reported it stolen—and since then the two of them don't even seem to bother trying to get along."

"Did Thompson know Manning had borrowed the truck?"

"He's says he didn't." Julia twirled a strand of hair around her finger. "Hey, want to hear something ironic?"

"Um-hmm."

"Manning and I were together for a while."

Abigale felt the cognac rise in her throat. "Really?"

"Yeah. About four years ago. He ended up in my bed one night when we'd both had too much to drink. Manning was too much of a gentleman to treat it as a one-night stand, so he took me out on a few dates afterward. But it never went anywhere. We finally settled on a happy medium. You know; friends with benefits." Julia's lips curved into an impish grin. "Emphasis on benefits."

Abigale forced a smile as she raised her glass to her lips, using the liquor as an excuse not to reply.

"Then he moved out to Los Angeles for a couple of years, and since he's been back we haven't been together. Until the other night, but I guess that doesn't really count." Julia unfolded herself from the sofa and held up her empty glass. "Need a refill?"

"No, I'm fine."

The cork squeaked as Julia twisted it from the bottle, and Abigale listened to the glug-glug of cognac filling Julia's glass. "Have you and Manning been in touch at all over the years?" Julia asked as she sank back on the sofa.

"No."

"That must have been weird seeing him tonight."

"A little."

Julia took a long draw from the glass. "He still won't talk about it."

"What do you mean?"

"Manning. He refuses to talk about what happened with Scarlet. Even after all these years."

Abigale didn't respond.

"And it's not because he's forgotten it, either. I think it's just eating away at him inside. I tried to get him to talk to me about it once. Thought it might help him to let it out, you know? But he just froze up. Got this dark look in his eyes that would've scared me if it hadn't been Manning. I think that's what's at the root of his drinking problem."

"Manning has a drinking problem?"

"Big time."

"I can't believe that," Abigale murmured. "Manning was always so adamantly against drinking because of his father. Remember when Margaret was out of town and we had a party at the barn, and Manning gave Percy hell for showing up with a case of beer?"

"Yeah, well, times have changed. Manning got caught up in the drinking scene when he went to college and he became quite the partier. But his drinking has really spiraled out of control since he's been back from L.A. I guess he must have inherited the gene."

"What did he do in Los Angeles?"

"He ran a pretty successful show barn, even taught some of the stars. Can't you just see him fitting in out there? The studios used his place to shoot a lot of films and he got to play a couple of bit parts. I have DVDs of the films. I'll show them to you sometime.

"Anyway, it sounded to me like he was a big success, but Margaret came back from visiting last year and was none too happy about his lifestyle. From what I hear, she did everything she could to get him to come back home. Even threatened to cut him off. Take him out of her will. But Manning stayed in L.A. Then this summer Richard and Margaret double-teamed him and convinced Manning to come back here."

"What did they do?"

"Richard told Manning he was worried about Margaret, that running the farm had gotten to be too much for her to handle but no one could convince her to slow down. He asked Manning to try to convince Margaret to hire a full-time manager, which of course Margaret refused to do. Then Margaret started dropping hints about how Richard couldn't hunt three days a week like he used to, but that since Manning had moved away there was no one Richard was willing to let lead the field. You get the picture. Long story short,

Manning fell for it hook, line, and sinker and came back home to help out.

"I know Margaret and Richard had good intentions, but I really think it was a shitty thing for them to do. Manning had made a name for himself in L.A., you know? But the minute he got back here that old Scarlet cloud was still hanging over him. I mean, give the guy a break. It was, what, seventeen years ago? But people still gossip about it."

Julia's eyes widened and she threw a hand over her mouth. "Oh, my God. I'm so sorry. What a stupid thing to say, to you of all people!"

"It's okay. You were just being honest." Abigale managed a smile.

"Yeah. Brutally."

"Don't worry about it. Tell me more about Manning's drinking. You said it's spiraled out of control."

"Well, for example, a couple days ago Manning was at the Blackthorne Inn, where I work, and Stevie—he's the bartender—thought Manning was too drunk to drive, so I brought him home with me. Manning has a total blackout about the night."

"Really."

Julia nodded. "That's what I meant when I said we were together the other night but it didn't really count. I had no idea at the time how bad off Manning was. But the next morning he couldn't even remember how he got to my house. Then he called me later that day, all frantic, wanting to know what time he'd gotten to the pub. Apparently Manning was supposed to meet Richard at the racecourse the afternoon he was murdered. But Manning was so drunk he can't remember if he kept the appointment, canceled it, or stood Richard up."

Loud barking erupted in the hall and toenails skittered over the wood floor. A beam of headlights swept across the room.

"That must be Margaret," Julia said, pointing to Duchess, who pranced by the front door, wagging her tail.

They heard the sound of car doors slamming and footsteps crunching on the gravel drive. The front door opened and Margaret scooted the dog back into the hall and stood aside as Manning stepped through the door behind her.

"How's Dixie?" Julia called.

Margaret's hand flew to her chest as she spun toward the library. "My Lord, you startled me. I didn't expect anyone to still be here. Abigale, I thought you'd be sound asleep."

Abigale stood. "I wanted to wait up to hear how Dixie is. Julia offered to keep me company. We were catching up on old times."

Margaret shucked off her barn coat as she walked over to them. "Dixie's doing much better. Javier is going to keep an eye on her through the night, but the vet thinks it's a mild impaction. He oiled her and gave her Banamine, and she just gobbled up a hot bran mash."

"I'm so glad to hear that," Abigale said. "Smitty told me a little about Dixie. She sounds like a fabulous mare."

Margaret nodded. "I'll take you down to see her tomorrow. She produced a pretty fancy colt I'll show you, too."

"I'd like that."

"Well, I'd better head home," Julia said. "Thanks so much for including me in your dinner party, Margaret. The pot roast was to die for."

"I'm glad you could join us," Margaret said.

Julia gave Abigale a tight hug. "It's so good to have you back here."

Manning stood watching them from the front door. His eyes grazed Abigale's, shooting a tingle through her. *They'd talk now. Alone. Clear the air.*

But Manning lifted Julia's coat off the hook by the door and held it out for her. "I'll walk you to your car," he said to Julia as she slipped on her coat.

Margaret had just returned from the barn when she heard Abigale's footsteps on the stairs. She flicked on the coffeemaker and grabbed a carton of eggs from the refrigerator.

"Good morning. I'm in the kitchen."

Muffled footsteps shuffled up the hallway and the door swung partially open. Abigale's face peered around the edge of the door. "Are you alone?"

"Yes, come on in."

Abigale was in her stocking feet and wrapped in the plaid flannel bathrobe Margaret had hung on the hook in her bathroom. She ran her fingers through her tangled hair. "I didn't hear anyone down here, so I thought I'd sneak down for a cup of coffee before I hop in the shower. I didn't expect to see anyone. How's Dixie this morning?"

"She devoured a bran mash and has a nice big pile of manure in her stall. The vet will be here in about an hour to check on her, but I think she's out of the woods."

"I'm so glad."

"You and me both." Margaret smiled at her. "You look well-rested. Grab yourself a cup of coffee and have a seat. I'll have breakfast whipped up in no time. How do you like your eggs prepared?"

Abigale reached for the steaming coffeepot. "Oh, no, Margaret, you don't need to cook breakfast for me. I never have more than coffee in the morning."

"That's why you're so thin." Margaret rummaged through a drawer for a spatula. "Are scrambled eggs okay?"

Abigale opened her mouth as if to argue, then caught Margaret's eye and broke into a smile. "Sure, scrambled eggs sound delicious. Can I help?"

"No, ma'am. Just sit yourself down."

"What's on the agenda for today?" Abigale asked, dropping down onto a kitchen chair.

"Well, let's see, Smitty and Manning have some painting to do at Longmeadow, and Wendy Brooks is coming by in about half an hour to discuss Monday's funeral arrangements with us. I'm sorry to spring that on you first thing, but we need to get preparations under way. Then I have an appointment at two o'clock this afternoon at Anne Sullivan's law office—she's Richard's lawyer—to go over Richard's will."

"So soon?"

Margaret nodded. "I need to get a look at it in case Richard specified any directives in his will about his burial. Richard named me as his executor."

"Do I need to be there?" Abigale asked.

"No, I don't suppose so," Margaret said. "I'll get a copy of the will for you to read."

Duchess leapt off the dog bed with a throaty bark, skidding into a chair as she tore toward the hall.

"Sorry about Duchess, she thinks she's a watchdog. She must have heard something out front. Perhaps Wendy arrived early." Margaret shoved the spatula into the eggs, yelling over her shoulder, "Duchess, get back here! Right now."

The doorbell chimed as the Lab padded back into the kitchen. She plopped on her pillow, a low growl rumbling in her throat.

"Come in. The door's open," Margaret called.

The doorbell chimed again.

"I'll be right back," she said, flipping the gas burner to low before heading for the front door. To her surprise, she opened the door to find Lieutenant Mallory and another deputy standing on the front stoop.

Lieutenant Mallory removed his hat. "Good morning, Mrs. Southwell. I apologize for showing up without calling first. We're following up on a new lead."

"I was just preparing breakfast, but come in. Please. We can talk in the kitchen if you don't mind."

When Margaret led the men into the kitchen, Abigale shot a look at her as if to say, "I can't believe you brought them in here." A flush spread across her cheeks, and she raised her coffee mug as if trying to hide behind it.

"Lieutenant, this is Richard's niece, Abigale Portmann. Abigale,

Lieutenant Mallory is in charge of the investigation into Richard's murder. He's here to tell us about a new lead."

"Good morning," Lieutenant Mallory said.

"Nice to meet you."

"Have a seat," Margaret said. "May I pour you each a cup of coffee?"

The lieutenant eyed the other deputy, who shook his head. "Thank you, no."

"All right, then." Margaret sat next to Abigale. "What do you have on your mind?"

Lieutenant Mallory set his hat on the table and leaned back in the chair. "I think you know we've been interviewing the members of the road crew working on St. Louis Road."

Margaret said to Abigale, "I told you about that yesterday, about the missing worker, Dario Reyes."

Abigale nodded.

"Our primary focus has been Reyes," Mallory said. "But we've also interviewed each worker individually to ascertain what if anything he might have seen Monday afternoon, or in the days leading up to the shooting, that could be of significance in the investigation."

Margaret turned to Abigale again. "They're trying to determine if your uncle might have struck up a conversation with Dario Reyes when he drove through the work site, maybe told him what was going on at the racecourse. If so, Reyes would have known Richard was working in an isolated place and might have figured he'd be an easy robbery target."

"Yes, and we're also trying to identify any other vehicles that might have been spotted in the vicinity around the time of the shooting," Mallory added.

Abigale frowned. "But Reyes's car was found abandoned nearby, so you know that's how he got there, right?"

"That's correct."

"So why the interest in another car? Are you saying you think he had an accomplice?"

"No, we have no reason to believe that. We're mainly trying to identify potential witnesses. And, of course, while Dario Reyes is our main suspect at this time, it is possible that he was not the shooter. We're following up on all leads."

"Have any of the workers confirmed whether Richard talked to Reyes?" Margaret asked.

"One of the workers we interviewed saw Reyes, as he put it, 'shooting the breeze with some dude in an SUV,'" Mallory said.

"Richard."

"Quite possibly. Although the witness can't remember anything about the description of the SUV or the driver. He did remember the description of another vehicle, however, which is why we're here."

"Oh?"

"Yes, ma'am. He remembered seeing a dark-green sports car drive through the area late afternoon Monday, just before they knocked off work. A BMW M Coupe. Apparently, he admired the car so it stuck in his mind."

The lieutenant paused, as if waiting for Margaret to say something. Margaret's stomach flip-flopped, but she returned his scrutinizing gaze.

He continued, "The worker noticed the vehicle had a foxhunting license plate. He thinks it was a personalized plate but doesn't remember what it said on it."

"What do you mean by a foxhunting license plate?" Abigale asked.

"Virginia offers license plates representing special-interest groups," Mallory explained. "One of those is a foxhunting plate. It has a unique design with a fox and hound across the bottom of the plate. Quite easily identifiable."

"We ran a check on all the foxhunting license plates, cross-referenced them with vehicle make and model. It was a relatively simple exercise, as you can imagine, since that model of BMW is relatively uncommon. In fact, we only came up with one match."

The lieutenant's eyes shifted from Abigale to Margaret. "A green 1998 BMW M Coupe, with a personalized foxhunting plate: TALLYO. It's registered to Manning Southwell. At this address."

"Manning is my son," Margaret said, managing to keep her voice steady.

Mallory nodded. "Yes, ma'am. That's what we surmised. We'd like to talk to him."

"Well, I'm afraid you've come to the wrong place. Manning uses my address for mailing purposes, but he doesn't live here."

"Where does he reside?"

"Off Zulla Road."

Mallory pulled out a notepad. "What's the address?"

"He rents the cottage at Clifden Cross. That's Ian and Claire McCullough's place."

"Do you know if we could find him there now?"

"There's no telling. What with planning the funeral and the races, we're running around like chickens with our heads cut off. I'll probably see him later today. I can ask him to call you."

"I'd appreciate that." Mallory fished a business card from his shirt pocket. "Here's my direct number in case you don't have it."

Margaret fingered the card. "I'll see to it that he gets this."

"I don't suppose you'd happen to know if your son was headed to Longmeadow when the worker spotted his car."

"I have no idea, Lieutenant. Like I said before, we've been running all over the place getting ready for the races. Manning has spent quite some hours at Longmeadow helping get the course ready, but I couldn't tell you for sure when he was there and when he wasn't."

"Any idea if your son spoke with Mr. Clarke by phone that afternoon?"

"Not the foggiest, but I'm quite certain that if Manning had knowledge about anything pertinent to Richard's murder, whether from a phone call or visit, he wouldn't just be sitting on that information."

"Sure, I understand." Mallory said. "We'd still like to question him."

"I'll pass on your request." Margaret's chair squawked as she pushed back from the table.

*A*bigale stared after them as they disappeared down the hall. Was the unspoken implication that Manning was a potential *suspect* in Uncle Richard's murder? The lieutenant hadn't come right out and said so, but if you read between the lines . . . What was it he'd said? Something about not being certain that Dario Reyes was the shooter. And then, in the next breath, he'd brought up Manning's car.

The front door thudded. A moment later, Margaret stormed past Abigale to the stove and snatched the frying pan off the burner. "Wouldn't you know it? The eggs are burned. I'll have to start over."

"Did that bit about Manning's car bother you as much as it did me?" Abigale asked.

"Why should it? They're just doing their job," Margaret said in a clipped tone. "Tying up loose ends."

Abigale frowned. "Is that really what you think?"

Margaret cracked an egg against the edge of the counter and plopped it into the sizzling pan. "What else would I think?"

Abigale stared at Margaret's back, noting her rigid stance, the angry way she whipped the egg with a fork. "I don't know. But I got the feeling they were bothered by the fact that Manning had driven through the work area. As if—I don't know—as if that was suspicious somehow."

"That's nonsense. Manning had a perfect right to be there," Margaret replied, cracking a second egg. She flung the shell into the sink. Abigale caught a glimpse of her profile and saw the hard set of her jaw. Margaret might say the visit from Mallory didn't bother her, but that's not how she looked. She looked worried. More than worried.

Cold fingers of fear wiggled up Abigale's spine. "Is Manning in trouble?"

No response.

"Margaret?"

The older woman's shoulders sagged, as if a puppeteer had relaxed his grip on her. She stopped stirring the eggs and rested the spatula on the stove.

"Talk to me. Please." Abigale patted the seat of the chair next to her. "Forget about breakfast. Come sit."

Margaret cut off the gas and walked slowly to the table, blowing out a noisy sigh as she sank onto the ladder-back chair. She lifted her gaze, her blue eyes dull. "Manning lied to me."

"Lied about what?"

Margaret clamped her lips together and shook her head, as if she couldn't bring herself to say the words. She squeezed her eyes shut and pinched the bridge of her nose with her thumb and forefinger. "Heaven help us."

Abigale's heart pounded in her throat. "Margaret, please. Talk to me."

"Manning told me he never went to Longmeadow after hunting on Monday. But that was obviously a lie. Because the construction worker saw him drive through the paving site. And if Manning was on St. Louis Road, he was on his way to Longmeadow. There would be no other reason for him to drive through that area."

"Manning didn't lie, Margaret. He didn't deliberately tell you he hadn't gone there when he had. He just doesn't remember."

"What are you saying?"

"Julia told me last night that Manning was so drunk on Monday he can't remember anything that happened."

"How does Julia know that?"

"She ran into Manning at the pub where she works." Abigale fingered the handle of her mug of cold coffee. "He spent the night with her."

Margaret's eyes flashed. "That's no surprise."

"Julia told me this wasn't the first time he's been drunk."

"The first? Far from it. Manning seems intent on honoring his good-for-nothing father's legacy, partying and sleeping around like there's no tomorrow. Not a care or responsibility in the world. I've bailed Manning out of more messes than you can count."

"It sounds like he needs professional help."

"Of course he does," Margaret shot back, her tone so sharp it made Abigale jump. "There's an excellent alcohol rehab facility right up the road in

Pennsylvania. I've given Manning all the literature about it, but you can't help someone who won't help himself."

She shook her head, disappointment swimming in her eyes. "The least Manning could have done was to fess up and tell me that he was so stinking drunk he can't remember whether he went to Longmeadow. But did he do that? *No.* He lied. Said he'd told Richard he couldn't meet him there. Now he has the police after him, questioning what he was doing in the vicinity at the time of Richard's murder, and you're telling me Manning can't even remember if he was there. Well, I'm tired of pinning up his diapers. He's on his own this time."

Abigale kept quiet. It wasn't her place to defend Manning.

A car door slammed outside. Duchess barked and scrambled toward the back door.

"That must be Wendy," Margaret said.

Abigale carried her coffee mug to the sink. "I'm going to run upstairs for a quick shower."

"That's fine. Wendy and I can go over race business until you join us to discuss the funeral arrangements. I'm sorry about this mess with Manning, Abigale. Nothing like being exposed to all the skeletons in the closet right off the bat."

The back door squeaked open and muffled footsteps drifted in, the sound of someone stomping on the mat.

"Don't apologize," Abigale said. "I—"

Manning stepped inside.

*B*oth women stared at Manning. Neither said a word. He looked from his mother to Abigale as he reached down to pet Duchess. "Did I interrupt something?"

Abigale jabbed a hand at her hair and tugged at the belt of her flannel bathrobe. "I was just leaving."

He arched an eyebrow as she disappeared into the hall. "Was it something I said?"

Margaret didn't return his smile. "I need to talk to you."

"Okay."

"Might as well sit down."

"Okay." He chose a chair across the table from her.

Margaret glared at him, her hands clasped together on the oak table in a white-knuckled grip. Her lips curved downward, exaggerating the lines around her mouth. It struck Manning how old she looked.

"I had a visit from Lieutenant Mallory this morning."

"Any breaks in the investigation?"

"As a matter of fact, yes."

"Good news?"

"Not necessarily."

Manning frowned. "What did he tell you?"

Margaret locked eyes with him. He wasn't quite sure what it was he saw in the look she gave him. Anger? Fear? Disgust? Whatever it was, it wasn't good. He waited.

"Lieutenant Mallory informed me that a witness reported seeing a green sports car drive through the paving site on St. Louis Road shortly before four o'clock on Monday."

Manning's pulse pounded so hard he was sure his mother could hear it. He shoved his hands in his pockets and leaned back in the chair.

"Turns out, they've identified the vehicle as your car and are curious why no one mentioned that you had been in the area around the time of Richard's murder. I'm sure you can imagine my surprise, since you told me you didn't go to Longmeadow."

Fire shot through Manning's gut. *Jesus Christ.* So he *had* gone to the racecourse. "I can explain—"

Margaret slammed her clenched hands against the table. "I'm not interested in an explanation. I'm interested in the truth."

He closed his eyes, ran both hands through his hair. "The truth is, I don't know."

"What's that supposed to mean?"

"I had too much to drink," Manning said, blowing out a sigh. "I have a blackout about that entire night. I've tried to piece things together, believe me, but I just can't remember whether I met Richard at Longmeadow or not." He told her about the incoming call from Richard on his cell, what Julia had said about him rushing out of the Blackthorne.

"So that's why Mallory asked if you'd talked to Richard by phone that afternoon. He probably saw it on the call record on Richard's cell phone."

"Probably."

Margaret gave him a long, cold stare. "You told me you didn't have a meeting with Richard. That you told him you couldn't make it that afternoon."

"Yeah, I know."

"So, that was a lie?" It was a statement, dressed up as a question.

He nodded.

"I'm sorry, was that a yes?"

"Yes. I lied."

"Why?"

"Why what?"

"Why did you *lie*?" She spat out the word, as if it was about to choke her.

"I don't know. When Percy asked me about meeting Richard at Longmeadow and I had no recollection of it, I guess I panicked."

"So you lied."

"Yes, Mother. I lied. For Christ's sake, how many times do you want me to say it?"

"Until you show some remorse for what you did!"

"You think I don't have remorse? Trust me, I have enough remorse for both of us."

"So what are you going to do about it?" she asked.

"I'll talk to Mallory and tell him the truth, that I was drunk and I don't remember going to Longmeadow."

"You expect him to believe that?"

"I don't know if he'll believe it or not, but it's the truth."

Margaret gave him a wintry smile. "Wonder if intoxication has ever held up as a defense in a murder case."

He narrowed his eyes. "What are you talking about?"

"Wake up, Manning. What do you think Mallory wants to discuss with you? Whether you had a nice afternoon drive on Monday?"

"You've got to be kidding! Mallory thinks I shot Richard?"

"I'd say it appears to be an angle he's exploring."

"That's ridiculous."

She didn't respond.

"Why in the world would I kill Richard? I loved him. He was like a father to me. You know that."

"That's neither here nor there as far as Mallory is concerned. He sees people kill people they love all the time."

Manning sucked in a breath. "I don't believe this. I thought they had a suspect. That road construction worker."

"They do."

"Okay, so if they find him and link him to Richard's murder . . ."

"Assuming they do, you'll be off the hook. Until the next time."

"What do you mean by that?"

"You have a drinking problem, Manning. That's what got you into this scrape. And, God forbid, it may be what put Richard in a situation where he ended up shot dead. Don't you think it's time you came to grips with it?"

He nodded as Margaret was talking. "I know. I've already had this conversation with myself. I had way too much to drink. The blackout scares the shit out of me. Trust me, it won't happen again."

"So that's your solution? You won't let it happen again?" Her voice was cold with contempt. "Like I haven't heard that from you before."

"Thanks for the faith in me, Mother."

"Why should I have faith in you? Give me one good reason."

Manning blew out a bitter laugh. "I've quit before, Mother. I can do it again."

"You've quit before? No, if you had quit before, you wouldn't be drinking now. Let's call a spade a spade: you went through a dry spell."

He looked away.

"You're an alcoholic, Manning," Margaret said, her tone a tad softer. "You can't just lay off the booze for a while. You need to own up to the problem and get help. This isn't something you can tackle alone."

"What, you want me to check myself into rehab?"

"That would be a good start."

Jesus. He threw his hands up in the air. "Hell, why not? What better way to avoid Mallory. And, let's see, I could also wash my hands of the races. And Richard's funeral. The timing couldn't be better."

"I'm not suggesting you do it this afternoon. I'm saying it's the only way for you to lick the problem. Take your life back, Manning. Do what your father was never strong enough to do."

C H A P T E R
28

*A*bigale wrapped her arm around the narrow trunk of a young oak as she hiked down the horse trail that led from the back of Fox Run to the Little River. Fallen leaves carpeted the path, making it slick beneath her feet. The meeting about Uncle Richard's funeral had seemed to drag on forever, bringing up so many questions—details—she never would have considered. Abigale had needed some time alone to clear her head after they'd finished. She'd told Margaret she'd meet her at the barn in an hour.

She scrambled over a log, cradling her camera against her chest. Late morning sunlight danced through the half-naked trees, creating a mosaic on the muddy hoof prints and brilliant leaves that defined the trail. She removed the lens cap and snapped several shots to take home to her mother.

The air was crisp and the woods held the musky aroma of damp earth and decaying leaves. Abigale closed her eyes and inhaled deeply, capturing the scent in her mind so she could describe it to her mother when she showed her the photos.

Leaves rustled nearby and she opened her eyes to see a gray squirrel scamper toward a poplar tree. It paused at the base of the trunk and eyed her, a nut of some kind clasped between its jaws. She slowly raised her camera, caught the image through the viewfinder, and zoomed in. The squirrel's weight was on its haunches, its front paws curled mid-chest, and its nose quivered as it mouthed the nut, an acorn. She snapped the shot, and the click of the shutter sent the squirrel scurrying up the tree.

Abigale lowered the camera and caught the glint of water through the trees. The river wasn't far off. She continued on the trail for a couple hundred feet until the canopy of trees parted at the edge of the river's bank. The path that led to the water seemed broader, less steep than when she'd last ridden down it; worn away by erosion, perhaps, or distorted by the tricks the years had played with her memory.

She crept along the edge of the bank until she reached the rock outcropping she was seeking. Abigale perched at the top of the rock and hugged her knees to her chest, welcoming the warmth that radiated from the sun-kissed stone. Memories showered her like a soft spring rain and she smiled, remembering the time Manning had shown off by accepting Percy's dare to cross the river walking backward over a fallen tree with his eyes closed. When Manning had been midway across, Percy had pegged a rock at him, doubling over with laughter as Manning lost his footing, dancing and flailing his arms as he struggled to avoid a backward plunge. The river was high, the water muddy from a recent storm, and Manning rose from the river with a roar, shaking the water from his hair as he leapt up the bank, his sneakers squeaking and sloshing brown water as he raced after Percy. They had all ended up in a water fight.

Abigale breathed a gentle sigh. Their lives had been so carefree that last summer. So innocent. Not yet scarred by war or terrorism. Or death.

She shook her head, trying to rid her mind of the angry exchange of words she'd overheard that morning between Margaret and Manning. She had managed to stay out of it, fighting the voice in her head that screamed at her to barge into the kitchen and stick up for Manning. What right did she have to intrude?

A red-tailed hawk swept down between the trees and Abigale reached for her camera. She spent the next thirty minutes ambling along the river's edge, capturing shots of a pair of bald eagles performing a mating ritual as they soared overhead and a huge red fox that watched her curiously from atop a ridge above the opposite bank.

She knew it was time to head back to the farm, but instead of hiking up the trail she'd taken on her descent to the river, Abigale veered off on a narrower path that traversed the steep hill at a more gradual incline. Her heart raced as she began the climb and she felt goose bumps prick her arms beneath the fleece jacket she'd borrowed from Margaret.

Abigale told herself this might not be the right path. Dozens of deer trails just like it crisscrossed throughout the woods. And after seventeen years, new passages would have been created, old ones abandoned. But instinct carried her forward.

A couple of minutes into her climb the trail disappeared into a wide swath of trampled undergrowth, fallen limbs, and uprooted trees, as if strong winds—perhaps even a tornado—had carved a lane straight along the side of the hill. She wove her way through the wreckage, sidestepping a crater left by the root-ball of a fallen oak, and ducked under a hanging sycamore limb, snapped like a matchstick from atop the towering tree.

On the other side of the debris she picked up the trail again, grasping at saplings as she clambered up a gully that led to the crest of the ridge. The terrain leveled out and she stood for a moment, her pulse pounding in her ears. *This was it.* She crept forward, boots shuffling through the leaves, her hands clenched so tightly at her sides that her nails carved half-moons in her palms. She dropped down on a log at the edge of the trail.

The image of Scarlet going down flashed through Abigale's mind, so vividly she could almost feel the ground rise to meet her, smell the warm, earthy dampness of that summer night. She squeezed her eyes shut. Still, the memory lingered, so intense she half-expected to hear Scarlet's throaty whinny, deepening in pitch as the mare struggled to get up, and Manning's voice, calm but stern, warning her to roll beyond the reach of Scarlet's thrashing hooves.

Abigale forced herself to look across the trail. Nature had reclaimed the spot, blanketed the earth with leaves, burying any evidence of the horror that had played out there. Her eyes swept the woods, then widened as she spotted a wooden cross, a few yards away, planted at the foot of a dogwood tree.

She pawed her way through the thicket and sank to her knees beside the cross. It stood about two feet high and was made from two strips of wood that had been carved to fit together at the center of the cross. The wood was unpainted and had aged to a silver gray. She ran her hand along the top of the cross. The edges had been beveled and sanded. It was smooth beneath her fingers.

Abigale looked down and realized the ground near the cross was clear of leaves and debris. Someone was tending to it.

29

Manning eyed the wood flooring on the top deck of the stewards' stand. The bloodstain—Richard's blood—stared stubbornly at him, still visible beneath the fresh coat of gray paint. "One coat's not going to cover it," he said to Smitty.

"I'm afraid you're right," Smitty agreed. "We'll have to give it time to dry, then hit it again." Smitty looked at his watch. "Problem is, I've got the vet coming to the kennels in about an hour to vaccinate the hounds. I'd best give him a call and see if I can push it back."

"Don't do that. You go on. I'll put the second coat on by myself."

"You sure?"

"Yeah."

Smitty glanced around the stewards' stand as if reluctant to leave, and Manning felt the lack of confidence in him as a slap in the face. Jesus, didn't Smitty trust him to finish the painting? *Smitty, of all people?* "You think I can't handle it?"

"Good God, it's not that," Smitty replied. "I was just thinking about Richard, what happened to him here. I wonder if it's sensible for you—any of us—to be out here alone."

Manning's gaze swept across the rolling terrain. "You really think whoever shot Richard is still around? Looking for another victim?"

"Probably not, but it doesn't hurt to be careful."

"Careful, sure. But not afraid. There's a difference."

"I hear ya," Smitty said.

Manning jerked a shoulder toward Smitty's truck. "Go on."

"All right. But keep your eyes open."

Manning felt a pang of regret as he watched Smitty disappear down the stairs. Now what? The last thing he felt like doing was killing time sitting around watching paint dry. His eyes swept the racecourse. Yellow crime-scene tape still wound around the vicinity of the stewards' stand, though half of it was torn loose, trampled into the ground. That definitely needed to be cleaned up before race day. He circled the stewards' stand, ripping loose the slippery yellow tape and tossing it in a pile. When he was finished, he grabbed the armful and stuffed it in the trash receptacle in the parking area.

Manning turned back toward the stewards' stand, then stopped and cocked his head to listen. He heard the far-off crunch of wheels on gravel, the faint whine of an engine. Despite his earlier resolve, he felt a twinge of unease. Shading his eyes with one hand, he fixed his gaze on the gravel drive. A sheriff's car topped the rise and relief washed over him, tinged with a prick of shame. So much for not letting fear take over.

The sheriff's car rolled to a stop beside him and two deputies got out. The radio on the driver's belt squawked. He reached down and silenced it, then nodded at Manning. "Afternoon."

"Hello." Manning eyed the deputy's name tag. *Mallory.*

Mallory cast a deliberate glance at Manning's BMW. "That your car?"

Manning's heart slammed against his chest. He sucked in a breath, nodded.

"So you must be Manning Southwell."

Manning figured the deputy probably already knew who he was, had most likely pulled his driver's license photo. "Yes." He extended his hand. "My mother told me you dropped by her house this morning. That you wanted to talk to me."

Mallory's grip was firm. His expression remained neutral. Not hostile, but not friendly either. "Then you're probably aware that your car was spotted in this area on Monday."

"That's what Mother said."

"Were you here with Mr. Clarke that afternoon?"

Manning shoved his hands in his pockets. How the hell could he explain it? Tell Mallory he didn't remember? If his mother was right, that might be digging a hole he wouldn't be able to get out of. Still, it was the truth. "I don't know."

Mallory exchanged a look with the other deputy. "You don't know?"

He shook his head. "I was supposed to meet Richard here to help work on the racecourse—and since someone saw my car, I guess that means I did—but

I really don't remember. I was drinking that afternoon. I guess I had a little too much."

"Too much to drink."

"Yes sir."

"Let me see if I have this right, Mr. Southwell. Are you saying you can't remember because you had an alcoholic blackout?"

"Yeah, I guess so."

Mallory's gray eyes turned steely, flickering over Manning as if trying to decide whether he was lying or just plain stupid. The other deputy took a step closer. The playing field flipped from neutral to hostile.

"You ever have a blackout before?" Mallory asked.

"Not this bad, but yeah."

"All right. Why don't you tell us what you do remember about Monday."

Manning did so, and finished by saying, "Look, what I did was irresponsible. No question. I drank too much and got behind the wheel. Did things I can't remember. But one thing I know for sure—blackout or not—I didn't shoot Richard. I never would have harmed him, no matter how drunk I was. I'll take a lie detector test, whatever you want. I have nothing to hide."

Mallory went over the timeline Manning had given him a couple of times, probably trying to trip him up, to see if he'd waver about what he remembered and what he didn't. He finally wrapped it up by telling Manning they'd most likely call him in for further questioning. Mallory also told him not to leave town without checking in with him first.

"Oh, one more thing, Mr. Southwell," Mallory said as he turned back toward the sheriff's car. He nodded at Manning's BMW. "I think it's safe to say your car has a bull's-eye on its tag from here on out. It'd probably serve you well to remember that the next time you've had a couple of drinks and think about crawling behind the wheel."

*A*bigale ran her hand across the oak stall front as she watched Margaret lead the dark bay colt back inside and slip off his halter. She'd scrubbed the thick boards in the aisle so many times, brushed countless cobwebs from the black steel grills. On crusty summer afternoons when it was too hot to ride, she and Manning would help out with chores in the stable, kept cool by the thick exterior stone walls. She smiled, remembering how quickly Manning got bored with cobwebbing, how he'd whisper in her ear to meet him in the hayloft, which was always hotter than hell. She'd usually ignored him, but not always. Her cheeks burned as she remembered the *not always* times.

"So what do you think?" Margaret asked as she slid the stall door closed and flipped the latch.

"He's gorgeous," Abigale replied, shaking off the memories. "How does he compare to Dixie when she was a weanling?"

Margaret's eyes twinkled and she held up her hand, showing her crossed fingers. "He's put together just as well as she is, but I think he's going to be a fancier mover. And you couldn't ask for a better attitude. Most laid-back colt I've ever handled. I've got big plans for him."

Abigale smiled. "Have you named him yet?"

"We're calling him Rebel, since Dixie's his dam. But I haven't come up with a show name yet." She gestured toward the stable office. "Follow me. I told you I'd show you Dixie's ribbons and trophies."

"The stable looks wonderful, Margaret," Abigale said as they walked up the asphalt aisle. "I can't believe it—everything still looks the same after all these years."

"This barn's been standing for over a hundred years, dear. As long as we take care of it, I imagine it'll look pretty much the same a hundred years from now." She chuckled. "Daddy and Granddaddy would both turn over in their graves if I ever let this place go."

"How many horses do you have here now?"

"Fifty. That's capacity. Forty are boarders, mostly show hunters. I have a handful of young prospects I'm bringing along and a couple of foxhunters. Manning's two hunters are stabled here. Of course, when Daddy was alive, Fox Run was strictly for foxhunters. He couldn't stomach the way folks babied their show horses."

"I guess Manning learned his love of foxhunting from his grandfather," Abigale said. "He used to tell me stories about his grandfather taking him hunting on the leadline. Manning idolized him."

"People said Daddy could think like a fox, that's why he was so good. I didn't inherit that instinct, but Richard often said he saw it in Manning." Margaret gave her the briefest of smiles. "Of course, it takes more than instinct to be a good master. It involves more work—responsibility—than I can imagine Manning ever being willing to shoulder."

Abigale kept quiet as she followed Margaret into the office, ignoring the impulse to jump to Manning's defense.

Margaret spent the better part of half an hour reliving Dixie's show career, glowing with pride as she regaled Abigale with tales of each victory.

"Is Dixie the winningest horse you've had in the barn?" Abigale asked.

"By far, of the horses I've owned. Of course, Dixie's show record didn't come close to Scarlet's."

Abigale forced a smile. "I guess not many horses have."

"That's for sure." Margaret stretched up and pulled a silver-framed photograph off the top shelf of the trophy case. She blew the dust off the top of the frame and handed it to Abigale. The frame was engraved: SCARLET IF CONVENIENT. "This is one of my favorite photographs of Scarlet. Remember that show? It was your first time showing her at a rated show and you walked away with three blues and the tri-color. Look at the smile on your face."

Abigale didn't need to look at the photograph to remember that horse show. It seemed as if every last detail was burned into her memory. That day had marked the beginning of her "relationship" with Manning—or the end, depending on how you looked at it. She handed the framed photo back to Margaret. "I took a hike this morning and went by the trail where Scarlet had the accident."

Margaret raised an eyebrow. "Oh?"

She nodded, swallowing the lump that rose in her throat. "Someone put a wooden cross there."

"Manning." Margaret set the photograph back on the shelf. "You should talk to him about it, you know. It would probably do the both of you a world of good."

Abigale glanced up at the photograph. "We can't turn back time."

"No, you can't, that's for sure. But sometimes you have to make peace with the past before it will allow you to move forward."

$\mathscr{A}$bigale cut across the stable parking lot, clutching the keys to Margaret's Subaru in one hand and the written directions to Uncle Richard's farm in the other. She had spent half a dozen summers being ferried back and forth between Margaret's stable and her uncle's farm and had told Margaret she was sure she'd be able to find her way, but Margaret had insisted on writing down the directions.

A layer of dust coated the silver Subaru, caking the edges of the stickers that lined the rear bumper: SAY NO TO SPRAWL; VIRGINIA IS FOR HORSE LOVERS; FARMLAND LOST IS FARMLAND LOST FOREVER. A decal sporting the international foxhunt emblem of an orange fox mask and a black hunt cap on a green background was stuck on the rear window.

Abigale drove past the bricked sidewalks and old-fashioned streetlights that adorned the tree-lined streets of Middleburg, noting happily that not much seemed to have changed in seventeen years, except that a few new hand-painted signs replaced some of those she remembered on the quaint storefronts. Books & Crannies was new. It looked like the quintessential independent bookstore: a huge bay window peeked out of the brick facade, chock-full with a cheerful display of books and flyers; a chalkboard on the sidewalk announced an upcoming book signing. She stopped for the red light next to a store called Wylie Wagg, obviously a pet boutique. A large plate-glass window framing the storefront was set up to look like a television studio. The network logo was *CNN: Canine News Network* and the news anchors—stuffed dogs—were named Woof Blitzer and Anderson Pooper. A red fire hydrant boasted a sign that read RELIEF PROGRAM. How clever was that! The light turned green and she moved on, making a mental note to come back and take photos to email to some of her CNN friends in Afghanistan.

She turned north at the corner by the Red Fox Inn, smiling at the hand-painted sign proclaiming it the oldest original inn, circa 1728. That *was* old, for America. But everything was relative. The walls of her parents' hotel in Switzerland dated back to the 1400s.

Abigale followed her instincts rather than Margaret's directions, meandering along Foxcroft Road, past farms bordered by dry-stacked stone walls and miles of black four-board fencing. Occasionally she met another vehicle and they both slowed, easing past one another with a smile and a wave. She drove past rolling pastures dotted with hay bales, fields with rows and rows of dried cornstalks, and horses, grazing peacefully: some already fuzzy with their winter coats, others, probably the clipped ones, wearing colorful blankets to ward off the chilly air.

A hand-painted sign by one farm entrance illustrated a burly black cow against a grassy background. The name of the farm glittered in gold letters: GREEN ACRES. A herd of black cattle lolled among the rolling hills; several lay sheltered beneath the sprawling branches of a gnarly tree at the top of a ridge. What was the old wives' tale they have in America: if cows lie down in a field it's going to rain? Abigale smiled as she glanced up at the faded blue sky.

When she reached the intersection with Mountville Road she knew exactly where she was. Manning and she used to hack through there when they went to school her uncle's horses over the outdoor course at Foxcroft School. She turned onto Mountville, then took the jog onto Leith Lane and followed it to Beaverdam Bridge Road.

As Abigale drove across the one-lane bridge, excitement quickened her pulse. Despite all her misgivings about being back, Uncle Richard's farm had always been a safe haven for her: a place where she'd felt sheltered from the rigor of school and her father's hardnosed expectations.

She topped the crest of a small hill and the brick pillars of Dartmoor Glebe rose into view. The black wrought-iron gates stood open, and Abigale eased the Subaru through the entrance and rolled to a stop. The long lane that led to the main house, graced on either side by lofty poplars, stretched before her. Beams of sunlight crept between the branches, spilling warm pockets of sunshine on the speckled pea-gravel surface. Beyond the fence to her left, a huge red fox trotted across the field. Abigale lowered the driver's window and cut off the engine.

"Hey there, Charlie," she whispered, reaching for her camera.

She zoomed in, clicking several shots as she observed the fox through the viewfinder. It ran toward her, then stopped, moved stealthily through the faded grass. What was it stalking? A mouse? It tilted its head inquisitively, its intelligent eyes bright, focused on its prey. It leapt and pounced, cat like, then pounced again. Abigale captured a shot as the fox shook its head triumphantly, a mouse clutched in its jaw.

32

argaret sat at the conference table in Anne Sullivan's law office across from Cyndi, Anne's secretary, who was punching numbers on the dial of the flying-saucer-looking speaker phone in the center of the table.

"Keep your fingers crossed that I'm able to get Anne on the phone. The ship-to-shore phone service hasn't been all that reliable," Cyndi said.

"Hello, *bonjour*," a woman's singsong voice drifted faintly from the speaker.

Cyndi jabbed the volume button. "Hello. Stateroom ten-oh-one, please."

"One moment, I'll connect you."

Two shrill rings jingled in quick succession.

"Hello."

"Hi, Anne. I've got Margaret here," Cyndi said.

"Hi, Margaret. Is Abigale with you?"

Margaret rested her elbows on the table and leaned closer to the speaker. "Hello, dear. No, Abigale went to Dartmoor Glebe. I think she's a bit overwhelmed by everything, haunted by old memories and the like. She didn't seem too keen to be present for the reading of the will, so I encouraged her to take some time for herself. I told her I'd fill her in later."

"That's fine. Cyndi can provide you with a copy to take to Abigale and I can speak with her once she's had time to digest it."

"Thank you, Anne. And thanks for arranging to do this by phone."

"You know I wish more than anything I could be there in person. Doug's been working with the captain trying to figure out how quickly we can get back home. We've been at sea for two days. We reach our next port-of-call tomorrow, but it has very limited air service. If we can even get seats on a flight out of there we'd have to take a circuitous route home. Our best bet may be to stay onboard until we reach Sydney on Sunday."

"For God's sake, Anne, you'd be crazy to even consider the puddle jumper, especially traveling with the children. I spoke with Doug this morning and I'll repeat for your benefit what I told him: I know the last thing Richard would want is for the two of you to cut short your trip. There's just no sense in you rushing home. It won't bring Richard back."

"I know, Doug told me what you said, but we want to come home."

Margaret exchanged a look with Cyndi. "Okay. It's your decision. Just remember what Richard said about you and Doug going on the cruise, even though you wouldn't be here for the races: after all you and Doug have been through this past year, you'd be crazy to let hunt business interfere with your family plans. He insisted you go. I'm sure if he were here today he'd say the same thing about you hopping on the next plane and flying halfway around the world to be here to lay him to rest."

"Thanks for saying that, Margaret." The rustle of papers crackled from the speaker. "So, let's get started. As you know, I drafted Richard's will. The original, which you have in front of you, was kept in our safe deposit box. Cyndi scanned it and emailed a copy to me."

Cyndi flipped open a file folder, turning it to face Margaret as she pushed it across the table.

"It's my understanding from Richard that he discussed with you his desire that you be named executor under his will."

"Yes, he did."

"So, as you can see in the first paragraph under Article One, you, Margaret Huntington Southwell, are named as executor and I am named as successor executor. Can I assume you are willing to serve in that capacity?"

"Yes."

"Good, then let's skip the boilerplate language and get to the meat of the will. If you look about halfway down the first page you'll see the heading *Article One, Special and Specific Bequests.* Do you see that?"

Margaret ran her finger down the page. "Okay, yes, I'm there."

"All right. Let me read this section out loud and you can follow along. Richard was very specific about the wording used here. After we go through it, I can fill you in on the background so you better understand his intent behind some of these bequests."

"Go ahead. I'm with you."

"'Many individuals have meant much to me in my life and I give the following gifts to those individuals, if they survive me, as follows:

"'To my niece Abigale Clarke Portmann, all interest I have in the real estate designated as Dartmoor Glebe. Abigale, this land is in your blood. It is the childhood home of your mother, my beloved sister Caroline, and has been the source of much joy and love for our family throughout the last eighty-plus years. With this bequest, I place the future of Dartmoor Glebe solely in your hands. It is my hope that in so doing, I will help you find peace with your past and open your heart to the future.

"'To my godson Manning Southwell, all interest I have in horses, hounds, vehicles, tack, equipment, and any and all hunt assets not named herein. Furthermore, all interest I have in the real estate designated as the Middleburg Foxhounds Kennels. Manning, in making this bequest it is my desire that you assume the role of Master of the Middleburg Foxhounds. Ultimately this decision will be made by the Board of Governors of the hunt, but I trust they will see the wisdom of my wishes. Undoubtedly, you possess the necessary skills as a horseman. Financial responsibility, you can learn. Leadership, I believe you can earn.'"

Margaret stared at the will, barely able to believe what Anne had just read aloud. *What in the hell had Richard been thinking?* Richard had always looked after Manning, sometimes despite her wishes to the contrary, but, still—*leaving the hunt and the kennels to Manning?* Good God.

"Are you aware of the fact that although the hunt kennels are located adjacent to Richard's farm, the facilities actually sit on a separate parcel?" Anne asked.

"I seem to recall Richard saying at one point that there were separate lots, but I never paid it much mind. I always just thought of the kennels as being at Dartmoor Glebe," Margaret replied.

"And for practical purposes, Richard treated the property that way. But Dartmoor Glebe proper encompasses just over two hundred acres, and the kennels an additional fifty. Because of where the kennels are situated at the back of the farm with no road frontage, Richard created an easement through Dartmoor Glebe for the access drive."

Margaret's mind raced, imagining what effect Richard's bequest would have on the hunt—and on Manning.

Anne said, "Anyway, I didn't mean to get sidetracked. I just wanted to make sure you were aware of the real estate configuration. Let me continue with the will. 'As the cost of operating the hunt is considerable and hunt revenues do not cover operating expenses, I direct my executor to set aside in the Manning Southwell Middleburg Foxhounds Hunt Trust an amount equal to five years of operating expenses for the hunt, to be paid to Manning Southwell in equal monthly disbursements. The hunt trust document more specifically addresses the requirements that must be met in order to receive the monthly disbursements, including the stipulation that said disbursements be used solely for hunt-related expenses and not other personal expenditures.

"'Furthermore, I bequeath to the hunt trust the additional sum of one million dollars. If at the end of the five-year period, the Middleburg Foxhounds still operates as a recognized hunt in good standing with the Masters of Foxhounds Association and Manning Southwell fulfills the requirements set forth under the terms of the hunt trust, the trustees of the hunt trust shall pay to Manning Southwell outright the sum of one million dollars, as directed under the terms of the hunt trust agreement. If the hunt is not in good standing and/ or Manning Southwell does not fulfill the requirements set forth under the terms of the hunt trust, the sum of one million dollars will be gifted to various charities, as specified in the hunt trust agreement.'

"Let me stop here and see if you have any questions," Anne said. "I assume Richard told you about these bequests, but I know the legal language can be confusing."

Margaret sank back in her chair. "Actually, no, Richard did not discuss his intentions with me."

"Really? I'm surprised. He told me he planned to do so. Although . . ."

"What?"

"I guess I'm not breaking confidence by revealing this to you, Margaret. Richard has voiced some concerns about Manning. He felt Manning's lifestyle had him on a downward spiral. Before I left on our trip, Richard told me he was going to talk to Manning and tell him about the terms of his will. He said he was going to give Manning an ultimatum, tell him that if he did not seek help for his drinking he was going to revise his will. Perhaps Richard didn't want to mention the bequest to you until after he'd had the conversation with Manning."

*A*bigale followed the drive as it meandered past the house toward the barn. She parked in back, using the key Margaret had given her to enter her uncle's house through the mudroom door. She expected the house to feel vacant, but instead was greeted by the smell of leather and boot polish and the sight of a row of Uncle Richard's boots tucked tidily beneath an array of coats and jackets stacked on brass horse-head hooks along the wall. Next to the door, a horseshoe-shaped painted plaque showed the hind-end view of a gray horse and a rider in a scarlet coat, with the words GONE HUNTING arched across the top. Along the outer edge, several sets of keys dangled on hooks formed from blacksmith nails. Abigale looped Margaret's keys over one of the nails.

Slipping off her jacket, Abigale draped it over a waxed raincoat on one of the hooks along the wall. Uncle Richard's tweed cubbing jacket hung next to it. She picked a flake of shavings off the shoulder and buried her face in the sleeve, inhaling the musty scent of wool mingled with the earthy aroma of hay. Memories flooded her, misting her eyes. She let the sleeve slip from her fingers.

Abigale followed the stone passageway that led from the mudroom to the kitchen, a spacious room that she remembered as always being warm and cheery, a hubbub of activity. Sunlight streamed in through wide casement windows, revealing a thin layer of dust on the large round-topped walnut table that squatted in the center of the slate floor.

The front hall opened into a large gathering room. Fluffy-cushioned sofas and chairs rested on a green-and-gold-hued oriental carpet that stretched across the wide-planked oak floor. A grand piano stood in one corner and a stone-chimney fireplace ate up a good portion of the far wall. Abigale rubbed her arms, imagining how good it would feel to have a crackling fire roaring in the hearth. She glanced at the stack of logs and crumpled newspaper deftly arranged on the fox-head andirons. All she'd have to do is strike a match. And then what? Sit in the enormous room by herself?

She slipped into the foyer, where oil paintings lined the mustard-colored walls almost to the ceiling. Horses mostly, of almost every size and color. Some pastoral scenes with gnarled trees, and sheep, and broad-faced cows. And a smattering of portraits: a young blond girl with a calico cat curled on her aproned lap; an old black man with the gray stubble of a beard and intelligent, smiling eyes; and a sun-beaten-looking woman wearing a faded blue dress and white bonnet. A gleaming mahogany hutch along the side wall supported an almost life-sized bronze of a well-muscled foxhound, his nose to the ground and stern held high as if he'd just picked up a scent. Abigale ran her hand along the arm of the velvet love seat nestled beneath the stairwell, once her favorite spot to curl up with her nose in a book, waiting for Manning to come and take her on one sort of adventure or another.

Gripping the hand-carved banister, she climbed the winding staircase that led to the second floor. The door to Uncle Richard's bedroom stood open near the top of the stairs. Abigale paused in the doorway, eyed the king-sized sleigh bed, its bedspread tucked military-tight across the high mattress, then stepped back and gently closed the door. She wasn't ready for this room yet.

Her mother's bedroom was next to Uncle Richard's and Abigale passed by without entering, heading for the room at the far end of the hall. The door was closed, and Abigale hesitated for a moment, then grasped the crystal handle and pushed against the door. It creaked open and she broke into a smile, remembering Manning's theory that Uncle Richard deliberately left the squeak in the hinges so he'd be alerted if she tried to sneak out in the middle of the night.

A shiver pricked her arms. The room was just as she remembered it: the canopy bed still swaddled with the girlish lavender bedding ensemble she had selected; the furniture the same white princess pieces adorned with pink and purple hearts. She recalled that when she'd outgrown the girlish décor Uncle Richard had offered to redecorate the room in a more sophisticated style, but she'd refused.

Abigale stepped onto the plush ivory carpet and approached the bed. Plunked in the center of a mass of frilly pillows was a grayish lop-eared bunny, a frayed lavender ribbon tied in a limp bow around its neck. She lifted it gently, a sad smile tugging at the corners of her mouth.

"Hi, old friend," she whispered, smoothing the matted fur between its ears. "There've been a couple of nights over the years when I could have used you."

Hugging the stuffed animal to her chest, Abigale opened the mirrored closet door. Her riding clothes hung in an orderly fashion, one show jacket still wrapped in dry-cleaner plastic; stacks of jeans, T-shirts, and sweaters were folded neatly on the shelves. Someone had obviously tidied the room since she'd last stayed there.

Her Disney princess jewelry box sat on one shelf, next to her hunt horn and the pair of spurs Uncle Richard had ordered custom-made for her. Abigale set the bunny on the shelf and ran her fingers over the neck of one spur, delicately curved into the form of a horse hoof. She picked up the hunt horn, its shine tarnished from years on the shelf, and pressed it to her lips. The note she blew was weak and tinny. Shaking her head, she wet her lips, sucked in a breath, and tried again. Despite the dent in the bell of the horn, she eked out some clear notes, then blew "gone away" with an intensity that left her ears ringing. Breathless but grinning, she lowered the horn and closed her hand around the misshapen bell. The dent marred the beauty and hindered the performance of the horn, but back when it had happened, her seventeen-year-old mind had viewed it as symbolic of Manning's devotion to her and she'd refused to have it repaired or replaced.

Abigale felt a burn creep up her face. She could picture that day so vividly: Manning as he'd ridden up to the barn, soaked to the skin, thunder rumbling in the distance. He wasn't wearing a riding helmet and his hair dripped in ringlets around his face. He slid from his horse and she'd flung her arms around him, burying her face in his neck before he even had a chance to roll up his stirrups.

"Whoa, hey, what's going on?" he'd asked, wrapping an arm around her.

She clung fiercely to him, paying no heed to his soggy clothes, anger and relief boiling inside her. "What were you thinking going back out to look for my horn with a storm brewing?" she demanded. "And what are you doing riding without a helmet?"

Manning tugged her arms loose from his neck. "It was just a little rain, no big deal. Besides—" he broke into a grin and reached into the pocket of his breeches—"look what I found."

Abigale squealed as he held up the horn. "You found it! Oh, my God, I can't believe it. Where was it?"

"On that trappy trail leading from up Goose Creek into the Bellevue woods. Remember after we crossed the creek with the hounds and Tally spooked and bolted around that rotted log? That must have been when the horn slipped from its case. It was buried in the high grass and at first I didn't see it, but I heard a clang when Samson grazed it with his hoof." He held it out for her to see, his strong fingers gracefully exploring the dented bell. "I'm sorry it's all banged up. I'll ask Smitty if he knows where I can get it fixed."

"I don't want it fixed." Abigale slipped her hand in his and leaned up to kiss him. "It's perfect this way. It will always remind me that you went back and found it for me."

Abigale shook off the memory and sighed, placing the horn back beside the spurs on the shelf. She turned to leave the closet when a stack of what looked like half a dozen or so letters tied together with a pale blue ribbon caught her eye. Abigale recognized her mother's handwriting on a note card on top of the pile and frowned, reaching for the packet.

She carried the letters into the bedroom and perched on the window seat in one of the dormer windows. Sunlight streamed through the glass and Abigale shifted position so her eyes were shaded from the glare. She untied the ribbon and lifted her mother's note.

Dearest Richard,

As we discussed during our last phone call, I am sending you the collection of letters Ralph confiscated. I'm not sure why I felt compelled to retrieve the letters from the rubbish, nor why I cannot bring myself to discard them now, as so much time has passed. I don't see what possible good could come from Abigale ever reading the letters, but, nonetheless, I send them to you for safekeeping. As you can see from the sealed envelopes, I did not read what was inside, although Lord knows I was tempted. I place the matter in your hands now, and trust with your wisdom you will do the right thing.

As always,

Caroline

Abigale's fingers trembled as she set aside her mother's note. Slowly, she lowered her eyes to the top envelope. It was addressed to her, with Manning's return address in the upper left-hand corner. The postmark was seventeen years old.

Oh, Daddy, what did you do?

$\mathscr{B}$y the time Abigale finished reading the letters, long shadows had crept across the room. Anger burned, so fierce her chest felt like a pressure cooker ready to blow. She thought back to those lonely months in Switzerland, how as days had turned into weeks her father had stood by and watched her suffer as she longed for some word from Manning. Yet he'd known all the while Manning had written—countless times! Her father had intercepted the letters. He'd even gone so far as to tell her Manning's silence confirmed he didn't love her. That she'd been a summer fling, nothing more. *How could her father have been so cruel?*

All these years she'd refused to accept that her father was right, that Manning had never really cared for her at all. She'd chosen instead to believe that Manning blamed her for Scarlet's accident. That had been easier to handle, thinking he hated her rather than that he'd never loved her. She gently shuffled the letters back into a pile and retied the ribbon, then ran her fingers across Manning's boyish script. Manning hadn't blamed her for the accident; the letters proved that. He'd written over and over that it was *his* fault. Asked her to forgive him. God, what must he have thought—how must he have felt—when she never responded? Despite the fact that she'd never received Manning's letters, she should have written to him, apologized for what she'd done. She'd thought about it often enough, even composed letters in her head late at night. But she'd listened to her father and . . . well, the letters went unwritten.

Abigale heard a door slam downstairs. A voice called, "Abigale?"

It was Margaret.

"I'm upstairs. Be right there," Abigale replied. She hastily tucked the letters on the closet shelf behind her jewelry box and ran her fingertips beneath her eyes, hoping there weren't telltale smudges of mascara.

As Abigale descended the stairs and rounded the curve in the stairwell, she saw that Manning was with Margaret in the foyer. He faced out the window, his back to her.

Margaret's head was tilted expectantly upward. "There you are. I just left the kennels and decided to swing by and take a chance you'd still be here."

"Is something wrong?"

"No, no, nothing's happened. I want to tell you about Richard's will." Margaret's lips pressed into a thin line as she shot a glance at Manning. "I've already briefed Manning and Smitty."

Manning turned, giving Abigale a ghost of a smile, and the breath caught in Abigale's throat. Words from his letters whirled through her head, ripping open feelings she'd buried, if not forgotten. Should she tell him she'd found his letters?

He raised an eyebrow as if to say, *Why are you looking at me like that?*

A blush flamed Abigale's cheeks. She turned to Margaret. "Do you want to go in the gathering room?"

"That's a fine idea. Manning can light the fire and get some of the chill out of the air. This house feels far too empty."

*M*argaret wasted no time laying out the provisions of the will, seeming genuinely happy that Richard had kept Dartmoor Glebe in the family by leaving it to Abigale. But her manner turned brusque, almost disapproving, as she outlined the bequest to Manning. She told Abigale the will made no mention of funeral plans and left a copy of the will for Abigale to read, then made a hasty exit, saying she had to attend an emergency hunt board meeting.

The entire time Margaret was talking, Manning leaned against the wall next to the fire and never said a word; his gaze was fixed toward the floor, as if he'd spotted something fascinating on the toe of his paddock boot.

When Abigale returned from walking Margaret to the door, Manning had abandoned the fireplace for the liquor cabinet. He'd draped his coat over the end of the bar and rolled up the sleeves of his white shirt. As she approached, he unscrewed the cap of a whisky bottle.

"Would you like a drink?" he asked.

She watched the brown liquid splash into a lowball glass until it was full to the brim. "No. Thanks," she said, sinking into one of the leather wing chairs that flanked the fireplace.

Manning twisted the top back on the bottle. "You sure?"

She nodded.

He tossed down a generous swallow, closing his eyes with a sigh.

"Bad day?"

"You could say that."

"Do you want to talk about it?"

Their eyes connected for a flash, then, as if a veil lowered over Manning's eyes, the moment was lost. He glanced away. "Not really."

Manning drained the glass and Abigale's stomach clenched as she watched him eye the whisky bottle. *Please don't pour another drink.* Her disappointment flared as his fingers wrapped around the neck of the bottle, but he opened the liquor cabinet and shoved the bottle inside.

The logs in the fireplace tumbled with a crackling display of sparks, and Manning grabbed the poker and jabbed at the wood.

"The fire feels good," Abigale said, wrapping her arms across her chest.

Manning nodded and returned the poker to its stand. He dropped into the chair across from her, hiking one leg over the other. Abigale noticed splatters of gray paint on his paddock boots and the hem of his khaki pants. He ran his fingers through his hair, revealing a smear of gray along his right wrist.

"Margaret told me you and Smitty were painting at Longmeadow today. Looks like it was a big project."

"Yeah." He glanced down at his boots. "I guess I should have worn different shoes."

"What were you painting?"

"The stewards' stand." Manning blew out a breath. "The deck needed to be repainted before the races."

"I guess with horses there's always work that gets put off until the last minute."

One corner of his mouth twitched in a humorless smile. "Right."

Manning's eyes shifted to the fire and he twirled a finger around a brass brad in the arm of the chair. His facial expression gave no hint of what was going through his mind, but the nervous jiggling of his foot and the twitch of his cheek muscle said enough. Abigale bet the bottle of whisky wasn't far from his thoughts.

"Margaret seemed pretty upset. Was it about Uncle Richard's will?"

"Only as it relates to me."

"I would think she would be happy about you taking over the hunt."

"Under different circumstances perhaps she would be." Manning's voice was quiet, his drawl barely more than a rumble in his chest.

"You mean if Uncle Richard hadn't died."

Manning lifted his gaze, and Abigale could see his eyes were ablaze. "No. I mean if Mother didn't think it gave me a motive to murder him."

"You can't be serious!"

"I wish I weren't."

"That's crazy. Just because Uncle Richard included you in his will?"

"There's more to it than that. Apparently Richard had second thoughts. According to what his lawyer told Mother, he was going to talk to me and threaten to change his will if I didn't make some lifestyle changes."

"So you knew about the provisions of his will?"

"No. That's just it. I had no idea. I gather that he was going to tell me about it in the hopes that it would give me an incentive to be more responsible. To prove to him that I was worthy of the bequest."

"But he didn't tell you."

"That's the million-dollar question."

Abigale frowned. "I don't get it. You don't know if he told you?"

Manning tilted his head against the back of the chair and closed his eyes. "No. I don't."

The reality of what Manning *wasn't* saying finally hit Abigale. "Oh, my God. Margaret thinks Uncle Richard might have told you on the day he was murdered. Only you were too drunk to remember whether you even went to the racecourse, let alone whether or not he told you about his will."

He opened his eyes, his expression as bleak as a winter's day. "Guess the gossip mill's alive and well. You've been back what, twenty-four hours, and you're already up to date on my drinking habits?"

"No one's gossiping. Julia told me."

"Ah."

Abigale forced herself to ignore the look of betrayal in his eyes. "Are you saying Margaret thinks if Uncle Richard did tell you about changing his will, you might have become so angry you grabbed his rifle and shot him?"

"Bingo."

"That's ridiculous."

"Apparently Mother doesn't think so."

"She can't really believe that."

"Maybe she does. Maybe she doesn't. I'd say at the very least she's unsure. And Mother doesn't deal well with uncertainty. The fact that I can't remember is entirely unacceptable to her. She keeps demanding that I try harder. As if she can order away my blackout."

"Did Uncle Richard's attorney actually say he was going to talk to you about his will that day? The day he was murdered?"

"I don't think she knew when he was going to talk to me. Just that he planned to do so."

"Don't you think he'd pick a more appropriate time than when you were working on the racecourse? Especially if it was obvious that you'd been drinking?"

"Who knows? Maybe the fact I was drunk would have made it the perfect time to have the conversation."

Abigale considered that for a moment. She'd never known her uncle to do anything important spur-of-the-moment. He was almost as methodical as her father. Everything planned to perfection. Especially important conversations. No, she just couldn't believe he would confront Manning about his drinking in such a casual manner. Particularly if Manning was drunk. "Was it supposed to be just the two of you working on the racecourse that day?"

Manning's eyes flattened and he shook his head, giving her a look as if to say, *what part of 'I don't remember' don't you understand?*

"Okay, if Uncle Richard did ask you to work with him that day—just you—would that have been odd?"

"That we'd work alone?"

She nodded.

"No."

"So there's no reason to think Uncle Richard arranged for it to be just the two of you so he could talk to you privately about his will?"

He lifted a shoulder. "I don't know."

God, how could he be so nonchalant about it? "Manning, it's important. Why are you acting like you don't care? Don't you want out from under the cloud of suspicion?"

"Is that a serious question?"

"Yes."

"Of course I do." His tone was flat.

"So help me out here. Let's try to figure out a way to show that you didn't know about the will."

"What if I did?" His blue eyes bore into hers, as hard and cold as a shaft of steel. "What if we discover that Richard did plan to tell me about it the day he was murdered?"

Abigale's throat closed up and she forced herself to swallow. "Then we'll figure out a way to show it didn't matter."

His expression softened and he hunched forward, resting his forearms on his knees. "I didn't kill him, Abby. It's driving me nuts not being able to remember where I went or what I did that evening. But whatever else happened, I *know* I didn't kill Richard. I told that to Mallory today. I'll take a lie detector test if he wants me to. Whatever it takes. I can't live with this."

His voice cracked and he paused, running a hand across his mouth. "Richard was like a father and big brother to me, all bundled into one. When you left, Richard was the one who helped me get through it. Not Mother. Not my friends. *Richard.* He stood behind me and he stood up for me when everyone else in the community was pointing fingers. You think I'm a mess now? You don't even want to imagine where I'd be if Richard hadn't intervened."

Manning pushed out of the chair and walked to the bar. Abigale expected him to pull the whisky bottle out of the cabinet, but he grabbed his coat instead. "I've got to go," he muttered, heading for the door. "Thanks for listening."

"Manning . . . wait . . . can we talk for another minute?"

He stopped and half-turned toward her, a pained look on his face. Cleary, he was finished talking.

"Not about Uncle Richard's will. About something else." She heard the tremble in her voice, and could tell from the look he gave her that he'd noticed it, too. "About us."

Manning studied her for a moment, then walked back and dropped down in the chair across from her. Their eyes met. "Go ahead."

"I went for a walk in the woods behind Fox Run today. I saw Scarlet's grave. The cross you put there." Tears stung Abigale's throat, swam in her eyes.

"Abby, let's not—"

She held up a hand. "Please. This is something I've wanted to say for a long time."

He looked as if he'd love to get the hell out of there, but he mumbled, "Okay."

"I know I'll never be able to make it up to you," she continued. "Never be able to make it right. Life doesn't give us a do-over. But for what it's worth, I'd give anything to be able to turn back the hands of time. *Anything.*"

"Make it up to me?"

She nodded.

His brow creased into a frown. "What are you talking about? It was my idea to go on the moonlight ride."

"But I insisted on riding Scarlet. You wanted me to ride one of the old schoolies."

"Christ, Abby, so what? Would it have been better if one of the schoolies had broken its leg and had to be put down?"

"That's just it. One of the schoolies wouldn't have. If I had listened to you, we would have gone on a moonlight ride, had a blast, and the worst that would have happened is that Margaret might have caught us and made us clean tack for a week. But I insisted on riding Scarlet. A horse I didn't own, that I had been given the privilege to show thanks to your mother going to bat for me with the Symingtons. And you warned me not to."

Manning opened his mouth to say something, but Abigale ignored him. "You warned me that it wasn't a good idea. That Scarlet was too spooky out of the show ring, that she didn't have enough trail experience. But I wouldn't listen. And then, when she got all freaked out and wouldn't cross the river and you suggested we go back to the barn, I still fought you. I begged you to take the long way home, up the Snowy River trail. *The Snowy River trail.* What was I thinking? I was so intent on proving that I could ride Scarlet better than anyone, that she loved me so much she'd do anything I asked her to. And then the hoot owl flew off and she spooked off the trail into the sinkhole—"

"Don't do this, Abby."

She plowed on, hot tears pouring down her cheeks, "I will never, ever forget the look in Scarlet's eyes when she stopped scrambling, gave up trying to get out of the hole. It was as if she knew right then she wasn't going to make it. She lay there and looked up at me, her big eyes as much as saying, *Hey, I took care of you in the show ring. Now you need to help me.*"

Manning shook his head. "There was nothing else you could do. Her leg was broken. She was going into shock. You did all you could for her by staying with her and keeping her calm."

Abigale had cradled Scarlet's head in her lap while Manning rode for help, watched shimmering moonlight fade into a dull dawn as the vet put the mare down—as the tractor growled through the woods, digging Scarlet's final resting place in the murky earth. "*Nothing else I could do?* I could have left her in her stall to start with."

"But you didn't. *We* didn't!" Manning's eyes flashed and his face tightened with anger, or painful memories. "It was an accident. Let it go. No one blamed you."

"Exactly. That's just it. I was whisked back to Switzerland, where no one knew what I'd done. You were the one who had to live with it. You and Margaret."

Manning blew out a breath. "It wasn't that bad. People forgive and forget. The Symingtons never filed a claim against Mother."

"No, but they pulled all their horses out of her barn. Uncle Richard told me. And Julia told me how rough it was for you. That people still talk about it." She pressed her lips together, swallowed hard. "I will never forgive myself for letting my father say those things to you, Manning. I'll never forgive him."

"He was just trying to take care of you."

"No." Abigale swiped her fingers across her cheeks. "My father—God rest his soul—was trying to manipulate my life. When I got back to Switzerland, he refused to let me have any contact with you. He told me I was behaving like a lovesick child, said that you had clearly moved on to greener pastures, as evidenced by the fact that I never heard a word from you."

Manning's eyes narrowed. "I called you. More than once. Your father told me you refused to speak with me. So I wrote to you."

"I never refused your calls, Manning. And I never received your letters. My father confiscated them. Apparently my mother felt guilty about it—just not guilty enough to tell me. She packed up your letters and sent them to Uncle Richard. I found them this afternoon, upstairs in my old room."

"Jesus."

"I am *so* angry at my father. And my mother, too, for that matter. What right did they have messing with our lives like that?"

"I guess they thought I was a bad influence." He snorted and shook his head. "Which I was. I talked you into sneaking out of the house. Riding through the woods in the middle of the night."

"It was more than that. I think my father was afraid we were getting too serious. What was it he said to Margaret, something to the effect they were damned lucky you hadn't gone and gotten me pregnant and *really* screwed up my future?"

Manning shoved his fingers through his hair. "Look, Abby, I don't appreciate the way your father handled it—deceiving both of us—but I can't say I blame him. I'd probably be just as protective with my daughter."

"He wasn't protective. He just wasn't going to risk having anything derail the future he'd mapped out for me. From the time I was a little girl—hell, maybe from the time I was born—he'd dreamed that I would attend the Hotel School at Cornell. Return to Switzerland to help him run our hotel. Eventually take over when he retired. God forbid he'd let something as insignificant as my happiness—or yours—interfere with that."

Manning gave her a tired smile that didn't reach his eyes. "I don't know what else to say. It was a long time ago. We can't change what happened."

No, they couldn't. "You're right. I just wanted you to know I'm sorry."

*A*bigale stood by the front door, watching the taillights of Manning's car grow smaller until they disappeared into the night. Wherever he was going, she suspected it involved the company of a bottle. And she almost couldn't blame him. Even if Manning hadn't had a cloud of suspicion hanging over him, the last thing he needed in his life was the burden of running the hunt. She'd been in town only a day and she could already see that. What had Uncle Richard been thinking? Didn't he know it would turn Manning's life upside down, dumping that kind of responsibility on him, especially without giving him some kind of warning? Without finding out if he would even want it?

And what about leaving Dartmoor Glebe to her, when she hadn't even set foot on the property in years? Of all people, Uncle Richard knew her life revolved around her photography. That she was finally living her dream. He was the one who had gone to bat for her with her mother, convincing her mother to give her blessing for the assignment in Iraq. What could he have possibly expected her to do with Dartmoor Glebe? Live here?

The paintings on the walls seemed to close in on her, as if taunting her for her lack of gratitude. What kind of person was she, worrying about the turmoil her uncle's bequest had caused, when anyone in her right mind would jump for joy at such a gift?

She longed to call her mother and pour her heart out, but there was no way she could do that. Not now, with her being so sick. Loneliness washed over her, and suddenly, she ached for the safe harbor of Emilio's embrace. Yearned for his ability to help wipe away her grief, as he had done so many times in Afghanistan when she'd been overcome by the horror she'd viewed through her lens. The thought of hearing his velvet voice spread warmth through her.

She glanced at her watch and saw it was the middle of the night in Afghanistan. Emilio wouldn't mind if she woke him; she knew that. He was used to getting leads at all hours of the day and night. But was it really fair to run to him and cry on his shoulder, after she'd insisted on a clean break? *No.*

Darkness had crept into the house, and Abigale flipped on lights as she walked to the kitchen. The back window faced the barn and she saw the Dutch doors to the stalls were fastened, but a soft glow shone from the hayloft and a shaft of light beckoned through the aisle doors. A glimmer of an idea tugged at the hollowness in her chest. Maybe there was someone else she could talk to . . .

She snatched her coat from the mudroom and hiked the short distance to the barn. The whine of country music floated from inside and Abigale grabbed the handle of the aisle door and threw her weight against it, tugging it open just enough to slip through.

About halfway down the aisle, a slender dark-haired man dressed in coveralls whistled to the music as he swept a corn broom over the rubber pavers. He slid open the stall door of a sleek black horse and brushed a tidy two-by-two-foot square in the shavings at the opening to the stall.

"Hello," Abigale called as he pulled the door closed.

He looked up and waved, then trotted over to the radio and lowered the volume. "Sorry, I didn't hear you come in."

"That's all right. Don't let me interrupt. I was just wondering if Smitty is around."

"Smitty's down yonder at the kennel, but he should be by shortly. You must be Abigale," the man said, leaning his broom against the stall front. He was about her height and looked to be in his fifties, with the leathery skin of someone who'd spent most of his life outdoors. He tugged off his work glove and extended his hand. "I'm Michael."

"Nice to meet you." Abigale was surprised at the force with which his callused hand engulfed hers. She bet he didn't spend much idle time around the barn.

"I'm sorry for your loss, your uncle passing like he did," Michael said, scrunching up his face. "I've worked for Mr. Clarke for going on near twelve years, and I just want you to know he's the best man I've ever had the privilege to call my friend."

Abigale's throat swelled. "Thank you."

"He was—" Michael's voice cracked and he clamped his mouth shut, snorting a breath through his nose. "I guess I don't have to tell you." He gave a quick nod, putting an end to the unspoken sentiment. "Anyway, like I said, I expect Smitty'll be sticking his head in here before too long. If you want to hang around, I'd be happy to give you a tour."

"Sure, I'd love that."

The black horse banged his front hoof against the stall door and Abigale glanced at Michael. "I'm not holding up their dinner, am I?"

"Nah, they were fed an hour ago. He just wants attention." Michael slid the door open and thumped the horse affectionately on the neck. "This here is Henry. He's Mr. Clarke's favorite."

"He's gorgeous."

The horse stretched his muscled neck and nibbled at Michael's jacket pocket. "Spoiled rotten, that's what he is," Michael said.

He gently shoved the horse's head away and fumbled in his pocket until he came up with a sugar cube. Henry greedily attacked the cube, then licked Michael's palm as if to say *is that all there is?*

"Is he a thoroughbred?" Abigale asked.

"Yes, ma'am. Never raced, though. Mr. Clarke bought him as a two-year-old with the intention of making him into a hunter."

"How old is he now?"

"Just turned six." Michael flicked a wayward strand of the horse's mane back in order. "He's a beauty, but he can be a pistol to ride. Manning's the only one besides Mr. Clarke who gets along with him."

Something thumped in the hayloft above them, and Abigale jumped back as Henry whirled around in the stall.

"Goddammit, Larry, what the hell you doing up there?" Michael shouted, craning his neck to peer up at the hayloft.

A plump-faced boy peeked over the edge, baseball cap turned backward on his head. Abigale guessed him to be in his late teens.

"I was just stacking the hay bales like you asked me to."

"Stacking or throwing?"

"Sorry, boss." The boy's face reddened and he ducked away from the opening.

Michael rolled his eyes at Abigale. "I swear, that boy's got two left hands and is slower than molasses. If your uncle hadn't hired him as a favor to Larry's mama, I'd have sent him packing a long time ago." He shouldered the horse away from the door and gestured toward the aisle. "Come on. I'll show you the rest of the crew."

Michael introduced Abigale one by one to the rest of the herd. Twelve horses in all. The last stall they reached housed a sturdy dapple gray with a puffy silver mane and big, kind eyes.

"He looks like an overgrown pony," Abigale exclaimed, letting him nuzzle her hand. "Sorry, big guy, I don't have any treats for you."

"Last but not least, we have Braveheart," Michael said, fishing a sugar cube out of his pocket and slipping it in Abigale's outstretched hands. "A real gentle giant, he is."

"How big is he?"

"Sixteen-three hands. Seventeen hundred and twenty pounds." His chest puffed up with pride as he said it, as if he could somehow take credit for the horse's size. "But you'd never know it to ride him. He's a real athletic son-of-a-gun. Can jump the moon, too."

"Can he keep up in the hunt field?"

"You better believe it. He's got plenty of fuel in his tank. Depending on what territory they're hunting, Mr. Clarke sometimes leads the field on him." The corners of his lips drooped as he stroked the horse's broad shoulder. "In fact, Braveheart gave Mr. Clarke his last good ride, didn't you, boy?"

"Uncle Richard hunted him the day he was murdered?"

Michael nodded. "Henry had thrown a shoe and the ground was a little sloppy from the rain, so Mr. Clarke decided to take Braveheart." His eyes crinkled and he let out a chuckle. "He said it was a good day to be riding a horse with four-wheel drive."

Abigale hugged the horse and inhaled his warm, sweet scent. "Were you here when Uncle Richard returned from hunting?"

"Yes, ma'am. Mr. Clarke was on the run, rushing off to the steeplechase course. But we chatted for a little bit and he told me he had a glorious day. Viewed two foxes and had one helluva run, in spite of the bad footing. He said Braveheart lived up to his name."

Abigale smiled and smoothed the horse's forelock. "Did you talk with him about what his plans were at the racecourse?"

"Not really. I just know he was planning on meeting up with Manning."

Her heart quickened. "What did he say about it?"

"About meeting Manning?"

She nodded.

Michael eyed her uncertainly. "Just talked about how with all the rain he was worried about the footing for the races. He mentioned something about opening up the drainage ditch on the far side of the course and I asked if he needed my help, but he said no, Manning was going to meet him there and they'd be able to handle it just fine, the two of them."

"That's all he said?"

"As far as I recall. Is there some specific reason you're asking?"

"I'm just trying to piece together my uncle's last moments, that's all. Looking for some closure, I guess."

Michael's expression relaxed and he nodded. "We're all doing the same thing. I know I'm second-guessing whether I should have tried to talk him out of working on the course that afternoon. I thought about it, seeing as it was such rotten weather and all and he'd already been out hunting for three hours. But I held my tongue."

He shook his head, looking as though he could kick himself. "If I hadn't gone to a hay seminar that evening I might've noticed that he didn't return home, but I got home late and didn't pay any mind to the fact that the house was dark. I just figured he'd gone to sleep. It never entered my mind to check on him. One thing your uncle didn't like was folks fussing over him. I reckon it made him feel like they thought he was getting old."

Abigale said, "Maybe that's why he wanted to work on the course that afternoon."

"To prove that he could?"

She nodded.

"You just may be right about that." Michael pursed his lips together and cocked his head, watching Braveheart nuzzle Abigale's hand for another treat. "Or maybe he just wanted some busywork to keep his mind off things."

"Was something bothering him?"

He eyed her as he nudged Braveheart back into the stall and closed the door, as if weighing how much he should say. "I don't know if it was a big deal or not, but he seemed like he had the weight of the world on his shoulders when he came to the barn before hunting that morning. I asked him if everything was okay and he said, 'we've got a fox in the henhouse and I've got to figure out the best way to take care of it.'"

"A fox in the henhouse?"

"Yes, ma'am. Those were his exact words."

"What did he mean by that?"

Michael shrugged. "Beats me. I asked him if I could do anything to help and he said no, he'd get it straightened out."

"That was it?"

"Yes, ma'am. Then he loaded Braveheart on the trailer and off he went. There wasn't no more discussing it."

Abigale felt her impatience rise as she poked around the tack room, waiting for Michael and Smitty to finish discussing the exercise routine for one of the hunt horses recovering from an injury. Dozens of photographs of Manning stared at her from the walls, adding to her edginess.

She stopped pacing long enough to study a faded color photo of Manning and Percy in the winner's circle at Charles Town Race Track. The two of them stood side-by-side near the head of a sweaty chestnut horse, both grinning from ear to ear; the green-and-blue-clad jockey on the horse's back raised his fist in a victory gesture.

The door to the barn aisle opened. "Sorry that took so long," Smitty said, stomping his boots on the mat before setting foot in the tack room. "We've got this whip horse, blew his suspensory ligament. The vet gave the green light to start him back into work, and Michael and I were just divvying up the riding schedule."

"No problem."

Smitty jabbed a finger toward the photo Abigale had been looking at. "That was the first horse Manning and Percy ever ran at the track. Not bad, winning your first time out of the starting gate, eh?" He chuckled. "Look at those big old grins on their faces."

Abigale smiled. They looked as if they'd just won the lottery. "Did their luck continue?"

"Well, now, that's a different story," Smitty said, winking. He sank down on the leather couch and patted the cushion next to him. "Come sit and tell me what's on your mind."

She dropped down next to him, wondering if she looked as nervous as she felt. She wiped her palms on her slacks. Maybe this wasn't such a good idea. "I don't know where to start," she said, hating how meek her voice sounded.

"I reckon the beginning is as good a place as any."

That made her smile and she felt her jitters disappear. She sucked in a deep breath. "Okay. I suppose you've heard about Uncle Richard's will."

Smitty nodded.

"So you know about Manning inheriting the kennel and the hunt assets."

"Sure do. In fact, I just left the hunt board meeting a little while ago and it's official now. Manning's been voted in as master."

Her eyes widened. "That was fast."

"Had to be. What with the upcoming races and all."

"Was there opposition?"

"Nah, not really. Margaret runs a tight ship as president of the board. She saw to it Manning got the votes he needed. But that's not to say there wasn't some discussion about the matter. Several board members, Thompson for one, have strong reservations about whether Manning will be able to step up to the plate. But in the end there was consensus to give him a shot at it. Really, what choice did the board have, with Richard leaving the kennels and all to Manning?"

"Nothing like trial by fire."

"He'll be all right," Smitty replied. "I'll help as much as he needs. And Margaret will, too. He'll have plenty of support."

"Are you sure about Margaret?"

"Of course. Why?"

She told Smitty what Manning had said about his mother viewing the bequest, or at least Uncle Richard's thoughts about changing it, as providing Manning with a motive for murder.

"Oh, that's hogwash," Smitty said, pawing at the air. "Margaret doesn't really believe that. She's just upset because Manning was drunk and he can't remember enough about what happened to defend himself. Margaret doesn't think for one second that Manning murdered Richard, and anyone who knows Manning half a lick knows that Richard's will didn't provide him with any kind of motive for murder. Being master is probably the last thing Manning wants."

"So why did Uncle Richard leave the kennels and the hunt to Manning if he knew Manning wouldn't want it?"

"I imagine the simple answer is Richard didn't expect to go when he did. When Richard made his will he was probably looking years down the road, and figured on gradually grooming Manning to take over. If what you said about him planning to tell Manning about the will is true, I expect he would have been hoping it would give Manning some direction in his life. He never would have used it as a threat against Manning. That wasn't how Richard operated."

"So you're not worried it will be viewed as giving Manning a motive?"

"Nah, and Margaret probably isn't either."

"I wish she'd let Manning know that."

"Give her time. Right now, Margaret's about overcome with grief over Richard's death, despite appearances that she's holding it all together. I think she's lashing out in pain at anyone who she thinks might have been able to help prevent the tragedy."

"Even her own son?"

"That's Margaret," Smitty said, shrugging a shoulder. "If Manning really needs her, she'll come through for him."

"I think he needs her now," Abigale murmured.

"Still watching out for him, aren't you?" Smitty asked, giving her a gentle smile.

"Yeah, I guess I am." She flopped back against the cushion, picking up a pillow embroidered with the hunt logo and hugging it to her chest. "My shrink would probably say I'm trying to make amends for not sticking up for Manning when my father dumped all the blame on him for Scarlet's accident."

He studied her thoughtfully for a moment. "This must be rough on you, being back here, especially under these circumstances. How are you holding up?"

"I'm fine," she said quickly, then blushed when she saw him cock an eyebrow.

"Is that so?" Smitty reached out and drew her to him, engulfing her in a whiff of pipe tobacco and the musty corn-chip odor of hounds. She buried her head against his chest, ignoring the scratch of his wool sweater against her cheek. A sob escaped her throat and he rubbed his sturdy hands along her back. "There, there, it's okay," he murmured. "Just let it all out."

Finally, she dropped her guard and just let the tears flow. Gave in to anger over the senselessness of Uncle Richard's death, and her mother's illness; the resentment she still felt toward her father, even after all these years, for the way he'd dragged her away from Manning. It squeezed at her heart until she felt she couldn't breathe.

Smitty drove Abigale back to the house and shoved the gearshift into park. "I don't like the thought of you driving back to Margaret's all alone. You sure you won't let me give you a lift? You can leave Margaret's car here and we'll swing by and pick it up tomorrow."

"I'm fine, Smitty. Really," Abigale said. She opened the passenger door, flooding the cab with light. "Besides, I'd kind of like to spend some more time here going through Uncle Richard's things, if that's okay."

"No need to ask permission," Smitty replied. "It's your house now."

Wow. It was, wasn't it? Would she ever think of Dartmoor Glebe that way?

He must have sensed her reaction, because he covered her hand with his and said, "I reckon that'll take some getting used to."

"That's for sure," she murmured, gazing out the open door at the stately ivy-covered home.

"Give it time, Abigale. Your uncle wouldn't expect you to love this place as much as he did, at least not right off the bat. When the time's right, you'll know in your heart what you want to do with Dartmoor Glebe."

She leaned over and gave him a peck on the cheek. "Thank you. For everything."

"Nothing to thank me for," he replied, but his face flushed with pleasure.

Abigale slid out of the cab and started to close the door, then jerked it back open.

"Wait—I just remembered something I wanted to ask you about."

She relayed to Smitty what Michael had said about her uncle being preoccupied about a fox in the henhouse. "Do you have any idea what he meant by that?"

"No, can't say as I do." Smitty narrowed his eyes and chewed on his lip for a moment. "Unless . . ."

"What?"

"I was just thinking about something Percy said the other day. Probably just gossip."

Her heart sped up. "What did he say?"

"Oh, just that one of the hunt members, Charles Jenner, had ended up in the wrong stall again."

"The wrong stall?"

Smitty ducked his head and gave her a sheepish look. "You know, cheating on his wife."

"Oh."

"Percy said rumor has it that it's a married woman this time."

"This time?"

"Charles has a bit of a reputation, although his wife seems oblivious to it. Or pretends to be." He snorted. "In the past, Charles has been discreet enough to graze in other pastures, if you know what I mean, but Percy said this gal is a member of the hunt—and married at that. That's why I thought of it when you said the bit about the fox in the henhouse. Richard wouldn't take too kindly to those kinds of goings-on."

"What would he do?"

"Probably tell Charles to keep his breeches on, or to find another hunt to join."

Abigale laughed. "And what would Charles do?"

"Oh, I imagine he'd zip it up. There was more riding on Charles staying on Richard's good side than just his hunt membership. He's got a contract to buy Percy's property, Mulvaney Farm, and is fixing on developing it. He was wining and dining Richard something awful; trying to work some kind of deal where if Charles agreed to cluster the homes in such a way that we could still hunt a portion of the property, Richard would speak out publicly in favor of the development."

"Would Uncle Richard have agreed to that?"

Smitty hunched both shoulders up toward his ears. "Don't know. He was struggling with it. If we can't hunt Mulvaney Farm, Margaret's farm would be landlocked. Cut off from the rest of our territory. The fact is, Charles has a right to develop the property; and he could sure close it to the hunt, no question about that. So Richard was between a rock and a hard place. He's for preservation of open space, that's a fact. But if he opposed Charles's development flat out, there was no question we wouldn't be hunting there anymore. On the other hand, if Richard reached some kind of deal with Charles, he'd be compromising his principles about land conservation."

"Why did Charles need Uncle Richard's blessing, if he had a right to develop the land anyway?"

"Well, now, there's rights and then there's *rights*. Charles is hoping to make it some kind of fancy equestrian community, with a clubhouse and restaurant and all, and it's not zoned for that. It's strictly single-family residential. He'll have to apply to the county for a special exception, which is why he wanted Richard's blessing."

"How could Uncle Richard help?"

"It's all political, and your uncle had a lot of influence in this community. Folks looked up to him. If he brokered the deal, it might be an easier pill to swallow."

Abigale thought about it for a moment. "If he builds an equestrian center on the property right next to Margaret's, won't that hurt her boarding and lesson business?"

"Margaret says not. She claims the clientele he'd attract wouldn't be serious horse people, that he'd be catering to new money. You know, folks looking to build McMansions on postage-stamp-sized lots, pay too much money for horses they can't ride, that kind of thing. Says it won't compete with her business at all."

"I wouldn't be so sure."

"Richard wasn't either. I think part of his agenda was to work out some kind of compromise that also protected Margaret. And Richard was trying to help Percy, too, for that matter. From what I hear, the shine on Percy's trust fund has grown pretty dull. I think Percy might be in a heap of financial trouble if this deal doesn't go through."

"What a can of worms!" Abigale said. "No wonder Michael thought Uncle Richard seemed preoccupied."

"You got that right. But don't you go worrying yourself about it. It'll all get straightened out in time." Smitty waved a hand at the house. "You'd better go on and get yourself inside now. The temperature's dropping like a rock. Feels like a storm's brewing."

39

The cozy warmth of the kitchen felt good, and Abigale was in no hurry to get in the car and drive back to Margaret's. She found a bottle of chardonnay in the refrigerator and poured a glass, reflecting on what Smitty had told her about the hunt turmoil. Her perception of the duties of a master had always been that it was mostly ceremonial. More of an honor than a job. She'd had no idea so much politicking was involved. *Wonder how Manning would handle that?*

Abigale sipped the glass of wine as she wandered past the gathering room to her uncle's study at the far end of the house. She turned on the desk lamp and dropped down on the high-backed swivel chair, letting the rich leather swallow her as she sank against the tufted padding. This part of the house held almost no familiarity to her. Not that it had been off-limits to her exactly; she just remembered it as Uncle Richard's quiet place where he went to be alone with his books.

The room could easily have been in an old English manor home. In fact, other than the electrical lighting, it could have been transported from another century. She could almost imagine Heathcliff brooding on the Windsor chair beside the rugged stone hearth.

Nary a computer nor other form of modern technology was in sight. Even the telephone was a replica of an old-fashioned candlestick phone. Heavy brocaded drapes framed the deep casement windows, no doubt hung to shield the artwork and antiques from the strong southern sun. And to protect the books. The room was overcome with books. There must have been over a thousand of them, lined precisely along the oak-paneled shelves. A wheeled ladder allowed access to the ones out of reach.

Abigale ran her eyes over the spines, wondering which books had been her uncle's favorites, and which he hadn't yet gotten around to reading. She promised herself she'd go through them, when she had time. But the piles of papers stacked neatly across the generous desktop demanded her attention first.

The desk blotter that gobbled up the center of the surface was empty except for a legal pad and leather-bound journal, lined up side by side. She brushed her fingertips across her uncle's initials embossed in the top rail of the blotter, remembering when she and her mother had purchased it from a store on Banhofstrasse in Zürich, as a Christmas gift a few years back. The Waterman fountain pen she had bought for her uncle in Paris—with the money from her first photo shoot—rested in the pen well.

Abigale slid the chocolate-brown journal closer and flipped it open, using the silky green ribbon that peeked out at the edge of the page bottoms. It was a day planner, opened to the day her uncle had died. A chill wiggled through her and she rubbed her hands along her arms as she scanned the entries on the page: JAY BARNSBY; HUNTING; LONGMEADOW—OPEN DRAINAGE DITCH; TJ.

None of the entries noted a specific time. Rather, Uncle Richard's bold script sprawled among the lines, irrespective of the times printed at the left of the page; it was more like a list than an actual schedule of appointments. Abigale read the notations again, wondering who or what "TJ" was.

She flipped back a page: DR. PALEY—FALL SHOTS; HUNT BOARD MEETING; LONGMEADOW—REPAIR TIMBER. The preceding pages held more of the same, mostly entries about work to be done at Longmeadow and innocuous daily appointments. She thumbed through the days until a single notation caught her eye: TIFFANIE. The name was sandwiched between HUNTING and NATIONAL SPORTING LIBRARY RECEPTION. Who was Tiffanie?

Abigale kept a finger on that page as she flipped back. There, six days earlier: TIFFANIE JENNER. She stared at the name. Jenner. Was she related to Charles Jenner—the man she and Smitty had just been talking about? His wife, perhaps? She wet her fingers and rifled back several days: MEETING WITH TIFFANIE JENNER—DOGWOOD LANE.

She sipped her wine as she eyed the entries: TIFFANIE JENNER; TIFFANIE JENNER; TIFFANIE; TJ. So TJ must refer to Tiffanie Jenner. Uncle Richard had an appointment with her the day he was murdered. A meeting that most likely had never occurred, since the reference to TJ was listed after the notation regarding Longmeadow.

The phone twittered a shrill *ring-ring* and Abigale jumped, sloshing the glass of wine. Damn it! A splatter landed in the center of the open page, swelling the word HUNTING into an indecipherable smudge of blue ink. She dabbed at the page with her sleeve and grabbed the phone.

"Hello."

"You're still there."

"Hi, Margaret." She set the base of the candlestick phone on the desk, freeing up a hand, and continued to blot the page of the journal with her sleeve. "Yes, I'm just going through some of Uncle Richard's things."

"I was getting worried about you. I didn't expect you'd stay there so long."

Abigale glanced at her watch. "It's only eight o'clock."

"Only?" Margaret gave a gruff laugh. "I guess you're used to the European custom of dining fashionably late."

"I hope I didn't hold up your dinner."

"Don't you worry yourself about it. I didn't make anything that I can't heat back up," Margaret replied, warmth creeping back into her voice. "When can I expect you?"

Abigale wasn't hungry. At all. "I didn't know you were expecting me for dinner, so I made a snack here," she said, feeling guilty for lying. "I'm really sorry. I should have called."

"Well, no, that's all right. You don't have to report to me. I was just worried, that's all."

"I'm so sorry."

"Consider it forgotten," Margaret said, the finality in her tone putting an end to the discussion. "How much longer do you expect to be there?"

"I'm not sure. I just started going through the papers on Uncle Richard's desk." She glanced at the wine-splattered page in the journal. "Hey, I have a question. Is Tiffanie Jenner Charles Jenner's wife?"

"Yes, she is. Why, did you meet her?"

"No, but Uncle Richard had several appointments with her in his day planner."

"That's because Tiffanie volunteered to organize the VIP reception at the races. An offer which in hindsight Richard probably wished he had declined."

"Why?"

"Tiffanie was brown-nosing so hard it was driving Richard crazy."

"What was she brown-nosing for?"

"Colors. Tiffanie is lobbying for her husband to be awarded his hunt colors, never mind that they only joined the hunt last season. Tiffanie throws a nice party, don't get me wrong, but she makes sure everyone knows it. Her husband's no better. That might be enough to earn colors with some hunts, but not ours."

"I heard Charles Jenner's name mentioned earlier today. Smitty said there's a rumor he's having an affair."

"I haven't heard that, but it wouldn't surprise me. Charles has a history of it. Who was the source of the rumor?"

"Percy."

Margaret snorted. "Then I'd take that with a grain of salt."

Good advice. Unless Percy had changed over the years, Abigale would not consider him a reliable source. "Smitty told me Charles wants to develop Percy's property."

"That's true. Another reason Richard was up to his ears with brown-nosing from Tiffanie and Charles."

"You mentioned Tiffanie is hosting a party. Was Charles doing something else to try to win Uncle Richard's favor?"

"Mostly just pestering Richard with good intentions. Charles has more newfangled equipment than you can shake a stick at and he's always wanting to lend one thing or another to the hunt, most of which he hasn't a clue how to operate."

"That doesn't sound so bad."

"It is if you're fixing to nail a fence board back up, and Charles insists on hooking his nail gun up to a generator when you could just pound a couple of nails with a good old-fashioned hammer in the blink of an eye."

Abigale smiled. "I get the picture."

"Charles isn't so hard to stomach, I guess. He just doesn't know any other way than throwing his money around—never mind that the ink's still wet on it. But I wouldn't turn my back on Tiffanie for an instant."

"Why's that?"

"She's a social climber of the highest order. I often wonder if there's anything she wouldn't do to be accepted in the right circles. From what I've seen, she knows no limits. No wonder Charles strays from time to time."

"What has she done?"

"Well, for example, she wanted to enroll her daughter in preschool: she has a three-year-old, cute as a button, but spoiled rotten. Anyway, the class was full, so her little Brooke was placed on the waiting list." Margaret cackled. "You'd have thought the President's daughter had been denied admittance to the Easter egg hunt on the White House lawn. Tiffanie called everyone, trying to figure out a way to pull strings and get Brooke enrolled in the class."

"Did anyone help?"

"Nope." Margaret's tone was smug. "She hit a brick wall. But that didn't stop her. Tiffanie figured if she couldn't bring Mohammed to the mountain, she'd bring the mountain to Mohammed. She got Charles to pony up the money for a full-time teacher's assistant so the school could accept more students to the class."

"Did the school agree?"

"How could they not? It benefited all the kids."

"Oh, my."

"Anyway, we've wasted enough time talking about the Jenners. You'll meet them soon enough and you can form your own opinion. I'd better stop bending your ear and let you get on the road. It's already raining something awful and there are storms in the forecast."

Abigale tilted her head toward the window and heard the soft melody of rain pinging against the glass. A perfect night to curl up by the fire with her glass of wine and a good book.

"I think I might stay here tonight, Margaret."

There was a long silence. "You don't have any of your belongings."

"That's okay. I always carry essentials in my bag. I'll be fine for tonight, and I can pack up the rest of my things tomorrow."

"The rest of your things? You mean you don't intend to stay here at all?"

Abigale hadn't realized until the words were out of her mouth that she really wanted to stay at Dartmoor Glebe. And not just for one night. "I'm not sure, Margaret. It just feels right for me to stay here. I feel closer to Uncle Richard."

"I can understand that. You do whatever makes you feel best. I just worry about you being in that big house all alone."

"I'll be fine."

"Um-hmm. Make sure the doors are bolted. When I got there today the front door was unlocked."

What was this all about? Abigale had never known Margaret to lock anything. "Has Middleburg changed that much over the years?" she asked. "As I recall, you used to leave your car running when you went into the post office to get your mail."

"No, it hasn't," Margaret replied. "But whoever shot Richard rifled through his wallet and could have gotten his address from his driver's license. It stands to reason he might try his luck at burglarizing the house."

Abigale glanced at the darkened hall and felt a tiny shiver run up her back. The house suddenly felt less cozy, but not enough to make her change her mind. "Okay. I'll check the locks. Don't worry. I'll be fine. I'll talk to you in the morning."

"All right. And just so you know, Thompson lives in the gatehouse at the front of the property and Michael lives in the tenant house back by the kennels. Either one of them could be there in a flash if you have a problem. Let me give you their phone numbers."

Abigale scribbled the numbers on a legal pad. "Thanks, Margaret. Good night."

"Good night, dear."

Just as Abigale was about to hang the earpiece on the base, she heard Margaret's voice.

"Wait! Abigale?"

"Yes?" she said, raising the earpiece.

"There's a gun in the drawer of Richard's nightstand. Just in case."

*A*bigale jerked awake, her heart pounding. It took her several seconds to shake off the fog of sleep and remember where she was. She realized she must have had a bad dream, though she remembered nothing of it, just felt a drumbeat hammering inside her chest.

The digits on the Disney clock beside the bed glowed red in the dark room: 11:23. She had kicked the covers off in her sleep and chilly air pricked goose bumps on her arms. Abigale grabbed the blanket and puffy comforter, pulled them back up to her chin, and turned onto her stomach, greedy for sleep.

A throaty growl of thunder rolled in the distance, and the wind whistled across the gutters as it pelted rain against the windows. She snuggled into the cocoon of the mattress, lazily cognizant that the rumblings outside her window were claps of thunder rather than explosions and small-arms fire, night sounds all too commonplace in Afghanistan.

A muffled thump from downstairs joined the cacophony of sounds, almost like a cabinet door banging closed. She wiggled deeper under the covers. Probably a loose shutter blowing in the wind. She'd mention it to someone tomorrow.

Bang. There it was again, tugging at her consciousness. Abigale squeezed her eyes shut, fought to ignore it. *Bang-bang.* A double thump, louder this time. She envisioned a shutter crashing against a window pane and felt a twinge of guilt for lying there, all nestled down in the bed. Uncle Richard would never have disregarded the threat of damage to Dartmoor Glebe. She could almost hear him, as she had summer after summer, cautioning the window-washing crew that the original glass panes were irreplaceable.

Abigale sighed and smothered a yawn. Flinging off the covers, she shrugged into the robe she'd dropped on the foot of the bed. Lightning flashed, making dark objects seem to jump out at her, and she fumbled for the light switch by the door.

Light from the bedroom spilled into the hall, giving her some guidance as she felt her way down the long passageway toward the stairs. A shiver shimmied down her back and she wrapped the robe tighter, yanking at the belt. Had the temperature really dropped that much, or did the howl of the wind add to the feel of chill in the air?

She switched on the lamp by the landing and headed down the stairs, flinching as another bang echoed from the darkness below. It sounded farther away than it had when she'd been upstairs, which meant the loose shutter was probably at the far end of the house, beneath her bedroom. That was her luck, wasn't it? No way it could have been a window closer to the door. She decided she'd check it from the inside first.

Her bare feet padded softly on the oriental carpet in the foyer as she cut through the darkness, and she felt a cold prickle flutter in her stomach. The lamp above bathed the ceiling with a dim glow, but the downstairs was black as pitch. If Margaret hadn't voiced concerns about her staying there alone Abigale would probably have thought nothing of it, but Margaret's words rang in her ears, unleashing her imagination.

"Shit." She reached down and rubbed her shin where it had collided with the corner of the hutch.

Abigale groped unsuccessfully for a light switch, then gave up and let her hand trail along the wall, mindful not to dislodge a painting, as she felt her way toward the hall. Her feet touched the cool oak-planked flooring and she rounded the corner, breathing a sigh when she saw the glow of light coming from the study. She thought she'd turned the lights off before she went to bed, but she'd nodded off in the study reading *A Portion for Foxes* and had been so groggy when she decided to go upstairs that she must have forgotten the lamp. Thank God for that.

Halfway down the hall, she froze. The last bang sounded as though it came from *inside* the study. Abigale held her breath, straining to hear. Nothing but a far-off grumble of thunder. Had she imagined it?

She crept forward, then jerked back. What was that? A low rumble, but not thunder. Not outside. More like something rolling and thudding to a stop. *In the study.*

The hair on the back of Abigale's neck pricked to attention. Was someone in the house? She threw a quick glance into the dark abyss behind her and flattened herself against the wall, eyes glued on the study door.

Abigale craned her head toward the study, straining to hear over the war-drum beat of her pulse pounding in her ears. She forced deep breaths and felt her heart slow, slam less violently against her chest.

No more sounds from the study. Just the faint whistle of wind. Rain pelting against the windowpanes. "Get a grip, Abigale," she muttered. This wasn't a war zone. Bad guys weren't lurking around every corner.

Smiling at her foolishness, she padded forward, the dark hall once again swaddling her with familiarity. Almost as if her uncle was beside her. In fact, given that she was now fully awake, after she fastened the shutter she might pour another glass of wine and ride out the storm in the study.

Abigale was about to enter the study when a shadow danced across the wall of bookcases to her left. *What the hell was that?* She drew back, her knuckles white where she gripped the door molding. There! It moved again. The shape was indistinct, but it was large, rising up along the shelves of books and mushrooming against the ceiling. It moved slowly, looming across the room. Then, the raspy sound of someone clearing his throat.

Fear trickled icy fingers down Abigale's spine. Margaret's warning rang in her ears: *The murderer took Richard's wallet and knows his address.*

She pressed her shoulders to the wall and slowly crept away, her wet palms fumbling behind her for guidance. Carefully, she slid one foot sideways across the other, never taking her eyes off the study. She heard the thump of wood against wood, followed by what sounded like a stack of papers smacking down.

Abigale inched her way back twenty feet or so, then stopped and listened. From that vantage point she could no longer see the interior walls of the study, couldn't monitor the shadowy movements.

Should she make a dash for the car? The keys were hanging by the back door. But her cell phone battery was dead, the charger in her duffle back at Margaret's. She wouldn't be able to call for help from the car. She remembered Margaret telling her that Michael and Thompson lived nearby, but if she drove to get one of them, the intruder—*her uncle's murderer?*—might get away. She wasn't willing to risk that. No. She'd call from here.

Her eyes darted to her left, spotting the dim outline of the winding staircase. The phone in the kitchen was closest, but she preferred to put more distance between her and the intruder before calling for help. Casting one final look in the direction of the study she turned and fled, cringing as the sound of her slapping footsteps seemed to thunder through the silence.

*A*bigale flew across the foyer and sailed up the stairs, eating up two steps at a time. She barely slowed as she flung open the door to her uncle's bedroom. The light from the hall streamed a path halfway to the bed, beyond which she saw only inky darkness. Stumbling beyond the light to the bed, her hands slid along the mattress until her fingers hit the edge of the nightstand. She searched blindly for a light, grasping the cold metal feet of a lamp base. Her hands ran up along the thick crystal column, searching for a switch at the neck of the lamp. Nothing. *It must be on the cord.*

She felt her way back down the lamp and located the cord that emerged at the back of the base, slid her shaky hand along the rubbery cord to the in-line switch, and flicked it with her thumb and forefinger. The switch slid through her fingers and Abigale jerked her hand back, swiped her sweaty palm against the bedspread, then groped for the cord again.

The instant her knuckles scraped against the cut crystal, Abigale realized she'd aimed too high, shoved too hard. Both hands flailed in the dark, stretching for the falling lamp as it crashed to the floor. The clatter seemed deafening in the stillness of the bedroom, but was it loud enough to be heard downstairs? Abigale's heart pounded against her chest. She held her breath, listening.

The rain drummed a beat on the nearby window, making it impossible to hear much of anything else. Abigale tore her gaze away from the top of the staircase long enough to peer in the direction of the nightstand, making sure she didn't dislodge something else as she groped for a phone.

Her hand brushed across the glossy dust jacket of a book, bumped up against a metal picture frame. But no phone. It had to be on the nightstand on the other side. Abigale's eyes flickered toward the stairwell as she scrambled on all fours across the king-size bed.

A lamp perched in the center of the opposite nightstand but she ignored it, preferring the safety of the dark in case the intruder had heard the crash and came upstairs to investigate. Her fingers skimmed the polished wood, skipped deftly around a crystal decanter. Something metal, heavy, sat in front of the lamp. It didn't budge when she ran her hand along it: a rectangle, about a foot long and almost a hand's width across. She frowned, exploring with her fingers. Beneath the metal rectangle was a smooth stone base, marble maybe. What—ah, of course! It was the bronze of Sommerset that Uncle Richard had commissioned when he retired the horse from racing. The artist had sculpted Oinkers, the potbellied pig who was Sommerset's constant companion, nestled between the horse's front legs.

Abigale slid her hand to the left of the bronze. Yes! An old-fashioned European-style desk phone. She lifted the receiver and reached for the dial. It was push-button, but the keypads were arranged in a circle to resemble a rotary phone. Her fingers trembled as they flew over the dark keys. There were twelve in all. Okay, zero through nine, plus the asterisk and number keys. But which keys were nine and one? She felt a metal lever at about three o'clock on the dial, figured it must be where the numbers began, and started counting counterclockwise from there.

One, two, three. *Wait.* Did the dial start with one, or zero? *One.* It had to be one. She mouthed a silent prayer and counted to nine, pressed the key, then punched the first key twice.

Silence.

Shit. Okay, so the first key had to be zero. She hesitated. Should she just press zero? Did phone operators even still exist in America? No, 9-1-1 was a safer bet. An operator would eat up valuable time transferring the call. Her fingers skipped ten keys to the left, then back to the second button.

"Come on, come on," Abigale whispered, glancing over her shoulder. She couldn't see the stairway from that side of the bed and the half-open bedroom door shielded her view of the hall. She scooted up against the headboard and stared at the two-foot-wide strip of light in the doorway, as if her vigilance could will the intruder away.

Nothing moved in the hall. Abigale blew out a breath and tore the silent receiver away from her ear, pressed the lever. She bent over the nightstand, her face inches away from the phone dial, but could make out nothing on the keys. *Damn it.* Why couldn't Uncle Richard have had a cordless phone like everyone else?

"Okay, third time's a charm." Abigale counted clockwise this time, down from the lever. Gambling that zero was first, she pressed the second key, which should be *nine*, and was fingering her way around to one when she sensed a movement behind her.

She whipped her head toward the door. What was that? A shadow? The creak of a floorboard?

There it was again. A slow, deliberate squeak. Measured footsteps.

Abigale replaced the receiver and slipped to the floor, huddling against the side of the bed. She ducked her head and peered at the door. From beneath the bed she had a sliver of a view, enough to see if someone entered the room.

A shadow appeared first, then two largish, light-colored athletic shoes, legs draped in a black track suit. Undoubtedly male. He crept forward, the nylon track suit rustling, then stopped just short of the end of the stream of light. Abigale froze in her contorted position, fighting to ignore the cramp that seized her muscles, spearing a burn across her lower back.

Darkness and the element of surprise worked to her advantage, but that wouldn't get her far. She needed a weapon. She considered the lamp, but God only knew where it was plugged in. If she made a move, he'd be on top of her in a heartbeat; and if the cord held the lamp back for even an instant she'd never have a chance to swing at him. There had to be something else. The objects she'd felt on the nightstand raced through her mind. The bronze was heavy enough, but maybe too heavy for her to heave with the kind of force that could do damage. Then she remembered Margaret's parting words from their phone call. *There's a gun in the drawer of Richard's nightstand. Just in case.* Hope surged, leaving Abigale almost giddy for an instant. But which nightstand?

The intruder's breathing grew louder, and Abigale could tell he'd turned his head in her direction. She tensed, ready to spring toward the nightstand if his feet moved an inch. He took a step back, then turned toward the door. Abigale's heart sank as she watched him turn right, heading down the hall rather than toward the stairs.

She spun around and ran her hand up the front of the nightstand. Open shelves lined with books ate up the bottom half; above that she felt the beveled edges of two drawers. She grabbed the knob of the lower drawer, eased it open, and slipped her hand inside. A long, narrow velvet box was tucked in one corner, probably containing a watch or jewelry of some sort. Other than that, the drawer was empty.

Abigale yanked open the top drawer. Yes! Her hand closed around the pistol, feeling the familiar ruggedness of the Luger's carved handle, the worn leather strap that protruded from just below the barrel. She fingered the empty cavity in the butt of the handle. Shoving her hand back in the drawer, she fished around for the clip; she felt a pen and notepad, a couple of small foil packets. Condoms? Oh, God. Too much information. In spite of the circumstances, she felt her cheeks burn with embarrassment at the thought.

She patted down the rest of the drawer. No clip. Where was it? The ammunition had to be close by. It made no sense otherwise. She ran her hand inside the drawer again. All the while, the nightstand across the bed tugged at her, as if screaming *it's over here.* She frowned in that direction. Would Uncle Richard have done that? If he had a gun in his nightstand, it would be because he wanted quick access. In the middle of the night. No way would he put the clip out of reach of the gun . . .

Abigale shoved the top drawer shut and grabbed the velvet box from the drawer below, feeling a surge of adrenaline as she held the solid weight in her hand. She placed the gun on the floor and flipped open the box. Her fingers traced the outline of the clip.

The creak of a board in the hall made her jump and she grabbed the gun, shoving the clip into it as she flew across the room. Flattening herself against the wall, she peered through the crack in the open door and caught a glimpse of a short white shirtsleeve as the intruder stepped back into the room. A second later, the overhead light flicked on.

Abigale shouldered the door out of her way as she flicked off the safety and cocked the gun, aiming the Luger at the man's back. "Stop right there! Put your hands up. I have a gun."

The man half-raised his arms. "Okay, take it easy."

"All the way up!"

He spread his fingers and shoved his arms in the air. "All right."

"Now turn around. Slowly."

"Listen, just calm down."

Abigale jerked the gun up, fixing her aim on the back of his close-cropped dark hair. *"Now."*

"All right." He wiggled his raised hands, turning slowly toward her. "My hands are up, okay? I'm not going to do anything. Just take it easy."

He faced her full on and his dark eyes narrowed as he dropped his hands. "Abigale? Jesus Christ, I heard a noise up here and came to investigate. I thought there might be an intruder."

Abigale stared wide-eyed at Thompson as she lowered the gun, resting it against her thigh. She eased out a long breath and swallowed against the tightness in her throat. "What are you doing here?"

Thompson jabbed a hand toward the hall. "I came to get some files from Richard's study. Then, like I said, I heard a noise up here and came to investigate." He offered an apologetic smile. "I had no idea you'd be here. I'm so sorry. It just never entered my mind to think anyone would be here."

"How did you get in?" She had locked all the doors after her conversation with Margaret. She was sure of it.

Thompson fished in the pocket of his track pants and palmed a single gold key. "I have a key to the front door. I do all the bookkeeping for the hunt, and the files are kept here in the study. Richard gave me carte blanche to come and go whenever I needed to access the files. Of course, I was always respectful of Richard's privacy. I'd never have been so rude as to intrude in the middle of the night when he was here."

He ran a hand across his mouth and snorted, giving an angry shake of his head, clearly irritated with himself. "God, what an idiot I am! I must have scared you half to death. I am so sorry. I can't apologize enough."

"It's all right. No harm done." Abigale glanced down and wiggled the gun in her hand. "I probably scared you just as much as you scared me."

The lines around Thompson's eyes crinkled as his face relaxed into a smile. "You got my attention, that's for sure." He aimed a finger at the gun. "Is that thing loaded?"

She nodded.

He arched a quizzical eyebrow. "Really?"

"Why, does that surprise you? A girl has no business handling a loaded gun?"

"Well, yeah, kind of. No, not the girl part." He held up a hand to smother her retort. "But that gun looks like an antique. Is it safe to shoot?"

"It's almost old enough to be an antique. It's a relic from World War Two." She released the clip into her palm, then offered the gun to him. "See the Reichsadler?"

Thompson ran his fingers over the barrel. "Is that a swastika?" he asked, raising it and peering closely at the engraving.

Abigale nodded. "Hitler's emblem. A wreath of oak leaves surrounding a swastika, held in the talons of an eagle."

He held the gun gingerly, as if bad karma might rub off on him. "Holy cow. How did Richard end up with it?"

"My grandfather took it off a German soldier he'd shot dead. He smuggled it back to the States after the war."

"Do you know how to shoot it?" Disbelief tinged Thompson's tone.

"Quite well, actually. Uncle Richard taught me to shoot it when I turned sixteen."

"That's a hell of a sweet-sixteen gift."

"*I* thought so."

Thompson eyed her through thick, dark lashes, the corners of his mouth creeping upward into a slow grin. "I'm beginning to understand what Margaret meant when she likened you to Ruffian. 'A filly through and through, but more than able to take on the boys.' That's how she described you."

Abigale felt heat rise in her cheeks and Thompson's smile seemed to broaden. The man knew how to lay on the charm, no doubt about that. He wasn't overtly sexy, he didn't have the undress-you-with-his-eyes air that Manning possessed. Nor did he have Manning's rugged good looks. Thompson was more refined, genteel, his features almost too perfect. Handsome, in a gentlemanly way. She regarded his neatly trimmed hair, the white cotton T-shirt tucked tidily into the waistband of his track pants. So proper. The antithesis of Manning, really. She tried to picture Thompson losing control, or drunk, but couldn't.

Thompson handed the gun back to her. "I'd better get out of your hair and let you get back to sleep. I'll never forgive myself for my stupidity, barging in on you like I did. It won't happen again, I assure you."

She put the Luger and clip back the way she'd found them in the drawers of the nightstand. When she finished, Thompson handed the house key to her. "I'll take the files I use most often home with me and coordinate future access with you."

"You don't have to give up the key," Abigale said.

"No, I insist. I wouldn't feel right keeping it."

Abigale accepted the key from Thompson and accompanied him downstairs. She leaned against the door to the study, watching as he gathered up manila file folders. Some he slipped back into the drawers in the filing cabinets, others he stacked on the edge of the desk.

"What possessed you to work on bookkeeping at this hour of the night anyway?" Abigale asked. "Trouble sleeping?"

"Right. The perfect cure for insomnia." Thompson flashed a tired smile, which faded as quickly as it appeared. His brow creased as he flipped through a file folder, hesitated as if considering the contents, then added it to the pile on the desk.

"Seriously, you have a day job, right? Do you have to stay up half the night doing bookkeeping for the hunt?"

Thompson shook his head. "I generally get it done on weekends, but you hit the nail on the head when you surmised I had trouble sleeping. I thought I might as well do something productive, and since I live so close it was no big deal to run up here and get the files I needed."

"Margaret told me you live in the gatehouse."

"Yeah, I board my horses with Richard, too. So it's great to be close by."

"Except when the paperwork starts calling to you in the middle of the night."

Thompson smiled. "Nah, it's not usually like that. Keeping the books for the hunt is no burden. But I guess you know we had an emergency board meeting this evening and voted Manning in as master."

"Yes."

He paused, open file folder in hand. "Well, to be honest, it troubles me to think of Manning trying to make a go of it financially. For the sake of the hunt, I hope he succeeds. And if he wants me to continue to handle the bookkeeping, I'll gladly do so. But frankly, I'll be very surprised if Manning doesn't inform me that my services are no longer needed. With that in mind, I thought I'd better spend some time tidying up the files—make sure everything's in order for whoever takes over the responsibilities." He dropped the folder into the drawer and slid it shut. "I just hope Manning has the good sense to know he'll need someone to help him and not try to tackle this himself."

"What makes you so sure Manning won't be able to handle the finances?"

Thompson snorted a little laugh. "Are you serious? Well, let's see, I can think of a handful of reasons right off the bat. There was his racing fiasco. I hear that set Margaret back a hundred grand or so. Then there was his stint at playing professional polo. That would have driven Margaret to the poorhouse in a hurry if Richard hadn't stepped in as Manning's sponsor."

He held out his hand and spread his fingers, ticking off each damning piece of evidence he named. "Then there's the fact that he doesn't have a real job. Sure, he teaches a lesson here and there, but what little money he makes from that he probably squanders on booze. Granted, he made a bundle selling that horse he bought at the track and turned around as a show horse. But not a week went by before he blew it all on a sports car. I think Manning has some romantic notion of himself as the Great Gatsby, and he hasn't come to grips with the fact that his bank account is more befitting a character in a Steinbeck novel."

Abigale drew in a breath, ready to pounce back in Manning's defense, bring up what Julia had said about the success he'd had in California until Margaret and Richard had tricked him into coming home. But she bit back the words.

"Oh, Christ. I've offended you, haven't I?" Thompson asked.

She managed a tight smile. "No offense taken. You were just voicing your opinion."

"No," he said with a groan. "I was out of line. For the second time tonight, I beg your forgiveness."

*A*bigale slept fitfully, tortured by unwelcome dreams, swirling images of Scarlet and Manning. She woke herself with a garbled moan, clawing her way to consciousness past a foggy figure brandishing Uncle Richard's Luger. A weak stream of sunlight peeked through the curtains and she saw from the bedside clock that it was almost seven-thirty.

Her head throbbed, probably from the coffee schnapps she'd downed to help her fall asleep after Thompson had left. She flipped onto her back, trying to summon up the motivation to get out of bed.

Something pinged against the window. Not rain. It sounded more like sleet dancing across the panes. She opened one eye and squinted at the stream of sunlight. That made no sense. *Ping.* There it was again. Against just one of the dormer windows. *Ping. Ping. Ping.*

She jerked fully awake. It sounded like . . . No. It couldn't be.

Abigale flipped back the covers and raced across the room. Kneeling on the cushioned window seat, she flicked the curtains apart with one hand. The glass was dry, with no hint of precipitation. She leaned closer, then jumped back as a torrent of gravel hit the panes. She yanked on the curtains, sending the brass rings skidding across the curtain rod.

Manning looked up at her, a wide grin spread across his face. He stood between a jittery black horse, the one Michael had told her could be a handful to ride—Henry, she thought his name was—and the big gray, Braveheart. He gripped both sets of reins in one hand and a fistful of gravel in the other.

Abigale flipped the double locks on the window and cranked it open.

"Sleeping in, I see," Manning said, smiling at her in a way that reminded her of him as a boy.

"God, Manning, I was sound asleep." Abigale cringed at the sound of her voice, still thick with sleep. She could only imagine what she looked like. She yanked her hair back and twisted it into a knot at the nape of her neck.

"Yeah, I figured. Either that or you were ignoring me. Used to be, it never took me more than a couple of tosses to get your attention. I've been out here pitching pebbles for a good five minutes." He flung the gravel on the drive and wiped his palm against his breeches.

Abigale stared at him, feeling trapped in a time warp. Joyful memories bubbled to the surface, only to collide with darker, painful ones. "What are you doing here?"

He nodded at the gray horse. "I tacked up Braveheart for you. Let's go for a hack."

"*Now?* Don't you have to be at Longmeadow?"

"Not for another couple of hours." He jiggled both sets of reins and gave her a crooked grin. "Come on."

She made a face and Manning chuckled. "Still not much of a morning person, huh?"

"Manning, I hardly got any sleep. I haven't even had a cup of coffee yet."

"Riding's better than coffee. Come on."

"I haven't been on a hunter since—" Their eyes met and she stopped, then shook her head. Manning cocked an eyebrow, as if challenging her to finish the sentence.

"Other than a trek through the mountains in Afghanistan, I haven't ridden in years," she said quietly.

"Then it's time you got back on."

$\mathcal{M}$anning let both horses graze on the lawn while he waited for Abigale, mindful of the fact that Michael would groan when he saw grass slobber on the bits. Abigale stepped out the front door ten minutes later, a velvet hard hat tucked under her left elbow, coffee cup clutched in her right hand.

"My feet must have grown a full size since I last had these boots on. My toes are already numb." She glared at Manning as she marched toward him, her riding boots crunching against the gravel drive. "And don't you dare look at my breeches. They're one size too small, too. At least."

Manning raised his hands in mock surrender. "I wasn't," he replied, noting appreciatively how the beige fabric clung to the firm muscles of her thighs, stretched tight across the curve of her hips and buttocks.

Steam rose from the cup and Abigale raised it to her lips and blew across the top, then slurped a generous sip.

"Feel better now that you've had some caffeine?" he asked.

"I'm getting there."

"Good." He lopped Henry's reins over his arm and gave the horse a gentle shove out of the way as he pulled Braveheart up next to Abigale. "This is Braveheart. He looks like a tank but rides like a dream. You'll love him."

Abigale gulped down half the cup of coffee, then set the cup on the front step and patted the horse on the neck, smoothing his thick mane with her graceful fingers. "I met Braveheart last night when I went down to the barn. He's adorable."

"Good. So you already know each other." He snapped the stirrup leathers down. "These should still be adjusted to the correct length."

"That's my saddle!" Abigale exclaimed.

"Of course. What did you expect?"

"I—I don't know. I just didn't expect Uncle Richard to keep all my things. Everything's just like it was when I left. Even my room."

Imagine that, Abby, Manning thought. *Almost as if Richard was waiting for you to come back.* He said, "Come on, I'll give you a leg up."

Manning waited while she put on her riding helmet and gloves, then cupped his hands for her knee and boosted her easily into the saddle. She toed both boots into the stirrups and he eyed her legs from the front of the horse. "Length okay?"

"I think they could come down a hole." Abigale dropped her left foot from the iron and tugged up on the stirrup leather to loosen the buckle.

"I'll get it," Manning said.

He slid the leather through the buckle, dropped it a hole lower, then did the same on the other side. "How's that feel?"

Abigale wiggled her feet and the irons hit just below her ankle bones. "Good."

Without thinking, Manning positioned her foot in the stirrup and gave her a pat on the knee. A perfectly innocuous gesture, but part of an old in-gate ritual he and Abigale used to carry out just before she entered the show ring. She'd insisted it was a good-luck charm, that Manning was her "true north" and his touch guided her around the hunter course. It seemed corny now, but it had sure fed his ego at the time. The familiarity of the act caught at his chest, igniting an ache he'd thought he was rid of. Abigale must have remembered it, too, because her muscles tensed beneath his hand.

"Sorry," he murmured. He slid his fingers beneath the girth to make sure it was tight, then backed away, tossed the reins over Henry's head, and swung lightly into the saddle. "I thought we'd head out the back way toward Dogwood Mountain. Then if we have time we can loop around through Seven Chimneys on our way back."

Abigale's eyes narrowed. "Don't do that."

"Do what?"

"Don't baby me. I know you're avoiding Seven Chimneys right off the bat because of the galloping field. You think I'm not up to it."

Manning fought a smile. She'd nailed him on that one. "That's not it at all. I just thought you'd enjoy a hack through the woods. The color is at its peak."

"Bullshit."

*S*even Chimneys was as pristine and peaceful as Abigale had remembered. They entered through the gate at the back of the lower pasture and followed the creek as it meandered through the cow pasture toward the vineyard on the other side of the farm. The creek was swollen from the storm and the horses' hooves made soft sucking noises, like loud wet kisses, as they walked along the mossy bank. Henry spooked at a cow that let out a mournful moo as they approached, scooting sideways into Braveheart, but the big gray just snorted softly and plodded ahead. Henry settled back to a walk alongside him.

Manning hadn't spoken much since they'd left Dartmoor Glebe, other than to give an occasional warning about trappy footing, or to draw her attention to a herd of deer, at least a dozen of them silhouetted on a nearby rise, and a peregrine falcon that flew overhead. She didn't object to the lack of conversation. The silence between them wasn't awkward; quite the contrary. They'd settled into it with a familiar ease.

They reached the galloping field and Manning glanced over at her and arched an eyebrow.

"Need you ask?" she said, shortening her reins.

"Henry gets a little strong when he's behind. Mind if I lead?"

"Go right ahead."

Manning eased Henry into a canter and she leaned forward and clucked at Braveheart to follow. The field stretched across almost five acres of well-manicured turf, allowing a horse to stretch into a brisk gallop, but Manning kept Henry checked at a canter as they loped across the gently rolling terrain. Abigale knew he was keeping the pace slow for her benefit, but she didn't care. Braveheart had a long, flowing stride that left her feeling as if she were sitting on a cloud, each powerful thrust of his haunches rocking them forward with a steady rhythm that made her want to whoop aloud. *Da-da-dum. Da-da-dum. Da-da-dum. Poetry in motion.*

The wind whispered against her face and she gulped in a lungful of the fresh morning air, catching a whiff of fading grasses and musky earth. Goose bumps rose on her arms as the plaintive calls from a flock of southbound geese floated down from the pale sky. Nothing equaled the sheer sense of freedom she felt on the back of a horse. Nothing. Not the rush of her skis, spraying powder as she carved down a mountain-face of virgin snow; nor free-falling from a plane, in that terrifyingly glorious eternity before her chute whooshed open. Both were pure adrenaline fixes, but lacking the completeness she felt on a horse.

Braveheart was enjoying the canter, blowing contentedly with each stride, and she ran a gloved hand along his neck. The tangy scent of his sweat stung Abigale's nostrils and a warm glow spread through her chest. She was home again.

Far too quickly, they reached the end of the field, and Manning twisted in the saddle and looked back at her as he brought Henry to a walk. He must have read the look on her face, because he flashed a broad smile. "I told you Braveheart was a pleasure to ride."

"I love him. He must be a blast to hunt."

"He is—hey, are you okay?"

"I'm fine." Abigale brushed her fingertips across each cheek. "The wind made my eyes water."

Manning knew better; she could read it in the tender look her gave her. "You should hunt him while you're here."

"Maybe I will."

He swung open the gate into the next pasture and waited for her to ride through. "They put in a cross-country course up by the vineyard. Want to hop him over a couple of jumps?"

Jumping Braveheart was like flying in slow motion. He didn't have the speed of a thoroughbred, but his huge stride gobbled up the distance and he sailed over each fence as if it were just another canter stride.

"It feels like I'm sitting on a couch," Abigale said with a laugh as she pulled him up next to Manning.

He smiled. "That's why Richard bought him. His back was starting to bother him and he needed a comfortable ride. Richard didn't like to admit he was in pain, except maybe to Mother, but I noticed he was choosing to hunt Braveheart more and more. He pretty much backed off on hunting Henry, except when he was leading second field and wasn't going to jump much."

"Is Henry green over fences?"

"Not in terms of quitting. Henry will jump anything you point him at. But he'll pick a long spot or add another foot or so to the height of the jump if he thinks it looks spooky. It's hard to sit him when he overjumps like that, but he's a phenomenal athlete. He should probably be an open jumper rather than a field hunter."

He gathered up the reins. "Want to see him over a fence?"

"Sure."

Manning trotted a low log jump, then let Henry canter to a hedge. The horse slid over the jump, quick and catlike.

"Wow, his knees were up around his ears!" Abigale exclaimed.

"Watch what he does over a bigger fence," Manning said, cantering toward an oxer that looked to be a good four feet high with a three-foot spread.

Henry's ears pricked forward and he leaned into the bridle. "Easy," Manning murmured, checking him back. She could see that the horse wanted to leave long, but Manning steadied him and made him wait. They hit the perfect spot and Henry arced gracefully over the jump, clearing the front rail by at least eight inches, his front legs folded tight and square. As he stretched across the oxer, Abigale heard a muffled *pffttt*. An instant later, she saw the girth dangle beneath the horse's belly.

The events after that seemed to happen in slow motion. Henry landed and scooted away from the jump, his head low between his front legs. Manning worked to get Henry's head up but seemed unaware that the girth had broken.

"The girth!" Abigale shouted.

"What?" He turned his head to look at her, and in that moment Henry kicked up his heels and let out a buck that sent Manning and the saddle flying. It looked to Abigale as if Manning was launched ten feet in the air before plummeting to the ground.

Manning's right forearm took the brunt of the blow; then his head smacked the ground, hard, as the momentum slammed him onto his back. His velvet hunt cap flew off and tumbled away. Manning still gripped the reins in his left hand as he was dragged on his back, bumping across the field behind the fleeing horse. Abigale heard herself scream.

Manning jerked the reins and Henry rocked back on his haunches. For an instant it looked like the horse would stop, then the right rein snapped near the bit; the thoroughbred kicked out and shot back into a gallop, ripping the broken reins from Manning's grasp.

"God *damn* it!" Manning rolled to one side, then scrambled to his feet.

Abigale trotted Breaveheart over to him. "Are you okay?"

"Yeah." He raised his arm, winced, then gestured toward Henry. The horse was on a flat-out run, still trailing the broken reins, racing toward the tree line at the far end of the field. "You have to stop him. He's running toward Foxcroft Road."

"Isn't the field fenced in?"

"There's a coop. He'll jump it." Manning's breath came in short gasps, the color drained from his face. "If he gets to the road, God only knows where he'll end up."

Abigale gathered her reins but hesitated. "I don't feel right leaving you here all alone."

"I'm fine."

"Manning—"

"I'm fine. I just got the wind knocked out of me. Now go!"

*H*enry slowed when he got to the tree line, and Braveheart's huge, galloping stride quickly ate up the distance between them. The thoroughbred screamed as he trotted along the fence, looking for a means of escape. Braveheart seemed to kick into overdrive and whinnied to his stable mate, a deep, throaty call that heaved his sides against Abigale's legs. Henry swung his head in their direction, just long enough to raise Abigale's hopes that he might stay in the field; then the horse found the coop, popped over, and galloped out of sight.

Abigale was close, no more than ten strides from the coop, when she heard the screech of brakes, tires squealing against asphalt. She sat back and tried to pull up Braveheart, but he grabbed the bit in his mouth and plowed for the jump.

"Whoa!" Abigale yanked on the reins, but she might as well have been a fly on his back for all the reaction she got. All she succeeded in doing was to throw him off stride.

"Damn it," she muttered, her breath rushing out with a hiss. Her long absence from the saddle had caught up to her. No way seventeen years ago would she have let this horse—*any* horse—run her to a jump.

Braveheart came in tight to the coop and managed to clear it, but tossed her out of the saddle. She lost both stirrups, landing hard on the pommel. Pain shot through her crotch, bringing tears to her eyes.

The big horse must have sensed she was off balance and seemed to stall in mid-stride, allowing her to wiggle back into the saddle and slip both feet in the stirrups. She gathered Braveheart at a walk and blew out a shaky breath.

"Good boy," she murmured, patting him on the neck.

They were on a narrow path, the muddy surface littered with Henry's deep hoof prints. Through the thicket of trees, she caught a glimpse of a silver pickup truck stopped on the road about twenty feet ahead, then heard the *putt-putt-putt* of a diesel engine and the shrill yapping of dogs. Abigale trotted the remaining distance to the road, dreading what she would find.

The driver's door hung open and a slim woman stood with her back to them by the front of the truck, hands on the hips of her faded jeans. Three terriers danced around her feet. She spun around as Braveheart's steel shoes clomped onto the paved road.

"He went that way," the woman called, shielding her eyes with one hand and pointing at a gravel drive on the opposite side of the road.

Abigale saw angry tire marks on the asphalt behind the truck, but the front of the vehicle appeared to be undamaged. "He wasn't hit?"

"No, thank God. I was able to brake in time." Her voice had the slight trace of an accent. French, Abigale guessed.

"Where does that lane lead?" Abigale asked. The drive was wide enough for only one vehicle at a time, with narrow grass shoulders on both sides that ran abruptly into wobbly-looking American-wire fencing. Dense woods flanked the lane on the left and a pasture ran along the right. Abigale saw a round metal trough perched in the center of the pasture at the top of the hill. Black cattle grazed knee-deep in the yellow-green grass.

"It's the back entrance to Beaver's Ridge Farm. They only use it to access this cow pasture."

"Is there a gate?"

The woman shook her head slowly. Sunlight filtering through the trees caught glints of gold in her spiky dark hair. "There is, but I don't think they're religious about keeping it closed. There's a cattle guard to keep the cows in. And a people gate next to it, so riders can get through. But it's probably hit-or-miss whether or not the vehicle gate across the drive is closed."

Abigale felt a lump form in her chest. "Great."

"Think he'll try to jump the cattle guard?"

"I wouldn't be surprised."

"Hope he has more sense than that," she replied. "Want me to stay here in case he heads back this way and gets past you?"

Abigale crossed the road and eyed the narrow lane. "If he stays in the fenced lane, I think I'll be able to get him. But would you mind checking on his rider? He took a pretty bad fall. He insisted he wasn't injured, but I'm worried about him."

"Of course. Where is he? Right there at Seven Chimneys?"

"Yes. In the jumping field."

"You got it. Just let me put my dogs back in the truck and pull it off the road."

Abigale trotted Braveheart down the lane, praying that Henry did have good sense. "Thank you, God," she whispered when she saw that the vehicle gate hung wide open but the horse hadn't jumped the cattle guard. Henry stood next to the people gate at the end of the lane, gazing over the fence at the herd of cattle. As Abigale neared the horse, she saw his glossy black coat was crusted with sweat down his neck and between his hind legs.

"Good boy," she said softly. Henry nickered at Braveheart and showed no inclination to flee when she grabbed the end of the broken reins. She removed her belt and looped it through the ring on his snaffle bit as a lead shank. Henry walked quietly alongside Braveheart, head low and relaxed, as she led him back down the lane.

As she topped a slight rise, she saw the woman's silver truck bouncing up the lane toward her. The woman must have spotted her, because the truck braked to a stop. The passenger door flew open and Manning hopped out as the engine cut off.

"He's okay," Abigale called.

Manning nodded that he'd heard, then turned and spoke to the woman in the truck. The driver's door opened and the woman climbed out, shooing back the dogs as she eased the door shut. She walked to the bed of the truck, returning a moment later with a halter and lead rope. Manning reached out for it but she shook her head. Abigale was close enough to see the scowl darken Manning's face, the stubborn thrust of his jaw, but he withdrew his hand, too much of a gentleman to argue, she guessed.

As Abigale pulled the horses up near the truck, the terriers scampered across the front seat, yapping ferociously. She felt the lead go tight as Henry jerked his head up and started to jig. The woman shushed at the dogs, succeeding in silencing them for all of about five seconds.

"Terriers. Don't you love them?" she said, stepping forward and slipping the halter over Henry's head.

Abigale smiled as the dogs scrambled over each other in the driver's seat, juggling for position as they lunged at the window. "What breed are they?"

"Cairn. Fearless little buggers. Too smart for their own good."

Manning shot a look at the dogs as he walked over to Abigale. "You okay?" he asked.

"I'm perfectly fine." She tilted her head toward Henry. "I don't think Henry hurt himself. He seems to be walking okay."

Manning squatted beside the thoroughbred and ran his hand down each leg. Seeming satisfied, he rose and grasped the lead shank near the halter, above where the woman had hold of it.

"I've got him," Manning said.

She opened her mouth as if to say something, then shrugged and backed away, letting the lead slip through her fingers.

"I called the barn," Manning said. "Michael's on his way with the trailer. We can load up down by the road."

"Okay."

"I'll meet you down there." He led Henry onto the grass strip to get around the truck, ignoring the way Henry snorted and shied at the frenzied dogs.

"He's in a mood," Abigale said quietly.

"Male pride rearing its ugly head, I imagine," the woman replied. "I'm Michelle de Becque, by the way."

"I'm Abigale Portmann. Thanks so much for your help."

"No problem." Michelle stepped to the side and motioned for Abigale to go first. "You go on. I'll turn around up in the pasture and meet you by the road. I've got his saddle in my truck."

"Thank you."

"He's hurt, you know," Michelle said as Abigale started to ride off.

"Who?"

"Prince Charming. His right arm. I'd put money on it being broken, considering the way he's babying it."

Abigale looked down the drive at Manning and realized for the first time that he was leading Henry from the off side, using his left arm. He was left-handed, which was probably why she hadn't noticed earlier that he wasn't using his right arm.

"He'd trekked across the field, lugging his saddle, and was almost to the road by the time I met up with him," Michelle continued. "I spotted right off that he was protecting his right arm and tried to get him to let me carry the saddle. But it was like my offer fell on deaf ears."

46

*A*bigale spun toward Manning as soon as Michelle's truck rounded the curve and disappeared down Foxcroft Road. "That was embarrassing."

"What was?"

"Your attitude."

Manning frowned, his lips parting with an oh-so-innocent air. "What was wrong with my attitude?"

"You were rude."

"How was I rude?" he demanded. "I thanked her."

"Uh-huh. And refused her offer to stay and help us load the horses."

"We don't need her help loading the horses."

"No, of course we don't. Why would we want help? Better for you to handle it all by yourself, broken arm and all."

"I don't have a broken arm."

She arched an eyebrow. "Really?"

Manning narrowed his eyes and looked away. "Michael will load the horses. That's what he does. He doesn't need help."

"Especially not from a woman."

"Is that what you think, that I didn't want her help because she's a woman?"

"I think that your ego is bruised because you fell off, and your stupid male pride won't let you accept help."

"That's ridiculous."

"What's ridiculous is that you wouldn't let her carry your saddle. And the way you got all pissed off when she wouldn't give you the halter to put on Henry."

"God, Abby." Manning looked away as he blew out an angry laugh; then he locked eyes with her. "Ego has nothing to do with why I wouldn't let her carry the saddle."

"Really."

"Yeah. *Really.*" He shoved Henry's lead rope at her. "Hold him."

Abigale shifted Braveheart's reins to her other hand and grabbed the rope, watching as Manning stormed over to where the saddle straddled the top fence board. He leaned his right shoulder against the saddle and lifted the flap with his left hand.

"Come here."

She led the horses over to the fence.

"See that?" Manning asked.

Abigale eyed the saddle and felt his glare on her. "Both billet straps are broken."

"Not broken."

"No?"

"No." He nodded at the straps. "Feel them."

She looped Braveheart's reins over her arm and ran her fingers over the torn leather. The left half of each strap was jagged, as if ripped apart by force. But from the stirrup hole in the center to the right, the tear was smooth.

Abigale looked up at him. "They were cut."

He nodded, his eyes flashing a stormy blue. "Cleanly sliced. And cleverly concealed under the buckle guard, so the cuts wouldn't be noticed when buckling the girth. The straps were solid enough to hold until Henry jumped that oxer. Which I guess was the point."

"What do you mean?"

"If they had broken at a walk or even a trot, it wouldn't have been a big deal. Odds were, by cutting just halfway across to the center hole, the straps wouldn't break until the horse put more strain on the girth—going over a jump, or galloping uphill. Obviously increasing the chance of injury."

Manning's fall flashed through Abigale's mind: that agonizing eternity when he'd sailed into the air, then plunged slowly toward inevitable impact. She shuddered, thinking how lucky Manning was he hadn't broken his neck. Mud smeared the sleeve and shoulder of his jacket; it was streaked down his back so thick it held clods of grass. The damp, earthy smell mingled with the seductive scent of saddle leather and the subtle aroma of Manning's cologne. The urge to touch him was almost irresistible. She eased slightly away. "I can't believe this. Who would want to harm you?"

"It wasn't intended for me." Anger weighed his mouth down and darkened his voice.

"What do you mean?"

Manning lowered the saddle flap, grabbed the cantle, and tilted it toward her. He ran his thumb across the block letters engraved on the brass nameplate: REC.

It all made sense, then. Manning's mood. Why he'd been so territorial about the saddle. "It's Uncle Richard's saddle."

"Yeah."

"Why were you riding in it?"

"My saddle's at Fox Run. Besides, Richard had this saddle custom-made to fit Henry's back. I use it whenever I ride him."

Their eyes locked, sky and earth, and Abigale felt her world swirl around her as the significance of the discovery hit home. "Oh, my God, Manning, it wasn't a random killing. A robbery gone bad. Someone targeted Uncle Richard."

"No doubt he was targeted," Manning replied. "But tampering with a saddle and cold-blooded murder are worlds apart. Sure, Richard could have been badly injured, even killed, when the saddle broke; but if someone wanted to murder him, that'd be taking a long shot. Tampering with the saddle seems more like something someone would do out of spite."

"Or as a threat."

"Yeah," he said slowly. "But if someone was trying to put pressure on Richard—to threaten him—what accelerated the situation to make them shoot him? Why was he murdered before he rode in the saddle? Before the threat had a chance to play out?"

"Unless . . . he did ride in the saddle."

Manning arched an eyebrow.

"You said it yourself, that it wouldn't have broken—didn't break—until you jumped and put stress on it. Maybe it was cut before Uncle Richard hunted that day, but it didn't break."

"It's possible, I suppose. But we hunted hard and fast that day. Plenty of action. Besides, if it was cut and didn't break, why did things escalate?"

"I don't know. It doesn't make sense. But there was something going on that Uncle Richard was worried about. With the hunt, I think. I can't shake the feeling that it's tied to this." She relayed what Michael had told her about

Uncle Richard saying there was a fox in the henhouse.

"Jesus Christ."

"Uncle Richard never said anything to you about it?"

"No."

"Maybe he confronted someone that day. Hunting. Or before, or after. Or that afternoon at the racecourse." Anger and frustration clawed at Abigale, making her want to scream. "Damn it. The more we learn, the less we know."

"Except it looks less and less certain that Richard's murder had anything to do with a highway worker."

Yeah. And more and more crucial they discover whether Uncle Richard planned on meeting anyone besides Manning at Longmeadow the day he was murdered. "Have any details about Monday come back to you?" she asked. "Bits and pieces? Anything?"

Manning's eyes darkened. He shook his head, then looked away.

"Oh, great," Manning muttered as they pulled up to the barn. "A welcoming party."

Abigale followed his gaze and saw Margaret stride up the barn aisle toward them with Duchess at her heels. "It's just your mother."

Manning snorted as if she'd said something amusing. He shoved the door open and climbed out of the truck.

Abigale eyed Manning and Margaret as the two of them walked to the back of the trailer. Margaret was doing all the talking. Manning looked as though he was bracing himself for attack. She took her time getting out of the truck, then stood back and watched as Margaret helped Michael unload the horses. The clank-clank-clank of the blacksmith's hammer echoed from the far end of the barn and she saw Larry, the boy who worked for Michael, halfheartedly sweeping the aisle. Thompson longed a bay horse in the nearby round pen. The vet drove up just as Michael unloaded Henry off the trailer.

"Don't that just figure," Michael said. "The vet never shows up on time, except when I'm running behind."

"That's all right, Michael. We'll put the horses away," Margaret said. "You go do whatever it is you need to do with Doc Paley."

Michael ran his eyes over both horses, as if reluctant to relinquish the duty. "They need a good going-over, to make sure they didn't hurt themselves none."

"Got it," Manning said, grabbing Henry's lead, the hint of a smile relieving some of the tension in his face. "Go on."

"All right," Michael said reluctantly, still eyeing the horses as he walked over to the vet truck. He shouted over his shoulder at the barn, "Hey, Larry, get Rocky out of his stall and bring him on out. Doc Paley's here."

Margaret chuckled. "You know Michael's going to go back and check both horses as soon as he's finished with Doc Paley."

"Yep," Manning agreed.

"Speaking of injuries . . ." Margaret waved a hand at Manning's mud-covered back. "Looks like you took a pretty good tumble."

"Yeah, the billet straps broke over a jump."

"You hurt?"

"Just my pride," Manning replied, shooting a sideways glance at Abigale.

Abigale caught Margaret's eye, gave a little shake of her head, and pointed her index finger at Manning's right arm.

"You sure about that?" Margaret asked.

"I'm fine, Mother."

"Well, you don't look fine to me. You look like your right arm's hurting you something fierce. And you're pale as a ghost." Margaret stepped forward, squinting as she gave him a closer inspection. "You're sure wearing a good bit of real estate. Even got mud in your hair. Your helmet come off?"

Manning didn't respond.

Margaret glanced at Abigale and raised an eyebrow. Abigale nodded.

"All right, so you've probably got yourself a concussion. Let's go on in the tack room and take a look at your arm. Abigale, you okay taking care of Braveheart?"

"Of course."

"Good." Margaret snatched Henry's lead rope from Manning and called to Thompson, who was leading his horse across the drive toward the barn. "Can you lend a hand here?"

Abigale let Thompson use the wash stall first, grazing Braveheart while she waited. After giving him a liniment bath, she ran a comb through his puffy mane and thought about how hard it must be to braid. She smiled as she allowed herself the indulgence of painting his plate-sized feet with hoof dressing; she could almost hear Uncle Richard scolding her as he had the first time she'd used that *goddamned oil* on the feet of one of his hunt horses, telling her that hoof dressing interfered with scenting in the hunt field, that it was a show-horse thing. But Braveheart wasn't going hunting today. Abigale slid the brush across his hooves, making sure the shine reached clear around to his heels. She felt strangely soothed by the way the dark goo filled the nail holes above his shoes.

She led Braveheart down the aisle to his stall, loving the way his wet coat gleamed with dark gray dapples, smelling of menthol from his bath. She slipped the halter off and watched the big horse nosedive into a fresh pile of alfalfa. Sliding the stall door shut, she hung the halter and coiled the thick black lead rope around itself like a spring, securing it by tucking the end through the bottom loop the way Uncle Richard had taught her.

The barn was peaceful now. The blacksmith had packed up and left, and Michael was outside, trotting a horse for the vet. Thompson had finished with Henry and disappeared into the tack room about five minutes before. Abigale inhaled, capturing the smells of hay and shavings, fly spray and horse manure. Heaven.

She swept and hosed down the wash rack, packed the brushes and hoof pick she'd used back in the grooming box, and carried the box to the storage closet. The door was cracked open with the light on. She swung the door wide as she stepped inside, almost smacking into Larry's broad back.

"Oops, I'm sorry," she said, jumping back as he spun around. "I didn't know you were in here."

Larry gaped at her. A flush crept up his stocky neck and flared across his chubby face. "Uh, I . . . I, uh, I got Mr. Clarke's saddle out of the truck and was just putting it in here," he stammered. "Mrs. Southwell's in the tack room and I didn't want to interrupt."

"That's all right, Larry. Sorry I startled you." She swallowed a smile, imagining he was taking his sweet time with the saddle to avoid less desirable chores.

Abigale eyed the saddle as she plunked the grooming box on the shelf. It was splayed upside down on the horse vacuum. The sight of the severed billet straps turned her stomach, fueling the burn of anger. She backed out of the closet and knocked lightly on the tack-room door.

"Come on in," Margaret called.

Manning was seated near Margaret on the couch, holding an ice pack to his arm. Duchess sprawled on the floor by their feet. Thompson leaned against the counter by the sink, his hand wrapped around a glistening bottle of Deer Park water.

Margaret waved her inside. "We were just talking about—why are you limping?"

Abigale flashed a look at Manning and caught a glow of conspiracy in the smile he gave her. "Because I stuffed my size-eight feet into size-seven boots," she replied.

"Well, for God's sake, take them off," Margaret said. "The bootjack's over by the coatrack."

Abigale was red-faced and out of breath by the time she'd managed to tug her feet out of the boots. "These are up for adoption," she said, plunking them down next to a pair of mud-crusted muck boots.

"Custom Vogels." Margaret nodded approvingly at the boots. "You'd get a pretty penny for those if you put them on consignment at Middleburg Tack Exchange."

"Fine by me." Abigale sank down in a club chair and tried to wiggle some feeling back into her toes. "I'll donate the proceeds to the panel fund," she said, referring to the money set aside for maintaining trails and building coops in the hunt territory.

"Thanks—" Manning and Thompson spoke in unison, then glared at one another.

Thompson broke the standoff first, bowing his head. "Pardon me, Master."

"Yeah, like it or not, I am," Manning muttered.

"So," Margaret said, ignoring both of them and directing her attention to Abigale, "before you came in we were going around in circles trying to make sense of the fact that someone tampered with Richard's saddle."

"It changes everything, doesn't it?" Abigale asked.

"I certainly think so. I called Lieutenant Mallory. He's on his way here."

"I don't imagine they'll be able to get any evidence off of it."

"No, probably not," Margaret said. "But they'll start poking around, try to narrow down the time frame when it might have happened, try to establish who had access, et cetera."

"That shouldn't be too hard," Abigale said. "It's not like this is a public barn."

"You're right. Assuming the saddle was meddled with here."

Abigale frowned at her. "Where else?"

"At Monday's hunt." Margaret said it as if it should be obvious. "Someone could have slipped into the trailer when Richard was off chitchatting, slit the billet straps with the saddle already on the horse. Could have been done in the blink of an eye, with no one the wiser. I know the slices were concealed under the buckle guard, but if I was going to do something like that I'd do it once the horse was saddled. Make sure it wasn't discovered when buckling the girth.

"Of course, it could also have been done after hunting, setting it up for the next time Richard rode. That would have been easy as pie. When Richard stayed around for a tailgate, he usually untacked his horse. Put the saddle in the trailer's tack room. Someone could have tampered with the saddle then; but that'd be mighty risky, bargaining that it'd escape Michael's keen eye when he cleaned the tack."

"Was there a tailgate the last time Uncle Richard hunted?"

Margaret nodded.

"We should also find out if Richard stopped in town on his way home from hunting," Thompson said. "It wasn't unusual for him to pick up supplies at the feed store. Or, for that matter, he might have made a detour to the Coach Stop. He did that more than once when I was with him. He'd see a vehicle parked out front and say 'so-and-so's in there. I need to have a word with him.' He'd park the truck and trailer on the street and off he'd go. If Richard did that, anyone could have had access to his saddle."

"I just can't believe that someone wanted to murder Uncle Richard," Abigale said. "It wasn't some random shooting, some highway worker who tried to rob him and got spooked. Someone actually planned it. Someone he knew."

"We don't know that for sure," Thompson said. "Whoever tampered with Richard's saddle most likely targeted him directly. But I have a hard time seeing how that ties in with the shooting."

"You think it was just a coincidence?" Abigale demanded, exasperation putting more bite in her tone than she intended.

"I don't know what to think. I just can't make sense of it."

"That's why I think we should keep this quiet," Margaret said. "Just between us and those close to Richard. And the authorities, of course. If Dario Reyes didn't shoot Richard, best not to tip off whoever did that the focus of the investigation may have shifted. In the meantime, we all need to be vigilant. Abigale, that means that you shouldn't stay alone at Dartmoor Glebe."

Abigale's eyes widened. "Isn't that a little extreme?"

"I agree with Margaret," Thompson said. "Think about what happened last night."

"What happened last night?" Manning demanded.

"Nothing," Abigale replied.

"I let myself into the house with the key Richard gave me," Thompson said, ignoring the look Abigale gave him. "I was doing the quarterly accounting for the hunt and needed to get some of the financial files. Of course, I had no idea Abigale was sleeping there. It was very late and when she heard me moving around downstairs I about gave her a heart attack. Anyway, the point is that any number of people could have a spare key. You know Richard. He was everyone's best friend."

"No doubt about that," Margaret agreed. "Seemed like Richard always had a house guest of one sort or another. Course, I don't imagine he gave them all keys, but better safe than sorry."

"Okay. So I'll get the locks changed," Abigale said.

"Forget it, Abby. You're not staying here alone," Manning said.

Abigale glared at him.

Margaret said, "Was it that bad, staying at my place?"

"No! Of course not."

"Then do me a favor and get your things. I packed up what you had at my house and brought your bag over this morning. Before I knew about any of this. It's in your room."

CHAPTER

48

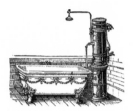

The session with Lieutenant Mallory only added to Abigale's frustration. The lieutenant had seemed properly disturbed about the saddle, and he'd treated Manning with some deference; this led her to believe maybe Manning wasn't a suspect after all, or if he had been, that the saddle incident had changed things. But the interview session had been tedious, and no obvious leads had turned up from Mallory's questioning of Michael about who had been in the barn or had access to the saddle.

She'd escaped to the house to pack her bag and steal time for a quick shower. As much as it bothered her to pack up and leave Dartmoor Glebe, she had to admit the solitude of the big house felt threatening now. Even the clangs and gurgles as the water worked its way through the pipes seemed to sing with a menacing note. Still, she lingered long enough to let the warm water ease the stiffness from her muscles, wash away some of her stress.

Margaret had unpacked her clothes for her, folding them neatly on the closet shelves. Abigale threw on her favorite pair of jeans and black cashmere sweater, then stuffed the rest of the clothes back in her duffle. She took one last look around before zipping the bag, and her gaze rested on the stack of Manning's letters. Abigale eyed them for a moment, then tucked them gently in a side pocket. At the last minute, she also tossed in her hunt horn and spurs and grabbed Uncle Richard's journal from the study. She wasn't sure why she did it; it wasn't as if she was never coming back. She just wanted them with her.

Abigale turned off the lights, made sure the doors were locked, then tossed the duffle in the back of Margaret's Subaru and drove to the barn.

Margaret stood with Manning by the open door to her truck, a scarlet hunt coat draped over her arm.

"I have to go to Longmeadow, Mother. Now. I was supposed to meet Smitty there an hour ago."

"I already spoke with Smitty. He has Charles Jenner there to help him—"

"Some help that is."

"And," Margaret continued, holding up her hand to quiet him, "Smitty recruited a couple of guys from the training track. Thompson's on the phone with his office now, delaying his appointments until this afternoon so he can help. They'll be able to set the hurdles just fine."

Manning moaned. "I don't believe this. My arm isn't broken. I can move my fingers." He wiggled his swollen fingers. "See?"

"Good. Then it won't take but a quick visit to the ER for an X-ray to confirm that."

"Jesus Christ." He looked away, shaking his head back and forth, then spun back to face her. "You want me to have it x-rayed? Okay, I'll have Doc Paley x-ray it. If he says it's broken, I'll go to the ER."

"Fine by me. If you can get Doc Paley to agree to it."

Abigale pressed her lips together, fighting back a smile as she watched the chess game between the two of them. Thompson leaned against his nearby Ford Explorer, arms folded across his chest, a look of amusement on his face. He caught her eye and winked.

Manning stormed off toward the barn, muttering, "I don't have time for this."

Thompson unfolded himself and walked over to Margaret's car. "Things are all set at my office. I can stay at Longmeadow as long as Smitty needs my help."

"Thank you, Thompson. You're a godsend. If I don't have to run Manning to the emergency room, I'll join you at Longmeadow."

"I can drive Manning to the hospital," Abigale said, then quickly added, "or help out at the racecourse."

"Thank you, dear. Let's see what verdict we get from Doc Paley. I hope it doesn't take too long." Margaret shot a glance at her watch, then at the scarlet coat she was holding. "I have to run Richard's coat to the dry cleaner while I can still get same-day service. I thought we'd drape it on the altar, along with his boots. We've invited all MFHs attending the service to wear scarlet. And of course the pallbearers will be in scarlet."

Margaret glanced at Thompson as she leaned into her truck and hung the coat over the back of the passenger seat. "I've got Manning's coat in here, too.

If yours needs cleaning, I'll be happy to drop it off for you. Just add it to the heap. I'm going to go see what the story is with the X-rays."

Thompson started to shake his head, then hesitated and cocked an eyebrow. "You sure you don't mind?"

"If I minded, I wouldn't have offered."

He smiled. "Then I'll take you up on the offer. Let me run down to my house and get it. I'll be right back."

*M*argaret fiddled with the collar on Richard's coat as she waited in line, thinking about how true it was that the robin's-egg blue fabric had brought out the blue in his eyes. She'd heard ladies tell him that over more years than she liked to remember, but she'd never told him so herself. Now that it was too late, she wished she had. Tears misted her eyes and she blinked hard, stiffened her spine. She was turning into a sentimental old fool.

"Hello, Mrs. Southwell." The blond girl at the counter smiled a greeting, her ponytail dancing across her neck as she shoveled the pile of clothes from the previous customer into a green nylon bag.

"Morning." Margaret couldn't remember her name. She was one of the Williams girls, but they'd all helped their parents at the cleaner at one time or another and she'd stopped trying to keep track of who was who. "I spoke with your mother earlier this morning and she told me she'd do me a favor and get me same-day service on these."

"Yes, ma'am, she told me." The girl lifted the coat on top of the pile. "Wow, these are heavier than they look."

"Keeps out the wind and rain," Margaret replied. "You'll be sure to wrap the buttons, now, won't you?"

"Oh, yes ma'am. Don't you worry."

"Margaret, hello!"

Margaret turned to see Tiffanie Jenner. *Just what she needed.* "Good morning, Tiffanie."

Tiffanie's eyes drifted to the pile of coats on the counter. She nudged next to Margaret and fingered the collar of each coat with her French-manicured nails. Tiffanie tugged Richard's coat across the laminate counter. "The tailor did a lovely job attaching the collar on this one. Do you know who did the work?"

"Richard had all his coats tailored in London," Margaret said.

"How nice. No one does work like the Brits, do they?"

Margaret grunted in response. "I can pick them up today after five, is that right?" she asked, turning toward the Williams girl.

"They'll be ready for you."

"All right. Be sure to thank your mother for me."

"Sure thing," the girl said, rushing around the counter to open the door for a woman with an armful of horse blankets. She held the door for Margaret, too, giving her a cheery smile. "See you later."

Margaret was climbing in her truck when the cleaner's door burst open again and the Williams girl flapped an arm at her. "Mrs. Southwell, wait! Look what I found in one of the pockets."

The girl held a gold watch in her outstretched hand. *Richard's watch.*

"Dear Lord." Margaret marched back to the girl and folded her hand around the watch, clasping it to her chest. "Bless your heart for finding it."

The girl blushed. "We always check pockets before we send things off so we don't end up ruining something valuable, like your watch. Or in case there's gum or food or such in there."

Margaret started to tell the girl that it wasn't her watch—it was Richard's— but something stopped her. She said, "I usually look through the pockets before I bring things in, especially hunt coats. It just must have slipped my mind." She followed the girl back to the counter, almost bumping shoulders with Tiffanie who hurried by on her way out.

Margaret grabbed Richard's coat and slipped her hand in the breast pocket. "I'd better check and see if there are any other treasures stashed away."

"Oh, no, Mrs. Southwell, that's not the coat I found the watch in," the girl said, reaching into the laundry bag. "The watch was in this coat here."

She spread Manning's coat on the counter.

The force of her words hit Margaret square in the gut, stealing her breath away. She gripped the counter to steady herself.

The girl tilted her head, her hazel eyes wide. "Are you okay?"

"Are you certain that's the coat you found it in?" Margaret demanded. She saw confusion cloud the girl's eyes at the sound of the tremble in her voice.

"Oh, yes ma'am. It was in this pocket right here." Her nail-bitten fingers plucked at the top corner of the left side pocket. "See how it's torn right here?

That caught my eye right off, and then I checked inside the pocket and found the watch. The rip is in the seam, so it would be simple to repair. Would you like us to mend it while we have it here?"

A visit to the emergency room confirmed the vet's diagnosis of a broken arm, which did nothing to help Manning's mood. Abigale kept quiet and let the ER doc be the bad guy and insist Manning's arm be put in a cast. Manning had argued with him, but in the end he'd given in—though he'd grumbled about how it was a waste of time. When Manning was ready for discharge and the nurse insisted it was hospital policy he be escorted out in a wheelchair, Abigale left him bickering with the nurse and slipped out to bring the Subaru to the curb.

Once Manning was in the car, Abigale resisted the urge to help him fasten his seat belt. He stabbed the silver tab at the receptacle with his left hand until it finally clicked in place, then flopped back against the seat.

"Should I stop at a pharmacy now for the pain medication, or do you want me to drop you off at your place so you can rest while I run back to town to get the prescription filled?"

He rolled his head against the headrest until he was looking at her. "You're joking, right?"

"No."

"I'm not going home to rest, Abby. I'm going to the racecourse."

"Don't be ridiculous." She pulled Margaret's Subaru out of the hospital parking lot. "You're going to have to help me get back to Middleburg; I'm totally lost with all these new roads."

"Turn left at the light and follow the signs to Leesburg. And I'm not being ridiculous. I'm going to Longmeadow. If you don't want to drive me, I'll drive myself."

"Wow, that'll be interesting with a cast on your right arm. Your car's a stick shift, isn't it? Being left-handed won't help you out there."

Manning sighed and closed his eyes. "I have a small fracture in my arm, Abby. It's no big deal. Just please stop giving me a hard time and drive me to Longmeadow. Whose side are you on, anyway?"

He sounded so disheartened, Abigale felt a stab of guilt. "I'm on your side."

"Then stop treating me like a child. I get enough of that from Mother."

"That's unfair, Manning. It's just because she cares—"

"She treats me like I'm twelve."

Abigale laughed, and she thought she caught the glimmer of a smile play on his lips.

"And that's on a good day," he said, opening his eyes and sliding a glance at her. "You know it's true."

"Okay, I agree. Margaret can be a little controlling."

He arched an eyebrow. "A little?"

"But this has nothing to do with treating you like a child, Manning. You have a broken arm and a concussion—"

"A *mild* concussion."

"You have a broken arm and a mild concussion, and the doctor told you to go home and rest. I know you feel responsible for the work being done at the racecourse, but let's figure out some kind of compromise here. How about if you call Smitty and see if he has it under control? They might even be finished by now. We were at the ER for over two hours."

Manning didn't say anything for a minute, then pulled his cell phone out of his pocket and flipped it open. He thumbed down his list of contacts and pressed the call button.

"Hey, Smitty. How's it going?"

Abigale had reached the outskirts of Leesburg and Manning motioned for her to follow the bypass toward Warrenton.

"I'm fine. They slapped a cast on my arm and I'm good to go. Are you still at Longmeadow?"

He stretched his neck from side to side as he listened. "You supervised, right? You didn't leave Jenner alone to screw up anything?"

She heard Smitty laugh, the lilt of his Shenandoah Valley accent.

"Okay, if you're sure. I'll see you there tomorrow morning to flag the course. Nine o'clock, right?"

Abigale smiled at him when he snapped the phone shut. "Feel better?"

"Mildly."

"So, are you going to tell me how to get to your place?"

His expression dimmed, as if someone had turned off the light. He looked away and a sigh whispered through his lips.

"What?"

"I don't want to go home, Abby. I'll go nuts just sitting there alone."

"You won't be alone."

"I won't?"

She shook her head. "No. The ER doc said you need neuro checks every hour for the next twenty-four hours."

"Oh, great," he said with a groan. "Mother will love it when she hears that. I'm sure she's always wanted to set up round-the-clock guards for me. She'll probably have someone show up at my door every hour with some kind of casserole."

*M*anning's cottage was tucked away behind a knoll, out of sight of the rambling manor house at Clifden Cross. Tangles of ivy hugged the white stucco exterior, tapered into an arch above the fire-truck-red front door. A weathered trellis draped with ropes of wisteria vines sheltered a stone patio that had a to-die-for view of the Blue Ridge. Sunlight glistened off a pond nestled in a hollow.

"This is lovely, Manning," Abigale said.

"Yeah, it's a nice place. I'm fortunate to be able to rent it. The owners, Ian and Claire McCullough, don't spend much time here, so they like the idea of having someone living on the property."

"Do they live in Ireland?"

Manning smiled. "No; good guess, though, based on their names and the name of the farm. They live in Los Angeles."

He thumbed the brass lever on the door handle and elbowed the door open. "Come on in."

The door led directly into a large room that looked like something out of a travel brochure for an upscale B&B: wide-planked oak flooring, tapestry-draped windows, sporting-art oils on sage-green walls. A massive claw-footed coffee table squatted in the center of an oriental rug, surrounded by two leather club chairs and a comfy-looking overstuffed couch strewn with needlepoint pillows.

Abigale looked around, wide-eyed. "Wow."

"Yeah, like I said, it's a nice place."

"Did you furnish it?"

"Are you kidding? The only things in here that are mine are those trophies and ribbons over there." He gestured toward a mahogany sideboard that was littered with tri-color ribbons, assorted silver cups and trays, and an engraved champagne cooler.

"That's a nice collection."

"Makes it feel like home. Come on, I'll show you the kitchen. The bedroom's over there," he added, nodding toward a door across the room, next to a broad brick fireplace.

The kitchen was small but cozy, very Country French. A glass-paneled door led out onto the patio. Abigale set her shoulder bag on the counter next to a porcelain rooster. "Do you need me to pick up any groceries when I get your prescription filled?"

Manning lifted a shoulder. "Like what?"

"I don't know, like—" Abigale tugged on the stainless-steel refrigerator door—"food. My God, Manning, this is pathetic."

The glass shelves were bare, but for an open case of Bass Ale and a half-empty jar of salsa.

"I usually eat out," Manning said, shrugging it off with a crooked smile.

"I can see why. The idea of Margaret organizing people to bring casseroles is sounding better and better."

"Be careful what you wish for."

Abigale laughed, feeling the warmth of his smile wash over her. "Speaking of Margaret, we should give her a call."

"Be my guest."

"Come on, Manning. Give her a call. I'm sure she's worried about you."

He handed the cordless phone to her. "You do it. She'll want to quiz you about everything the ER doc said."

Something in his tone of voice told her not to push it. "What's the number?" she asked.

Abigale punched in the numbers as Manning recited them to her. Margaret answered on the first ring. "Hi, Margaret. It's Abigale. I just brought Manning back to his house."

"And?"

"He's doing okay. The vet was right, he did break his ulna. The doctor called it a nightstick fracture. He explained it as a partial fracture that occurs when just one side of the bone is fractured, like if you held your arm up to defend against a blow. Manning finally admitted that his arm hit a rock when he landed, so that's probably what did it."

"Will it require surgery?"

"No, it wasn't dislocated, so they were able to cast it. The doctor considered giving him a removable brace, but it took him all of about two minutes to pick up on the fact that Manning would not be an ideal patient, so he put him in a hard cast. It should heal fine. The doctor said it will just take time and hurt like hell."

Manning turned away and yanked open a drawer by the sink, noisily shoving objects around.

"Well, thank the Lord he didn't need surgery. Does he have a concussion?"

"Yes, a mild one—wait a minute, hold on, Margaret." She covered the phone with her hand. "What are you doing?" she asked Manning.

"Taking aspirin?" His expression said, *Are you going to jump on my back about this now, too?*

"The doctor specifically said you can't take aspirin when you have a concussion. It could worsen bleeding if there is any and potentially cause a brain hemorrhage. Take Tylenol."

"I don't have Tylenol," Manning muttered, tossing the aspirin bottle back in the drawer.

"There's some in my bag. I'll get it for you as soon as I'm off the phone."

She slid her hand off the mouthpiece and turned her attention back to the conversation with Margaret. "Anyway, we're supposed to keep an eye on him for the next twenty-four hours. The doctor wants us to do hourly neurological checks throughout the night."

"Sounds like he needs to be under lock and key if he's already disobeying orders about aspirin."

Abigale let the remark slide. She turned her back on Manning's accusatory glare and walked to the window, where she watched a cardinal flutter down to a bird feeder suspended from a weeping cherry tree. "I can stay here and keep an eye on him. My internal clock seems to be stuck on Kabul time, so I'll probably be awake half the night anyway."

There was a long silence. Finally, Margaret said, "Or you could bring him here. We could take turns with the hourly checks."

"I think Manning will be more comfortable sleeping in his own bed." Abigale turned to face him. "In fact, he looks like he's about to fall asleep standing up. I'll get him settled, and then I'm going to run into Middleburg to fill his prescription."

Margaret exhaled loudly into the phone. "All right. Call me if you need me."

"I will. 'Bye, Margaret."

"Thank you," Manning said when she placed the handset on the base. He flashed a tired smile. "I owe you."

She arched an eyebrow. "Do you believe I'm on your side now?"

Manning's smile flattened. "I shouldn't have made that remark earlier. I've always believed you're on my side, Abby." His voice was quiet, deep, and so dark with emotion she felt as if he'd reached inside her chest and wrapped his hand around her heart. Seventeen years vanished in the blink of an eye.

Abigale swallowed and looked away. She knew what would happen if she took one step toward him. She grabbed her bag, rummaged through it for the Tylenol and placed the bottle next to the sink. "I'll be back shortly. Try to get some rest."

Manning leaned against the counter, regarding her through cool blue eyes as she walked to the door.

*M*argaret wasn't keen on the idea of Abigale spending the night at Manning's, even though she'd prompted her to talk to Manning about what had happened with the mare, air all the dirty laundry, hash things out, and get on with it. She'd bet money they were heading toward more than talking. You'd have to be blind not to see the fire rekindling. In both of them. There was nothing she could do, though, except let them ride it out. And be around to pick up the pieces afterward.

She tossed the phone harder than she'd meant to, and felt Duchess jump against her leg as the handset clunked against the oak table. "It's okay, girl," she said, reaching down to rub the dog's velvety ears. Duchess sat up and rested her head on Margaret's knee; her soulful brown eyes flickered back and forth, as if searching Margaret's face for the cause of her temper.

"You know me too well, don't you?" Margaret murmured, absently stroking her on the head. "Things are a far cry from okay."

Richard's watch lay on the kitchen table in front of her, glowing in a beam of afternoon sun. As if taunting her to make a decision. She ran her fingers along the gold band, shuddering as goose bumps pricked her arms. It felt so cold, impersonal. So lifeless. Of course, what did she expect? It was just an object. Separated from Richard, it meant nothing. She closed a gentle fist around it. If only it could talk.

No matter how hard Margaret tried, and she'd thought of little else since leaving the cleaner, she could come up with no good reason why Richard's watch had turned up in Manning's coat pocket. Unless the Williams girl had been mistaken about which coat she'd found the watch in. She was young, probably had boys on her mind. Might even have been text-messaging while she worked, like all the kids seemed to do these days. It was no wonder more and more kids were being diagnosed with ADHD. She'd have a hard time paying attention, too, if she had a goddamned cell phone constantly alerting her that she had a new message.

Of course, even assuming the girl had been correct, that didn't mean there wasn't a perfectly innocent explanation. Maybe Richard had left the watch somewhere and Manning had picked it up and slipped it in his pocket, intending to give it to Richard the next time he saw him. That was entirely possible. Richard was forgetting things more and more lately. Just the other week, he'd been distracted after hunting and had driven halfway out of the pasture before he'd realized the back trailer ramp was down. He'd laughed it off, but Margaret knew the slipup had bothered him.

The fact that the watch was found in Manning's scarlet coat gave Margaret some comfort. That meant that no matter how Manning had ended up with the watch, it must have happened at the hunt. Once the hunt was over, Manning would have changed into his tweed jacket. Etiquette dictated it. If Manning did meet Richard at Longmeadow—and the fact that his car was spotted by the road crew implied he probably did—he would not have been wearing his scarlet coat.

But a chill crept over Margaret as a memory niggled the back of her mind. It had been raining the day Richard died. Raw. They'd had a good go of it hunting, but they'd arrived back at the trailers damp and chilled to the bone. She remembered how the Brunswick stew Wendy had provided for the tailgate had warmed her. She also remembered that Manning was still wearing his scarlet coat at the tailgate. When she'd commented on his lack of manners, Manning had shrugged it off, told her he was toasty warm under the heavyweight wool, that it repelled the rain much better than his tweed jacket did. She'd noticed later that he'd lent his rain jacket to Julia.

The image of Manning in his scarlet coat burned in Margaret's mind like a hot coal. Surely Manning would have taken the bulky coat off when he got back to the truck to drive his horse home. Or, at the very least, when he arrived at the barn. Even dry, the coat would be uncomfortable to drive in. Especially in the confines of Manning's sports car. It made no sense that he would still be wearing the coat if he met Richard at Longmeadow. But then again, it was Manning. Logical thinking—rules—didn't always apply to him, especially when he was into the booze.

Margaret shoved the chair back, disgusted by the game she was playing with herself. Making excuses. But, as damning as the evidence was, she couldn't make herself believe Manning was guilty. Not of murder. It just wasn't in him. Drinking too much? You bet. Shirking responsibility? He was a pro. But Manning loved Richard. And despite the fact that Manning seemed to be mad at the whole world lately, she'd never heard him exchange an angry word with Richard. Ever. Besides, when Manning did get mad he didn't blow a fuse. Get worked up enough to shoot someone. He sulked. Confessed his woes to a bottle of whisky. Nope. She'd blame Manning all day long for getting drunk that afternoon, but she wasn't ready to believe him guilty of Richard's murder.

She scraped the chair across the kitchen floor to the sink, Duchess trailing underfoot. Grabbing the back of the chair, she stepped up on the rush seat, stretching to hook her fingers through the horse-head-shaped handle of a small porcelain pitcher on the top shelf. Margaret pulled the pitcher down, blew off a coat of dust, and slipped the watch inside. Thank God she hadn't told the Williams girl the watch was Richard's. Or that the coat the girl had found it in belonged to Manning.

C H A P T E R

53

*A*bigale juggled the grocery bags as she let herself in the front door, trying to be as quiet as possible in case Manning was resting. She gave the door a gentle shove with her hip and elbowed it closed. The door to Manning's bedroom stood open, and she could see the curtains were drawn, the lights off. Thank God. It looked as though he'd finally given up the macho pretense and surrendered to sleep. She'd put the bags in the kitchen, then go check on him.

Halfway across the room, she heard a sharp clang in the kitchen, like glass clanking against glass. *Clang . . . clang . . . clang.* She darted for the kitchen, smelling the sour stench of beer before she even reached the door.

She froze in the open doorway, then flinched at the clatter as Manning shot a beer bottle into the trash. His back was to her, oblivious to her presence. She stood silently, watching him twist the top off a bottle of Bass Ale, hold it high above the sink, and ceremoniously drain it down to the foam. He tossed the empty bottle in the trash, then grabbed another.

Good God. How long had he been at this? Had he consumed as much as he was emptying into the sink? She drew in a breath and stepped into the room.

"Manning?"

He spun around, half-empty bottle in hand. His hair was wet; he must have showered, and he'd changed into khakis and a faded navy hoodie, the right sleeve bunched up like an accordion above his blue cast.

Abigale dumped the tangle of grocery bags on the counter. "What's going on?"

Manning turned back to the sink and upended the bottle. "I'm pouring beer down the drain."

"I can see that."

He snorted, flashing a humorless smile over his shoulder.

She clamped her arms across her chest. "Talk to me, Manning."

Manning held the bottle by two fingers, let it slip, and watched it collide with the other bottles. He crushed the empty cardboard beer carton against the counter with his cast and stuffed it into the trash.

Abigale took a step forward. "Manning—"

"Wait." He held up a hand. "I'm not finished."

She watched him yank open a cupboard door and grab a full bottle of Maker's Mark. He wedged the bottle against his side with his cast, used his left hand to pull the tab, and peeled off the red wax seal. The cap squeaked as he unscrewed it. Manning narrowed his eyes, concentrating on the caramel liquid flowing into the sink.

The scent of sour mash teased Abigale's nostrils, igniting a craving in her throat. And she didn't even like the taste of whisky! She could only imagine how it must be torturing Manning. He shook out the last drop and chucked the empty bottle in the trash. His eyes slid over to meet hers.

"There."

Abigale bit her bottom lip and studied him for a minute. "Finished?"

He nodded. "Yeah."

"Want to talk about it?"

"Nope."

"Fair enough." She pulled a carton of orange juice and a loaf of bread out of a grocery bag. "Are you hungry?"

"Not really."

"You should eat something. The pain meds are supposed to be taken with food." She lifted a white paper bag and dangled it in the air. "I stopped at the Upper Crust and got you a ham-and-cheese croissant."

He shook his head. His eyes flickered toward the trash.

Abigale knew she had to get him out of there. She pulled her camera from her shoulder bag. "I saw a blue heron down by the pond when I drove in. I thought I'd go try to get some shots of it. I'd love it if you'd come with me."

"You'd love it?"

She blushed. "Come with me."

The corners of his lips twitched, curving into a ghost of a smile. "Sure. Why not?"

*M*anning's legs were as wobbly as a newborn foal's, his feet so numb he was tempted to look down to see if they were still there. He felt just like he had when they'd given him anesthesia to remove his wisdom teeth. Another couple of seconds and it'd be lights out.

"Someone's driving down to your house," Abigale said.

Grateful for an excuse to rest, Manning stopped and looked up. A red Volkswagen Jetta sped down the driveway. "It's Julia."

"I'm sure the word's spread by now. You'll probably have a steady parade of visitors."

"Great."

They'd already hiked halfway from the pond to his house, up a hill that was nothing more than a gentle slope. But it felt like he'd been climbing Mt. Everest.

"Are you okay?" Abigale asked. She was only a couple of feet away, but her voice sounded as if she were talking through a tunnel. Her face swam in front of him, making it hard to focus. He saw her lips move but couldn't make out what she was saying. It was as if someone had stuffed cotton in his ears.

He felt her grab his arm and lower him to the ground, then heard her yell, "Julia!"

Cool hands caressed the back of his neck, gently pushing his head between his knees. Manning closed his eyes. Whoa, that was a mistake! Darkness swirled around him, making his head swim like on the teacup ride at the county fair. The one he and Percy used to ride over and over again as teenagers, daring each other to another spin, until one of them finally stumbled off to a corner to upchuck corn dogs and funnel cakes.

Manning forced his eyes open. No way in hell he was going to vomit in front of Abigale. He stared down at faded grass, a lone leaf that must have blown in from one of the sugar maples that lined the drive. He sucked in a breath, waiting for the world to stop whirling around him; he focused on the leaf, green at its very base, then flaming from mustard to blaze orange.

He heard the sound of someone running, feet rustling behind him through the grass. "What happened?" Julia shouted.

"He almost passed out," Abigale called back. "Can you see if there's ice in the freezer? If not, bring a cold towel."

"Sure thing."

A clammy sweat pricked Manning's scalp and he felt oddly hot and cold at the same time. But the spinning had stopped. Slowly, he lifted his head and found himself looking into Abigale's eyes.

"Are you okay?"

"Yeah." He blew out a sigh. "Just give me a minute."

Sweat trickled down his cheek and Abigale wiped it away with her fingertips. "Julia went to get some ice. She'll be back in a sec."

She smoothed his hair off his forehead, irritating and pleasing him at the same time, and rested the back of her hand against his brow the way his mother had when he was a kid. "This is my fault. I never should have let you take Vicodin on an empty stomach. Or walk down to the pond."

"That's bullshit," he muttered.

The house door slammed, and he looked over his shoulder to watch Julia race gracefully down the hill in her riding boots. "I found ice," she yelled, waving a folded towel.

Julia sank to her knees beside them and exchanged a worried glance with Abigale. "Hey, what happened to Superman?" she asked, handing him the ice.

He managed a smile as he pressed the ice to the back of his neck. "Must have been kryptonite in that rock I landed on."

"There must have been. You look like hell."

"Thanks."

The growl of a motor drifted down the hill, and Manning turned to see Percy's truck swerve off the drive and bounce across the grass toward them.

*A*bigale glanced out the window as she plugged her cell phone charger into an outlet above the kitchen counter. She guessed Manning wasn't feeling as jolly as he was acting, but he was putting on a good show for Percy. "It was good timing, Percy showing up when he did."

"Yeah, no kidding," Julia replied. "Percy annoys the hell out of me sometimes, but today he looked like a knight in shining armor, driving down the hill in that big old truck of his. I think Manning would have passed out if he'd tried to walk the rest of the way up to the house."

Julia crumpled the grocery bag she had just emptied and tossed it in the trash can. "God, did Manning have a party last night?"

"Far from it. He emptied all the bottles into the sink."

Julia arched an eyebrow. "Oh? That's interesting."

Abigale nodded. She grabbed a plate off the counter. "I'm going to take this out to Manning."

"Okay." Julia popped the oven door open a crack and peered inside. "This looks like it's almost done. I'll be out in a couple minutes."

"Perfect timing," Percy said when Abigale opened the back door. "Be a doll and bring us a couple of beers."

Abigale just smiled and set the plate down in front of Manning, along with a can of Coke. "I thought the Coke would help settle your stomach, but I can get you a bottle of water if you'd prefer."

"Coke's fine," Manning said.

"What?" Percy's eyebrows shot up. "You brought him a Coca-Cola? The man needs a cold brewsky."

"Manning's taking pain medicine, Percy. He can't have alcohol."

"That never stopped you before, did it, bud?" Percy said with a snort, punching Manning playfully on the shoulder.

Manning smiled, flipping the tab on the soda can.

Percy regarded Manning through half-closed eyes, a lazy smirk twisting his lips. "Good thing I don't mind drinking alone." He raised a palm toward Abigale as he lumbered to his feet. "No, no, stay right there. I'll help myself."

Abigale ignored Percy and slipped into the chair next to Manning. "Are you feeling better?"

"I'm fine." As if to prove it, he tipped the can and took a sip.

She nudged the plate closer to him. "I warmed up the croissant."

"I'm not hungry right now, but thanks." Manning pushed the plate away.

"You have to eat something. If the sandwich doesn't appeal to you, I'll get you something else."

His expression tightened, jaw muscles clenched. "The sandwich is fine, Abby. I'm just not hungry right now."

"I bought Jell-O. And chicken noodle soup. Would you rather have that?"

He shook his head.

"Or, you can wait for the egg-and-sausage casserole Julia brought. She's heating it up now."

"God, Abby," Manning said with a groan. "You just don't let up, do you?" He picked up the croissant and shoved it in his mouth. Flakes of pastry floated to the table as he bit off a chunk.

She pressed her lips together, holding back a smile, and resisted telling him to take small bites.

The kitchen door flew open, Percy bellowed, "Hey, Manning—I mean, *Master*—what the fuck? You're out of beer?"

"I have a case in my car," Julia said, slipping through the door behind him. "It's not cold, though." She set the casserole on the wrought-iron table, tossing the potholders beside it.

"I don't care," Percy replied, handing her a stack of plates and utensils. "Beggars can't be choosers."

Julia scooped a heaping pile of casserole onto a plate and handed it to Manning. He eyed the steaming mound of eggs and chunks of sausage; the color drained from his face. "Thanks," he said, plunking the plate on the table and leaning back in his chair.

"Hey, your cell just dinged. I think you got a text message," Julia said, handing Abigale her cell phone. "I brought it out in case it was someone important."

Abigale thumbed the message button.

"Based on the look on your face, it must have been from someone good," Julia said.

"It's from my friend Joe in Afghanistan. We work together at Reuters." She opened the text message, smiling as she scrolled down. "He sent a picture."

"Let me see," Julia said, scooting her chair over next to Abigale's.

Abigale tilted the screen so Julia could see the photo.

"Oh, my, three hunky guys. Who are they?"

"This is Joe, here on the left. The one in the center is Alex. He's an AP photographer."

Julia tapped a long red fingernail against the screen. "Who's the hot one with the bedroom eyes?"

"That's Emilio. He's a reporter for *Corriere della Sera.*"

"Aw, look at the way he has his hands clasped across his heart. Is he doing that for you?"

"No."

Julia grinned. "He is. Look, the subject line says *Heartbroken in Kabul.* How cute!"

Abigale pulled the phone away. "They're just joking around. We were all friends. We watched each other's backs."

"I don't know if I believe you. You're blushing. Isn't she, Manning?"

Manning lifted a shoulder indifferently and gave Abigale a faint smile.

"I'm ba-ack," Percy sang, slamming a case of beer on the table. He yanked the cardboard open, snatched a bottle, and twisted the top off with a pop. "Anyone else want a beer?"

"I'll take one," Julia said. She wrinkled her nose. "I hate warm beer, but what the hell. I heard somewhere that warm beer gets you drunk faster."

Percy opened a bottle and handed it to Julia, then grabbed another and held it out to Abigale. She shook her head.

He nodded at Manning, raised the bottle as if he was going to pitch it to him, then jerked back his arm. "Oh, I almost forgot. Nurse Ratched here won't let you have one."

"Fuck you, Percy," Manning said.

Percy laughed and dropped down in his chair. "Ah, this looks good." He eyed the plate in front of him, smacking his lips. "Cholesterol city, here I come."

He shoveled a forkful into his mouth and made a thumbs-up sign. "Fantastic."

"You're going to have a heart attack by the time you're forty," Manning said.

Percy laughed, speared another forkful and washed it down with a swig of beer. "Yeah, but I'll die a happy man."

He stabbed his fork in the air at Manning, "Speaking of dying, sounds like you dodged a bullet today."

"That's a bit of an exaggeration," Manning said. "I broke my arm." He glanced at Abigale, adding, "Barely."

Percy said, "Yeah, but the billet straps gave way over a jump, right?"

Manning nodded.

"Lucky you didn't break more than your arm." Percy chewed thoughtfully. "Why the hell were you riding in Richard's saddle, anyway?"

Abigale shot a look at Manning. "How do you know Manning was riding in Uncle Richard's saddle?"

Percy shrugged as he ran his fork through the eggs. "I don't know. Heard it somewhere."

Abigale half-listened to the banter, which grew louder and raunchier as Percy and Julia downed more beer. She couldn't shake the thoughts that had eaten at her ever since Percy had made the comment about Uncle Richard's saddle. First of all, how did Percy know Manning hadn't been riding in his own saddle? Lieutenant Mallory had agreed with Margaret that they shouldn't discuss any details about the saddle incident. So, how had Percy found out? And so quickly?

She thought back to the conversation she'd had with Smitty about Charles Jenner wanting to buy Percy's property, and about how they wanted Uncle Richard to speak out publicly in favor of the deal. Did they want it so badly that they'd have resorted to threats? Or intimidation? *Or worse?*

Abigale studied Percy across the table: cutting up, poking fun at Manning, at himself. The class clown. Would he stoop to blackmail if he wanted something badly enough? She found it hard to believe him capable of it. But then, she really didn't know Percy anymore. She really didn't know any of them.

Except Manning. She might not know what he'd been doing the last seventeen years, or all that he'd been through, but when he turned those blue eyes on her, the old bond burned so strong it hurt her chest. Like it or not, she felt as if he could still read her thoughts. And right now, she could tell he was wishing like hell Percy and Julia would go home.

Percy caught her eye and thrust out his bottom lip. "Don't look so worried, Nurse Ratched. Manning's going to be okay."

Manning balled up a napkin and threw it at Percy. "Knock it off."

"It's okay," Abigale said to Manning. "Percy's wit is lost on me. I have no idea who Nurse Ratched is."

"She was the nurse from hell in *One Flew Over the Cuckoo's Nest*," Julia told her.

"Sorry, never saw it. But—" Abigale smiled at Percy—"since you already think I'm the evil nurse, I'm going to break up this party and insist Manning get some rest."

Percy whooped. "Good luck with that. This party's just getting started." He waved his beer bottle at Manning. "Tell her how it is, my friend."

Manning shrugged. "You heard the lady."

"Oh, man, you are so fucked," Percy said.

Julia shoved her chair back, rolling her eyes at Abigale. "Come on, Percy. Time to hit the road."

Percy rose with a lot of moaning and groaning, then threw a few more good-natured jibes at Manning.

"You going to help us flag the course tomorrow?" Manning asked.

"Yeah, I'll be there."

"Thanks." Manning held his left hand up as Percy tucked the case of beer under his arm. They clasped hands as Percy walked away. "And thanks for stopping by."

Julia leaned down and gave Manning a hug, whispering, "Don't worry, I'll follow Percy and make sure he gets home all right."

Manning waited until they both disappeared around the corner, then heaved a noisy sigh. "Thanks for playing bad cop and making them go home."

"It went on a bit long."

"Yeah. And Percy's a lot less funny when I'm sober."

She smiled, studying him for a minute. "It seems like the two of you are still good friends."

He stretched his shoulders and shrugged. "We hang out, but we're not as close as we were back in the day."

"Did something happen?"

"We were partners in a racing stable during college and it ended badly. In fact, we barely spoke for years." He shrugged. "Since I've been back from Los Angeles we've pretty much patched things up."

Abigale bit the inside of her lip, measuring her words. "Did it strike you as odd that Percy knew you were riding in Uncle Richard's saddle when you were injured?"

He frowned. "Odd how?"

"Odd that he knew. I mean, we all agreed that we wouldn't mention it to anyone. So how did Percy find out?"

"You've been away too long. You've forgotten how quickly news travels in this town. So-and-so tells so-and-so, eases his conscience by making them promise not to repeat it, and so on."

"Yeah, I get that. But so quickly? And who told? I sure didn't. You didn't. Both Margaret and Thompson agreed to keep quiet about it."

The look Manning gave her said *so what*? "Michael, Larry, Doc Paley, Kevin."

"Who is Kevin?"

"The blacksmith. Look, Abby, does it really matter? Someone obviously said something to someone. Nothing we can do about it now."

Manning's tone was clipped, as if it was an effort to get the words out. Abigale knew she should drop it, let him get some rest. Still, she had to ask. "What if someone didn't tell Percy?"

"What do you mean?"

"What if he already knew."

His eyes narrowed. "What—you think Percy tampered with Richard's saddle? No. No way."

"Are you sure?"

"Yeah, I'm sure. How did you come up with that, anyway? Just because Percy knows I was riding in Richard's saddle, you think that means he cut the billet straps? That's as far-fetched as Mother suggesting I'm a suspect in Richard's murder because I can't remember what I did that afternoon." Manning scowled at her. "Jesus Christ, Abby."

"That's not the only reason," Abigale said, regretting that she'd ever brought it up. "It's also something Smitty told me the other night."

She repeated what Smitty had told her about Percy's land deal. Halfway through, Manning was already shaking his head. "Percy's going to sell that property one way or the other, Abby. If Charles Jenner doesn't get his equestrian subdivision approved, Percy will sell it to someone else. It's a valuable piece of property. There are other buyers out there."

Abigale held her hands up in surrender. "Okay. I didn't realize Percy had so many other options. Smitty made it sound like it was a make-or-break deal with Charles Jenner and they really needed Uncle Richard's help."

"Maybe for Jenner, but not for Percy. Besides, even if it was, Percy would never do something like that."

"All right. I'm sorry I brought it up. I didn't mean to upset you."

"You didn't upset me. I'm just pissed off. I feel like shit." He raised his arm in the air. "And I can't stand this goddamned cast."

Abigale looked at her watch. "You still have two hours before you can take more Vicodin. Why don't you lie down and elevate your arm for a little while?"

"And what will you do, sit there and watch me sleep?"

"Do you have Internet access?"

He nodded.

"Say no more."

*A*bigale sank onto the couch, sighing as the deep cushions swallowed her with a soft caress. She pulled her MacBook onto her lap and watched firelight flicker off the screen as the computer booted up. She'd won the fight with Manning about who would sleep on the couch, but he'd insisted on starting a fire for her before he'd trod wearily off to bed.

She hoped he'd be able to sleep for awhile. He'd been snoring softly when she'd last checked on him. And she'd been able to cajole him into swallowing half a bowl of chicken noodle soup when he'd taken his pain meds, so with any luck he wouldn't get nauseated again.

Abigale plugged the cable from her camera into the laptop and waited for the pictures to load. She'd caught up on her email earlier when Manning was resting, spent some time poking around the Internet. Googled Percy Fletcher, Charles and Tiffanie Jenner. Found a slew of articles about the proposed development. She'd discovered a group called Foxhunters Online and followed a long string of discussions about her uncle's murder. She'd had no idea how well-known and well-loved her uncle was. And not just in Middleburg. There were posts from foxhunters in Tennessee and Nebraska. Even one from Ireland.

Most of the online chatter seemed to take it as fact that he'd been murdered by a "Hispanic road worker," but the discussion flared more than once into accusations of racial profiling. There was one particularly fiery post chastising people for convicting Dario Reyes before he'd even been located by the police and given the opportunity to speak out. It concluded by cautioning people to wait and see, that things are often not as they appear. Almost as if the writer knew something. The post was from a woman identified only as Michelle, with an email address of chiencheval112@aol.com. Could it be the same Michelle she'd met that morning, Michelle de Becque? *Chiencheval.* Dog and horse in French. It was certainly possible. Of course, it was just as likely the post was from France, given that the Internet group was international. Abigale sent an email message, identifying herself and asking if the woman would be willing to talk to her privately.

One by one, the images from Abigale's camera popped up on the screen and she saved them all to the hard drive. The shots of the soldier on the flight from Ramstein had turned out well. She spent a few minutes adjusting the brightness on the picture of the soldier holding his son's photo, corrected a shadow on his face. She smiled as she noticed a soldier seated across the aisle saluting the injured soldier. *Nice.* She hadn't noticed that when she'd snapped the shot. No surprise. When she focused on a subject in her lens, she blocked out everything happening around her. A skill she'd learned from a veteran photojournalist in Iraq. She wrote a short email to the soldier wishing him luck and attached the photographs.

Abigale scrolled to the end of the downloaded photos, to the shots she'd taken down by the pond. She'd snapped a couple of Manning without him knowing, and she clicked on the first one, enlarging it to full screen. She zoomed in on his face. There was no denying Manning still took her breath away. He wasn't exactly classically handsome. His hair was too unruly, his nose a tad crooked from when he'd broken it as a kid, and a faint scar ran the length of his right jaw. But his eyes were deep enough to drown in. The curve of his lips held the promise of a kiss. She advanced to a shot of Manning leaning against a willow tree, his arms folded across his chest. His shoulders looked about a mile wide.

"God, get a grip," she muttered, jabbing at the keyboard to exit full-screen mode. She viewed the shots of the blue heron, a couple of which were nice. The shots of the red fox in the field at Dartmoor Glebe captured the moment just as she'd hoped they would. Her mother would love them. She scrolled up to the shots she'd taken in the woods behind Margaret's. The shot of the swimming rock was bathed in soft morning light, the river glistening gently in the background. Beautiful.

"What are you looking at?" Manning asked. His voice, deepened by sleep, seemed to rumble across the quiet room.

Abigale jumped. "God, Manning! You scared me. What are you doing up?"

"I couldn't sleep." He rubbed his eyes as he flopped down next to her on the couch. He wore a pair of orange UVA athletic shorts and a gray T-shirt. He propped up his bare feet on the coffee table. "Are those the pictures you took at the pond today?"

Abigale snapped the laptop lid down. "It's just a hodgepodge of photos."

"Can I see?"

She splayed her hands across the lid, embarrassed for him to see the shots she'd taken of him by the pond. "I still need to edit them."

"I don't care if they're not edited." He grabbed the lid with the thumb and forefinger of his broken arm and tugged it open a couple of inches.

Abigale slid her hand over his, stopped him.

"What the hell?" Manning stared at her for a minute, then grunted, pulling his hand away with a hollow laugh. "Never mind, I get it."

"You get what?"

"You were looking at the photo you got on your cell tonight. The one with your boyfriend in it."

"My boyfriend?"

"Yeah. *Emilio.*"

"He's not my boyfriend."

"No?"

"No."

He smiled. "Does he know that?"

"Screw you, Manning. For the record, we broke up before I left Kabul. And I wasn't looking at photos of him." She raised the lid. "I was viewing the photos I've taken in Virginia to select some to send to my mother."

Manning's eyes shifted to the screen. "That's the river behind Mother's." He peered closer. "Is that our swimming rock?"

Abigale nodded. "I took a hike yesterday morning and snapped a bunch of shots. Here, I'll go back to the beginning." She scrolled back to the first picture and enlarged it.

"Can you do a slide show?"

"Sure." She clicked it on automatic and slid the computer over to Manning.

He settled lower into the cushions and raised his knees. The legs of his nylon shorts slid back, revealing well-muscled thighs. Manning balanced the computer on his lap and angled it slightly in Abigale's direction, shifting so his shoulder rested against hers.

Abigale's stomach clenched as the pictures slowly advanced toward the shots she'd snapped of the cross. She felt the muscles in Manning's arm stiffen, but neither of them said anything as the photos of the cross faded one into the other on the screen. She eased out a breath when the scene shifted to the shots of the fox. The corners of Manning's mouth hinted at a smile when he saw the snapshots of him by the pond. When the slide show ended, Manning shut the laptop lid and set the computer on the cushion next to him.

"Those are nice," he said. "You obviously have a gift for photography. Something beyond what you learned at Cornell."

"Actually, I never took a photography class at Cornell."

"I thought you did."

She shook her head. "I begged my father to let me study photography, but he wouldn't even discuss it. As far as he was concerned, it was the Cornell Hotel School or no school."

"So where did you get your training?"

"I joined the staff at *The Cornell Daily Sun.* All of my photography training was strictly hands-on."

He arched an eyebrow. "That's impressive. I hope you gave the *Sun* credit when you won your Pulitzer."

She smiled.

A log settled in the fireplace, scattering sparks across the hearth. Manning gazed thoughtfully at the fire. The reflection from the flames danced in his eyes. "I came to see you once at Cornell."

"You did?"

"Yeah. I played polo for UVA and we had a match at Cornell. I knew you were going to school there, so I decided to look you up."

"But you never found me."

"Yes, I did."

She frowned. "I don't understand."

Manning rubbed his hand along his jaw. "Your roommate answered the phone and told me you were studying outside at—what's it called—the hill?"

"The slope."

"Right. The slope. So I went there."

"And?" Abigale demanded when he didn't continue.

"And I saw you with a guy. You were lying on a blanket with your books all spread out, but you weren't doing a lot of studying. I found out later he was your fiancé."

Abigale's chest ached, imagining how Manning must have felt that day.

"Why didn't you say anything?"

He shrugged. "You looked so happy. I figured there was no point. But, for the record," he cracked a grin, "we beat the hell out of Cornell in the polo match that day."

She smiled, her thoughts drifting back to her time at Cornell. Manning was right; she had been happy there. Happy to be in America, at Cornell, on staff at the *Sun*. Happy with Peter. Not with the same manic, head-over-heels, partners-in-crime passion she'd had with Manning. But Peter was her rock. An island to cling to as the stormy future her father had crafted swirled around her, threatening to suck her under.

"What did your father say when he found out you were pursuing photography despite his wishes?" Manning asked.

"He didn't. My father was oblivious. As far as he knew, I was happily on track to spend my life as an hotelier."

"He must have figured it out at some point. You're famous."

"Hardly," Abigale said, rolling her eyes. "My father did eventually learn about my passion for photography, but it wasn't until after I graduated from Cornell. When he discovered Peter, my fiancé, had the passion for the hotel business that I lacked, he tagged his future son-in-law as his heir-apparent to run the hotel. Then my father no longer had a reason to dictate my future. At least not my career."

"So he let you become a photojournalist and ship off to a war zone?"

"Are you kidding? I started out interning for a Swiss fashion magazine. It wasn't until after my father's death that I was free to pursue photojournalism."

Manning's expression darkened. "I'm sorry about your father. And your fiancé. I wanted to write you—started to several times—but decided I was probably the last person you wanted to hear from. That must have been hell for you and your mother. You weren't skiing with them when it happened, were you?"

"No. It was my father, Peter, and six of our hotel guests. Americans. The avalanche danger was high that day and my mother begged my father not to go. She tried to talk him into skiing at St. Moritz, only sixty kilometers away. But helicopter skiers are adrenaline junkies. The risk only seemed to fuel their enthusiasm, so my father agreed to take them. Two of the Americans died along with Peter and my father."

"Jesus."

"The conversation between my parents wasn't unlike many I heard between Margaret and Uncle Richard, arguing about whether the footing was too treacherous to hunt on a given day." She gave a hollow laugh, remembering. "Uncle Richard used to say he owed it to the hunt members to go out, the same argument my father made. And Margaret's response was always the same as my mother's: that he owed it to the hunt members not to risk their necks hunting in sloppy footing. The only difference is Uncle Richard usually had the sense to yield to Margaret's better judgment. My father didn't. I can still picture my mother that day, framed in the arched front door of our hotel as my father drove away. She stared after the van until it disappeared beyond the shadow of the castle, no doubt hoping he'd change his mind."

Manning slid his hand across hers. "I'm sorry."

Pain swelled in Abigale's chest, whether from the memory of Peter and her father's death or Manning's touch she wasn't sure. Ten years had passed since the skiing accident, and time had mercifully dulled the pain. But the old wounds from the breakup with Manning still felt raw. She swallowed against the tightness in her throat.

He entwined his fingers with hers, raised their joined hands, and studied them for a moment in the firelight. "I've missed you, Abby. I'm glad you're back."

"Me too."

Manning's grip tightened and he pulled her hand to his mouth, pressed his lips lightly against her knuckles. A shiver ran to the pit of her belly.

"Don't," she murmured, passion and panic playing tug-of-war within her.

His lips parted, breath whispered across her fingers. "Why not?" Desire flared in his eyes, turned them the dusky blue of an approaching storm.

She tugged her hand away from his mouth. "Because. I have to leave, go back on assignment."

"Tonight?"

The smile in his voice dissolved Abigale's panic and ate at her willpower. "No."

"Good."

Manning cupped his fingers under her chin and ran his thumb over her mouth, so gentle it made her want to cry. He bent his head, brushed his lips against hers, lingered, then captured her mouth with his, pulling her deeper and deeper until she couldn't get enough of him.

The far-off ringing of a phone woke Abigale. She opened her eyes to see sunlight streaming through a crack in the curtain and wondered lazily what time it was. Night had just begun to fade to gray when they'd fallen asleep.

She was spooned up against Manning, his broken arm curled protectively around her. His breath teased the back of her neck. She shifted ever so slightly, easing the stiffness out of her sore muscles. Their lovemaking was a mindless blur, Manning's hands everywhere, caressing, demanding, tender, greedy; his hungry mouth; the slide of skin against skin; hard muscles pinning her to the bed; a voyage of rediscovery, a journey into unchartered territory. Emotion welled in her chest and a tear trickled down her cheek, pooled in the hollow of her throat. Life would tumble back down on them, she knew that. But whatever happened, she'd carry the memory of last night—this moment—in her heart.

Manning tightened his arm, drew her closer. She looked over her shoulder and saw his eyes were open. She rolled to face him and Manning smiled, a slow grin like the sun breaking out from behind a cloud. He planted his left elbow on the bed and propped his head up against his palm. "Good morning." His fingers skimmed her hair from her face and traced the line of her cheekbone.

"Hey," she said softly. "How's your arm?"

"It hurts like hell." Manning kissed her mouth gently. "We'd better do something to take my mind off it."

Abigale's lips curved against his. "Let me get you a Vicodin. Or at least Tylenol."

"I don't want a Vicodin." Manning nuzzled her ear, then nibbled his way down her neck as he pulled her closer. "Or Tylenol. But I think you need to check my vital signs."

Her arms curved around his neck. "I'm pretty sure your vital signs are fine."

A smile softened his blue eyes and he pushed the sheet away. "Then I'd better check your vital signs." His hand slid down to her breast, teased her nipple with his thumb.

"That one works," he said lowering his head. "Let's check the other one."

His mouth found her breast, and he slowly drove her insane with his tongue as his hand trailed lower.

"You're still wet," he murmured.

A soft moan caught in Abigale's throat as he rolled on top of her and slid inside.

*M*argaret knocked again, louder this time. Placed her ear to the door, listened for the sound of footsteps. Still quiet as a church inside. She tromped back to her truck and fished a key out of the cup holder.

Her Subaru was parked in the drive, so Abigale and Manning hadn't left for the racecourse yet. Why the hell wasn't anyone answering the door? She jabbed the key in the lock and shoved, and was greeted by a faint odor of wood fire. The curtains were drawn, the lights off. Sunlight poured into the kitchen and she poked her head inside. Empty. She spun around. Eyed the open door to Manning's bedroom.

"Hello?" she called.

"Mother?" Manning's voice came from the bedroom, husky-sounding as if he'd been asleep.

"There you are. I was beginning to think no one was home."

"Hold on!"

She stopped just shy of the bedroom. Heard the scuffle of feet, a door click shut.

"Are you decent?" she asked, averting her eyes.

Sheets rustled. "Yeah. Sure. Come in."

Manning lay on his back, arms folded in front of him. His blue cast pinned the white sheet to his chest. She heard a clunk as the shower cut on in the bathroom. Saw a trail of clothes on the floor. Orange gym shorts, a pair of jeans. A black bra.

"Abby's in the shower," Manning said, his eyes swimming with guilt.

"So I surmised."

It had been years since Margaret had seen Manning look like he even cared that he'd been caught with his hand in the cookie jar. Maybe there was a ray of hope in that.

"Are you on your way to Longmeadow?" he asked with forced casualness.

Margaret nodded. "I called earlier but there was no answer, so I stopped by on my way to see how you fared through the night." She paused. "Looks like you managed just fine."

"Yeah." Manning tugged at the sheet with his broken arm. "Give me a minute and I'll get dressed."

"I'll wait for you in the kitchen."

Manning padded into the kitchen a few minutes later, barefooted, wearing the orange shorts she'd seen on the floor and a wrinkled gray T-shirt. He moved gingerly, as though he wasn't sure which part of him hurt the most.

"Coffee's brewing," Margaret said, switching on the oven. "I thought I'd heat up this egg casserole I found in the refrigerator."

"None for me, thanks."

"It looks good. Did Abigale make it?"

Manning shook his head. "Julia."

"Oh? When did she bring it by?"

"She and Percy came over yesterday afternoon."

"That was nice." Margaret had noted the absence of beer in the refrigerator, thought perhaps Abigale had put it away somewhere. But if Percy and Julia had stopped by, that explained it.

"Yeah." He smiled, pulling a carton of orange juice from the refrigerator. "Kind of like old times, Abby and Percy going at each other."

"What's that you're saying about me and Percy?" Abigale asked as she slipped into the room, all scrubbed and perfumed, her wet hair twisted up in a clasp.

Manning's face lit up when he saw her. "Hey."

"Hi." She smiled at him through lowered lashes, almost shyly. "Good morning, Margaret."

"Morning. Coffee's ready. Help yourself."

"Thanks." Abigale opened several cupboards and finally found a coffee mug.

"I've got the egg casserole heating in the oven."

"It smells good," Abigale said, looking at Manning. "How's your stomach?"

Manning wrinkled his nose.

"You have to eat something."

He palmed a bottle of Tylenol and pointed at the glass of orange juice he'd poured. "Breakfast of champions."

"Wrong. Especially if you think you're going to work on the racecourse today." Abigale took the bottle from Manning, shook out two tablets, and handed them to him.

"Only two?"

"If you need more than that you should probably spend the day in bed."

Margaret saw Manning give Abigale a wicked grin before he tilted his head and tossed back the pills. She caught Abigale's blush. *Lord.* The two of them were acting like lovesick teenagers. Yet she found herself smiling as she watched them, despite the fact she was sure no good would come from their reunion. She guessed part of her wanted to believe Abigale might be Manning's salvation.

All night she'd battled whether to confront Manning about the watch, but in the end she'd decided against it. What was the point? He'd say he had no idea how it got in his coat pocket. Or that he couldn't remember. Anger and grief tightened her chest, making it hard to breathe. *Maybe the truth was, she didn't want to hear his answer.*

"I'll leave the two of you to eat your breakfast," Margaret said, snatching her pocketbook off the counter. "I've got to get over to Longmeadow."

"I'll see you there," Manning said. "I'm meeting Smitty at nine to flag the course."

"I'm not sure that's a good idea," Abigale said.

He cocked an eyebrow and cracked a grin. "What, flagging the course?"

"You know what I mean. I'm not sure you should work on the course today. Look how swollen your hand is. You should keep your arm elevated and iced."

"Uh-huh."

"Abigale's right, Manning," Margaret said. "We'll get on fine at Longmeadow without you. Better you should take it easy today and get your strength back. We'll need you at the races tomorrow."

"Gang up on me, I don't care," Manning said. "I'm still going to Long-meadow."

Margaret wasn't surprised that Manning would quarrel with her, but for him to argue about going to work rather than trying to get out of it? That was out of character. In fact, now that she thought about it, he'd done the same thing yesterday when he'd argued about having to go to the hospital when he was supposed to help Smitty set the national fences. She studied him curiously and saw a look in his eyes she hadn't seen in a long time. As if the storm had finally blown through, whisked away all the thunderclouds. Maybe Richard had been right in thinking that Manning would rise to the challenge of being master.

"Actually, we could use your help," Margaret said, ignoring the look of betrayal Abigale shot at her. "I'd asked Michael to fill in for you, but he's running behind at the barn. Larry didn't show up for work today. So, if you feel up to working, I'll be happy to give you a ride." She glanced at Abigale and added, "After you've had some breakfast."

"Jesus, what is it with the two of you and food?" Manning flung open a cupboard. He rummaged around, then grabbed a box of Pop-Tarts.

"How old are those?" Margaret asked.

He lifted a shoulder as he tore into the silver wrap. "Who cares? I'm eating."

Margaret exchanged a look with Abigale, who rolled her eyes. "What are your plans today, dear?" she asked.

"I don't have any," Abigale said. "I thought I might get started going through Uncle Richard's papers, but please let me know if there's anything I can do to help you get ready for the races."

"I do have an errand I'd love to delegate," Margaret admitted.

"What is it?"

"I have some table linens for the VIP reception tomorrow that need to be dropped off at Tiffanie Jenner's place."

"I'm happy to do that. I want to meet her anyway."

"No you don't," Manning said, through a mouth full of Pop-Tart.

"Why not?" Abigale asked.

He took a swig of orange juice. "She's a pain in the ass. She'll want to be your best friend because you're Richard's niece. And because you inherited Dartmoor Glebe."

Margaret frowned at him. "Manning."

"What? You know it's true."

*A*bigale clutched the stack of linens to her chest, steadying them with her chin as she stretched up and pulled down the hatchback on Margaret's Subaru. The old car looked forlorn parked between the hulking black Hummer and the black Mercedes-Benz SUV. She wiped her hand on her jeans, wondering how the other two vehicles could be so clean when the back of the Subaru was caked with road dust. Sure, the Jenners' driveway was paved, but they had to travel on gravel roads to get there. She imagined someone dashing out to wipe off the Jenners' vehicles as soon as one was parked.

Abigale eyed the immaculate landscaping, the neatly mowed fields, the mature dogwood trees evenly spaced lining the long drive. Of course. *Dogwood Lane.* She remembered that from the first notation about Tiffanie Jenner in her uncle's journal.

Margaret had described the house as a McMansion, and Abigale saw why. It was at least ten thousand square feet, probably more, covered with what looked like enough bright-red brick to pave the square in central Baghdad. The roof was slate, undoubtedly the real thing, and the keystone above each window bore the impression of a fox head. A four-tiered fountain bubbled merrily in the middle of a cobblestone courtyard surrounded by boxwoods. Abigale admired the lush moss that checkerboarded the stone pavers; she knew from years of listening to her father and various gardeners discuss the walkways behind the hotel that it wasn't an easy feat to keep crabgrass from creeping in.

She climbed the flared stairs to the front door and pressed the button for the bell, listening to the melody chime inside. A few moments passed and she wondered if she should push the button again when she saw movement through the stained-glass panel in the door. The woman who opened the door was about Abigale's height and Hollywood thin. Her honey-colored chin-length bob was tucked behind her right ear, to which she clutched an iPhone. She flashed the emerald-cut diamond rock on her left hand with practiced ease as she motioned Abigale inside.

Abigale stepped into an entry hall that soared the full three stories of the house, crowned in the center with a crystal chandelier almost large enough to be lowered in Times Square on New Year's Eve. The woman gave Abigale a pained look and opened and closed her hand, as if to say the person on the other end of the phone wouldn't shut up. Abigale smiled politely.

Tiffanie said, "Belinda, I understand *completely* what you're saying, but just because the children have used the same old costumes for the last umpteen years doesn't mean we shouldn't get new ones for the pageant this year. My contact in New York promised to email pictures first thing on Monday and assured me he'd have the costumes here in time if we make our selections by the end of next week."

Abigale averted her eyes, studying a foxhunting mural painted on the entry wall.

"I told you before, the cost is not an issue. Charles will pay. Listen, Belinda, I have to go. I have company. We'll get together next week and make the selections. 'Bye."

Tiffanie slid the phone into the pocket of her mustard-colored blazer, cashmere from the looks of it, which was stylishly coordinated with her Chanel mustard-and-black ballet flats, black wool slacks, black silk turtleneck, and cream, gold, and black Hermès scarf. More New York than Middleburg, but stunning nonetheless.

"I'm so sorry to have kept you waiting. I'm Tiffanie Jenner. And you must be Abigale."

"Yes, hi." Abigale shifted the bundle of linens. "Margaret asked me to drop these off."

Tiffanie eyed the linens but made no attempt to take them. "Yes, Margaret called and told me you were on your way. Can you stay a minute? Would you like an espresso?"

"That sounds wonderful."

"Lovely. Follow me."

Tiffanie led Abigale to a kitchen that belonged on the pages of *Architectural Digest*, complete with wood-burning pizza oven, trompe l'oeil walls, and mammoth Viking range. Dozens of gleaming copper pots that Abigale would bet had never touched the stove hung suspended over the center island.

"Where would you like me to put these?" Abigale asked, extending the armful of linens.

Tiffanie waved a hand at the black granite counter. "Just set them there." She pressed her deep red lips together, causing a tiny row of lines to appear like crescent moons on either side of her mouth. "I don't know what to do about those."

"What do you mean?"

Tiffanie reached out a slender finger and pressed a button on the front of a shiny espresso machine. "I bought some fabulous linens for the reception," she said, raising her voice to be heard over the grinding noise spewing from the machine. "When I told Margaret, she said it was nonsense to waste money, that she had a set the hunt has been using for years. She all but ordered me to return the ones I bought and use hers."

Abigale set the linens on the counter. "Can you still return them?"

"I probably can, but I'd rather not." Tiffanie poured two shots of espresso into a bone china cup and handed it on a saucer to Abigale. "The ones I bought are gorgeous."

She brewed an espresso for herself and tugged back one of several bar stools tucked under a high counter at the end of the island. "Please, have a seat."

Tiffanie perched on the edge of a stool one over from Abigale's. "What would you do if you were in my situation?"

You don't really want me to answer that, Abigale thought. She said, "That's a tough one. But I'm sure you'll handle it just fine."

Tiffanie eyed Margaret's linens and wrinkled her nose. "Much as I hate to offend Margaret, Richard did put me in charge of the reception . . ."

She sipped her espresso, shifting her wide brown eyes to Abigale. "I'm so sorry for your loss, by the way. You must just be devastated. Richard was such a wonderful man. The hunt will never be the same without him."

"I understand you worked with my uncle quite a bit organizing the race reception."

"Yes. And as ornery as Margaret can be—don't tell her I said that— Richard could not have been more agreeable. I have to admit, I was nervous when I first met with him to discuss the reception. But he could not have been more patient with me. Everyone told me he was such a perfectionist about the races and would try to micromanage all the details, but he pretty much turned the whole VIP reception over to me. Within no time he went from being this larger-than-life master to treating me like I was important to the hunt."

"I'm sure he really appreciated your help."

"We worked well with one another. In fact, we planned to get together as soon as the races were over and talk about planning several other hunt fundraisers. Richard was especially excited about an idea I have for a skeet-shooting competition."

"Do you shoot skeet?"

"Not since we moved down here. But it was big socially in Connecticut."

Abigale swallowed a long draw of espresso, trying to figure out how to broach the subject of the proposed real-estate development Smitty had told her about. "Your home is beautiful. Have you lived here long?"

"A little over a year."

"Did you live in the area before that?"

Tiffanie held her coffee cup with her little finger crooked daintily in the air, the way they teach in etiquette school. "No, we moved here from Connecticut. Charles's idea, not mine."

"Charles is your husband?"

"Yes," Tiffanie replied in a flat tone. "Charles is from a Podunk town in the Midwest and really wanted to raise our daughter in a small town. I told him I wasn't Dorothy and Kansas wasn't an option, so we compromised. He proposed Middleburg and I figured I could live with that. So we did the whole *Green Acres* thing."

Abigale laughed. "Except Eva Gabor ended up on a ramshackle farm and your place is gorgeous." She felt a little disingenuous saying it, but the Jenners' farm was impressive in a flamboyant, grandiose way. Even though she'd trade it for an old farmhouse in a heartbeat.

"Thank you." A frown wrinkled Tiffanie's slender nose. "If I'd lived down here while Charles was building the house there are some things I would have done differently, but I stayed in Connecticut so Brooke—that's our daughter—could finish her first year of preschool. That was a mistake. For several reasons."

"That must have a lot of perks, being married to a builder. I guess you don't have to spend a lot of time sitting around waiting for repairmen."

"He's a developer, actually," Tiffanie said, as if the distinction was obvious. "He doesn't waste his time with individual building projects. Other than our own, of course."

"What kind of developments does he do?"

"Planned communities. Themed subdivisions. Last year he completed a Christian-themed community in Tennessee with big old church-looking pillars at the entrance and religious names for all the streets. Pretty tacky, if you ask me, but those houses sold like hotcakes."

"Sounds like he did a good job designing a community to fit in with the local area."

Tiffanie shrugged, as if praise for her husband held no interest for her.

"Is he doing a project in this area?"

"Um-hmm."

"What theme will it have?"

"Equestrian, what else?" Tiffanie sighed daintily. "Charles is ready to break ground as soon as he finishes cutting through all the red tape, but it almost takes an act of God to get subdivision approval in this county. They act as if a few more homes are simply going to ruin paradise. That's how Charles got the opportunity to buy the land in the first place. Percy Fletcher—do you know him?"

"Yes."

"Well, Percy had a prior deal to sell the land. The buyers had plans to develop it into an equestrian community, but they got tired of jumping through hoops with the county and walked away. Percy was desperate to sell, so he approached Charles about developing the land."

Desperate to sell? Was Manning wrong about Percy not having a motive to see that the subdivision was approved?

"Charles jumped on the deal like a cat on a mouse, dollar signs in his eyes. He redesigned the entire project, of course. Upgraded everything. He says it will be his 'signature' development. If he ever gets a green light from the county." She flicked her hand, as if the situation were a bother. "The whole thing's a nightmare."

"Switzerland has very tough building regulations as well," Abigale said. "I remember my father almost tore his hair out trying to get approval to build an addition to our hotel. In the end, it came down to politics. Knowing the right people."

"It's the same all over the world. In fact, Charles asked Richard to speak out in favor of his project at the zoning hearing."

"Did Uncle Richard do so?"

"He never had the chance. The hearing is still a couple of weeks away."

"But he agreed to help?"

"I'm not sure if Richard had officially told Charles yes, but I'm sure he was prepared to. I spoke with Richard about it the last time we got together to discuss the reception and he all but told me so."

"Was that the day he died?" Abigale asked.

"God, no. The details for the reception were finalized and approved by Richard weeks ago."

Abigale thought back to the notation her uncle had written in his journal. "But didn't you have plans to get together with Uncle Richard the day he died?"

Tiffanie gave her an odd look. "My only plans for that day were to go hunting, which as it turned out I probably should have canceled. It was a sloppy day and my horse pulled a shoe in the deep footing. I had to hack in early."

61

$\mathcal{M}$anning leaned against the Gator beside Smitty, trying to ignore the sound of Percy popping the tab on a can of beer. He forced himself to concentrate on what his mother was saying to Wendy and Thompson about tomorrow's race-day assignments.

"I think that covers everything, except we still need to designate an outrider who'll be responsible for escorting the horses to and from the paddock," Margaret said.

"What do you mean?" Manning asked. "That's always been my job."

"Not this year." Margaret flipped the cover on a small spiral-bound notepad and shoved it in her jacket pocket.

He frowned at her. "Why not?"

"You'll be occupied with other things."

"Like what?"

"Politicking," Margaret said. "Buttering up the sponsors, making sure they're happy. Posing with them for trophy presentations."

"I don't want to do that," Manning said with a groan. "You should be in charge of the sponsors. You probably know all of them."

"I'll do it," Percy said. "It sure beats directing cars."

Margaret clamped her lips together and shot a look at Percy. "It's not my place to do that, Manning. You're the master. That's what the master does."

He breathed out an acknowledgment, though he felt like saying *why doesn't the master get to decide what the master does*?

"Besides," Margaret added, "with your broken arm you aren't in any condition to be an outrider tomorrow anyway."

Manning's arm hurt like hell, but he still preferred being on a horse to schmoozing VIPs. "The doctor said I can ride. That's why he put the cast on," he muttered, knowing it would make no difference.

"Speaking of riding," Smitty said, "I got a bunch of hounds I need to hunt. Any decision on when we'll meet?"

Margaret nodded. "Wendy and I discussed it with Abigale, and she agrees that a hunt before Richard's service is appropriate. Hounds will meet at Dartmoor Glebe at ten Monday morning. Richard's service will be at four o'clock that afternoon. The hunt will be private. Members only. But the service will be open to the public."

"Will Doug make it back by then?" Smitty asked.

"Hopefully. They're on a flight from Sydney that gets in early Monday morning. I've asked him to lead the second field if he's not too exhausted from the trip."

"That's good. It wouldn't seem right, Doug not being here." Smitty's voice broke and he turned away, patting the fender of the Gator. "Guess if we're all finished, I'd best be getting this loaded up."

Manning said, "Come on. I'll drive the Gator and meet you at the parking area, give you a hand hooking up the low boy."

"Thanks. Much appreciated."

Manning helped with the trailer hookup and watched Smitty drive the Gator onto the low boy. "You're going to need the Gator tomorrow; why don't you just leave it here overnight?"

Smitty winked at him, then spoke with an exaggerated drawl. "Why, Mastah, it wouldn't be fittin' for you to drive all those VIPs around in this tomorrow, looking like it does. I'll be giving it a good washing when I get it back to the kennels."

"That's funny, Smitty, and, by the way, thanks for standing up for me with Mother. I really appreciated you trying to convince her to let me be an outrider."

Smitty chuckled, gripping Manning's shoulder and squeezing it a couple of times. Then his smile flattened and he pulled Manning so close he could see the white stubble on Smitty's chin. "I know it's gotta be tough as hell on you right now, son. It's a real big pair of boots you're stepping into. But you're going to do just fine. I imagine you'll feel a right bit better on Monday after you lead the field for the first time."

"You mean *if* I lead the field on Monday."

"Why wouldn't you?"

"Mother may have other plans."

"Hogwash. You're the master, aren't you?"

"Yeah, so I hear. Obviously in name only."

Smitty's eyes crinkled into a kind smile. "Margaret's just trying to keep things together right now. Once we get past the races and Richard's service she'll step back."

"We both know that's not true, Smitty. Mother doesn't trust me enough to back off an inch. Maybe I can't blame her. But I don't know how long I'll be able to stand this benign dictatorship. I don't mind riding a difficult horse, but I'd rather not do it with someone else holding the reins."

"I hear ya," Smitty said, his head jiggling up and down like a bobble-head doll's. "I've been in your shoes and it ain't much fun. But she'll come around. In the meantime, just keep reminding yourself that Richard believed in you enough to leave the hunt to you. That ought to count for something."

Yeah, it would, Manning thought, *if Mother hadn't told me Richard was about to change his will.*

*M*argaret barely gave Manning a fleeting glance when he opened the passenger door of her truck and climbed in. Her attention was on Thompson, who stood outside the open driver's window, one arm braced against the door.

"Make sure you bring the checkbook tomorrow," she said.

"I've already written the checks." Thompson patted his breast pocket. "I've got them right here."

"That's fine, but bring the checkbook anyway. I'd like to present the donation check to the environmental council at the conclusion of the races tomorrow."

Thompson gaped at Margaret. "We never write the check to the charity until we've done a final accounting of revenue and expenses."

"I know that's how we've done it in the past, but I'd like to present a check tomorrow in honor of Richard. Surely you already have a pretty good feel for the bottom line."

"Yes," Thompson said slowly. "But I'm not sure all the online payments have been credited to our account. This is the first time we've used this merchant services vendor. Besides, you know the gate proceeds can vary wildly depending on the weather."

"It won't vary that much. We have a good forecast for tomorrow."

"I don't want to argue with you, Margaret, but that's not best accounting practices."

"To hell with best accounting principles. We're not some Fortune 500 company. You know Richard always made up the difference if there was a shortfall in race revenue and the numbers didn't justify the amount of donation we wanted to make. So I'm saying that this year we should go ahead and write the check. We've got plenty of money in the bank. We'll sort out the accounting later."

"Okay," Thompson said coolly. His expression made it obvious that it clearly was not. He took a step back from the truck. "I'll bring the checkbook. See you in the morning."

Margaret rolled up the window and cranked down on the gearshift. She eased off the brake, glancing at Manning as she turned to look out the rear window to back up. "What's so amusing?" she asked.

Manning shook his head. "Nothing."

She pursed her lips as she stomped on the brake and threw the truck into drive. "Do you find it humorous that Thompson takes his position as treasurer so seriously?"

"No, Mother. I was just wondering when you're going to start including me in conversations about the future of the hunt."

"I didn't realize I wasn't. Or that you cared, for that matter."

"How could I not care?"

She arched an eyebrow, as if that was a question that didn't need to be answered.

He said, "The board elected me master, right?"

"You know it did."

"Right. And Richard left the hunt assets to me. With the challenge to see if I could make a go of it."

She shoved the gearshift into park and turned to face him, her expression a mixture of confusion and curiosity. "Go on."

"How can I do that if no one lets me make decisions?"

"You can make deci—"

"No." He shook his head. "You haven't asked my opinion about a single thing. No one has. You decide everything like I'm not even there. Like I inherited some title that doesn't really mean anything."

A faint smile tugged at Margaret's lips. "It hasn't even been forty-eight hours since the reading of Richard's will."

"Yeah, I know that."

"So, what did you expect? Would you rather we'd just dumped the hunt, the races, everything, in your lap? Left you to sink or swim? When you have no experience running anything?"

Anger gripped Manning's chest and pounded in his temples. She didn't get it. Probably never would. He looked out the window. "Forget it. Sorry I brought it up."

"No, I will not forget it," she snapped. "You started the conversation, so let's finish it. Tell me how I should handle it?"

"Just give me a chance, Mother. At least act like my opinion matters."

"It isn't just about you, Manning. It's about honoring Richard's memory. About ensuring that the hunt and the races live on long after him, in a manner that would make him proud."

"Despite his bad judgment in leaving the hunt assets to me."

"That's not what I said."

"You didn't have to," he replied quietly.

"Your mother was uncharacteristically quiet this evening," Abigale said as she drove the Subaru away from Margaret's house. "Is everything all right?"

Manning shrugged. "We had a slight difference of opinion this afternoon."

"About?"

A hollow laugh caught in his throat. "Me."

Damn it. Why couldn't Margaret cut Manning some slack? Abigale glanced over at him. "You okay?"

"Better now that I'm with you." Manning knocked his knuckles against the passenger window. "Hey, pull over here."

"Into the orchard?"

"Yeah."

Abigale stopped the car but didn't pull off the gravel drive. "It's late, Manning. You should go home and get some sleep. Tomorrow's going to be a long day."

"No way I'd be able to sleep right now." He ducked his head and looked at the sky through the front windshield. "Come on. There's a full moon."

Manning opened the door before she could object and grabbed an armful of polar-fleece horse coolers from the backseat. "Just pull off the drive."

He waited for her by the edge of the orchard. When she reached his side, Manning laced his fingers through hers and tugged her into the first row of trees. The full moon bathed the orchard in a soft glow. Neither of them spoke as they stumbled over roots and dodged low-hanging branches. They both knew where they were heading.

"It's a little overgrown," Manning said when they reached their spot. "But it still has a clear view of the sky."

He dropped the coolers on the ground and shook one to unfold it. Abigale grabbed the other end and helped him spread it across the high grass. "Margaret just had these all washed for tomorrow, you know," she said.

"Good, then we won't get covered with horse hair," Manning replied, grinning. He pulled her down beside him on the blanket, grabbed a folded cooler and propped it under her head as a pillow, then flung the remaining one over them as a cover. He slid his left arm under her neck and drew her close to him, gently encircling her with his cast. "There."

Abigale nestled her cheek against his solid chest muscles and gazed at the stars in the washed-out sky. She'd always liked the orchard best when there was a mere sliver of a moon. When the stars twinkled like diamonds against a velvet heaven. But tonight she loved the way the moonlight spilled down on them. She tilted her head so she could see Manning's face and traced her fingers along his jaw. The stubble of his whiskers tingled along her fingertips. She closed her eyes, inhaling fresh air, overripe apples and musky leaves, and listened to the beat of his heart.

"Are you warm enough?" Manning asked.

"It's perfect," she whispered.

Manning looked down at her, his eyes dark as the night sky. "Yeah, it is," he murmured, tangling his fingers in her hair as he pulled her lips to his. His kiss was insistent, demanding, as if he needed to lose himself in her. She felt the world sink away until there was nothing left but his mouth on hers, his body, hungry, pressing her against the ground.

64

"And the flag is up!" the race announcer barked. Eight sleek, prancing, well-muscled thoroughbreds lunged forward, like arrows shot from a bow, and thundered past the stewards' stand.

Manning leaned close to Abigale and removed a pair of binoculars from around his neck. He raised them so she could look through them. She adjusted the focus, fixing the lenses on the turquoise and yellow silks of the jockey atop What A Day, the horse she'd picked to win. Manning slid his left arm around her waist and kept his right hand on the binoculars.

The loudspeaker above their heads blared with the announcer's quick drawl. "Executive Girl leads over the first of thirteen fences, followed by Silent Song. What A Day moves into third place as they round the first turn."

Abigale pulled back from the binoculars. "Do you want a look?" she asked Manning.

He shook his head. "Nah, I'm just holding them as an excuse."

"For what?"

"To be near you," he murmured, his mouth close to her ear.

Abigale smiled, losing all interest in the race. It was the first time she'd been alone with Manning since arriving at the racecourse. He'd been going nonstop, schmoozing the VIPs, shepherding sponsors to trophy presentations, keeping things on schedule. She handed the binoculars to him, noting how handsome he looked in his tweed sport coat and silk tie patterned with running foxes. *A Virginia gentleman.* "Last race of the day. How are you holding up?"

"It actually hasn't been as bad as I thought it would be, once I figured out most of the sponsors really don't give a damn about the races. They're just here to have a good time."

As if on cue, a middle-aged man nearby clinked glassed with the fellow next to him, grinned, and said, "Hey, Victor, who in the hell invited all these horses to our cocktail party?"

Manning gave her a wry smile. "See what I mean?"

Abigale observed the dozen or more people on the top deck of the stewards' stand and realized only a handful appeared to be watching the race. "Do you know all these people?" she asked.

"About half of them." Manning tipped his head toward Percy, who stood a few feet away, his back to the racecourse, deep in conversation with a tall bear of a man who had blue VIP and yellow Paddock passes strung around his neck. The man's gut threatened to pop the button on his expensive-looking tweed sport coat, and a thick lock that had sprung loose from his slicked-back salt-and-pepper hair dangled in front of one eye, bouncing every time he blinked.

"The man Percy's talking to is Charles Jenner. Tiffanie's husband. He's sponsoring this race."

"Oh, interesting. That's not how I pictured him." Abigale eyed the man, trying not to be obvious.

Charles glanced over and caught them looking at him, and raised his glass in a toast. "Good afternoon, Master," he called in a deep baritone, paying no mind to the bourbon that sloshed on his hand, staining the monogrammed cuff of his white dress shirt.

Manning nodded a return greeting. "How'd you picture him?"

"I don't know. More pulled together, I guess. Like Tiffanie."

A gasp murmured through the crowd and Manning's head jerked toward the racecourse. He peered through the binoculars. "Shit," he said, shoving the binoculars at her. He unclipped a walkie-talkie from his belt and shouted into it as he dashed for the stairs. "Horse and jockey down at the hurdle on the far turn."

Abigale pushed her way to the rail of the stewards' stand. A horse lay flat on its side, the jockey crumpled in a heap a few yards away. Neither moved. An outrider galloped along the back side of the course toward the injured pair, his red coat blazing like a splash of paint on a faded green canvas. She heard the roar of an engine and saw Manning shoot across the track in the Gator with Margaret in the passenger seat, a man she recognized as the course physician crouched in the bed of the vehicle. A vet truck pulled onto the racecourse near the far turn, followed by a truck hauling the horse ambulance.

The remaining seven horses flew around the turn toward the finish line and a cheer roared from the spectators. "It's Silent Song by three lengths as they approach the wire," the announcer called, "followed by What A Day and Goodnight Moon. Goodnight Moon makes a move, and it's Silent Song by two, with Goodnight Moon in second. Silent Song and Goodnight Moon are neck-and-neck as they come to the finish with Goodnight Moon pulling in front, and it's Goodnight Moon by a head! Goodnight Moon wins the Jenner Development Maiden Hurdle!"

Abigale's eyes were glued to the far turn. The jockey was on his feet, limping, pacing as if trying to walk off pain. The horse still lay motionless. She clutched the binoculars, wanting to look through them but afraid of what she'd see. The Gator jerked to a stop. Manning, Margaret, and the course physician spilled out like ants from an anthill. The doctor clutched a black bag.

Abigale raised the glasses and focused on Manning as he dropped to his knees next to the horse's head. She zoomed in and saw the horse's eyes were open. Manning turned to look at the approaching vet truck and ambulance, still a hundred yards away, and shouted something as he unbuckled the girth. Margaret bent down to help Manning tug the saddle off the horse.

The doctor said something to the jockey, who nodded and waved a hand at the horse. The doctor knelt next to Manning, probing the horse's chest in front of the girth area. The horse raised his head and jerked his front legs as if trying to get up. The doctor barely escaped being nailed by the horse's front hoof. He jumped back, his hand smeared with blood.

Manning grabbed the horse's head and forced it back down. Margaret scrambled to the other side of the horse and knelt against its neck. Abigale held her breath, then blew it out in a rush as she saw the horse stop struggling. She knew as long as they were able to restrain the horse's head and neck he wouldn't be able to get up.

The doctor grabbed a fistful of gauze from his bag and packed it against the horse's chest. Blood instantly soaked the snow-white dressing. He grabbed another handful. Then another.

Manning stroked the horse's head. His lips moved slowly and she knew he was talking to the horse. She could almost hear his voice, murmuring, reassuring. Ice seemed to flow through her veins, wrenching her back to a moonlit night, another injured horse. She yanked the glasses away and tried to erase the memory, to block out the sound of Manning's voice, reassuring Scarlet, calming the mare, even though he knew there was no hope. An ache swelled in Abigale's chest like the whine of a teakettle until she felt she couldn't breathe.

"Hey, can I borrow your binoculars?" Percy asked.

Abigale thrust the binoculars at Percy, spun from the rail, and wove her way through the crowd to the stairs. "Excuse me," she murmured repeatedly, dashing past people until she reached the ground level, where she was pressed up against a sea of humanity. Words and laughter buzzed all around her, smothering her. Abigale was jostled by two young men carrying a cooler and bumped up against something rubbery—a trash can, swarming with bees. The stench of rotting food and beer roiled her stomach, and she pushed her way into the swell of the crowd.

The throng of people snaked along a bluestone path, barricaded on each side by a snow fence. There was no pushing or shoving; no one seemed in a hurry, which only fueled Abigale's distress. She felt as though she was on the Autobahn, stuck in bumper-to-bumper traffic with no exit ramp in sight. She'd never considered herself claustrophobic, but she had to call upon every ounce of self-control not to elbow her way to freedom. She forced herself to breathe, counting the plaid squares on the tweed jacket of the man in front of her. Slowly, she inched forward.

A woman's voice called Abigale's name. She turned to see Michelle de Becque wave over the wide-brimmed hat of the woman behind her. Abigale let the people behind her slip forward until she was next to Michelle.

"Hi," Michelle said, smiling broadly. "We meet again, under slightly better circumstances this time—hey, are you okay?" Her green eyes narrowed with concern. "You're pale as a ghost."

"I need to get out of this crowd," Abigale said.

"Oh, my God. All right." Michelle grabbed her arm and drew her to the right side of the path. "There's a gate into the paddock area up ahead. We can exit there."

They shuffled with the mob until they reached the entrance to the paddock enclosure. A uniformed officer stood behind a closed gate with a white cardboard sign that read PADDOCK BADGE HOLDERS ONLY. A yellow Paddock badge was stapled to the sign.

"Excuse me, we need to get through here," Michelle said to the officer.

The officer's thumbs remained hooked in his belt. His eyes roamed down to their badges. "Sorry, this is for Paddock badge holders only." He tipped his head. "The exit gate is farther along."

"Please, she's not feeling well," Michelle insisted. "I think she might pass out. She needs to get out of the crowd."

Abigale could see people staring at them and felt like a fool. "I'm—"

Michelle's fingers dug into her arm, silencing her.

The officer's eyes settled on Abigale's face, then flickered back to Michelle. He released the gate. "Okay, bring her through."

"Thank you," Michelle said, keeping her grip on Abigale's arm as they slipped through the opening.

The officer pointed to a nearby bench beneath a shady oak tree. "Take her over there. Do you need me to call the paramedics?"

"No!" Abigale said.

"I think she just needs to sit for a minute," Michelle said, steering Abigale to the bench.

Abigale dropped down on the hard wood, turning her back toward the stream of people. "How embarrassing!"

"Don't be silly," Michelle said, sitting beside her. "I hate crowds too."

"Crowds don't usually bother me. I just lost it when I saw that injured horse. It felt like everything closed in around me."

"I know, it was terrible. I think the horse is going to be okay, though. They put up a screen, so I couldn't really see what was going on, but the horse got up and walked onto the trailer."

Abigale sucked in a slow breath, then eased it out. Despite the cool afternoon air, perspiration prickled her scalp. She lifted the clasp that held back her hair and felt cool air whisper across the back of her neck.

"You've got a little more color in your cheeks," Michelle said. "Feeling better?"

Abigale nodded. "You've come to my rescue twice now. Thank you."

"Just lucky timing, I guess," Michelle replied. "Hey, I saw your Prince Charming earlier. He apologized for seeming ungrateful for my assistance the other day. Said you gave him hell after I'd left."

Abigale thought back to that afternoon. "I guess I did."

Michelle smiled. "How long have the two of you been together?"

Eighteen years? Two days? "It's complicated," Abigale said.

"The good ones usually are." Michelle turned, looked at the thinning crowd on the pathway. "It looks like things have eased up. Feel up to making a go of it?"

"Can I ask you something first?" Abigale asked.

"Sure."

"Are you familiar with Foxhunters Online?"

Michelle's eyes slid away. She bit her bottom lip, as if considering what to say, then finally replied, "I got your email."

Abigale's heart lurched. Her hunch had been right! Michelle de Becque was *chiencheval112*.

Michelle said, "I know someone—this is all off the record, by the way—who knows someone, who knows someone who knows Dario Reyes. My friend told me Dario says he didn't murder your uncle. But he's afraid to come forward because he knows he's already as good as convicted."

Disappointment tumbled down on Abigale. Was that the only reason Michelle had posted the comment online? Because Dario said he didn't do it? Of course Dario Reyes would proclaim his innocence!

"But it gets more complicated," Michelle continued. "According to my friend, Dario was there, on the road, when the murder happened. He heard the shot."

"*What?*"

Michelle nodded, giving her a *see what I mean* look. "He's a witness, not a suspect."

Abigale asked, "Did he see who did it?"

"I'm not sure. He saw a vehicle drive out of the racecourse after he heard the shot. That's all I know. I don't know if he saw who was in the vehicle, the license plate, whatever."

"He saw the killer's car?"

"That's what my friend told me."

"He has to come forward!" Abigale exclaimed.

"I hear you. That's what I told my friend. But Dario's afraid."

"But if what your friend says is true, and Dario tells that to the authorities, he'll clear his name. And possibly help them find the person who murdered my uncle." He would also lift the cloud of suspicion hanging over Manning, but Abigale didn't say that.

"I know," Michelle said, nodding. "But you have to look at it from his perspective. Dario's lived his whole life as a victim of racial profiling. He doesn't trust the cops. He's afraid they'll lock him up first, ask questions later."

"Doesn't he know they'll find him eventually? That the fact he's gone into hiding makes it look worse for him?" Abigale asked.

"Probably. But he's still not going to turn himself in."

Abigale thought for a moment. "Okay. What about talking to me?"

"What do you mean?"

"Ask your friend to convince Dario to talk to me."

"You?"

"Yes. He can dictate where and when. I'll come alone. I just want to talk to him. Ask him what he saw. Maybe I can help him. We can help each other."

"You'd go alone to meet with the person who's accused of murdering your uncle?"

"Yes, if that's what it takes to hear what he has to say," Abigale said.

Michelle stared at her, as if trying to decide how much she could trust her. "You have to swear you won't tell anyone about our conversation."

"I swear."

"*No one.* Not even Manning."

Abigale gave a quick nod.

"All right. I'll ask."

*M*ichelle walked with Abigale to the VIP tent. By the time they arrived it was crawling with people. Abigale invited Michelle to join her at the reception.

"I've still got two horses to ride when I get home," Michelle said, turning down the offer. A brisk breeze kicked up her spiky hair, tousling it as if someone had raked a heavy hand through it. "Thanks for the invite, though. It looks like a nice party."

Abigale eyed the lavish buffet, complete with ice sculpture; she noticed the table linens were not the ones she'd delivered from Margaret. "Looks like Tiffanie went all out."

"Tiffanie Jenner?" Michelle asked.

"Yes, do you know her?"

"Not well. We both compete in the amateurs, so I've run into her at horse shows. She made a bit of a pest of herself last summer—tried to buy one of my horses that wasn't on the market. Kept insisting that *everything* is for sale at the right price." Michelle pointed toward the center of the tent. "Look, Manning just spotted you. God, what I wouldn't give for a man who looked at me that way!"

Manning excused himself from the group he was standing with and shouldered his way through the crowd toward them. He'd removed his tweed sport coat, and the right cuff of his yellow shirtsleeve flapped limply against his blue cast. His eyes held a flat, tired look.

"Where have you been?" he asked, brushing his lips against Abigale's cheek. "I was worried about you."

"Sorry. I ran into Michelle. We started chatting and lost track of time."

"Speaking of time, I'd better go." Michelle lifted her hand in a wave as she backed away. "Good to see you both again."

Manning mumbled goodbye to Michelle, then frowned at Abigale. "Percy said you ran out of the stewards' stand like a bat out of hell. Is everything all right?"

She nodded grimly. "I had a panic attack or something when I saw the injured horse. What happened to him?"

"He punctured himself in the chest with his hoof. I've never seen anything like it. The jockey said he left long to the fence and the horse rubbed the brush pretty good. His front legs must have been folded up tight, and the impact drove his hoof right through his chest wall."

"Is he going to be okay?"

"It looks like it. He lost a lot of blood, but they packed the wound and got him on the trailer to go to the Equine Medical Center. The vet doesn't think he did any major internal damage. He should be fine."

"Thank God."

Margaret bustled out of the tent toward them, waving urgently at Manning. "Tucker Reed from Capital Associates wants a photo with you. He sponsored the open timber race. He's waiting for you over by Tiffanie's god-awful ice sculpture."

Manning sighed and gave Abigale an apologetic smile. "I'll see you in a few minutes."

Margaret stayed with Abigale. She eyed the crowded tent with a disapproving shake of her head. "Richard would pitch a fit if he could see the spectacle Tiffanie's made of this reception. The only thing I can figure is Richard got so fed up with Tiffanie he just gave her carte blanche to do what she wished, because he certainly never would have approved all this fanfare."

"Are you sure?" Abigale asked.

"Of course I am. What makes you ask?"

Abigale frowned. "I just wonder if there wasn't something else going on between Tiffanie and Uncle Richard. Perhaps he wasn't as irritated with her as you think."

"*Something else* going on? What are you suggesting?"

"It's just—I found several notations in Uncle Richard's journal about meetings with Tiffanie, including on the day he died. But when I asked Tiffanie about it she denied it, claimed she and Uncle Richard did not have a meeting scheduled that day. That they'd finalized the plans for the reception weeks before."

"Are you saying you think she was lying?" Margaret asked.

"I don't know. I just got a funny vibe from her. Like she didn't want me to know they had plans to get together," Abigale replied.

"Why would she want to hide that?"

Abigale shrugged, averting Margaret's gaze.

"*Oh, no.* You think they were having an affair? No. Not a chance in hell. You've met Tiffanie. Do you honestly think she's Richard's type?"

"I don't know," Abigale said. "I just can't figure out why she would deny the meeting."

Margaret pressed her lips together as she thought about it. "You said you saw the notation about a meeting in Richard's journal?"

"Yes. And that was odd, too. Uncle Richard used Tiffanie's initials rather than her name. Almost as if he were trying to keep it a secret."

"Richard didn't use his journal as an appointment book. It was more of his to-do list. He'd whip it out and scribble in it whenever something popped into his mind that he didn't want to forget to do. The entry you saw about Tiffanie was probably just a note he wrote to remind himself he wanted to talk to her about something. Did it have a time associated with it?"

"No."

"See? It was probably just a reminder." Margaret waved her hand, dismissing the idea. "You're making way too much out of it, Abigale. We have more important things to worry about." She glanced at her watch. "Come on. We need to present the charity check before folks start to wander off."

*A*bigale wished she could do something to help Manning. It was probably a combination of emotional stress and the pain from his broken arm, but he looked absolutely wiped out. He clenched his jaw as if biting back words, and stared impassively at Margaret while she insisted he wear a sport coat for the check presentation photograph.

"It doesn't matter, Mother," Manning said.

"Yes, it does. See if you can borrow one from someone," Margaret replied.

"I'd lend you mine, but I think it will be too small," Thompson said, fingering the lapel of his blue blazer. "What size do you wear?"

"Forty-two long," Manning muttered.

Thompson gave a quick bob of his head. "Yeah, see? No way. I wear a thirty-nine regular."

"Look, Mother, I don't have to be in the photo. Why don't you present the check alone?"

"Nonsense. You're the master. Besides, we need more than one representative from the hunt."

Manning jerked his head at Thompson. "So have Thompson accompany you. You'd be happy to do that, wouldn't you, Thompson?"

Before he could respond, Margaret shouted, "Charles!" She raised her hand in the air, waving Charles Jenner over. "His jacket definitely won't be too tight on you."

"Jesus," Manning mumbled under his breath.

"What's the matter with your jacket?" Abigale whispered in his ear.

He shot a sideways glance at her. "It's covered with blood from the injured horse."

"Oh." She ran her eyes over him, noticing several dark smears on his khaki trousers. The look on her face must have mirrored the sick feeling in her stomach, because Manning reached down and squeezed her hand.

"Here. Put this on." Margaret handed Charles's tweed jacket to Manning.

The jacket swam on Manning, making him look like a little boy trying on his father's coat.

"That'll do," Margaret said. "Come on, Abigale. I'd like you in the photograph, too."

As Margaret marched away, Thompson slipped his hand inside his blazer and pulled out a check. "I guess you'll need this."

Manning took the check. "You still uncomfortable presenting this today?"

"Totally. But Margaret feels strongly about it, so . . ." Thompson hunched a shoulder.

"If it's any consolation, I'm with you on this one," Manning said. "Of course, we both know I have no influence with Mother."

"Obviously, neither do I," Thompson replied. "It's going to be interesting handling the hunt finances going forward. Richard took my advice on financial matters. I'm not sure how much control Margaret's going to want to have over things. That's assuming you even want me to stay involved. Now that you're in charge."

Manning let out a noncommittal grunt. He looked over at Margaret and the representatives from the environmental council. "Would you like to join the photo op?" he asked Thompson.

"No, that's okay. Thanks, though."

"Sure." Manning slid his hand to the small of Abigale's back. "Guess it's showtime," he said, guiding her toward the group.

"That was nice of you to invite Thompson," Abigale said.

"Yeah. I don't know what came over me. For a split-second it almost felt like we were on the same side."

Abigale pushed the power button on her laptop and waited for it to shut down. She'd signed on hoping to find an email from Michelle in her in-box, informing her that her anonymous friend was willing to set up a meeting with Dario Reyes. But she'd found mostly junk email. And an email from Emilio. He, too, was leaving Afghanistan. Back to Italy, not yet sure where he'd be reassigned. The email was forcibly lighthearted, but his valediction— *Mi manchi*—"I miss you"—left her feeling guilty.

Manning had fallen into bed as soon as they'd arrived back at his house, extracting a promise from her to wake him when she joined him. But she wasn't ready for sleep. Too many thoughts—doubts—were running through her head. Margaret had told her she'd spoken to Sheriff Boling at the races and they had no new leads in the case. The investigation into the saddle tampering had gone nowhere. Dario Reyes was still the prime suspect and the net they'd cast was tightening. The sheriff couldn't tell her more than that, but he'd hinted he was confident they'd catch Reyes soon.

Margaret had seemed somewhat encouraged by the sheriff's report, but there were too many unanswered questions for Abigale to jump on the bandwagon about Reyes. Not just yet. She pulled her uncle's journal from her duffle bag and flipped to the date of his death. Was Margaret right, that the notation about Tiffanie was simply a reminder Uncle Richard had written to himself, rather than an actual appointment? She read through the notations for that day again: JAY BARNSBY; HUNTING; LONGMEADOW—OPEN DRAINAGE DITCH; TJ.

Hunting obviously fell into the appointment category, while the notation about Longmeadow seemed more like a reminder. Who was Jay Barnsby? Did her uncle have an appointment with him that morning? She made a mental note to find out.

Abigale sighed, flipping the journal shut. What she needed to do was talk to Dario Reyes. Until then, she was just spinning her wheels. She felt confident she'd be able to tell whether Reyes was lying. Her instincts were good, finely honed by hairy experiences in Baghdad and Afghanistan, where survival often depended on sifting through the bullshit. She had no doubt she'd be able to read Dario Reyes. The question was, if what Michelle had told her was true, would he be able to identify the vehicle he'd seen drive out of Longmeadow? And had he seen who was in it?

As much as she hated to believe that someone who knew Uncle Richard— one of his friends—had killed him, she couldn't shake the hunch that he had known the killer. Too many things just didn't add up: the notation about Tiffanie in his journal, the way Tiffanie had acted when she'd asked her about the appointment, his comment to Michael about the fox in the henhouse. The fact that someone had cut the billet straps on his saddle and the whole business about Charles Jenner and Percy wanting his blessing for their land deal raised her antenna, too.

Abigale unfolded herself from the couch and switched off the light. Even though she doubted she'd be able to sleep, she had to try. They had an early start tomorrow. It would be a long day.

She hoped Manning understood why she didn't want to hunt in the morning. He'd seemed to. But she still felt as though she was deserting him, his first time leading the field as master. She'd be there, but she'd be on foot. Viewing it through her camera lens. Without the buffer of her camera, she wasn't sure she'd be able to handle it. All her memories of foxhunting involved her uncle. She understood how others—such as Margaret—might find healing in tomorrow's hunt, gain some kind of closure. But the thought of foxhunting without Uncle Richard left her feeling hollow inside. Abigale undressed and slipped into bed beside Manning.

$\mathcal{M}$anning watched Smitty lead the hounds toward him. His heart slammed against his chest and Henry danced beneath him, no doubt feeling his nerves. Habit drew Manning's hand to the void in front of his left saddle flap, where the leather pouch containing his flask was usually strapped. *Jesus.* Had he really thought he could get through today without it? A mind-numbing bolt of fear shot through him, as if he were a parent who had just discovered his toddler had disappeared in a crowded mall. Why the hell hadn't he accepted the stirrup cup of port Tiffanie had offered to him?

Smitty pulled his horse to a halt beside Henry and gathered the hounds. "Ready to do this?"

"Scared shitless."

Smitty chuckled. "What are you afraid of? You think they're not going to follow you?"

Manning smiled.

"You'll be fine, son. Richard's with us today." Smitty splayed his gloved hand across his heart. "Right in here."

Manning locked eyes with Smitty and saw the huntsman believed it. An uneasy calm settled over him. It was now or never. He removed his hunt cap as he faced the riders gathered in front of him.

"Today is a day none of us ever envisioned, not even in our worst nightmares. Richard was more than the leader of this hunt club. He was our friend. The void he left in the hunt, in our hearts, will never be filled. But together, we will get through this.

"The position of master is not something I sought, but I'll do my best to live up to the trust Richard placed in me. I will never come close to filling

Richard's shoes, but I promise to honor his memory." Manning's throat closed up. He swallowed, blinking back tears. "Please join me in a moment of silence."

Manning bowed his head, aware of a chorus of clicking as cameras captured the moment. Out of the corner of his eye he spotted Abigale nestled beneath the branches of a nearby sycamore tree. He knew this was as hard on her as on anyone. Maybe harder. She'd tossed and turned all night and had barely spoken to anyone since they'd arrived at the meet. As soon as he was on the horse she'd disappeared behind her camera.

"Thank you," he said, raising his hunt cap, then adjusting it back on his head. "I'll be leading the first field today and Doug will be taking second field." He looked over at Doug Cummings, who raised his hunt whip as a signal of confirmation. "Following the hunt, we'll have a brief tailgate hosted by Tiffanie and Charles Jenner."

They hadn't planned on having a tailgate, but Tiffanie had blindsided him as soon as he'd arrived at the meet, told him she "had it all arranged." The table was already set up. Flowers, champagne, the whole nine yards. What was he supposed to do, tell her no?

"Safe hunting," Manning said, gathering up his reins. He nodded at Smitty who blew on his horn and moved off to the first draw.

Manning steered Henry to Abigale before heading down the drive. "We're going out the front way. We'll cross the road and loop around through the woods to Hickory Ridge. There's a nice stone wall out of the woods into the back pasture if you want to take some jumping shots."

She stepped close and gave him a soft smile. "You said just the right thing. Uncle Richard would have been proud of you."

Manning still felt as if he were standing on the edge of a cliff, not knowing whether it was better to go ahead and jump or wait to be pushed, but Abigale's words managed to ratchet his panic down a notch. He nodded and urged Henry on.

$\mathcal{A}$bigale followed the hunt by car for over an hour, capturing some great shots over the stone wall and a nice photo of Manning leading the field down the road just outside the entrance to Dartmoor Glebe. She lost them when the hounds picked up a scent shortly after crossing Goose Creek. Abigale lingered by the creek for a while and listened to the sound of the hounds in full cry until the trees swallowed up their music. She felt the old adrenaline rush, for a moment regretting her decision not to hunt.

When she arrived back at Dartmoor Glebe, Tiffanie Jenner was barking orders at three women wearing white catering jackets. Abigale kept out of their way; she meandered around snapping shots of the house and grounds to send to her mother. As she emerged from the boxwood garden she heard someone call her name.

"Abigale!" Tiffanie waved at her, motioning her over to the food table. "Would you mind taking some photographs of my table?"

"No, of course not."

She took a couple of shots with Tiffanie standing beside a table that almost groaned from the weight of food piled on it. In the center, a vine of lush greens and white roses encircled the base of an enormous copper tub filled with a dozen or more bottles of champagne.

"It looks lovely," Abigale said.

"Thank you. I must say I agree with you," Tiffanie replied. "I want to send some photos to the local papers. I snapped some with my little camera, but I'm sure what you took will be much more powerful. Who knows, maybe you'll win another award."

Abigale bit back a smile. She doubted there was a Pulitzer lurking in the shots of Tiffanie's table.

"I'm glad I have this opportunity to be alone with you. There's something I want to talk to you about," Tiffanie said. She cast a glance at the caterers, then added in a low voice, "Let's step away."

They walked toward the garden. When they were out of earshot of the caterers, Tiffanie said, "I've thought some more about what you asked me at my house the other day, about whether I had an appointment with Richard the day he died." She said it in an offhand way, but her eyes shifted back and forth between Abigale and the catering staff.

"And?"

Tiffanie pressed her lips together. "I did get together with Richard after the hunt that day. But it wasn't planned. I just dropped by to chat with him about something. You threw me for a loop when you asked if we had a meeting scheduled—which we *did not*—I guess that's why I didn't recall our little get-together."

Their little get-together? Oh God. Had she been right when she'd suggested to Margaret that Uncle Richard might have been having an affair with Tiffanie?

"Where did you get together?" Abigale asked.

Tiffanie raised her chin in an almost defiant pose. "At Longmeadow."

"You were there, at the racecourse, that afternoon? *The day he was murdered?*"

Tiffanie's posture, the set of her mouth, dared Abigale to challenge her. But her eyes had a deer-in-the-headlights look. "I know what you're going to ask next," Tiffanie said. "You want to know if I saw anyone—anything—at Longmeadow that might provide a clue to Richard's murder. The answer is no, I did not."

"Have you reported this to the sheriff's office?" Abigale asked.

"There was no need. I was there hours before Richard was shot. I know nothing of any value."

Abigale felt heat rise in her cheeks. She made a stab at reining in her anger. "How do you know that? You have no idea what's relevant, what you might have seen that could help the investigation. How could you keep this to yourself?"

Tiffanie just stared at her.

"Are you so—" Abigale stopped herself, choking back the accusation she was about to hurl. If she wanted any information from Tiffanie, she had to calm down. She eased out a slow breath. "Who else knows about this? Does your husband know?"

"No! And that's the whole point," Tiffanie said.

"What do you mean, 'that's the point'? Why can't your husband know about it?"

"I went to talk to Richard about awarding Charles his colors. I thought it would be a nice touch if Richard presented Charles with his colors at the races. Since Charles was such a big sponsor and all."

"His colors?"

"Yes." Tiffanie's eyes flashed. "Charles deserved them. He's put in his time and God knows he's paid his dues. I didn't want him to have to wait until the end of the season. I have a scarlet coat on hold at Horse Country Saddlery and a tailor just waiting for the go-ahead to sew on the blue collar and hunt buttons."

Good God. "Did my uncle agree?"

"No. That's why Charles can't know I went to talk to Richard about it. Why no one can know. Richard refused to even entertain the notion of presenting colors at the races. He said it's always done at the end of the season." Tiffanie gave a dismissive roll of her eyes. "God forbid anyone around here would consider deviating from tradition. Richard also as good as told me that Charles won't be awarded his colors at the closing breakfast at the end of hunt season, either. Charles would be crushed if he knew that Richard didn't think he had earned his colors. Especially after all he's done for the hunt. It's embarrassing."

Abigale clenched her jaw. *Talk about self-centered!* "Why did you go to Longmeadow to talk to him about it? Why didn't you just call him?"

"Because I needed to know. If Richard had said yes, I was going to give the tailor the green light so Richard could present the scarlet coat to Charles at the races, rather than just handing him a strip of blue fabric and a handful of buttons. I've always thought that was such a tacky way to present colors. Anyway, I heard Richard talking at the tailgate after the hunt, saying he was going to Longmeadow. So I went there too."

Abigale could just picture it: Tiffanie cornering her uncle, demanding to know if her husband would get his colors. "Was he alone?"

"Yes," Tiffanie replied. "I wouldn't have had the conversation otherwise."

"Where was he?"

"In the stewards' stand." Tiffanie's expression remained composed, but her voice held the slightest tremble.

"What was he doing?" Abigale asked.

Tiffanie frowned at her. "Nothing."

"Was he just standing there?"

"He said he was waiting for someone."

"Did he say who?"

"No, he didn't. Look, Abigale, I already told you I don't know anything that will help find Richard's murderer. I went to see him. We talked. I left. End of story."

It was not the end of the story. Far from it. "Why are you telling me this now?"

Tiffanie tucked her hair behind one ear, her diamond ring glinting in the sunlight. "I figured you were going to keep asking questions and it might eventually come out. Then it could look like I was trying to hide something."

Which you are, Abigale thought.

Tiffanie said, "I figured if I told you and you understood the situation, that would be the end of it."

"No." Abigale shook her head. "I appreciate you telling me, but that can't be the end of it. You need to tell the authorities."

"Are you serious?" Tiffanie's voice shot up an octave. "Then everyone will know."

"Why do you care if people know?"

"Well, it won't help my marriage any, for one thing. Which is already on shaky ground." The tip of Tiffanie's nose reddened and she tossed her head, blinking rapidly.

True emotion? Abigale wondered. *Or just a good act?*

"Charles will kill me if he finds out I pleaded with Richard to give him his colors. He'd already warned me to back off." Tiffanie snorted daintily. "Charles thinks I'm being too pushy. That I should just let the chips fall as they will."

"Charles doesn't care if he gets his colors?" Abigale asked.

"Not enough," Tiffanie replied.

The sound of laughter drifted up the drive, the crunch of horseshoes on gravel. A group of riders came into view as they rode through the front gate.

"They're back. I've got to check the food," Tiffanie said.

Abigale ignored her. She wasn't about to let Tiffanie run off now. "Call Lieutenant Mallory. I'm sure he'll do whatever he can to help you keep a low profile."

"And if I don't call him?" Tiffanie asked.

"Then I will."

Tiffanie balled her fists and clenched her arms to her chest. The look she gave Abigale was pure hatred. "Give me some time to tell Charles."

"How long?"

"I don't know. Time. A week."

Abigale shook her head. "Twenty-four hours."

"Charles isn't even *home*. He left for California on business this morning. I can't tell him over the telephone."

Out of town on business? So Charles obviously wasn't going to attend Uncle Richard's funeral. Abigale knew it was petty to view Charles's absence as an insult, but she felt slighted nonetheless. Charles had been courting Uncle Richard—had asked him to go out on a limb to support his development—but didn't have time to show up at his funeral? "When will he be back?" Abigale asked.

"He takes the red-eye back Wednesday night. He'll be home Thursday morning."

Abigale said, "Then call Lieutenant Mallory by the end of the day on Thursday."

*M*anning had driven his BMW home from Dartmoor Glebe following the hunt and now was insisting on driving it to the funeral service.

"I'm tired of being chauffeured around by you," he said, putting an end to the discussion about who would drive.

His words stung and Abigale stepped away, reaching for her coat. "Okay."

"Hey, Abby, I didn't mean it that way. I really appreciate that you've driven me everywhere. But I'm okay to drive now." Manning grabbed her hand and drew her close, slipping both hands around her waist. He flashed a crooked grin. "It's a guy thing. I need a chance to show my masculine side."

She couldn't resist a smile. "No problem in that department."

He pressed his lips tenderly against her forehead and smoothed her hair, his blue eyes growing serious. "We're going to get through this together, okay?"

Abigale nodded.

"Come on." Manning helped her slip into her coat, making a show of ogling her bare legs as they walked to the door. "Nice legs."

She glanced down at the black pumps she was wearing. "I don't remember the last time I wore a dress. Or heels. I'll be lucky if I make it through the evening without falling on my face. I was going to buy flats, but the gals at Tully Rector's shop talked me into buying these."

"I like them. They show off your calves." Manning opened the front door, motioning for her to go first. "After you."

Abigale eyed the tweed coat he was wearing. "Aren't you going to wear your scarlet?"

"Mother has it. I'm going to wear the one she took to the cleaner last week. My nice one."

Abigale raised an eyebrow at the red coat that hung on a hook by the door. "That one isn't nice?"

"Not nice enough for Mother." As he pulled the door shut, he looked down at his freshly polished boots and clean breeches. "Keep your fingers crossed I pass inspection."

The church was in Middleburg, about a twenty-minute drive, and Manning handled his sports car the way she'd expect him to—fast and aggressive. It must have hurt like hell to shift gears with his broken arm, but Abigale pretended not to notice when he winced a couple of times. Nor did she comment on how swollen his fingers looked.

Manning tuned the radio to a classical station and Abigale's thoughts drifted to her confrontation with Tiffanie that morning. She wasn't at all convinced Tiffanie had told her the truth. At least not the whole truth. She couldn't square Tiffanie's story with the notation in Uncle Richard's journal. If the meeting was truly spur-of-the-moment as Tiffanie claimed, what was the reference in the journal about? Was it a coincidence? Uncle Richard wrote a note to himself, a reminder about something involving Tiffanie, and by chance Tiffanie decided to show up at Longmeadow? Unlikely.

Abigale's instincts told her she was missing part of the puzzle. Her uncle's comment about the fox in the henhouse kept running through her head. Did that somehow tie in with their meeting? Could Uncle Richard have wanted to talk to Tiffanie about Charles's affair? If so, it made sense that Tiffanie wouldn't want to reveal that to her.

Whatever the reason, she was convinced Tiffanie was hiding something. But why? Was Tiffanie really embarrassed to admit she had pressured Uncle Richard to give Charles his colors? Or about the fact that they'd discussed Charles's affair? Or had Tiffanie met with her uncle for an entirely different reason?

Tiffanie had feigned disinterest when she'd told Abigale about the subdivision her husband wanted to build on Percy's property. But was she really so indifferent to the project? The development would no doubt reap substantial financial rewards to the Jenners. And Tiffanie certainly seemed motivated by material possessions. Maybe the meeting had nothing to do with the hunt or Charles's affair. Perhaps Tiffanie had met with Uncle Richard to put pressure on him to publicly support the development. And if he had refused, or worse yet, told her he was going to oppose it . . .

She didn't think it likely that Tiffanie had shot her uncle. But she also wouldn't rule it out. What was it Margaret had said about Tiffanie, that she "wouldn't turn her back on her for an instant"? Tiffanie's voice rang in Abigale's ears, telling her she'd hacked in early from the hunt on the day of Uncle Richard's death because her horse had lost a shoe. So Tiffanie had been at the hunt that day; she could have slipped into Uncle Richard's trailer before the hunt and slit the billet straps on his saddle. Tiffanie had also mentioned being at the tailgate—hearing Uncle Richard mention that he was going to Longmeadow—so after she'd hacked in she must have hung around the trailers waiting for the others to return. She could have sliced the billet straps after Uncle Richard returned from hunting, setting him up for the next ride.

Then a thought struck her like a kick to the gut. *Maybe she was focusing on the wrong Jenner.* What if Charles was the one who'd tampered with the saddle? Or confronted Uncle Richard about the development? *Shot him?* Perhaps Charles's trip to California wasn't just a snub to Uncle Richard after all. Maybe Charles had deliberately scheduled the California trip so he'd miss the funeral—and avoid coming face to face with what he'd done.

For that matter, what about Percy? He had as much at stake as Charles if the subdivision wasn't approved. Perhaps more, if Tiffanie's remark about Percy being desperate to sell was true. Despite what Manning had said, she still found it suspicious that Percy had known Manning was riding in Uncle Richard's saddle when he was injured.

Abigale almost groaned with frustration. She needed to hear what Dario Reyes had to say about what he'd seen and heard at Longmeadow. Find out whether he could identify the vehicle Michelle claimed he'd seen leave the racecourse and determine if she thought he was telling the truth.

She had checked her email when Manning was in the shower and found nothing from Michelle de Becque. But the possibility that an email could now be sitting in her in-box nagged at her. She'd hated that Emilio was addicted to his BlackBerry, always thumbing through his messages. Yet, for the first time, she understood his addiction and wished she had a Smartphone, or had at least signed up for email access on her cell.

"Hey, you all right?" Manning asked, squeezing her knee. "You look like you're trying to solve the world's problems."

She forced a smile. "I'm okay. Just going round and round in my head about Uncle Richard's death."

"Yeah, I know what you mean."

Abigale felt a stab of guilt for not confiding in him, telling him what

Michelle had said about Dario Reyes. But she'd promised Michelle she wouldn't tell anyone, including Manning, and she'd keep that promise. At least long enough to give Michelle a chance to talk to her friend. If she didn't hear something by tomorrow, she'd reconsider.

"There's Mother," Manning said, pulling to a stop in front of the ivy-covered brick chapel.

Margaret stood outside the front door, a scarlet coat in dry-cleaner wrap draped over her arm. She was deep in conversation with an attractive, serious-looking woman in a black suit and a dark-haired, handsome man dressed in scarlet hunt attire. He was about Manning's height, but older, his temples powdered with a blush of gray. Abigale thought she recognized him but couldn't place him.

"That's Doug Cummings and his wife, Anne," Manning said. "Did you meet him at the hunt this morning?"

Ah. That was why he looked familiar. "I didn't meet him, but I saw him there. He led the second field, right?"

Manning nodded. "You'll like him. Doug's a good guy. He was a close friend of Richard's. Anne was Richard's friend, too. And his lawyer. She drafted Richard's will."

Abigale's eyes shot over to Manning. Anne was the one who'd told Margaret that Richard was having second thoughts about his will. That he was going to give Manning an ultimatum.

One corner of Manning's mouth twitched into a smile. "Don't worry, I don't blame her. Don't kill the messenger, right?"

C H A P T E R

71

The organ music stopped and Abigale glanced over her shoulder. Every pew in the small chapel was packed with people. Margaret told her a big-screen TV had been set up in the parish house next door to broadcast the service to the overflow crowd.

The six pallbearers marched up the aisle in pairs: Smitty and Manning first, followed by Doug Cummings and a man she didn't recognize. Thompson and another man brought up the rear. All six wore scarlet hunt coats, white breeches bleached snow white, and black boots spit-polished to a military gleam. One of the men she didn't recognize had a gold collar on his coat, the other hunter green, the colors of their respective hunts. Manning and the other three members of the Middleburg Foxhounds displayed robin's-egg-blue collars with navy piping.

Manning took his seat between Abigale and Margaret. Smitty and Doug sat to Margaret's right. Thompson and the other men sat in the second row. As the reverend asked them to join her in prayer, Manning slipped his hand through Abigale's, squeezed gently, and slid his other hand over Margaret's. Goose bumps pricked Abigale's arms when the vocalist sang "The Lord's Prayer," and she saw tears seep down the fine crinkles in Margaret's cheeks.

Doug rose to deliver the eulogy, pausing briefly as he passed the coffin. His blue eyes misted as he took the podium, and he fiddled longer than was necessary adjusting the microphone. But when he spoke his voice rang strong, echoing off the granite walls of the tiny church.

"We lost a dear friend last week. There are no words that can express the love and sorrow that fill our hearts. And yet we gather here today to honor Richard. Perhaps in so doing we try to deny the fact that he is gone, or at least prolong our farewell, possibly revere him in a way we dared not do in his presence. But the truest testimony to Richard lies not in what we say here today, but in the way he lived his life—with courage, honor, humility, and compassion.

"Richard was a Southern gentleman in the truest sense of the word. He treated those around him with charm—especially the ladies—and with respect. And it was genuine.

"Richard was a leader, in the hunt and in the community. Going places with him socially was like walking in the shadow of a rock star. Every five feet someone would stop him, want his attention. And yet no question, no concern, was too trivial for Richard to spend time talking about." Doug paused and smiled. His eyes shone with a mixture of sadness and affection. "I often accused Richard of campaigning for mayor of Middleburg, and I'm not so sure he didn't have designs on serving in that capacity one day."

A light titter wafted through the church. Abigale felt the heavy weight that seemed to be lodged in her belly ease some. She drew in a long, slow breath. Manning gave her a sideways glance, the barest of smiles.

"Richard loved horses, hounds, and open space," Doug continued. "He was a foxhunting purist and the finest master I have ever had the privilege to ride behind. He hunted with skill and instinct—keen for great sport, yet ever mindful of the safety and enjoyment of those riding behind him.

"I remember hunting with Richard one day as a child. I was probably eight or nine, and my father had me ride with him near the front of the field, something several of the more senior members took exception to. Richard wasn't master then, but he was riding up front near us when we approached a jump in the fence behind Stony Bank that was giving everyone problems. It was a brand-spanking-new coop—a good three foot nine, four feet—and a nearby oak tree cast a dark shadow across the fresh boards. The first horse spooked at the shadow, as did the one behind it, and it turned into monkey see–monkey do, with one horse after the other refusing the coop.

"Richard was in front of me on that retired open jumper of his, Rufus, who would have stepped over the jump with his eyes closed. But Richard pulled up, turned to me, and asked for a lead over the fence. I was on a tough little pony that would jump anything I aimed her at, so I kicked on and she sailed over the coop, knees tucked up around her ears. Richard jumped right behind me and the other horses followed. Thanks to Richard, one of the old-timers took to calling me his lucky charm and from that day forward always insisted I hunt up front with him.

"I'm sure many of you have similar hunting stories to share. When hounds went out this morning, our hearts ached that Richard wasn't there. Yet, let us not weep for what we've lost, but rather celebrate what we shared. Richard lived his life to the fullest, and if he were here today it is his life, not his passing, that he would want us to remember."

Doug turned toward the coffin. "I will miss you, my friend."

The reception following the burial was in the parish house, where a slide show flashed across the big-screen TV. Abigale found it painful to watch, yet her eyes kept returning to the photos. As if she had to burn the images into her mind, so she'd never forget the way her uncle looked. She shuddered, remembering how she'd panicked about a year after her father's death when she wasn't able to envision his face.

An old black-and-white shot of her uncle and Margaret appeared on the screen. They were on horseback, dressed in tweeds for cubbing. Margaret held a lead line attached to the bridle of a small paint pony. A boy of no more than four or five was on the pony, his legs barely reached the bottom of the saddle flap.

Abigale glanced to her left and saw Doug standing beside her. "Your eulogy was lovely. Thank you," she said.

"I was honored to be asked to deliver it." Doug nodded at the TV screen. "Is that Manning?"

"Yes. Cute photo, isn't it?"

"He looks like a natural."

Abigale smiled.

"Manning did a great job leading the first field this morning," Doug said. "Richard made a good choice."

"It's nice to finally hear someone say that."

Doug arched an eyebrow. "Has Manning been taking some heat?"

"It's just that Margaret doesn't seem thrilled with my uncle's decision. And Thompson made it clear to me he has no confidence in Manning's ability to handle the hunt finances."

"Manning shouldn't take it personally. Part of that reaction is simply that no one can envision the Middleburg Foxhounds without Richard. He *was* the hunt. *Anyone* following in Richard's footsteps would have to prove himself."

"Even to his own mother?" Abigale asked.

"Point taken," Doug said, his mouth curving down in a sympathetic smile. "Listen, tell Manning I'm there for him if there's anything I can do to help. I mean that."

"Thank you. I will."

A tall, thin-faced man interrupted them. "Excuse me," he said, extending his hand to Abigale. "I just want to give you my condolences about your uncle. I'm Jay Barnsby."

Jay Barnsby. That was the name in her uncle's journal. "I've actually been wanting to meet you," Abigale said.

"Really? To what do I owe that pleasure?"

"I saw your name in a note my uncle wrote in his journal. I just wondered if you could shed some light on it."

"I'll be happy to try. What did the note say?" Barnsby asked.

"It was just your name. Written on the page of the day my uncle died. Did you have an appointment with him that day?"

"No. But I did receive a phone call from him."

Abigale's heart sped up a notch. "What did he want?"

"Well, now, that I can't tell you," Barnsby replied in a slow drawl. "I was out of the bank that morning and when I returned, I received Richard's voicemail. It was very short. Just said he had something he wanted to discuss with me. He said he was going hunting and he'd try to reach me again later."

"The bank?"

"Jay's president of Middleburg Merchant's Bank," Doug explained.

"Oh." That seemed like a dead end. But it did confirm Margaret's theory that her uncle used his journal more as a reminder than an actual appointment book. Maybe Tiffanie was telling the truth when she claimed they didn't have a meeting planned. "Do you have any idea what my uncle wanted to discuss with you?"

Barnsby said, "Not for certain, but my guess is it was about a large deposit he was expecting for the hunt account. He'd mentioned it to me in passing awhile back and told me he'd be in touch to discuss investment options."

"That must be the donation from Walt Fleming's estate," Doug said.

"That's right. Richard also mentioned a large amount of cash would run through the account from the steeplechase races." Barnsby's eyes flickered from Abigale to Doug. "I guess Thompson would be the one to talk to about it now that Richard has passed?"

"Manning Southwell is the master now," Doug replied. "Why don't I bring him by the bank. We can discuss the options."

"That sounds like a good plan." Barnsby nodded at Abigale. "It was a pleasure to meet you. Please accept my deepest sympathies about your uncle. He was a great man."

"Tell Manning to give me a call and I'll set up an appointment at the bank," Doug said to Abigale as Jay Barnsby walked away. "I'm sure Manning knows several folks at the bank, but I serve on the bank board, so maybe I can make some additional helpful introductions. In fact, I have a meeting at the bank tomorrow morning. We could get together after the meeting if it works for Manning."

"Thanks, I'll let him know."

Abigale felt a hand on her arm and turned to see Michelle de Becque.

"Thank God they finally left. I thought I'd never get you by yourself," Michelle said. "I have good news."

Hope fluttered in Abigale's chest. "Did you speak with your friend?"

"Yes. He agreed to talk to you. He'll meet you at my farm tomorrow morning."

*M*anning knew as soon as he saw Mallory in the doorway of the parish house that the lieutenant wasn't there on a social call. He watched Mallory's eyes roam the room.

"What are you looking at?" Abigale asked, twisting around to follow Manning's gaze.

"Mallory." He tilted his coffee cup toward the lieutenant, who was working his way across the room.

Margaret pursed her lips. "Why would he show up here?"

"I don't know, but he doesn't look happy." Manning said a silent prayer that Mallory's appearance didn't have anything to do with him. Abigale slipped her arm through his, and Manning saw his own flicker of fear mirrored in her eyes.

"Evening, Lieutenant," Margaret said.

"Good evening, Mrs. Southwell." Mallory nodded a greeting at Manning and Abigale. "I'm looking for Michael Parker, but I don't see him. Do you know if he's here?"

"He was," Margaret replied, spinning around as she surveyed the room. She shot a finger toward the far corner. "There he is. Talking with Smitty."

"Thank you, ma'am," Mallory said.

"Hold on, Lieutenant." Margaret stopped Mallory as he turned away. "Mind sharing what you need to talk to him about?"

Mallory eyed them for a moment, as if deciding whether to reveal the information. "Someone who works for Mr. Parker has been reported missing."

Margaret's brows scrunched together. "Larry?"

"Yes, ma'am. Larry Fisk."

"*Missing?* As in he's run away? Or met with foul play?"

"That's what I'm trying to determine."

"Good Lord!"

Manning saw heads turn. A troubled silence settled over the room. "Why don't we go where we have some privacy," he suggested in a low voice. He tilted his head toward the front hall. "No one's using the nursery. I'll get Michael and meet you there."

Abigale shot him a questioning look. "Go with Mother," he said softly, as he headed toward Michael.

As Manning led Michael down the hall toward the nursery, Michael said, "I don't mind telling you, Lieutenant Mallory makes me nervous. He's questioned me twice now. First about the day Mr. Clarke was murdered and then again the other day about the saddle. I never can tell if he believes what I'm saying."

That makes two of us, Manning thought, reaching for the door handle.

Mallory stood near the doorway, looking as though he felt out of place amidst the jumble of toys and pint-sized furniture. "I understand Larry Fisk hasn't shown up for work in a couple of days," he said to Michael.

"That's right. Now, of course, he wasn't supposed to work today. Mondays are his day off. But he left me high and dry all weekend."

"Did he call in sick?"

"No, sir. I didn't hear from him. Not a peep."

"Has he done that before?"

Michael thought for a moment. "Not really. Larry's not all that much help when he's around, but he usually shows up more or less on time."

"Can you think of any reason he would fail to show up?"

"Like what do you mean?"

"Anything happen that would have made him skip work?"

Michael's gaze slid to the floor. His Adam's apple danced in his neck as he swallowed. "Well, now, I did have a few words with Larry Friday afternoon."

Manning exchanged a glance with his mother. *Jesus.* Was Michael responsible for Larry's disappearance?

"Tell me about that," Mallory said.

Michael squared his shoulders, as if gathering up strength. "Right before you got there to do your questioning about Mr. Clarke's saddle, I asked Larry to drag the back pasture—you know, run the chain harrow over it to break up the manure, spread it around. Anyhow, after you questioned me and all and everyone had left, I realized I didn't hear the tractor running, but Larry still wasn't back at the barn. So I jumped in my truck and went looking for him. Found the tractor parked in the run-in shed back there. Larry was fast asleep."

"So that's when you had words with him?" Mallory asked.

"Yes, sir. I about ripped him a new one." Michael's face flushed and he glanced at Margaret. "Pardon me, Mrs. Southwell."

"Do you think that could account for Larry not showing up for work over the weekend?" Mallory asked.

"I don't imagine so. It's not the first time I've had to light a fire under the boy. Besides, by the time Larry had finished up for the day it had blown over. He didn't act like anything was wrong when he left." Michael paused and frowned at Mallory. "Have you talked to Larry's mama?"

"That's why I'm here," Mallory said. "Larry's mother called to report her son missing. Apparently Larry usually shows up at her house on Mondays for a hot breakfast and to drop off a pile of dirty laundry. When he didn't come by this morning, she tried to reach him. He didn't answer his phone, so she drove over to his apartment and found a stack of dirty dishes in the sink, but no sign of her son. She says from the looks of the dishes they'd been there awhile, and there was no evidence of recent activity in the kitchen. She got worried, called the barn, and found out Larry hadn't shown up for work all weekend."

"If she called I didn't talk to her, but she might have spoken to Elizabeth," Michael said. "That's who fills in on Mondays when Larry's off."

"That's right," Mallory replied. "Mrs. Fisk spoke with Elizabeth Carey and learned that Larry hadn't been at work all weekend. That's when she gave us a call."

"What about at the training track where he rents the apartment?" Michael said. "Did anyone up there see him over the weekend?"

"We've asked around up there and no one remembers seeing him or his car since Friday morning. But then again, they don't remember not seeing him either."

"Meaning Larry doesn't have much to do with his neighbors." Margaret said.

"That's right," Mallory replied. "Pretty much keeps to himself. Apparently he spends most of his spare time playing games on his Xbox."

Manning felt Abigale's hand on his arm. "Friday was when you had your riding accident."

Manning frowned at her. "Yeah. So?"

"So that's when the saddle broke," she said quickly. "After I finished grooming Braveheart, I went to put my grooming supplies in the closet and Larry was in there with Uncle Richard's saddle. He acted like I'd caught him doing something he shouldn't be. At the time, I just figured he was goofing off and I didn't think anything else about it. But maybe there was more to it."

"Like what?" Manning asked.

"Maybe Larry was the one who tampered with the saddle. When the saddle broke and you were injured, he might have gotten scared he'd get caught so he ran away."

"That doesn't explain why he would have acted suspiciously when you caught him with the saddle in the closet. That was after the fact."

"Right, but maybe he was trying to cover up what he'd done."

Manning frowned. "How?"

"I don't know. Maybe rough up the billet straps so it wasn't obvious they'd been cut."

"Much as I moan and complain about Larry, I just can't see him doing something like that," Michael said. "The boy might be lazy, but he's not a bad seed. And he looked up to Mr. Clarke something fierce."

"Okay." Abigale gazed out the window as she thought it over. "So what if Larry saw someone *else* messing with Uncle Richard's saddle? Maybe he didn't realize at the time what they were doing, but after the saddle broke on Friday he remembered it. And when I saw him he was checking out the saddle, confirming his suspicions." She looked at Michael. "Did Larry say anything about the saddle to you?"

"No, ma'am."

Abigale's expression turned grim. "Maybe Larry decided to keep his suspicions to himself until he confronted the person directly. And when he did he went missing."

*A*bigale drew in a slow lungful of air, finding some comfort in the fresh, woodsy odor of the bagged pine shavings she was perched atop. She glanced at her watch. It hadn't been five minutes since Michelle had left her alone in the storage barn, but it might as well have been an hour. She wiped her palms against her pant legs. *Everything* rested on her being able to talk to Dario.

It was no longer just about catching Uncle Richard's killer. Or clearing Manning's name. It might be about saving Larry's life. If whoever had tampered with the saddle was the same person who'd shot her uncle, then odds were that person had kidnapped Larry. If Dario could identify the person he'd seen leaving Longmeadow after he heard the gunshot, or give a description of the vehicle, they might have a chance at finding Larry before it was too late.

A worm of doubt about Larry still niggled at her. She'd wrestled with it most of the night. Larry wasn't at work the last day Uncle Richard hunted. Michael had confirmed that. It was a Monday, Larry's day off. That meant if the saddle had been tampered with that day, at the barn or the hunt, Larry hadn't been the one to do it. Of course, that cut both ways. Larry also wouldn't have been present to see who did. The one thing being off work that day did provide Larry with was opportunity. He could have been at Longmeadow. All the more reason it was crucial she talk with Dario. If Dario described seeing Larry's car leaving Longmeadow—an old Ford Focus with a bad muffler— well, then, they'd know Larry was a killer, not a victim.

Without warning—no approaching footsteps, no knock—the doorknob turned. The white metal door slid silently inward, no more than a foot, and a young man slipped through. He turned the inside knob and closed the door without a sound.

They eyed each other: Abigale from her perch on the shavings, he with his back against the door, his hands thrust into the front pockets of his jeans. Michelle had told her his name was Miguel. He was the friend of one of her grooms. That was the extent of what Abigale knew.

Abigale swallowed and ran her tongue across her lips. Should she stand, offer her hand? She sensed that if she moved he'd disappear through the door. "Thanks for agreeing to talk to me."

Miguel's eyes darted beneath slick brows, shining like bright, black marbles in his round face. She guessed him to be in his early twenties.

"Michelle, she say you can help Dario."

"I might be able to, if he'll agree to talk to me. Michelle told me Dario saw someone drive away from Longmeadow the night my uncle was murdered. If he can give me a description or information that helps us find whoever shot my uncle, he'll be cleared as a suspect."

He shook his head. "The cops'll still be after him. For not turning himself in, resisting arrest. Some crap like that."

"I'll find an attorney. We'll work out a deal for Dario if he cooperates by talking to me. You have my word."

Miguel was young, but the look in his eyes told her he'd seen more than his share of the darker side of life and had plenty of reasons not to believe her. "Why should he trust you?"

"Because it's my uncle who was murdered."

"Don' that put you on opposite sides?"

"Only if Dario killed him."

A frown tugged at his full lips.

"Did he?"

Miguel shook his head. "The cops, they jus' trying to make him take the heat."

"Then Dario should tell me what he saw and help me find my uncle's killer."

"How he know you not working with the cops?"

"I'm not. No one knows I'm even talking to you except Michelle. I'll come alone, meet him anywhere he wants."

He gave her a long look. She stared back, her heart thumping so hard in her chest she could barely breathe.

"I tell him," he said finally. "No guarantee."

"I understand."

Miguel reached behind his back to grab the doorknob.

"How will you get in touch if Dario agrees to talk to me?" Abigale asked.

"Michelle have your cell number?"

She nodded.

"If Dario want to talk, I call."

"How soon do you think I'll hear?"

He shrugged. "Depends on Dario."

"It's important that I speak with him. As soon as possible. It might save someone's life."

Miguel's dark eyes softened. He gave her a quick nod. "I see what I can do."

*A*bigale stopped by Dartmoor Glebe after she left Michelle's. She needed time to think. Time to be alone.

A storm was forecast to hit overnight, some tropical depression sitting off the coast that was supposed to pummel them with rain for the next few days. Before the rain settled in she wanted to capture more shots of Dartmoor Glebe to send to her mother.

The sky was already blanketed with a wispy sheet of clouds, making for ideal lighting conditions. She strolled around the grounds until the sun sank behind the Blue Ridge and shot a memory card full of photographs. She'd brought along the hunt horn and spurs Uncle Richard had given her, and she arranged them on a moss-covered log in a cluster of trees in front of the house and shot them from various angles with the house in the background.

When she arrived at Manning's he was hunched over his computer. Sheets of paper littered the hinged writing surface of the secretary desk, and a couple of file folders were scattered near his feet. He glanced up from the computer screen, sighing as he yanked his fingers through his hair.

"What are you doing?" she asked.

"Beating my head against the wall." Manning leaned back in the swivel chair as she bent down to kiss him.

He grasped her arm as she started to rise. "Hey, what kind of a kiss was that?"

Abigale smiled as he pulled her onto his lap. He tugged her mouth to his and kissed her tenderly. "I missed you today," he whispered. She sank into his kiss, tumbling to a place where all that mattered was his mouth, his hands, and the force of his arms around her. "Mother invited us to dinner," he murmured against her lips. "We need to leave soon."

"Mmm." Abigale buried her face against his neck. His skin was warm against her cheek, the spicy scent of his aftershave soothing and erotic at the same time. Manning wrapped both arms around her and stroked her back, her hair—

She jerked back, stared wide-eyed at his right arm. "You got your cast off."

"Yeah."

"When—why? You didn't tell me you were going to the doctor today!"

Manning took her hand and guided her off his lap. "I didn't," he said, standing up.

Abigale's eyes shot from his arm to his face. "What do you mean, you didn't?"

"I didn't go to the doctor."

"Did you go back to the ER?"

Manning shook his head, his eyes hardening into a don't-argue-with-me look. "Kevin cut it off."

"Kevin?"

He nodded.

"As in, your *blacksmith?*"

"Yeah."

"Why?"

"Because my arm was swollen and it hurt like hell, itched like a son-of-a-bitch, too. I couldn't stand it any longer."

"Did it enter your mind to go to the doctor rather than your blacksmith?"

"Christ, Abby—" His eyes flashed and he clamped his mouth shut, then blew out a heavy rush of air. "I was at the barn, talking to Kevin. He commented on how swollen my hand was and I told him I felt like ripping the goddamn cast off. He offered to use one of his tools to cut it off and I took him up on it." Manning looked away, stretching his neck from side to side as if to ease tension. "Look, let's not fight about it, okay?"

"It's your arm," she said, giving him a tight smile.

Abigale knew Manning's arm was bothering him when he didn't object to her driving them to Margaret's in the Subaru. He even admitted he'd had a rough go of it driving home from the barn without the cast, and had ended up shifting gears with his left arm. She managed to curb the impulse to point out that maybe there was an advantage to the cast after all. No doubt he'd figure that out on his own soon enough.

*M*argaret was talking on the phone when they let themselves in the back door. She waved them into the kitchen. "All right. Thank you for letting me know, Lieutenant. I appreciate you keeping me informed."

"What was that about?" Manning asked as Margaret hung up the phone.

"They found Larry's car in the parking lot at Dulles Airport."

Abigale's pulse quickened. "So he did run away!"

"Not necessarily," Margaret replied. "I just said the same thing to Lieutenant Mallory and he pointed out that if Larry did meet with foul play, the parking lot at Dulles is a logical place for someone to dump his car."

No one spoke for a moment. Abigale said, "I assume they're checking to see if he boarded a flight."

"Of course. They haven't found him on a passenger manifest yet. But Mallory said they're investigating all possible modes of transportation out of Dulles. If Larry did run away, he could have jumped on a shuttle bus from Dulles and gone any number of places."

Abigale exchanged a glance with Manning. "So finding the car there really doesn't tell us much of anything."

"Not really." Margaret grabbed a platter of roast chicken off the counter and set it on the table. "Come on. Let's sit down and eat before everything gets cold."

As she filled their plates, she said to Manning, "Tell me about your meeting at the bank this morning. Doug told me Jay Barnsby met with you personally."

"He did. Doug, Jay, and I talked in general about the hunt account and what services the bank offers, and then he had the branch manager oversee the paperwork adding me to the account. I'm already set up for online banking."

Margaret's eyebrows shot up. "Online banking? That seems like an unnecessary expense. Don't you think you should get a better grasp of the bookkeeping before you start piling up charges for services you'll probably never use?"

Manning's expression flattened as if someone had lowered a curtain, blocking out the light. "I didn't add the service," he replied, stabbing his fork into a piece of chicken. "The hunt account already has online banking. They just authorized me as a user. Besides, it's free."

"Well, Richard certainly didn't bank online." Margaret's tone had an edge to it, almost accusatory. "He didn't even know how to turn on a computer. And he had no regard for anything financial if he couldn't hold it in his hands, read it on a piece of paper. Must be something Thompson authorized."

"I don't know who authorized it," Manning said, "but it was a good move. No one writes checks anymore. Online banking allows you to get up-to-date account information. It's easier to stay on top of things. Especially when you accept online payments, like the hunt does for the race tickets."

"How do you know so much about it?" Margaret asked.

"I used online banking in L.A.," Manning said, handing the platter of chicken to Abigale. "The system there allowed me to pay bills online and download the transactions directly into my bookkeeping software. It even allocated the payments to different expense categories—feed, bedding, whatever."

"*You* paid bills?" Margaret said.

"What, you thought I bought all my barn supplies with my charm?"

"Don't get sassy with me, Manning. I assumed you had someone handle it for you."

"I did in the beginning. Then I figured out the only way to really keep an eye on costs was to manage things myself."

Margaret looked as though she couldn't have been more surprised if Manning had just declared he was running for president. Her expression teetered between incredulity and pride. "Well," she said, finally, "I didn't realize you had that experience. That should help you understand the hunt finances."

"Yeah." Manning chewed thoughtfully. "I spent most of the afternoon looking through the files you gave me, though, and some of it just doesn't make sense to me."

"What doesn't make sense?" Margaret asked.

Manning narrowed his eyes. "A couple of things don't seem to jibe. For starters, I can't get the figures you gave me to reconcile with the online account balance. And the deposits for ticket sales from the races seem way off."

"Those figures I gave you are from last month's board meeting," Margaret said dismissively. "You'll get revised financials tomorrow. I set up a meeting for both of us with Thompson tomorrow afternoon at Dartmoor Glebe."

"What about the deposits?" Manning asked.

"Same thing. The paperwork you got from me is outdated."

Manning said, "But that's just it. What I'm looking at online is up to date. Actual deposits. And it doesn't match the revenue figures you gave me."

Margaret waved off his concern. "Sounds like you're spending too much time fretting over things. I'm sure Thompson can explain it to you."

"Terrific," Manning said without enthusiasm. "That's something to look forward to. I'm sure Thompson will welcome the opportunity to make me look ignorant."

Margaret's eyes flashed. "If you're going to go into it with an attitude like that, we might as well cancel tomorrow's meeting. I have better things to do with my time than massage egos. The sooner you learn to work with Thompson, the better off you'll be."

"That went well," Manning said, yanking the Subaru door shut.

Abigale inserted the key in the ignition but didn't start the engine. "You shouldn't let her get to you like that."

"Easy for you to say."

She gave him a sympathetic smile.

"Christ." He thumped the dashboard with his left fist. "I can almost deal with the fact that Mother has no faith in me, but the killer is that she refuses to even entertain the notion that Thompson might be at fault for anything. I thought I did a pretty good job keeping my cool until she jumped all over my back when I mentioned what Kevin told me about Thompson adding his horses to Richard's shoeing bill. She acted like I'd accused the Pope of stealing money from the collection plate."

"I think she was just suggesting that there's probably a logical explanation and you should give Thompson the benefit of the doubt. Ask rather than accuse."

"I wasn't accusing. I merely said I noticed the shoeing and vet expenses looked really high compared to what I paid in L.A., and that when I mentioned it to Kevin he told me the shoeing bill included Thompson's horses. *That's all I said.* Mother made the leap that I was accusing Thompson of something underhanded."

Abigale gently fingered his broken arm as the interior light dimmed. "It probably didn't help any that you mentioned the conversation took place while Kevin was cutting your cast off."

Manning sighed. "Yeah. Probably not."

Frustration seemed to radiate off him in the dark car. "I can't—Jesus—I can't do this whole master thing. I'm boxed into a no-win situation. I'm the master, but I have no authority. The board—Mother—runs the show. Fine. I don't care. Let 'em. Let Thompson handle the finances. All I want to do is hunt anyway. Except—and this is a biggie—the hunt itself has no money. In fact, it loses money hand over fist. The hunt probably wouldn't even exist if Richard hadn't kept pumping in a steady stream of money all these years."

"But he left you money to fund it now, right?"

"Yeah. He did. Five years' worth of operating costs. And an additional million dollars in five years with the caveat that I'm successful at keeping the hunt alive that long."

"Don't you think you can do that?"

"That's just it. The hunt lost money when Richard was master, right? Can I do any better? I don't know. Not if I can't call the shots. Not if the board dictates how things should be run and Thompson handles the money. And when I start asking questions, trying to understand the numbers so I can try to make a go of it . . ."

He looked out the window at the house, rapping his knuckles against the glass. "Mother jumps down my throat."

"Go back inside and talk to her," Abigale said softly. "Tell her what you just told me."

"No."

"Why not?"

Manning shook his head. "I'll get the financials from Thompson tomorrow and figure it out myself."

The light in the downstairs window clicked off, plunging the house into darkness.

He turned to Abigale. "Let's go home."

*A*bigale spent most of the morning trying to stay out of Manning's way while he alternated between staring at the computer screen and rifling through papers strewn across his desk, muttering things like "what the hell" and "this makes no sense."

She reluctantly uncurled herself from the couch in front of the smoldering fire and padded to the kitchen for more coffee, her bare feet whispering across the hardwood floor. She glanced through the rain-streaked window. The steel-bottomed clouds that had pressed down from the heavens all morning were still unleashing a steady torrent of rain.

Sipping her coffee, Abigale checked her cell phone for what seemed like the hundredth time to make sure she hadn't missed a call or text message from Miguel. Nothing. The landline rang, but Manning ignored it, so Abigale picked it up in the kitchen and carried the cordless phone to him, covering the mouthpiece with her hand.

"It's your mother," she said, extending the phone to him.

Manning's face darkened. He shot her a look, mouthing a sarcastic "thanks" as he reached for the phone. "Hello?"

The conversation lasted less than a minute. Manning disconnected the call and stared thoughtfully at the handset.

"Everything okay?"

"Yeah." He frowned at her. "Mother is coming over here. She wants me to show her the financials that I have questions about."

"That's great. What turned her around?"

"I don't know. She just said she'd been thinking about it overnight and wanted to get together with me before the meeting with Thompson this afternoon."

Abigale stroked the back of his neck. "Just keep your cool if she jumps down your throat again. Once she realizes you're not criticizing the way things were done in the past, that you're just asking questions in order to understand things, she'll be on your side."

His broad shoulders expanded as he sucked in a deep breath, then let it escape. "I hope so. Because the more I look at these numbers, the less I know."

"You'll figure it out." Abigale pressed her lips to his forehead. "I'd better get dressed so I can get out of your hair before Margaret arrives."

She was wearing one of Manning's dress shirts, and he grabbed a handful of blue cotton as she turned away. "Uh-uh. Not so fast."

Tension swept from Manning's face as if washed away by the tide. His lips parted, curving into a smile. He reeled her back, his eyes dancing greedily up her thigh and across her abdomen, settling on her chest. He popped open a button and pulled her into a kiss.

Abigale planted a hand on his shoulder as she tore her mouth away. "I've got to go, Manning. I still need to shower."

"Good idea. Me too," he murmured, slipping his hands up inside the shirt. "We can save water."

"You have a one-track mind," she said, gently shoving his hands away.

A low chuckle rumbled in his throat. "Of course I do. I'm a guy."

Abigale's cell phone buzzed in her breast pocket. She'd set it on vibrate so she'd be able to slip away to answer it if she got a call about a meeting with Dario. She snatched the phone and saw a number she didn't recognize. The area code was 703. *Virginia.* She punched the call button. "Hello."

"It's Miguel."

Abigale's heart slammed in her chest. She turned away from Manning and walked over by the window. "Yes."

"Dario, he agree to talk."

Thank God. "Just tell me where and when."

"I take you to him. You know Big Lots?"

"No."

"It's a store in Sterling. I meet you in parking lot."

Abigale heard Manning shift in his chair. She felt his gaze on her. "Okay. I'll find it. What time?" she said quietly.

"Five o'clock today."

"I'll be there."

Abigale drew in a breath as she ended the call. *She was actually going to meet with Dario Reyes.* She itched to tell Manning, ached to let the whole story burst out—how Michelle had arranged for her to meet with Miguel, that Miguel was going to take her to Dario. Everything. But she fought the urge. She knew Manning would never let her meet with Dario alone. And if Miguel caught wind that anyone else was involved, he'd disappear like a scared rabbit. Her one chance to talk to Dario would vaporize. She couldn't allow that to happen. This was something she had to do alone.

CHAPTER

79

There were only a handful of cars in the parking area in front of Big Lots. No surprise. The pounding rain and relentless wind had probably kept all but those in need of absolute necessities hunkered down at home. Abigale glanced at the clock as she pulled the Subaru into a parking space a few rows away from the store entrance. She'd been slowed down by standing water on the roadways and a couple of intersections where the traffic signals were out, but had still managed to arrive with seven minutes to spare. She switched off the engine and eyed the other vehicles in the lot. None of them appeared to be occupied.

Two entrances led to the parking lot, one directly in front of her off Sterling Boulevard and another that fed off an access road to her right. Her eyes flickered back and forth between the two. An occasional vehicle splashed by on Sterling Boulevard, spraying water in its wake, but none of them turned into the lot.

Rain hammered the Subaru's roof, blowing sideways in the neon glare of a nearby security light. A shopping cart skittered across the lot and slammed into the cart return area. Abigale had heard on the car radio that there was a flood watch in effect for the entire D.C. area throughout the night. And the forecast was no better for tomorrow. She shivered. It almost made her long for the unforgiving Afghan sun.

The inside of the car windows were fogging up, and Abigale stretched forward to run her jacket sleeve across the front windshield. As she settled back in the seat, she caught the sweep of headlights to her left, then heard the growl of an engine as a truck glided into the spot next to her. She wiped a circle with her fist and saw Miguel peering at her from behind the wheel of a battered brown pickup truck. He had to have been parked at the far back of the lot, watching to make sure she was alone. Another man sat in the front seat beside him.

The truck's passenger door opened and the other man slid out. He wore jeans and a black hoodie pulled snug across a baseball cap with a broad rim that shadowed most of his face. Even without getting a good look at his face, she was sure the man was not Dario Reyes. She'd studied the photo of Dario released by the sheriff's office, committing his description to memory. Dario was five foot eight and 145 pounds. This man had to be at least six feet tall and probably weighed close to 200 pounds.

Miguel leaned across the seat, waving his hand impatiently for her to get into the truck. Abigale hesitated. The presence of the man with the hoodie bothered her. *Who was he?* A shiver crept up her spine, but she grabbed the handle. She hadn't come this far to back down now. She shoved open the door and climbed out. A gust of wind knocked her back against the Subaru as fat raindrops splattered her face and trickled down her scalp.

She motioned for the man with the cap to climb into the truck ahead of her, but he shook his head. *He wanted her to sit in the middle.* He gripped her arm, lifting her up as she climbed into the cab. As she slid across the bench seat toward Miguel, the man jumped onto the seat beside her and slammed the door. He thumped his fist against the dashboard. *"Vayamos! Muévalo."*

She understood enough Spanish to know what that meant. *Let's go. Move it.*

Miguel threw the gearshift into reverse and the truck jerked back out of the parking space. Neither man spoke as the truck lurched toward Sterling Boulevard. Abigale sucked in a deep breath, trying to assure herself these men were nothing compared to the informants she'd met with in the Middle East. But she couldn't shake the fear that she'd just made the stupidest move of her life.

*M*oments after they'd settled in Richard's study, Thompson ticked off Manning.

"What do you mean you don't have the most recent profit-and-loss statements?" Manning demanded.

"That's not exactly accurate," Thompson replied. "I have them. Everything's up to date. I just didn't run printouts for you."

"Why not?" Manning asked.

Thompson glanced at Margaret. "I'm sorry. I didn't realize you wanted to get into that kind of detail today. I thought Margaret just wanted me to give you a primer—hunt economics 101."

"Hunt economics 101?" Manning scoffed. "I'm not as ignorant as you think, Thompson."

"All right, both of you calm down," Margaret said. "We're all part of the same team. For the good of the hunt, the two of you need to put aside your differences and forge a solid working relationship."

"This is a waste of time," Manning muttered.

Margaret ignored the remark. "Thompson, Manning has been looking over the financials you handed out at last month's board meeting and he has some questions. I'm sure you can answer many of them without having any printouts with you. Let's start there."

"By all means," Thompson said. "Ask away."

Manning wanted to start with the shoeing and vet expenses, but he figured Thompson would likely react the same way his mother had when he'd brought it up the night before. He splayed his hands across the stack of papers on his lap. He didn't need to refer to them. Most of the numbers were already committed to memory. "Let's start with the races," he said. "I assume the hunt incurs much of the expense and receives a good portion of the revenue in advance of race day."

"Not necessarily," Thompson replied. "Checks and invoices will trickle in for another month or so."

Manning nodded impatiently. "Sure, I can see that. Especially with race-day expenses that are invoiced. But let's talk revenue. The race entries are paid in advance. So are program ad sales. I assume the sponsors pay in full up front."

"Don't assume." Thompson flashed a knowing smile at Margaret.

"We give a little leeway to some of the regulars," Margaret said. "We'll collect it eventually. Always do."

"Okay. But most pay up front, right?" Manning said.

Thompson rolled a shoulder. "Sure."

"Do the vendors pay up front?"

"Yes."

"And you sell advance tickets online. So, other than the late payers, you basically receive all the revenue up front, except for the gate receipts on race day."

"And program sales. Souvenir items. Pony rides," Thompson said.

"Yeah, but that's piddly stuff," Manning said. "The bulk of the money is collected before race day."

"What's your point?" Thompson asked.

Manning feathered the stack of papers. "It doesn't show up. I see lots of expenses, but little income."

"The financials Margaret gave you are from last month. Those numbers are old news."

"I'm not talking about last month's financials," Manning said. "I'm talking about deposits. I don't see credits that reflect anywhere near the revenue that should have been received."

"What figures are you looking at?"

"The bank account. Checks and deposits."

"Where did you see the bank records?" Thompson's eyes darted to the papers in Manning's hands. "I hope Richard didn't leave old statements floating around for the world to see."

"I wasn't looking at old bank statements. I've been going through the account online."

"Online!" Thompson exclaimed. "Who authorized access for you? It takes a board resolution to authorize a new signatory to the account."

"Not if you're the master," Manning replied, surprised by how good it felt to call himself that. He hadn't said it to be arrogant, but he couldn't deny the surge of pleasure he felt from the look of resentment on Thompson's face. "The account was set up giving signatory to Richard and any subsequent master or masters. Doug produced the board resolution voting me in as master and Jay Barnsby had me authorized on the account."

"Well, I wish I'd been informed," Thompson said, shooting a look at Margaret. "I've been the sole authorized user—Richard had no interest in online banking—so I'm not geared toward coordinating banking activities with anyone. There's a risk for disaster if the right hand doesn't know what the left hand is doing."

Manning said, "I haven't been doing anything. I've just been observing."

"Okay," Thompson said slowly.

"So, back to the account. Why am I not seeing deposits for race revenue?"

Thompson managed to look bored and irritated at the same time. "Do you really want me to go into detail? It's far more complex than you probably care to know about."

"Try me."

"All right. There's more than one bank account. I keep a separate account for the races."

"Why's that?" Manning asked.

"For one thing, I decided to set up an online merchant services account for ticket sales for the races this year. I thought it would be a good trial. If we're happy with the process, we can use it in the future for members to purchase tickets to the hunt ball, even pay their membership dues online."

"You couldn't set that up with the hunt account?" Manning asked.

"I could. But we needed a separate race account anyway in order to get the ABC license to sell liquor." Thompson wet his lips, looked at Margaret. "You remember how we went round and round about that at the board meeting and I finally discovered that we could get the license if we set up a separate nonprofit LLC for the races?"

Margaret nodded. "I remember it seemed like a convoluted process, but the bottom line was you came up with some way for us to be able to sell booze."

"That's right." A slight smile lit Thompson's eyes. "As Richard used to say, 'There's more than one way to skin a cat.' Anyway, the merchant account dumps the online payments into the race account, not the hunt account. That's why you didn't see many deposits."

"But I saw checks for race expenses written on the hunt account," Manning said. "If the race revenue flows into a separate account, shouldn't the expenses be paid from the same account?"

Thompson smirked at him, as if he were a naïve child. "Sure, in an ideal world. But at the time I wrote the checks we didn't have sufficient funds in the race account to cover them, so I used the hunt account. If you've been online, you probably saw that I used the hunt account for the donation check to the environmental council. Once all the online payments process through the race account, I'll transfer funds to the hunt account."

Manning frowned. "No, I didn't see the donation check. Which means it hasn't cleared the account. You wrote the check for ten thousand, right?"

"You know I did," Thompson replied.

"Then the donation check will bounce. The hunt account has a balance of less than ten thousand dollars."

"Bounce! What in God's name are you talking about?" Margaret demanded.

"Manning's making this more complicated than it has to be," Thompson said, flapping his hand dismissively at Manning. "We have overdraft protection on the hunt account. The check won't bounce, but you'll recall, Margaret, I was against the idea of presenting the check at the races and you overruled me."

"That's true," Margaret said.

"Well, no harm done," Thompson said. "I knew how important it was for you to honor Richard that way. If we didn't have overdraft protection I wouldn't have gone along with it, but I knew it was just a temporary cash-flow problem. Trust me, it will all sort out in the end."

Trust him? Far from it. An uneasy feeling crept over Manning. Maybe his judgment was colored by his aversion to Thompson, but there was too much smoke and mirrors for his liking. Two accounts, with a line so blurred it might as well not exist.

"Why doesn't the race account show up in online banking?" Manning asked.

"You have to log in to each account separately," Thompson replied. "They're different LLCs with different tax ID numbers. You probably didn't request online access to the race account."

Manning went on full alert, confusion rocketing to distrust. How could he request access when he didn't know the account existed? "Was Richard authorized on the race account?"

"I honestly don't recall. Possibly not. There would have been no need. Richard never wrote checks. I handled everything." Thompson glared at him. "Look, Manning, I don't like where this conversation is heading. I've busted my ass—sorry, Margaret—for this hunt, and I resent you marching in and questioning how I operate. If you want to deal with the finances by yourself, be my guest. I guarantee you'll end up appreciating the way I've managed things. It's not easy handling the books for an outfit that operates in the red. I pride myself on the fact that the bills always get paid on time."

How hard is that when all you've had to do is tell Richard to deposit more money in the account? Manning thought. But he refrained from saying it.

"We all appreciate your efforts on behalf of the hunt, Thompson," Margaret said. "But I think with Richard's passing and Manning taking a fresh look at things, it has spotlighted how you were single-handedly managing the hunt finances. Not only does that put a big burden on you, it's not good business practice. This seems like a good opportunity for us to spread out the responsibilities, relieve some of your burden."

"Fine with me," Thompson said, though his tight-lipped look implied otherwise.

"Good." Margaret glanced at her watch. "I'd like to wrap this up. I left Duchess locked up at home. Do either of you have anything further to discuss?"

Manning had plenty more to ask, but first he wanted to see the race account. "How do I get authorized to access the race account?" he asked.

"I would think a simple call to the bank is all it should take," Margaret said.

Thompson shook his head. "I'm not sure. It may take a board resolution."

"Will you find out?" Margaret asked Thompson.

"Sure. No problem."

"When?" Manning asked.

"Christ, you're really champing at the bit, aren't you?" Thompson said. "I'm snowed under at the office, but I'll try to drop by the bank before the end of the week. Beginning of next week at the latest."

"In the meantime, why don't you print out the financials for Manning and give him bank records for the race account," Margaret said.

Thompson's shoulders sagged as he blew out a loud breath. "I guess I could do that. But I've got to tell you, I'm feeling double-teamed here."

"Nonsense," Margaret said. "The sooner you help Manning get up to speed on things, the sooner he'll be able to help shoulder some of the bookkeeping burden." She nodded at the built-in filing drawers beneath the bookcase. "Are the bank records in these files?"

"No. They're at my house."

"Then why don't you run down and collect them. You can print off the financials at the same time. Manning and I will swing by for them on our way out. There are a few other files I want to gather for Manning before we lock up here."

Thompson shot a look at his watch. "I have a business dinner to attend."

"That's all right," Margaret said. "We won't be long here."

Thompson snatched his jacket from the back of his chair. "Give me ten minutes."

Neither Manning nor Margaret spoke until the front door banged closed.

"Thanks for backing me up," Manning said.

Margaret pressed her lips together and eyed him thoughtfully. "I don't know if your suspicions are correct—I hope to God they're not—but I think you've raised some legitimate questions."

"I just can't believe Richard let Thompson have free rein with the finances," Manning said. "Thompson paid the bills, kept the books, and reconciled the bank accounts. With no checks and balances. And apparently no oversight from Richard."

"Now don't go blaming it all on Richard. The board knew Thompson was handling everything. In fact, Doug raised a concern about it at one board meeting and we all just brushed it off." Margaret shook her head. "Now that I think about it, we really just turned the finances over to Thompson with blind faith. When Dottie Weymouth quit hunting and retired from the board, we were thrilled that Thompson volunteered to fill her shoes as treasurer. We knew Thompson was an accountant. We just assumed the books would be in good hands. Stupid of us, I guess, considering he'd only been a member of the hunt for a couple of years."

"See, the fact that Thompson's an accountant just adds to my doubts about the numbers," Manning said. "He specializes in auditing companies to see if they're cooking the books, for God's sake. Generally, auditors have no mercy. They're usually the type who'd go around a battlefield shooting the wounded. Yet Thompson's all loosey-goosey about the two accounts, moving money back and forth to suit the needs of the moment."

"I hear you." Margaret pushed herself up off the love seat. "I think I'll place a call to Doug now and ask him to have Jay Barnsby take a look at those two accounts."

"Sorry, Margaret, I can't allow you to do that."

Thompson's voice came from behind them. His tone hard, confident. Chilled with an air of authority.

The hair pricked on the back of Manning's neck as he spun toward the hall.

Thompson stood in the doorway, a pistol gripped in both hands. Aimed squarely at Margaret.

"Don't even think about it, Manning. I can see you're trying to figure out a way to play hero. You make a move, and I'll blow Margaret's brains out. Then turn the gun on you. You think I won't do it?" Thompson's lips twisted into a sneer. "Ask Richard."

*N*either Miguel nor the other man had spoken a word since they'd left the parking lot at Big Lots. They'd been driving for about twenty minutes, and had turned off Sterling Boulevard into a residential area about five minutes ago. Miguel made a series of turns that seemed to be taking them in a circle. Abigale figured the indirect route was to ensure they weren't being followed. And to make sure she wouldn't be able to lead the cops back to Dario.

The truck splashed through standing water so deep Abigale felt the floorboards vibrate beneath her feet. Water sprayed up over the hood and the truck fishtailed to the left as the wheels fought for traction, then righted again.

"Mierda!" Miguel swore.

The truck slowed, then pulled up to the curb in front of a four-story apartment complex. Warped orange shutters hung like faded beacons against tired brown siding. Rivulets of mud meandered past cast-off toys in a dismal yard of crabgrass and mud.

"We meet Dario here," Miguel said. "Inside."

Abigale eyed the bleak building. She had managed to rein in her initial rush of fear by reminding herself that she was the one who had requested the meeting with Dario, that the fact Miguel had brought someone with him probably just meant he was being cautious, making sure he had protection in case she double-crossed him.

She was sandwiched between Miguel and the other man as they dashed up the cracked sidewalk and squeezed down an alleyway between two apartment buildings. Her jacket offered no protection against the icy rain that pelted her face. They skirted a Dumpster that looked as if it hadn't seen a garbage truck in weeks, where rodents scoured brazenly among rotting food and garbage bags, indifferent to the rain or the threat of humankind. A single caged bulb hung crookedly above a graffiti-covered metal door midway down the alley. By the time they halted in front of the door, Abigale's frozen legs shivered uncontrollably beneath her drenched jeans. Miguel banged once. The door swung toward them.

A young Hispanic woman with a mop of curly black hair and skinny-legged jeans held the door open, then clanged it closed behind them. She tossed her head in the direction of a staircase that ascended behind her. Her feet slapped the cement as she danced up the stairs ahead of them. Rap music blasted down from the second floor, the volume cranked so loud Abigale could feel the bass vibrate in her chest.

She stole a sideways glance at Miguel's companion. His ball cap still covered half his face, but even so, she could tell he was young. Maybe in his early twenties. His expression said *don't mess with me*. He shoved his right hand in the pocket of his hoodie, exposing the grip handle of a pistol. Abigale shot a glance at Miguel.

"Is okay," Miguel said hurriedly. "Jaime, he protect us."

Angry fists hammered a wall above them. A gruff voice bellowed, "Shut that fucking crap off!" The music instead got louder.

Miguel kicked a beer bottle out of the way and grabbed her arm. "Come on."

*M*argaret's jawed ached. She'd worked her lips so sore she could taste the metallic bite of blood in her saliva, yet the duct tape still clung to her mouth like a tick on a dog. She'd rubbed her wrists raw, too, having stretched and twisted the duct tape so much it now clamped around her like sticky ribbons of steel. And, damn it, she knew better than that. Every horseman who'd ever duct-taped a hoof knew that the tape only got stronger, tougher, the more you stretched it. Yet she hadn't been able to resist the urge to pull against the leg of the utility sink to which her wrists were bound, hoping she could use the metal as leverage to loosen the tape and slip a hand free.

She could tell by the muffled grunts whispering through the dark that Manning was struggling against his restraints, too. Thompson had bound Manning with his legs straddling the support beam in the center of the room, his ankles duct-taped together, his hands behind his back. Manning's face had blanched pale as a corpse when Thompson had grabbed his broken arm and wound the tape around his wrists. *God help him, the amount of pain he must be feeling with it twisted behind him like that!*

They were in the basement of Dartmoor Glebe, in the darkroom Richard had built for Abigale when she'd won her Pulitzer. Richard had loved the fact that in this digital age Abigale had a collection of old cameras, still liked to piddle around and shoot rolls of black-and-white, even develop her own film. He had planned to surprise her with the darkroom when—if—she ever came back to Virginia. As far as Margaret knew, Abigale had no idea the darkroom even existed.

Not only was the room windowless, but Richard had designed the space to be virtually soundproof as well. The darkroom shared a wall with Richard's workshop, and he had said he wanted Abigale to be able to lose herself in her work, not be disturbed by him hammering or drilling on the other side of the wall. *Quiet as a tomb* was how he'd described it. Painfully prophetic.

Margaret found it hard to judge how long they'd been locked in the darkroom. Her inability to see—or hear beyond the four walls—had robbed her of her sense of timing. She guessed it had been less than an hour. She had no idea whether Thompson was still in the house, but if he'd left, she expected he'd be back soon.

There was no way he could keep them hidden in the darkroom for long. Too many people knew about their meeting. Smitty. Abigale. When she and Manning didn't come home, Dartmoor Glebe was the first place they'd look, and Thompson the first person they'd contact. Besides, Manning's car was parked out front. And her truck was down at the barn.

But what the hell would Thompson do with them? Kill them, no doubt. Thompson had probably decided that as soon as he realized Manning had caught on to his financial shenanigans. She wondered if Richard had figured it out as well—that Thompson was cooking the books—and confronted Thompson, and that's why Thompson had shot him.

Fear, anger, and dread all swirled in Margaret's heart. But mostly anger. Thompson had killed Richard. Betrayed them all. And he might kill her and Manning in the end, too. But she wasn't going without a fight. If nothing else, she'd find a way to leave some kind of clue so Thompson didn't get away with this.

The girl waited for them at the top of the stairs. They caught up to her, then followed her into a long hallway of ugly beige walls. The stench of garlic and onions saturated the air. Miguel walked in front of Abigale, Jaime half a pace behind. They'd gone maybe twenty yards when the music abruptly cut off. Half a minute later, the door to one of the apartments flew open and three men strolled into the hall. Abigale's first impression was of testosterone and tattoos, low-slung jeans and close-cropped dark hair. One of them wore a white wife-beater undershirt. He folded his arms across his chest and tucked his hands under his armpits to pump up his muscles. The other two fell into place, flanking him on either side.

Abigale felt Jaime's hand on her back, pushing her forward. No one spoke. Miguel and the girl kept walking. Jaime slid around to Abigale's left, positioning himself between her and the men. The gaze of the one in the wife-beater undershirt focused on Jaime, and Abigale saw fear in his eyes. Jaime uttered something in Spanish, and the three men backed against the wall to allow them to pass.

The girl walked past two more apartments, then stopped and rapped lightly on an apartment door. "It's me."

The door instantly opened inward, revealing a tiny one-room apartment. The threadbare carpet was littered with dust bunnies, scraps of paper, and a couple of bags from fast-food restaurants. Battered aluminum blinds hung in a tangled mess from the lone window and a stained mattress was shoved against the wall. A closet-sized kitchenette was tucked into the corner next to a closed door that Abigale assumed led to a bathroom or closet. Light from a fluorescent bulb in the kitchenette flickered across the room, casting long shadows into the corners.

Dario Reyes stepped out from behind the door as it swung closed behind them. He draped his arm around the girl's shoulders. Jaime leaned his back against the door.

Abigale's heart pounded in her throat. She eased out a breath. "Hello, Dario. Thanks for meeting with me."

Suspicion and hope clashed in his dark eyes. "You his niece, the guy who get murdered?"

She nodded.

"I did no kill him."

"But you were there, in your car?"

"*Sí.* I run out of gas. I wait for my friend to come get me."

"Tell me what you saw," Abigale said.

Dario glanced at the girl, who gave him an encouraging nod. "I don't see who do it. I just hear the shot."

"Did you see a vehicle?"

Dario nodded. "*Sí. Dos.* The sports car and the SUV."

The chill that ran through Abigale had nothing to do with her wet clothes. "Tell me about the sports car."

"It was BMW."

"Was the sports car heading into Longmeadow when you saw it?"

"No. Back down St. Louis Road. To Middleburg." He shrugged. "I was no feeling well, so I close my eyes. Just chill and wait for my ride. The guy gunned the engine. It make me look and I see him drive off."

Abigale held her next question for a moment, not sure she wanted to hear the answer. "Did you see the sports car leave before or after you heard the shot?"

"Before," Dario answered without hesitation.

"Are you sure?"

He nodded. "An hour maybe."

"You saw the BMW leave Longmeadow an hour before you heard the shot?"

"*Sí.*"

Relief gushed through Abigale. *Dario could prove Manning was innocent.* "Tell me what you saw after the sports car drove away."

"I fall asleep; when I wake up it almost dark. My friend he should be there by then, so I think maybe he get lost. I take out my cell to call him. That's when I hear the shot."

"Just one shot?"

"*Sí.* From a rifle. I figure some guy shoot a deer."

"What happened next?"

"*Nada.* I try to call my friend, but my phone battery dead. So I just chill."

"You mentioned earlier that you saw an SUV. When was that?"

"Maybe ten minute."

"Ten minutes after you heard the shot?" Abigale asked.

"*Sí.*"

"Was the vehicle driving into or out of Longmeadow?"

"Out."

That had to be the killer. "Can you describe the SUV?"

Dario shrugged. "No really. It was dark."

"Do you remember anything? The shape of the headlights?"

"The guy don't have his lights on when he drive out."

"But you could tell it was an SUV?"

"*Sí.* He stop and close the gate after he drive out. Even in the dark, I can tell it is SUV."

Abigale thought of Larry's car. "You're sure it couldn't have been a Ford Focus?"

"No, it was SUV."

So it wasn't Larry. "Can you describe the driver?"

Dario shook his head.

"Nothing at all?"

"No."

"But you're sure it was a man?"

Dario thought about it. "No."

Damn it. He had to have seen something. Even if the headlights were turned off, the interior light would have gone on when he opened the door. Abigale asked, "When the driver opened the door to get out and close the gate, did you see the inside of the vehicle?"

He shook his head.

"Didn't the interior light come on?"

"No."

Abigale wondered fleetingly whether Dario was fabricating the story about the SUV to draw suspicion away from himself. "If it was too dark to see the car or the driver, how were you able to see him—or her—close the gate?"

Dario said, "I don't see him do it. But my friend pull over by the gate when he pick me up and I see it closed. So I figure the guy in the SUV must have close it when he get out of his car."

"And then he drove off down the road without his headlights?"

"*Sí*. He turn them on before he get to the curve."

"You couldn't see the vehicle then? The color, anything?"

"I think it was dark color."

Abigale thought of Tiffanie Jenner's black Mercedes SUV. "Could it have been a Mercedes?"

He shook his head. "It no have Xenon headlights."

"I thought you said the headlights were turned off."

"*Sí*, when he first drive out. But then he turn them on."

"Right, but the vehicle was driving away from you then. So how do you know what kind of headlights it had?"

"Xenon headlights, they light up the whole road blue." Frustration danced in Dario's eyes. "Look, I can no describe it any better. That's all I see. Just basic SUV. No fancy headlights, no roof lights, no jacked-up wheels."

Abigale figured she'd pushed the SUV questions as far as she could, even though she hadn't learned much. A basic SUV. That narrowed it down as much as describing a house in the Swiss Alps as a chalet. "Did you see or hear anything else?"

Dario shook his head.

"And you didn't see the SUV drive into Longmeadow. Just out."

"*Sí*."

So, had it been at Longmeadow all along? Even when Manning was there? Or had it driven in when Dario was asleep? Abigale regarded him for a moment. Or, was Dario making the whole thing up? "Why didn't you go to work the next day?" she asked.

"I was sick. I puke my guts out all night." His expression hardened. "Bad timing for me, *sí*?"

"Running didn't help any. You could have cleared it up if you'd talked to the authorities."

Something flickered in his eyes. "That's no how it work in my world. The cops, they would have throw me in jail."

The girl slipped her arm around Dario's waist. "Miguel say if Dario tell you what he see you can help him."

Abigale nodded. She needed to convince Dario to turn himself in. He might not have seen enough to identify Uncle Richard's killer or help them find Larry, but he could clear Manning.

The heater in Miguel's truck didn't work, and by the time Abigale climbed back in the Subaru at Big Lots her hand shook so violently she had a hard time inserting the key in the ignition. "Come on, come on," she muttered through chattering teeth. The engine roared to life and she turned the Subaru's heater on full blast, ignoring the cold air that gusted in her face. It would heat up soon enough. She fished her cell out of her bag and pressed the speed-dial button for Manning's house.

Manning didn't answer so she called his mobile, feeling a pang of disappointment when it went directly to voicemail. She tapped impatiently on the steering wheel while she waited for the beep.

"Where are you? I have some really good news. I can't wait to tell you. I'm on my way home. Call me."

Abigale disconnected the call and fingered the phone. She debated whether to call Margaret's to see if Manning was there, but decided against it. If he was at Margaret's and had deliberately ignored her call on his cell, he was no doubt having a conversation she shouldn't interrupt. The cell chimed in her hand and she saw she had a text message. She thumbed to her messages, frowning when she saw it was from Manning. Odd. He'd never texted her before.

She opened the message: *Went to PA with Margaret to look at some hounds. Not sure when I'll be back.*

Pennsylvania? She typed: *Did you get my message? I have good news.*

The windows in the car had fogged up, and Abigale slipped the knob to defrost while she waited for Manning to respond.

What's the good news?

She hesitated. She definitely didn't want to tell him about her meeting with Dario in a text message. *Can you call me?*

Several minutes passed before she received a reply. *Can't. Bad cell service. Can only text.*

Damn it. *Never mind. I'll tell you when you get home. How late will you be?*

We're staying overnight. Please let Smitty know. And can you feed Duchess? She's at Margaret's. Thanks. I'll talk to you tomorrow.

What the hell? Since when had Manning started referring to his mother as "Margaret" instead of "Mother"? And why in the world would he and Margaret decide on a whim to go off to Pennsylvania to look at hounds? It made no sense. Unless . . . She remembered Margaret telling her she had tried to get Manning to seek treatment for his drinking at a facility in Pennsylvania. Had Margaret convinced Manning to check himself in?

"*I*sn't that nice! Abigale has some good news to tell you, Manning," Thompson said, snapping Manning's cell phone shut. "You don't suppose she could be in the family way, do you?"

"Fuck you, Thompson."

"I'll take a pass on that. You're not my type."

Manning and Margaret were still bound on opposite sides of the room, but Thompson had removed the duct tape from their mouths. Manning exchanged a look with his mother. *Jesus Christ!* Thompson had gone off the deep end. Before Thompson had texted Abigale, he'd ranted for a good ten minutes about how no one in the hunt appreciated him. How Richard had always been one to "take, take, take," giving nothing in return, so he had decided to do a little "taking" of his own.

Thompson came right out and admitted that he'd been embezzling money from the hunt. He'd started out with the small stuff, paying vet and shoeing expenses for his personal horses out of the hunt bank account, then saw the opportunity to siphon off "more meaningful" sums by setting up a separate race account. He told them Richard had grown suspicious, confronting him about it at Longmeadow, and Thompson had shot him. Thompson showed no remorse about killing Richard, even seemed to believe that Richard had deserved it. In fact, the only regret he'd expressed was that he'd had to leave Richard's hunting rifle behind because it was too identifiable— he didn't want to risk getting caught with it.

Manning studied the brash, haunted look in Thompson's eye. Thompson's behavior reminded him of the cocaine addicts he'd been around in Los Angeles.

Arrogant, emboldened, yet paranoid at the same time. He never would have pegged Thompson as a cokehead. He seemed too straitlaced for that. But if Thompson did have a cocaine habit, it could be what had dragged him underwater financially. Or maybe he'd turned to coke to escape his financial troubles. Not that it mattered. Either way, they were screwed. Margaret had tried to reason with Thompson, talk him into releasing them, but he'd just laughed at her.

Thompson stuffed Manning's cell phone in his back pant pocket and grabbed the roll of duct tape. "I asked Abigale to feed Duchess for you, Margaret. Wasn't that nice of me?"

"Thank you," Margaret replied in a measured tone, obviously trying not to rile him. "You know how much she means to me."

"I do. And I will see to it that she's cared for when you're gone. You have my word."

"You're out of your fucking mind if you think you can get away with this," Manning said. Margaret shot him a warning glare, but Manning didn't care. They weren't going to talk Thompson out of killing them by being nice to him. But if he could get Thompson to reveal how he planned to kill them, they might have a chance. At least they'd be prepared. "What are you going to do, fake another botched robbery? You really think you can pull that off twice?"

Thompson tilted his head as if considering Manning's remark. "Actually, that's not a bad idea. Given the fact you both warned Abigale not to stay here alone for fear Richard's murderer might decide to burglarize the house. But I challenged myself to come up with a more creative solution for your demise."

"Yeah? You're a smart guy, Thompson, but you won't be able to think your way out of this one. Someone will come looking for us. Half a dozen people knew we had a meeting here with you today. My car's parked out front, for Christ's sake."

"Was," Thompson said. "Your car *was* parked out front. I've taken care of it."

He ripped off a strip of duct tape with his teeth, plastered it across Manning's mouth. "Ah, that feels good. You have no idea how many times I've wanted to shut you up, cut off your cocky remarks."

Manning jerked his head back, twisting to the side, but with his hands and feet bound he had no way to evade Thompson. He shut his eyes against a bolt of pain that sliced through his injured arm.

Thompson taped a longer strip across Manning's mouth and around to the back of his head, then turned to Margaret. "As for you, Margaret, I wouldn't be honest with you if I didn't admit this gives me a certain amount of pleasure. You've bossed me around—everyone, actually—for so long, I think it will be good for you to see what it feels like."

Margaret's eyes hardened defiantly. "Just answer one question for me."

"What's that?" Thompson asked.

"Did you put Richard's watch in Manning's coat pocket?"

Thompson smiled. "Of course. You see, that was a perfect example of you getting too bossy for my liking. You were starting to steer the murder investigation away from Dario Reyes and I just couldn't have that. So I gave you an incentive to stop pushing the *maybe-it-was-someone-who-knew-Richard* theory."

Margaret frowned. "It wasn't but a lick before I took the coats to the cleaner that we'd discussed whether someone from the hunt could have killed Richard. We started speculating when Manning was injured and discovered someone had cut the billet straps on Richard's saddle. I already had Manning's coat in my truck."

"That's right," Thompson said. "And after that discussion you told Manning you were taking his scarlet coat to the cleaners and offered to take mine as well. Your timing couldn't have been better. Frankly, I was at a loss trying to figure out how to blow up your insider theory, but, thank you, you presented me with the perfect opportunity. I got my coat and Richard's watch from my house, and when I put my coat in your truck I slipped the watch in Manning's pocket. As much as I hated to part with such a fine watch, I figured it was a win-win situation for me. You'd either turn the watch over to the sheriff and Manning would be implicated, or you'd keep it to yourself and make sure the sheriff backed off the insider theory. Quite honestly, my money was on you turning Manning in, but I guess I underestimated your affection for your golden child. Or maybe you just wanted to sweep a scandal under the rug."

Manning stared across the room at his mother. *Jesus. She'd found Richard's watch in his coat pocket?* No wonder she'd treated him the way she had. A lump formed in his throat as he realized she'd probably thought he was guilty as hell, but had covered up for him anyway.

"Actually, now that it's served its purpose, I'd kind of like to have the watch back," Thompson said. "Did you stash it at your house somewhere?"

When Margaret didn't reply, Thompson said, "Never mind. It will turn up at some point, when they go through your things. Won't that cause a stir? Wonder if anyone will think *you* killed Richard, Margaret?"

"Were you the one who cut the billet straps on Richard's saddle?"

Thompson wagged a finger at Margaret. "See, there you go again. Trying to run things. I agreed to answer *one* question. But just to satisfy your curiosity, yes, I did cut the billet straps. And I'm man enough to admit that was a mistake. It almost upset my plan. But it was a temptation too big to resist. I was in the barn that morning when Manning was tacking up Henry and the idea just popped into my head. The prospect of Manning hurt—or killed, if I got lucky—was simply too enticing to pass up."

He cocked his head and smiled. "I learned something from that experience, though. Never underestimate anyone, no matter how much of an imbecile you think they may be. Take Larry, for example. I would have sworn that lazy son-of-a-bitch was dumber than a fence post, but he saw me in the stall with Henry that morning after Manning had tacked him up, and he managed to put two and two together. I think Larry died happy, though. Before I put a bullet through his tiny brain, I told him I knew he wasn't as stupid as folks thought he was."

"Good God. *You killed Larry?*"

"Yes, I did. He's buried in the manure pit right behind Richard's barn. A fitting resting place, don't you think?"

Thompson tore off a strip of tape and wound it around Margaret's mouth. She glared at him as he yanked on the tape, but Manning saw her flinch with pain.

"Oh, Margaret, I'm sorry, that must hurt where you've rubbed your skin raw," Thompson said, clucking his tongue in mock sympathy.

Manning's hands balled into fists. *Goddamned son-of-a-bitch! Real ballsy, bullying a seventy-year-old woman who's bound and can't fight back. Just give me one chance, Thompson,* he thought. *I'll rip you apart with my bare hands.*

Thompson paused in the doorway, glanced around the darkroom as if making sure he hadn't forgotten anything, then flipped the switch, plummeting them into blackness.

"Oh, and don't worry about Abigale coming looking for you, Manning. I texted her that the two of you went on a little hound-shopping expedition. No one expects either of you home tonight."

bigale ended up bringing Duchess back to Manning's house with her, unable to resist the dog's pleading brown eyes. The rain had turned the long gravel drive into a channel of mud and ruts. Thank God the Subaru had all-wheel drive; she doubted Manning would be able to make it in his BMW.

The cozy house felt empty without Manning there and Abigale was happy she had Duchess with her. She flipped on all the lights and lit a fire in the hearth, then headed for the shower. Fatigue set in as she peeled off her wet clothes. She let the hot water beat down on her.

As the warmth seeped through her, disappointment that Dario hadn't been able to provide more information about the SUV began to eat away at her elation that he could clear Manning. Was she any closer to finding Uncle Richard's killer? *No.* In fact, what Dario had told her had eliminated the people she'd had suspicions about. Tiffanie drove a Mercedes SUV, which Dario claimed would have been recognizable by its bright bluish headlights. The black Hummer she'd seen at Tiffanie's house was out, too. It was too big, and covered with all kinds of gaudy running lights. Same thing with Percy's monster truck. It had roof lights, and running lights galore.

The fact that Dario claimed he hadn't seen the SUV drive into Longmeadow didn't answer the question of whether it had been there when Manning was there. Whether he'd seen the person—the killer—and would be able to identify him. If only he could remember! Or had the killer arrived later? After Manning left. While Dario was asleep.

And what about Tiffanie's visit? Assuming Dario was right about the Xenon headlights, he hadn't seen Tiffanie's Mercedes. But she'd been there. She'd admitted so herself. So that implied she had arrived and departed earlier. Before Manning got there. Tiffanie claimed that when she arrived at Longmeadow, Uncle Richard was waiting for someone. Was it Manning? Or the driver of the SUV?

She had given Tiffanie until 5:00 p.m. tomorrow to call Lieutenant Mallory. Once Mallory had a chance to question both Tiffanie and Dario, he'd be able to get a better fix on the timing, making sure both their stories meshed. But first, she had to find the right attorney to represent Dario. Someone who could work a deal if he turned himself in. She was counting on Manning or Margaret to know who the right attorney would be.

Abigale forced herself out of the steamy shower and dressed in one of Manning's T-shirts, then wrapped herself in his terry-cloth robe. She wasn't really hungry, but she had a low-blood-sugar, out-of-it kind of feeling, so she knew she had to eat something. She heated up some of the chicken noodle soup she'd bought for Manning and carried the hot mug to the couch in front of the fire. Duchess followed her like a shadow. When she settled down with her camera and laptop, the dog stood by her knees, eyeing the couch expectantly. Abigale didn't know whether Margaret let Duchess up on the furniture. Probably not. But she figured Manning wouldn't mind.

"Come on, girl," she said, patting the cushion next to her. The Lab jumped onto the couch and sprawled out, her head resting against Abigale's leg with a contented sigh.

She sipped the soup while she booted up her laptop and downloaded the shots she'd taken at Dartmoor Glebe the previous afternoon. She'd called her mother that morning, promising her she'd email pictures by tomorrow. Her mother had sounded stronger than she had in a long time. She'd even told Abigale she was going to talk to her doctor about making the trip to Virginia, saying she wanted to come home.

Abigale spent over an hour sorting through the pictures, deciding which ones to send. She lingered over the shots she'd taken of her hunt horn and spurs, trying to decide whether or not to send them to her mother. She knew the dented horn would conjure up memories of Abigale's relationship with Manning, and she didn't want to upset her mother. On the other hand, her mother had saved Manning's letters for her. Maybe it was finally time to talk about it.

She had taken half a dozen different shots of the horn and spurs on a moss-covered log nestled in a clump of trees in front of Dartmoor Glebe. She eyed each shot critically. For most, she'd focused on the horn and spurs, and the house was blurred in the background. But she'd shot several with the house in focus and the foreground blurred. Her mother might like those more. She selected one, enlarging it so it filled the laptop screen. The house looked so tranquil—wait . . . was the front door open? She zoomed in. *It was.*

Abigale quickly scrolled back to the first photo in the series. The door was closed. She clicked on the next one. Still closed. The third photo showed a man standing at the front door. She clicked ahead and saw the man's arm extended, pushing the door open. In the next one, he walked inside. Then, wide-open door, and, finally, closed door.

Who was he? She hadn't noticed anyone around when she'd shot the photos. But, then again, she'd been focused on her work. And he probably wouldn't have noticed her, because she was hidden in the trees. She enlarged the shot of him opening the door and zoomed in on his head. He was in partial profile, but it was blurred. Still, something about him was familiar . . . She leaned closer, squinting at the screen. She caught a glimpse of the tip of a bow tie peeking out next to the lapel of his tweed jacket. Was it Thompson? She zoomed out, then back in, gradually. Studied his physique. His posture. *Yes.* She was sure of it.

But that made no sense. Thompson had handed her his key to Dartmoor Glebe the night he'd come in the house during the storm. How had he opened the front door yesterday? She remembered checking to make sure all the doors were locked when she'd gone to pick up her things. She zoomed in on the shot where Thompson was pushing the door open. His left hand was on the door handle, his right on a key in the dead bolt. So where did he get a key?

Abigale sank back against the couch, staring at the slide. She was sure there were some spares floating around. Margaret had said as much. But who gave one to Thompson? And why had he used it? When he'd returned his key to her last week, he'd told her he didn't feel comfortable entering the house unannounced.

She thought about calling Thompson, just coming right out and asking him. He might be offended, but she wanted to know. Besides, Thompson had been with Manning and Margaret this afternoon. He might be able to shed some light on why they had suddenly decided to drive to Pennsylvania. She glanced at the clock on her laptop. It was after ten o'clock. She'd call him first thing in the morning.

C H A P T E R

87

*M*anning awoke with a start, his heart slamming against his chest. He'd heard something. What was it? He strained to hear. There it was again. A faint scraping sound. Back and forth. It was coming from inside the room. Had his mother figured out a way to cut herself loose? It didn't sound like something cutting through duct tape, more like metal scraping against stone, like fingernails on a chalkboard. He pictured the way she was tied, with her arms around the leg of the freestanding utility sink. Maybe she was working on the screws, trying to remove the metal leg. That had a long shot at succeeding. But right now, a long shot was all they had.

He had no concept of what time it was—no idea how long he'd dozed off—but he figured it had to be morning by now. It seemed as though hours had passed since Thompson left, though living in complete darkness took away one's sense of time. So did lack of nourishment. It wasn't that he felt like eating, but his stomach grumbled noisily for food and his throat felt as if it was lined with sandpaper.

The scraping sound was unremitting. A slow back-and-forth, with an occasional screech. He cocked his head, angled to hear better. Suddenly, the door burst open and light flooded the room. Blinking against the brightness, Manning saw his mother drag her bound arms down the sink leg and scoot to face away from the sink. They locked eyes and he raised an eyebrow, but she just gave a slight shake of her head.

"Time to rise and shine," Thompson said, swinging the door closed. His muck boots squeaked on the cement floor, leaving muddy treads as he crossed the room.

"Look here, Manning. I brought you breakfast." He plunked a bottle of Early Times whisky on the stainless-steel developing table, then reached down and tugged at the tape on Manning's face. His mouth tightened with annoyance as the strips stuck together.

"See, that's the problem with duct tape." Thompson whipped a box cutter out of his back pocket. "It's a sticky little bugger." He slid the blade to the locked position, then whipped it across the tape behind Manning's ear. White-hot pain shot down Manning's neck.

"Oops. Looks like I nicked you," Thompson said, ripping the strips of tape from Manning's face. "Don't worry. There won't be time for infection to set in." He balled the duct tape into a wad and tossed it into the utility sink like a basketball. "And he scores!"

Manning clenched his jaw against the searing pain, exchanging a look with Margaret. If Thompson retrieved the tape from the sink, would he see what Margaret had been working on? She must have had the same thought, because she leaned back and rested her head against the center of the sink basin.

Thompson unscrewed the cap on the whisky. "Sorry I couldn't spring for Maker's Mark, Manning. I'm on a bit of a tight budget these days. But I figured beggars can't be choosers, right?"

Manning yanked his head back as Thompson pressed the bottle to his lips.

Thompson chuckled. "No sense trying to be virtuous at a time like this. Consider it your last supper." He waved the bottle slowly in front of Manning's face. "Come on. You know you want it."

The brown liquid sloshed in the bottle, sending Manning's thirst spiraling. And not just for something wet. He'd fought like hell not to drink booze since Abigale had arrived, but the sour mash aroma kicked his longing into high gear. His licked his parched lips but clamped his jaw shut.

"Come on." Thompson shook the bottle enticingly, the way you'd try to lure a dog with a treat.

Manning turned his head to the side. "Get that the fuck away from me."

"Sorry, not an option." Thompson grabbed a fistful of Manning's hair, yanked his head back, and jammed the mouth of the bottle between his lips. Whisky glugged out, flooding Manning's mouth, and he gave in for a moment, let the beautiful burn sluice down his throat and quench his thirst.

No! Manning shoved aside the craving and fought the urge to swallow. Whisky pooled in his throat, gagging him. He whipped his head to one side, then the other, broke Thompson's grasp, and pulled away from the bottle.

Thompson jumped back as Manning choked, spewing a mouthful of whisky. As Manning coughed, gasping for air, he tried to wrap his mind around what Thompson was doing. There was more to this than Thompson giving him his "last supper." There was a reason Thompson wanted him drunk.

"Careful, some of that went down the wrong way," Thompson said. He set the bottle on the table. "I'll give you a minute to catch your breath."

Manning's chest heaved as he struggled to breathe. "What the hell are you doing?" he demanded in a strangled whisper.

Thompson flashed a cold smile. "We're going on a road trip. And you get to drive."

"You want me to drive drunk?"

"Something like that." Thompson grabbed the bottle by the neck. "Time for round two."

Even though Manning knew what was coming and fought like hell not to swallow, a healthy dose of whisky slid down his throat. Thompson waited until Manning stopped sputtering, then crammed the bottle in his mouth again. And again. A numbness crept over Manning, robbing him of his strength—even his desire—to fight. He felt the edge melt off his pain, ratcheting the throb in his arm down to a bearable ache.

"There you go. It feels good, doesn't it?" Thompson set the bottle down. "Just wait a minute. Don't get too greedy."

Jesus Christ. Manning closed his eyes and felt the room begin to spin. What the hell was Thompson up to?

Thump-thump-thump. As Manning's eyes flew open, he saw his mother kicking her feet against the floor.

"What's the matter, Margaret? Do you want to say something?" Thompson asked.

Her eyes flashed at him.

"Okay. Certainly. I didn't mean to exclude you from the party."

Thompson knelt beside her, avoiding skin this time as he sliced the duct tape with the box cutter. He stripped the tape from her mouth. "Sorry, there's just no easy way to do that."

Tears glistened in Margaret's eyes, but a fierce determination steeled her face. "What are you doing, Thompson?"

"Isn't that obvious?"

"You're getting Manning drunk. Why?"

Thompson rose, then spread both hands against the developing table.

"The two of you are going to suffer an unfortunate automobile accident."

A chuckle vibrated in Manning's throat, exploding into a hearty laugh. "That's your brilliant plan to kill us? Get me drunk and hope I get in an accident? I've got news for you, Thompson, I have a fair amount of experience driving drunk. We just might survive."

"No. You won't. You see, it's raining like a son-of-a-bitch outside. Flood warnings are in effect for the entire D.C. area until midnight tonight. The waters are raging in Goose Creek. Add the slick roads, a drunk driver, and you have a tragic combination. If the crash doesn't kill you, the floodwaters will."

*A*bigale checked the wall clock in Margaret's kitchen. Again. Three o'clock. And still no sign of the furnace repairman. She'd rushed over there shortly after nine a.m. when she'd received a text message from Manning asking her to go to Margaret's to meet the serviceman. She'd spent the day lounging around with Duchess, watching television. Waiting.

At least Manning was on his way back home. She still hadn't spoken to him, just received a couple of text messages. But he'd promised he'd be home by dinnertime. She couldn't wait to tell him about her meeting with Dario. And she also wanted to get his take on the photo she'd captured of Thompson entering Dartmoor Glebe. Abigale had tried calling Thompson earlier, but there was no answer at his house or on his cell and she didn't want to leave a voicemail. She had sent Manning a text with the picture, even though she doubted he'd be able to see much viewing it on his cell phone. He had texted her back, asking why she'd sent the photo, and she'd replied that she'd tell him when they spoke.

Abigale's cell rang and she snatched it up, relieved to see Manning's number on the Caller ID. "Hello?"

"Hey. It's me."

"I'm so glad you finally called. Where are you?"

"On our way home."

The call was full of static, but even so, Abigale could tell Manning's voice sounded odd. Strained. "It's a bad connection. I can barely hear you. Are you driving in bad weather?"

"Kind of."

"It's pouring rain here. There are all kinds of flood watches. Be careful."

"I will."

Manning's tone was flat. Abigale wondered if he and Margaret had been arguing. "Are you okay?"

"Yeah. I'm fine. Jus' tired."

Was he slurring his words? "How far away are you?"

"Uh, I dunno. A ways."

He *was.* "Is Margaret with you?"

"Yeah."

"Who's driving?"

"Me."

"Manning, have you been drinking?"

"Lissen, I've gotta go, Abby. Just—"

"What?"

"Develop your pictures."

Develop her pictures? What was he talking about? She used a digital camera. Manning knew that.

"Wait! Don't hang up. Can I talk to Margaret?"

"She can't talk right now."

Dread dropped like a lead weight in her stomach. She couldn't talk? Was Margaret really with him? She couldn't imagine Margaret letting Manning drive drunk. "God, Manning, I'm worried about you driving. Maybe you should spend the night wherever you are and drive home in the morning."

"I can't. Abby, lissen to me, okay? Know the photo you sent me of the hunt horn?"

"Yes."

"R'member that day you lost it and I rode back to get it in the storm?"

"Of course I do."

"Think about that."

What did that mean? "I don't understand, Manning. Are you saying you'll be okay driving even though it's raining? It's not the same thing. And you're not eighteen years old anymore."

"Jus' think about it. I've gotta go. I love you, Abby."

Abigale felt her world start to spin. Manning had never told her that before. "Manning, wait—Manning?" He was gone. She punched redial, but the call went immediately to voicemail.

She paced the kitchen, cell phone clutched in her hand. Something was wrong. She was certain Manning had been drinking. And he'd sounded so down, said things that made no sense. Developing pictures? And mumbling about the hunt horn? Why had Manning chosen this time to tell her he loved her? It was almost as if he was saying goodbye. She tried to push away the horrifying word—*suicide*—but it buzzed around her mind like a pesky fly. She had to find out if Margaret was with him.

She called Margaret's cell phone. Voicemail. *Damn it!* She scrolled through her list of calls, pressing redial when she found the number for the kennels. She'd spoken to Smitty last night, after she'd received Manning's text asking her to let him know that Margaret was staying in Pennsylvania overnight. Smitty hadn't known anything about Manning and Margaret looking at hounds in Pennsylvania.

"Hello?"

"Smitty, hi, it's Abigale. Have you heard from Margaret?"

"Hello, Abigale. No, I haven't. Have you?"

"No. I just spoke with Manning."

"You sound upset. Is something wrong?"

Abigale hesitated. Should she tell Smitty that she thought Manning was driving drunk? That he sounded depressed? "I'm just worried about him driving in this weather."

"Yeah, I hear ya. The roads are flooding something awful. I'd feel a lot better myself if they weren't in that sports car of his."

Manning's sports car? "Are you sure they're not in Margaret's truck?"

"Sure as I'm standing here. I just drove right past it; it's still parked in front of the barn at Dartmoor Glebe."

"That makes no sense. I assumed they drove Margaret's truck to Pennsylvania."

Smitty chuckled. "You ever driven Manning's BMW M Coupe? It's a right bit more fun to take on a road trip than a truck."

"Maybe, but what about Manning's broken arm? Shifting gears?"

"He's been driving it. Must be he's making out all right."

"But that was before he had Kevin cut his cast off."

"Well, where there's a will there's a way. I can't imagine Manning wanting to drive Margaret's old truck. And even though she'd never admit it, I think Margaret gets a kick out of riding in the BMW. Besides, if they're on the highway, there ain't much shifting involved."

"Yeah, I guess you're right. Will you call me right away if you hear from either of them?"

"Sure will."

"Thanks, Smitty."

Abigale grabbed Margaret's hunt directory and sank down on a kitchen chair. Duchess, who had been eyeing Abigale anxiously from her dog bed, lumbered over and flopped down by her feet with a weary snort. "I feel the same way, girl," Abigale murmured, patting her on the head.

She felt a little better after talking to Smitty. Maybe there was nothing to worry about beyond the safety of the BMW on flooded roads. Still . . . the whole trip just didn't make sense. She flipped through the hunt directory until she found the listing for Thompson. She hadn't wanted to call him at the office to ask why he had a key to Dartmoor Glebe, but she didn't mind interrupting him at work to ask about this. If he could shed some light on the hound trip, she'd feel a whole lot better. She pressed the keys for his office number.

"Good afternoon, Knightly and Knightly."

"Thompson James, please."

A few seconds ticked by. "Just a moment."

Abigale rubbed Duchess's stomach with her foot while she listened to elevator music.

"Hello, who is this?" a man's voice demanded.

It didn't sound like Thompson. "Abigale Portmann."

"Why are you calling here for Thompson James?"

Abigale hesitated. Maybe Thompson wasn't allowed to receive personal calls at work. "I need to speak with him. It's a bit of an emergency."

"Well, you won't find him here. James hasn't worked here for a couple of months."

Abigale stared at the number in the phone directory. "Are you sure?"

"Yeah, I'm sure. You a friend of his?"

"Yes. Sort of."

"Then pass on a message when you talk to him. Tell him Donald says he has one more week to settle his tab. He'll know what I mean."

The doubts about Thompson that had been nagging Abigale since she'd viewed the photo of him entering Dartmoor Glebe mushroomed into full-blown alarm. She'd heard Thompson make comments several times since she'd been there about how busy he was at work. Did he have a new job and the hunt directory just hadn't been updated? No. The night she'd met Thompson, he'd told her he worked at Knightly & Knightly. She remembered that clearly. Not that he used to work there; he'd said he was a partner. But according to the man on the phone, Thompson hadn't worked there in months. So Thompson had lied. She thought back to their encounter when he'd come into the house to look through her uncle's files. In the middle of the night. At the time, she'd written it off. Pegged Thompson as a workaholic. Was that it? Or was he doing something underhanded with the files?

Abigale pictured Manning, slumped over the computer trying to make sense of the hunt bank account. He'd found something in the numbers that bothered him. Something he planned to ask Thompson about. She wished she had paid more attention to his concerns, but she was so caught up in her own meeting with Dario that she'd barely given it any thought. And now, something was wrong with Manning. Something that went beyond his normal moodiness. Beyond his drinking. She could feel it. Did it have something to do with the meeting with Thompson? Had something happened at the meeting with Thompson that had caused Manning and Margaret to go on this mysterious trip to Pennsylvania?

Damn it! She jumped out of the chair and grabbed her cell phone. To hell with waiting for the furnace repairman. Duchess followed her to the mudroom, wagging her tail expectantly as Abigale shrugged into her raincoat.

"Come on, girl," Abigale said. "We're going to Dartmoor Glebe."

*T*hompson yanked the Luger out of Margaret's mouth and let her slump to the floor. "What a good son you are, Manning. I know how hard it must have been for you to lie to your precious Abigale. I could tell you wavered once or twice, but even in your drunken state you knew I'd pull the trigger on Margaret, didn't you?"

He powered down Manning's cell phone. "I think that was nice, though, the way you said goodbye to Abigale. And how you reminisced about riding back in a storm to retrieve her hunt horn. I'm sure she'll carry that memory with her for a long time."

Manning didn't bother to reply. Thompson had made a mistake showing him the picture Abigale had sent in her text message. Of course, Thompson didn't know that the trail near Goose Creek was where he'd found the hunt horn. *But Abigale did.* And when she discovered that something had happened to them, maybe she'd figure out he'd been trying to tell her to look for them by Goose Creek.

"Of course, Abigale will also remember the way you slurred your words," Thompson continued. "The sad fact that you were drunk. Poor girl, she'll probably blame herself for not doing more to prevent you from driving home. But then, that was the point of the call, wasn't it? We want to make sure they know right off the bat that you were intoxicated, so some deputy doesn't get a hair up his ass and conduct too thorough an investigation when they find your car in Goose Creek."

"You've thought of everything, haven't you, Thompson?" Manning muttered.

"I have. In fact, why don't you drink to that?" Thompson shoved the bottle in Manning's mouth. "Bottoms up."

He waited until Manning stopped sputtering and had caught his breath, then plastered a fresh strip of duct tape across his mouth. "Be careful not to puke now. If you asphyxiate yourself, you'll ruin all my plans."

Thompson tossed the roll of duct tape on the developing table and crouched down next to Margaret. "It's showtime," he said, slicing the duct tape that bound Margaret's feet.

Manning let his head drop to his knees. He tried to fight the fog that coddled his brain, but numbness sucked him toward oblivion. He was vaguely aware of Thompson hauling his mother to her feet and shoving her toward the door. Then darkness engulfed the room and he let it swallow him up.

*A*bigale pulled around to the back of the house—*her* house—and parked as close as she could get to the mudroom door. Wind whipped rain in her face as she opened the driver's door. She quickly slammed it, then tugged the back passenger door. "Come on, Duchess!"

Duchess trotted ahead to the house while Abigale scurried gingerly across the wet leaves on the stone walkway. Abigale fumbled to insert the key in the lock and the Lab nudged between her legs and the door, thumping her tail impatiently. "I know, just give me a second," Abigale murmured.

The lock turned and Abigale stumbled over Duchess as they both tumbled into the mudroom. She shoved the door closed and flicked on the light switch. Looking down at her jeans, she saw that they were drenched. Just from the short jaunt to the door. She bent down and plucked a crimson maple leaf off the sole of her boot. She shucked off her rain jacket and tossed it over an empty hook.

The house was gloomy and had a musty, unlived-in smell. There was still an hour or so until nightfall, but the darkened skies seemed to ooze into the house, dimming every crevice. Abigale switched on lights as she headed toward her uncle's study. She checked the front door just to make sure it was locked, that she hadn't misread the blurry photo and erroneously assumed Thompson had a key in his hand. She even reached out and jiggled the dead bolt to satisfy herself it was fully engaged.

Faint traces of footprints crossed the oak flooring leading from the oriental carpet down the hall toward the study, as if confirming that was where Manning's and Margaret's meeting with Thompson took place. She switched on her uncle's desk lamp and glanced around the room. Duchess sniffed the love seat and looked at Abigale with a pleading wag of the tail. "Sure, go ahead," she said.

The Lab leapt onto the cushion and circled around for a comfortable spot. Abigale eyed her uncle's desk and bookshelves, not really sure what she was looking for. Nothing seemed out of place. The file drawers were all closed. No papers were strewn around. Abigale's hopes melted to disappointment. What had she expected? A note, telling her what had happened? Evidence of some kind of scuffle? It was ridiculous when she thought about it, to blame Thompson for Manning leaving town, for his drinking. Thompson had likely been dishonest about some things—maybe even cooked the books—but Manning's troubles went beyond that. And the answer didn't lie here.

She thumbed the switch on the desk lamp. "Let's go, Duchess."

Duchess plodded along at Abigale's side, her tail drooping forlornly as if she sensed Abigale's mood. But when Abigale switched off the foyer light and crossed the kitchen toward the back door, the Lab held back.

"Come on, girl."

The dog just stared at her from the hallway.

"Duchess, come on."

Duchess skulked toward her, stopping halfway across the kitchen.

"What's the matter, girl?" Abigale walked over to the dog. "What is it?"

The Lab barked and bounded back to the hall. Abigale followed her and found her prancing in front of the basement door. What was she all wound up about? She bent down to pet the dog, then froze—Duchess's paws danced impatiently amidst a blur of human shoe prints. She whirled around, following the prints with her eyes. How had she missed the parade of shoe prints leading back and forth from the basement door to the mudroom?

Abigale squatted down. The prints had a thick tread mark, like those from work boots or muckers. They were fairly large, possibly from a woman with big feet but more likely from a man. She peered closer and saw the smattering of paw prints. A shiver shot up her spine. Duchess's paws should be dry by now. She reached down and smeared a fingertip through one of the fresher-looking shoe prints. It was still wet.

"Good girl," Abigale murmured, throwing an arm around the dog. Duchess let out a shrill bark and nudged the door with her nose. "No," Abigale whispered. "Shhh, take it easy now."

She jumped to her feet, her heart pounding in her ears. Should she go down there? A voice in her head screamed for her to call 9-1-1. She glanced at the bottom of the door. No light shined through the strip. Whoever belonged to the shoe prints had to be gone. But someone had been down there. *Recently.* She eased the door open and peered down the steps into blackness.

Duchess stood statue-still and cocked her head, listening. Abigale brushed her fingertips across the dog's silky ear. "Do you hear anything, girl?" Duchess looked up at her and whined.

Abigale sucked in a deep breath. "Okay, let's go," she said softly. She tugged on the cord that hung from the wall, bathing the stairwell in light. Slowly, she lowered her foot to the first step. Duchess leapt past her, toenails skittering across the cement stairs. "Easy," Abigale called in a loud whisper. "Wait!"

Duchess skidded to a stop and stared up at her. Abigale's boots tapped quietly as she hurried down the stairs. The stairwell bulb flooded a path of light a few feet from the base of the stairs. Beyond that was inky darkness. She remembered being down there as a kid: she and Manning used to play "rock, paper, scissors" to settle who would dash into the blackness and pull the next light cord. She doubted Manning was truly afraid of the dark, but she was. And, sometimes, he would wait until she was swallowed by the shadows and then let out an evil shriek. She always knew he might do it—and she swore that she wouldn't react—but no matter how much she steeled herself for it, she invariably jumped and screamed.

Abigale pushed into the dark, wishing Manning was with her now. Duchess pressed against her leg as they inched forward. Abigale's arms stuck straight out in front of her, blindly feeling for the dangling cord. Her fingertips brushed it but batted it away. Damn it. She groped the air and finally wrapped her hand around it.

She squinted against the sudden light, orienting herself. The basement was as she remembered it. The long center room was empty, except for a pile of outdoor furniture stacked along one wall. Her uncle's workshop was at the far end. Her eyes stopped at a door in the shadows next to the workshop. That was new since she'd last been down there. She looked down at the cement floor. The shoe prints were less noticeable than on the floor upstairs, but she saw a faint trail leading through the dim light toward the unfamiliar door.

"Come on, girl," Abigale murmured to Duchess. Every nerve in her body seemed on fire as she neared the door. She balled her hands into fists to stop the trembling. The door fit snugly against the frame and had a metal threshold across the bottom. No way to tell if a light was on inside. A dark bulb was mounted above the door frame, reminding Abigale of a signal outside a darkroom. She grasped the handle, half-expecting it to be locked, but the knob turned easily in her hand. Abigale pushed gently and the door swung open.

Muted light spilled onto a cement floor and the stale scent of booze tickled her nostrils, reminding her of a fraternity house on a Sunday morning. Was this some kind of liquor cellar? She groaned. Of course. Uncle Richard used to store the alcohol for hunt events down here. He must have decided to build a special room for it.

Relief and disappointment collided and Abigale slumped against the door jamb. Now the shoe prints made perfect sense. Smitty or someone else had probably been restocking unused boxes of liquor from the races. Or Uncle Richard's memorial service.

Abigale heard Duchess whine inside the room and she groped along the interior wall for a light switch. Her fingers fumbled across a small picture frame, knocking it off kilter. She slipped her hand higher, frowning as it bumped another frame. Why would Uncle Richard hang pictures on the wall of a storage room? She stepped into the room and squinted at the wall, catching the outline of a switch-plate cover. She flicked on the switch, then blinked rapidly as she stared at a wall of her framed photographs.

She sucked in a breath and spun around. *It was a darkroom.* Abigale stepped forward and ran her hand along the cool edge of a shiny new developing table. Guilt washed over her. Uncle Richard must have built the darkroom for her. And she'd never come back to visit. She fingered a roll of duct tape that lay on the table as she glanced around the room at the professional developing equipment.

Abigale heard the clink of glass and she peered over the table. Duchess's tail swept across an overturned bottle of booze as she nosed around the cement floor. Abigale crouched down beside the dog and grabbed the bottle. The stench of whisky almost took her breath away. The bottle was half empty, but the cap was screwed on tight. So where did the smell come from? She rocked back on her heels and fingered a splattered stain on the cement floor. Whisky. And it was damp. Someone—Manning?—had been drinking in here. Not long ago.

Manning's slurred speech rang in her ears, his illogical comments. Had he lied to her about going to Pennsylvania and been holed up here the whole time? Getting drunk? If so, where was he now? And where was Margaret?

She thought back on that afternoon's phone conversation. Manning had said something about developing pictures. When she'd asked him if he'd been drinking, he'd said, "Develop your pictures." *He must have been talking about this room.* But that suggested he wanted her to come here and find him. Her earlier suicide fears tumbled down on her.

"Oh, Manning," she whispered. "Where are you?"

Duchess looked over at her and wagged her tail, then went back to nosing eagerly around a thick beam that ran from floor to ceiling. Abigale frowned. What was that? She scooted over next to the dog and picked up a tangled mess of duct tape that lay on the other side of the post. It was sticky, but not tape-sticky. Something was smeared on it. She held it closer—and snatched her hand away as if it had burned her. The tape was covered with blood.

Abigale jumped to her feet. "Come on, Duchess. Now!"

Something had happened in this room. Something bad.

Abigale punched 9-1-1 on her cell phone as she raced up the stairs to the kitchen. She stumbled over her words as she tried to explain the nature of the emergency, then finally shouted that someone had broken into the house, figuring that would bring a patrol car quicker than a missing-person call. She jabbed the key to disconnect the call, then called the hunt kennels.

Smitty answered, and she said, "It's Abigale. Have you heard from Manning or Margaret?"

"Not a lick," he drawled. "They still not back from Pennsylvania?"

"No, and something's going on. I'm not sure what, but I found something in the basement. I called 9-1-1, but can you come over here?"

"Of course." Smitty's voice darkened with concern. "Where are you at? Margaret's?"

"No, I'm at Dartmoor Glebe."

"Just sit tight. Doug's here with me. We're on our way."

The remnants of the sandwich Thompson had for lunch roiled in his stomach as he maneuvered the truck and trailer around the tight turn onto Snake Hill Road. He'd encountered only a handful of vehicles since leaving Dartmoor Glebe. Too bad one of them was Doug Cummings. Not that he was all that worried about it. He'd waved casually at Doug and their vehicles had slipped past each other on the curvy two-lane road like oil through water, each disappearing into the storm. Later, after the BMW was found in Goose Creek, the memory of seeing Thompson driving down Foxcroft Road would probably be the last thing on Cummings's mind.

Water sluiced down the pavement as the rig lumbered up the steep incline. The back entrance leading to the stables at Coach Farm was just another hundred yards or so on the left. Once he turned in there, he'd be home free. He knew the Petersons were at a carriage-driving competition in New Jersey. And if anyone did happen to be around, he'd just say he'd come to pick up the carriage Richard had loaned them. He'd say Margaret had sent him—she wouldn't be around to contradict him—then he'd hem and haw a bit, and decide against loading the carriage on the trailer in such bad weather. He could even feign concern that Margaret would be irked with him for disobeying orders. Anyone who knew her would likely sympathize with him.

The thought of Margaret tied up in the cargo area behind the seats of the BMW pleased him. She'd been compliant, almost submissive, when she was in the basement, but when she'd seen the BMW inside the carriage trailer she had started kicking and struggling like a feral cat. It had probably hit home, the inevitability of what he was about to do.

Margaret's outburst had caught him off guard; even with her hands bound she'd damn near slipped out of his grasp. Not that she'd have made it very far, but still, timing was everything, and if Smitty or Michael or someone else had driven up the drive just at that moment and seen them struggling in front of the house he'd have been screwed. He'd hauled her right back into the trailer and ended up knocking her out to get her in the back of the BMW.

Manning, on the other hand, hadn't even put up a struggle once it had registered through his drunken fog that he had a gun barrel pressed against his neck. Of course, Thompson had counted on that. He knew even the most belligerent assholes could be overpowered if they were drunk enough. A lesson he'd learned from his stint as a waiter at an off-campus pub during college.

Thompson drove up the narrow gravel lane to Coach Farm and stopped the rig in front of the barn. So far, so good. No vehicles in the courtyard. Barn doors closed. No light peeked through the cracks. The place was deserted.

He snapped his waxed barn coat all the way up to his neck and patted his pocket to make sure the magnetic hunt logo he'd taken from the truck's passenger door was still there. If anyone saw him hiking back up the road after he sent the BMW into Goose Creek, he'd say a tree branch had brushed the logo off the door when he'd made the turn onto Snake Hill Road. That he'd seen it in the side mirror, didn't want to risk stopping the rig on the road, yada yada, had walked back to look for it. But if luck kept going his way—and no reason it shouldn't—he wouldn't encounter anyone. No one would be out and about in this weather if he didn't have to be.

An excited calm slithered through Thompson. He'd make it back to the truck unobserved, wait for the 9-1-1 call, and be the first responder. Make sure he was all over the scene, the bodies, to explain away any evidence that might be found that linked him to the accident. Same reason he'd shown up at Longmeadow, gone up in the stewards' stand when the call about Richard came in. Being an EMT had its advantages.

Thompson smirked, thinking about how Manning had accused him of being stupid for handling Richard's wallet after the dog dug it out of the bushes. Quite the opposite, actually. Nice how that had worked out.

He'd be even more thorough this time. Scour the darkroom from floor to ceiling. Mop his shoe prints off the kitchen floor, the hallway. Wash the tire tracks out of the trailer. Not that he expected anyone to have reason to search any of those places. But he wouldn't leave anything to chance.

Thompson jammed a baseball cap on his head and swung the driver's door into the rain. Time to get the show on the road.

*S*mitty and Doug arrived at the house in less than five minutes, dashing through the rain toward where Abigale stood waiting at the mudroom door.

"What's going on?" Smitty asked as soon as he ducked through the door.

Abigale quickly told them how odd Manning had sounded when she'd spoken with him on the phone, that she was pretty sure he was drunk. Then she relayed what she'd found in the darkroom. "If Manning was hiding out down there—drinking—that's one thing. But there's blood."

Doug and Smitty exchanged a glance. "Okay, show us what you found," Doug said.

"You go on," Smitty said. "I'll wait up here for the deputy and bring him on down when he arrives."

Abigale showed Doug the bloody duct tape first.

"Is this where you found it?" he asked, taking a pen from his pocket and turning the tape over to examine it.

"No, it was over there." Abigale pointed at the floor-to-ceiling support post. "I picked it up, just thinking it was trash, then dropped it when I realized there was blood on it."

Doug glanced at the post, then slowly eyed the rest of the room. His gaze lingered on Duchess who had followed them downstairs and was busily sniffing around the utility sink in the corner, her nose stretched out as if trying to capture a certain scent. Doug reached the sink in three strides and leaned over the basin. "There's more duct tape in here."

Abigale rushed to his side. Several tangled strips and one balled-up wad of tape littered the sink basin. Doug lifted one long strip gingerly with his pen.

Short strands of wispy gray hair dangled like spider legs from the tape. Abigale felt as if someone had socked her in the stomach. "That looks like Margaret's hair."

"Yeah." Doug dropped the tape back in the sink and gave her a look that left little doubt what he was thinking.

She shook her head. "No. I know what you're thinking. Manning would never harm his mother."

"I don't think he would either, Abigale, but we have to consider the possibility. You yourself said you could tell something wasn't right with Manning when you talked to him. And given the blood—" he shot a look at the sink—"and Margaret's hair . . ."

Abigale looked away and Doug gave her shoulder a gentle squeeze. "If Manning held Margaret captive here—even if, God forbid, he harmed her— we'll get help for him, I promise you. But right now we need to find him. And find Margaret."

She nodded, swallowing the salty tears that stung her throat. "I know."

"Okay, so think back carefully to your phone conversation. Did Manning say anything that provided a clue to where he might be?"

Abigale replayed the conversation in her mind. It did seem as though Manning had been giving her clues. He'd talked about developing pictures, obviously referring to this room. And he'd mentioned the photo of her hunt horn. What exactly was it he'd said? Something about riding back to get it in the storm—

Duchess scrambled away from the sink and banged into Abigale's legs, almost knocking her off balance. The Lab's golden coat rose into a ruffled line down her back and she let out a low growl, her eyes fixed on the doorway. Abigale listened, then heard the sound of men's voices, heavy footsteps.

"Sounds like the deputy's here," Doug said.

To Abigale's surprise, Lieutenant Mallory and another deputy followed Smitty into the room. She hadn't asked for Mallory when she'd called 9-1-1. Was it a coincidence he'd shown up?

Mallory must have seen the look of surprise on her face, because he said, "Just so happens we were checking out a flooding situation on Hibbs Bridge Road, so we were close by. What have we got here?"

Mallory listened without interrupting as Abigale recapped what she'd found. When she finished, he said, "Just so I get this straight, when you spoke with Manning on the phone this afternoon he told you he was in his car on his way home from Pennsylvania."

"Yes."

His expression hardened. "But the evidence in this room tells us he and Mrs. Southwell probably never went to Pennsylvania."

Evidence. The word shot through Abigale like shards of ice. "Maybe not."

"Manning's car went somewhere, though," Smitty said. "I saw it parked out front when I drove out late yesterday afternoon, and when I went back to check on the hounds last night it was gone."

"Okay. He hid the car somewhere so no one would come here looking for them." Mallory's eyes swept across the three of them. "Any barns or buildings on the property where he could stash it?"

Smitty nodded. "Yes sir, a couple."

"We'll have you show those to us when we finish in here." Mallory surveyed the room. He glared at Duchess, who had plopped down in front of the utility sink. "Let's get the dog out of here. We don't need the scene compromised any more than it already has been."

"I'll get her," Abigale said. "Come on, Duchess."

Duchess's brown eyes flickered, but her head didn't move from its resting place between her front paws. Abigale bent down and tugged gently on her collar. "It's okay. Come on."

The Lab lurched up slowly, her tail between her legs. "Good girl," Abigale said.

"Hold on. What's that?" Doug said as Duchess followed Abigale away from the sink. He squatted down by the sink leg. "It's a woman's ring."

Mallory quickly crouched beside him.

"That's Margaret's," Smitty said, eyeing the gold ring.

Mallory scooped the ring into a plastic bag and held it up toward the light. The fox-mask crown was worn smooth, the ruby eyes dulled with age.

"Richard gave the ring to Margaret years ago," Smitty said. "She wore it every day."

"Why do you suppose she took it off?" Mallory mused.

"Margaret don't make a habit of doing things for no reason. Might be she left it as some kind of clue," Smitty said.

"Could be." Mallory studied the ring thoughtfully. "But a clue as to what?"

"That she was here?" Doug said.

Maybe. Abigale looked at the three men. Or did Margaret leave the ring to draw their attention to the sink? "Are you sure there's not anything else under there?" she asked.

Mallory pulled the flashlight off his belt and flashed it around the floor, the underbelly of the sink. "I don't see anything." He ducked his head and crawled out backward. As he raised himself on one knee to stand, the flashlight beam bounced across the unglazed front of the porcelain basin.

"Wait, shine the light there again!" Abigale pointed at the sink front.

Smitty frowned. "It's all scratched up."

"It's not just scratched," Abigale said. "It says something."

"You're right," Doug said. "Look, there's a letter 'T' right here." He traced his finger just above the chalky surface, first following a horizontal, then a vertical line, each about six inches long.

Mallory shined the light along the scratch mark Doug had outlined, then slid it to the right. "There's another letter next to it. It looks like another 'T.'"

Doug shook his head. "I don't think so. Look here, the line doesn't stop at the bottom. It's faint, but there's a tail on the end. It's a 'J.'"

"Yeah, you're right," Mallory said. "It says 'TJ.'"

Abigale felt as though a floodgate opened in her brain when she heard Mallory say the letters. *TJ.* God! How could she have been so stupid? TJ wasn't Tiffanie Jenner. It was Thompson James. Now it all made sense. *The fox in the henhouse.* When Uncle Richard had made that comment to Michael, he must have been talking about Thompson stealing money from the hunt, not Charles Jenner having an affair. Uncle Richard must have become suspicious about the hunt finances just like Manning had, and he'd set up a meeting with Thompson at Longmeadow to confront him. That's why he'd called Jay Barnsby at the bank the day he died. That's why he'd written *TJ* in his journal. And the "basic" SUV Dario had seen drive out of Longmeadow after the gunshot was Thompson's Explorer.

"Thompson James. TJ is Thompson!" Abigale said. "That's who killed Uncle Richard. And now he's done something to Manning and Margaret."

Doug shot a look at Mallory, then said to Abigale, "Okay, slow down. Tell us what you're talking about."

Abigale told them first about her meeting with Dario.

"Are you telling me you knew the location of our prime suspect in Mr. Clarke's murder and you didn't contact the authorities?" Mallory demanded.

"I didn't know his location," Abigale replied. "I was taken to the meeting place by friends of his."

Mallory regarded her icily: "But you were in contact with individuals who knew Reyes's location and you kept it to yourself! That's called aiding and abetting."

"I didn't look at it that way," Abigale replied. "In my job, I meet with informants all the time. I know how crucial secrecy is."

"Reyes isn't a *source*, Ms. Portmann, he's a fugitive." Mallory glared at her, then waved a hand. "Continue."

Abigale told them about the notation in Uncle Richard's journal, the appointment Manning and Margaret had to talk with Thompson about the hunt finances yesterday—the day they "disappeared" on the mysterious trip to Pennsylvania—and the strange text message from Manning referring to his mother as "Margaret," which she now realized must have been sent by Thompson. She described the incident when she'd found Thompson going through the files in the middle of the night, and told them about the photo of Thompson unlocking the front door. About how she'd called Thompson's office and found out he hadn't worked there in a couple of months. Mallory took notes as he listened, his expression alternating between interest and skepticism.

When she finished, Doug said, "Jesus Christ. I passed Thompson on Foxcroft Road on my way here."

"Was anyone in the vehicle with him?" Mallory asked.

Doug shook his head. "Not that I noticed. But he was driving the rig Richard used to transport his carriages. He could have had Margaret and Manning in the trailer."

"He could've put Manning's BMW in there, too," Smitty said.

Mallory turned to the other deputy. "Find Thompson James. And put an APB out for the rig Mr. Cummings saw."

"I can give you a description of the rig," Smitty said. "And show you where Thompson lives. He rents the gatehouse right here at Dartmoor Glebe."

"All right. Come with me," the deputy said.

After they'd left, Mallory said, "I met Thompson James the day the dog dug up Mr. Clarke's wallet, and I wouldn't place odds on him being able to overpower Manning." He glanced at the whisky bottle. "If James did hold them captive here, he may have given Manning booze to try to gain an advantage over him, but he still must have had a weapon of some kind. Do either of you know if James owned a gun?"

Doug shook his head. "I know he went duck hunting with Richard a couple of times, but I think he used one of Richard's guns."

"*Uncle Richard's Luger.* Thompson knew where to find it," Abigale said.

Mallory's eyes narrowed at her. "Explain."

Abigale told him how she had used the gun for protection the night Thompson had surprised her with his midnight visit. "He was right there when I put the Luger back in Uncle Richard's nightstand. If Thompson needed a gun, he knew right where to find it."

Doug bolted for the door. "I'll check the nightstand."

Mallory's eyes roamed down his notes. "Tell me more about the phone call. You said you thought Manning was trying to give you some kind of message when he made the comment about a ride he took to find your hunt horn."

"Yes." Abigale shook her head. "But I can't figure out what he was trying to tell me. I don't know if he was talking about being out in the storm, or actually going to get the hunt horn, or what."

"Could he have been talking about something he saw or something that happened when he went on the ride? Was Thompson James on the ride with him?"

"No, we didn't even know Thompson then. It happened seventeen years ago."

"Seventeen years? I assumed it was recent." Mallory rubbed his hand across his forehead. "So what would he expect you to remember about that incident after all this time?"

Abigale gave a frustrated sigh. Maybe Manning hadn't meant anything beyond the fact that it represented how much he cared about her. He'd said it right before he told her he loved her. But the way Manning had said "just think about it" implied—

Doug rushed into the darkroom. "The Luger's gone," he said breathlessly.

Mallory's mouth tightened. He glanced at his watch and asked Doug, "What time did you see James on Foxcroft Road?"

"Maybe forty-five minutes ago. An hour, tops."

"So he has a good head start. Although . . . driving a rig like that will slow him down, especially in this kind of weather. If we're lucky, he might even hit a detour. We've got men out all over the county closing roads because of high water. They're saying Goose Creek might go over its banks before this is all said and done."

"Goose Creek, that's it!" Abigale said. She felt hope wash over her like a wave. "I dropped my hunt horn riding up the steep trail out of Goose Creek. That must have been what Manning was trying to convey to me. Thompson took Manning and Margaret somewhere near Goose Creek. That's why he was driving down Foxcroft Road when Doug saw him!"

Thompson shifted the BMW into reverse and backed slowly down the
trailer ramp. He considered whether he should close the ramp, just in case
anyone came by before he got back. He didn't want to risk anyone snooping
in the trailer and noticing the tire marks. On the other hand, he wanted to have
the option to quickly hide the car back in the trailer in the event he ran into
trouble. He decided on plan B and left the back wide open.

Margaret was still out cold in the cargo compartment behind the seats.
He'd removed the tape from her mouth and wrists so all he'd have to do with
her was buckle her into the passenger seat. Manning's wrists were still taped
as a precaution, but he could easily have gone ahead and removed those, too.
Manning was passed out in the passenger seat, head against the side window,
snoring up a storm.

Thompson knew he had danced a fine line with the booze. He needed
Manning drunk enough so he wouldn't put up a struggle or be able to get himself
out of the car after it hit the water. But Thompson also needed to be able to walk
Manning around to the driver's side. Manning outweighed him by a good thirty
or forty pounds, but Thompson knew from experience that as long as he could
keep Manning on his feet he'd be able to pull it off. He'd helped throw drunk
football players out of the college pub on more than one occasion.

Twilight was quickly fading, but Thompson left the headlights off. He
didn't want to attract attention to the car, neither now nor when it went into
Goose Creek. The longer it took to discover the car, the better.

Thompson stopped at the end of the gravel drive and made sure the glow
of approaching headlights wasn't visible in the distance. Nope. All systems
go. The engine growled as he sped onto Snake Hill Road and he gunned it a

little, feeling a thrill as the BMW fishtailed on the wet pavement. Nice car. It was a shame he had to total it.

He slowed as he crested the hill, checking his rearview mirror for head-lights. Nothing. Just gunmetal gray sky. Thompson eased the car about halfway down the steep incline, stopping about twenty yards above where Snake Hill Road met Foxcroft Road at a T, just shy of where the car would plunge into Goose Creek. He shifted to neutral and yanked up on the parking brake. Thompson reached down and fumbled for the empty beer can he'd placed in the car earlier. He wedged it under the brake pedal, just in case Manning was coherent enough to try to step on the brake. No one would think twice when they later discovered the beer can. Not with Manning in the driver's seat. He flung the door open and hopped out.

Thompson had conducted several dry runs without actually moving Manning and Margaret, and he knew he could get them into position in less than two minutes if he didn't hit a snafu. But time was of the essence. This was the most vulnerable part of his plan. If someone came along between now and when he sent the car into the creek, he was pretty much screwed.

He pulled the Luger from his jacket pocket and yanked the passenger door open, bracing a knee against Manning so he wouldn't tumble out. Rain almost blinded him as the wind smacked him in the face, but he didn't allow it to slow him down. He sliced the duct tape around Manning's wrists and stuffed it in his jacket pocket.

"Okay, big boy. Time to get up," Thompson said, swinging Manning's legs so his feet were on the pavement. He slipped Manning's arm around his shoulder, then slid his arm around Manning's waist and heaved him to his feet, jamming the barrel of the gun against Manning's side. Manning groaned, then mumbled something about hurting his fucking arm.

"Another couple minutes, you won't feel any pain," Thompson said. He stumbled under Manning's weight but managed to support him, bowed low against the wind, as he led him to the driver's seat, then stuffed him inside.

Thompson left the driver's door open and ran back for Margaret. He flipped up the hatchback, hoisted her out, and deposited her in the passenger seat. *Click.* Buckled her in. Just like clockwork.

He slammed the passenger door, pulled down the hatchback, and ran back to the driver's side. Manning had slumped forward, hugging the steering wheel. Thompson shoved Manning's chest back against the seat and yanked the seat belt into place. He lowered the driver's window and pushed the door closed, then slipped the Luger in his right-hand jacket pocket.

Thompson surveyed Foxcroft Road for any sign of headlights and checked behind him on Snake Hill Road, listening to make sure he didn't hear the sound of an approaching vehicle. All quiet, except for the soft thump of the windshield wipers and the purr of the engine.

Thompson's heart pounded in his ears as he leaned through the window opening. He guided the steering wheel with his left hand, making sure it was headed straight on course, and grabbed the brake lever with his right, his thumb poised to plunge the release button. Exhilaration pumped through him, a thrill like he'd never experienced. He hesitated for a split second, savoring it.

"Happy trails," he muttered, pressing the knob. He lowered the brake lever and the car instantly started to speed down the hill. Thompson ran with it for a few steps, steadying the steering wheel, until the speed became too fast and his feet began to drag. As he released his grip on the wheel and pulled back, Manning's left arm shot up and clamped his neck like a vise.

"You're coming with me," Manning mumbled.

"*What the fuck?*" Thompson tried to jerk away, but Manning pinned him against the door. His feet skidded uselessly along the wet pavement. Searing pain shot up his leg as he felt his right ankle snap.

As the BMW raced across Foxcroft Road, Thompson clawed at Manning's arm, trying to elbow him in the face. But even drunk, Manning's strength outpowered his. His right hand groped for his jacket pocket—the Luger—but he was trapped too close to the car to squeeze his hand inside the pocket. Terror clutched Thompson's chest; icy fingers seemed to squeeze his heart. *Jesus Christ. This couldn't be happening!*

The car smacked through the brush at the edge of the road. Briars grabbed Thompson's legs, ripping through his pants and tearing into his skin. A tree trunk slammed into his thigh, tossing his lower body alongside the car like a rag doll. Warmth flooded his leg as his bladder released.

Out of the corner of his eye he caught a glimpse of swirling water, and he felt a flicker of hope. The creek would be his salvation! Once the car plunged into the water, Manning would release his grip. Yes! Manning would let go and he'd be free. Somehow, he'd find the strength to get back to the bank. But not before he made sure Manning didn't escape from the car. He'd knock Manning out again, do something—anything—to ensure he and Margaret met their death in a watery grave. Adrenaline pumped through Thompson's veins as the car plunged down the bank toward the angry dark water.

*A*bigale and Doug rode in the back of Lieutenant Mallory's sheriff's car. Smitty had gone in the kennel truck with the deputy to search the outbuildings at Dartmoor Glebe. She'd talked him into taking Duchess along.

They had just crossed over the bridge on Foxcroft Road and were slowly cruising along the banks of Goose Creek. The graying light that had guided them when they started out had been swallowed by darkness. Abigale's eyes now tracked the beam of the searchlight from Mallory's car as it sliced through the night.

"Stop! What's that?" She perched forward on the vinyl seat and waved her hand to the left. "Back. And over a little."

Mallory stomped on the brake and swung the light as she'd directed. The ugly root-ball of a fallen tree glared at them in the spotlight. Abigale sighed and flopped back against the seat, fighting a sense of hopelessness. They didn't even know what they were looking for. Manning's car? Uncle Richard's truck and trailer? She could tell by the objects that Mallory was shining the light at that he was looking for something smaller. *Bodies.* But she refused to think about that.

Mallory shined the light at the rising waters. "The creek's almost over its banks. We're going to have to turn back soon. This road will be underwater before too long."

Abigale shot a look at Doug. *No,* she mouthed. No way was she turning around. She'd get out and walk if she had to. The glow from the front dash caught Doug's face and he nodded, indicating that he agreed with her.

"We're almost past the low part of the road," Doug said to Mallory. "It doesn't make sense to turn back. Let's keep following the creek. If the road floods so we can't get back over the bridge we can turn up Snake Hill Road and go around that way."

"All right," Mallory agreed. "I'll go as far as Snake Hill. Foxcroft Road angles away from Goose Creek at that point anyway."

They continued the slow trek along the creek, stopping occasionally to focus the light on something that caught their attention. But nothing panned out. Abigale was beginning to wonder whether she had misinterpreted what Manning had tried to tell her.

Mallory threw a glance over his shoulder. "We're almost to Snake Hill Road."

Abigale twisted sideways in her seat and pressed her forehead to the glass. Mallory's searchlight roamed slowly along the bank, sweeping across the debris tumbling downstream in the turbulent water.

"That's it," Mallory said, braking to a stop.

"*Wait.*" Abigale tapped on the glass. "Just . . . please . . . shine the light along here."

Mallory let out a sigh. "Goose Creek angled off back there." He danced the light across the dark water to the right front of the car. "This here is just a tributary that runs into the creek."

"I know. Technically it's not Goose Creek. But . . . still. Please."

Mallory and Doug exchanged a glance. Mallory shined the light at the water, rotating it slowly in an arc. *Nothing.*

The dark seemed to fold in around Abigale and she slumped back against the seat. Mallory drew the beam back toward the road.

"Wait, what was that!" she said, gripping the armrest.

A glint of red winked through a tangle of brush just above the water's edge. Mallory must have seen it, too. He shot the light down the bank.

Abigale tapped against the glass. "Look! It's a car's taillight."

Mallory whipped the steering wheel around and nosed the car onto the bank so the headlights shined down toward the river. He jammed the gearshift into park and grabbed the searchlight off the dash. Abigale groped frantically for a door handle until she realized the rear doors weren't operable from inside the sheriff's car. As Mallory pulled on the outside handle, she shoved the door open and shot out of the backseat. She heard Doug scramble out behind her.

"Hold on," Mallory said, grabbing her arm as she pushed past him. "Let me go first."

Abigale twisted out of his grasp. The wind whipped through the trees and she leaned into it as a strong gust socked her in the chest, pelting her with rain.

She fought her way through the brambles toward the embankment, ducking wet branches that slapped her face. Mallory and Doug crashed through the brush behind her.

The searchlight cast a shadowy path that flickered between the trees, shimmying across the dense undergrowth. Abigale felt elation and fear collide as the beam of light rested on Manning's battered BMW. The car looked as if it was suspended mid-roll—overturned onto the driver's side, halfway on its roof—wedged against a tree a few yards above the raging water. The tree trunk was all that prevented it from flipping over and plunging into the swollen creek. Abigale raced down the bank, grabbing at branches and tree trunks to steady herself.

"Stay back!" Mallory shouted as she neared the car. "I don't like the way that thing's leaning. It looks like it could go at any minute."

Abigale glanced at him over her shoulder as her feet struck something with a muffled thwack, pitching her to her knees. She flung both arms forward to keep from sprawling flat on her face. Her palms smacked against the tough fabric of a waxed rain jacket. "Shine the light down here," she cried, rocking back on her heels.

Mallory and Doug caught up with her, bathing the bank in the harsh beam of the searchlight. *Oh God.* Bile rose in Abigale's throat as the light caught Thompson's face. His mouth was open as if frozen in a look of disbelief, his head bent sideways at a nauseating angle. She jerked her hands back.

Doug dropped beside Abigale and gripped her shoulders, pulling her back from the body. But her eyes lingered. She'd seen dead people before— soldiers—and had struggled with witnessing loss of life. Emilio had never been able to understand how even the death of the insurgents had pulled at her heartstrings. But looking at Thompson's battered face, his terror-stricken expression, Abigale felt nothing more than a hollow rush of satisfaction. She hoped he'd suffered some of the pain he'd inflicted on others.

Mallory crouched down and pressed his fingers to Thompson's throat. A futile gesture, but still, Abigale waited for his nod of confirmation.

"Come on," Doug said, tugging her to her feet.

The three of them hopped over Thompson and tramped through the thicket to the car. As the searchlight flashed against the rain-streaked glass, the back of a weathered hand tapped against the window.

"It's Margaret," Abigale said, dancing on her tiptoes and craning to see inside. "Can we get the door open?"

"I don't think we can risk it, not with the way the car's tilted," Doug said, shouting to be heard as the wind whipped at his words. He looked at Mallory. "I think our best bet is to break the glass."

"I agree," Mallory said, handing the searchlight to Doug. He pulled a flashlight off his belt and shined it into the car. "It's Lieutenant Mallory, Mrs. Southwell. I'm going to break the glass. Try to cover your face."

Mallory hammered the butt end of the flashlight against the passenger window. Glass showered down into the car. The BMW rocked as someone moved inside and the roof screeched against the tree trunk. Abigale sucked in a breath, then released it slowly as the car held its position. If the car slid another foot down the bank, it would clear the tree and topple onto its roof like a domino.

Mallory flipped the light around and directed the beam into the car. "Are you injured, Mrs. Southwell?"

"I'm all right." Margaret's voice was weak. "I hurt my hip, is all. But I don't know about Manning. He keeps slipping in and out of consciousness."

"Okay. Just hold on. We're going to get you both out of there." Mallory backed away from the window. He squinted against the blowing rain at Abigale and Doug. "Do we risk trying to lift her out through the window?"

"What's the alternative?" Doug asked.

Mallory shook his head. "I'm not sure we have one. Time's not on our side."

"We can't wait for help. We have to get them out of there," Abigale said.

"I agree." Doug aimed the searchlight at the creek. "The car's hanging by a thread and the water's rising fast."

Doug handed the searchlight to Abigale and she aimed it at the car door as she backed out of their way. He leaned over the window. "It's Doug, Margaret. Lieutenant Mallory and I are going to lift you out through the window. Can you reach your seat belt buckle?"

"I think so," Margaret said.

"Good. Don't unbuckle it yet. Just let me know if you can reach it," Doug said.

Abigale's stomach clenched as the car groaned against the tree trunk. Doug jumped back and shouted, "Try to move around as little as possible, Margaret. The car's in a precarious position. We don't want to rock it more than we have to."

"All right." After a moment Margaret said, "Yes, I can reach it."

Doug said, "Okay, good. I'll tell you when to press the release button. Let us get a good hold on you first."

"Okay," Margaret replied.

Mallory moved closer to Doug. Both men spread their legs, searching for a good foothold, before reaching into the car.

"Can you reach an arm up around my neck?" Doug asked.

Abigale saw Margaret's right arm snake through the window opening and grip the back of Doug's neck.

"Ready?" Doug asked Mallory.

Mallory gave him a quick nod.

Doug said, "All right, Margaret. Release the seat belt buckle."

Abigale saw both men shift their weight as they caught Margaret. Her other hand shot around Doug's neck.

"Okay, hold on tight, all right?" Doug said. "We're going to try to move you as smoothly as possible. If you need us to stop just say so."

"Don't imagine it can hurt any more than when Champ bucked me off and broke my pelvis," Margaret said in a shaky voice. "Just go on and do what you need to do."

Abigale's fingernails bit into the palms of her hands. *Dear, God, please don't let the car slide toward the creek.*

"Okay," Doug said. "On three. One . . . two . . . three."

Both men pulled back and Abigale heard Margaret cry out in pain.

"Almost there," Doug said, scrambling to get an arm around Margaret's waist as her upper body cleared the window.

The glare of the searchlight bounced off Margaret's pale face. Her lips were caked with blood and an angry purple lump swelled across her forehead. Bits of glass from the broken window glistened in her hair. Abigale steadied the beam to guide Doug and Mallory as they slid Margaret free and lowered her to the ground several yards up the bank. Doug whipped off his rain jacket and spread it over her.

"We're going back for Manning," Doug said, trading Mallory's flashlight for the searchlight Abigale was holding.

Abigale tucked the flashlight under her arm and crouched next to Margaret. She knew it was up to Doug and Mallory to get Manning out. She wasn't tall enough to see inside the car, let alone lift Manning. Still . . .

She shot a glance over her shoulder as she reached for Margaret's hand. Doug was leaning into the car while Mallory shined the searchlight inside.

"They'll get Manning out," Abigale said, with more conviction than she felt.

"Thompson wanted to drown us in the creek," Margaret said hoarsely. "He forced whisky down Manning's throat, planned to make it look like a drunk-driving accident." She squeezed Abigale's hand. "Go to him, Abigale. Go help them get Manning out of the car."

Abigale twisted around. Doug was no longer leaning in the car. Both men just stared grimly at the vehicle, as if assessing what to do. Mallory said something and Doug shook his head.

Margaret waved her away. "Go."

Abigale jumped up and ran back to the car. "What's going on?"

"I can't reach Manning," Doug said. "And I'm afraid if I put more weight against the car to lean further inside I'll cause it to slide down the bank."

"Is Manning conscious?" Abigale asked.

"Not really. He's stirring, but he's not saying anything coherent."

Abigale stared at the car. "So what are we going to do?"

"I'll radio for help," Mallory said.

"We can't just stand here and wait for help to arrive," Abigale said. She jabbed an arm at the creek. "The water's rising too fast. You said so yourself. We're running out of time."

"Abigale's right," Doug said. "Who knows how long it will take for help to arrive, or whether they can even reach us with the flooded roads."

"At this point, it's our only option," Mallory said.

Rage ripped through Abigale. She would not stand by and do nothing. "No, it's not."

Mallory stared at her, his jaw thrust forward stubbornly. "What do you suggest?"

"I weigh less than either of you," she said. "Lower me into the car."

"What good would that do?" Mallory asked.

"I can see if he's injured. Unbuckle his seat belt so you can pull him out."

Mallory shook his head. "I can't risk letting a civilian put herself in danger."

"But you'll risk letting Manning drown inside the car?" Abigale shot back.

Doug put a calming hand on her arm. "Let's give it a try," he said to Mallory. "If the car starts to slide, we'll pull her back out."

Mallory regarded them through narrowed eyes. He blew out a loud sigh.

"All right. I don't like it, but I'll go along with it."

They boosted Abigale through the passenger window. She tensed with each movement, fearing the car's downward shift as they eased her into the cramped space. She heard Doug say something, but the rain hammering against the roof made it impossible to decipher.

"That's far enough," she called over her shoulder. The forward motion stopped, but Doug and Mallory each clamped an iron grip on her legs.

Manning's eyes were closed, but he winced and muttered something as the searchlight hit him square in the face. A gash beneath his ear oozed blood down his neck. An egg-sized knot on his left cheek swelled into a bluish halo beneath his left eye. The driver's window was open, and his left shoulder and the side of his head were smeared with mud.

Abigale gently shook his shoulder. "*Manning.* Can you hear me?"

His right eye opened to a slit and he squinted at her. "Abby?"

Abigale's eyes filled. She smiled at him. "Yes, it's me. Doug and Mallory are with me. We're going to get you out of here."

Manning shifted in the seat and the car pitched to the left.

"Watch it!" Doug yelled.

"Hold still, Manning," Abigale warned.

He opened both eyes, then flung his arm across his face to block out the searchlight. "What the—"

Abigale gripped his shoulder. "Manning, listen to me. The slightest movement could send the car down the bank into the creek. We're going to get you out, but you need to move very slowly, okay?"

He nodded, but Abigale saw confusion cloud his gaze. She wondered whether he had a concussion or if it was from the alcohol. Either way, she wasn't sure he'd be able to lend much help. "I'm going to unbuckle your seat belt. You need to brace yourself so you don't drop when it releases."

A moan hissed through Manning's lips as he groped for the steering wheel with his right arm. He drew in a sharp breath and flexed his hand.

"That's your broken arm. Use your left hand," Abigale said.

Manning's right arm fell back to his lap. He fumbled along the open window with his left hand and gripped the door jamb.

"Okay, good." She wiggled her fingers between the seat and the middle console and found the seat belt latch. "Here goes."

Abigale pressed the mechanism, but the catch didn't release. She punched the button again. It didn't budge. Frustration gripped her chest as she jabbed at it furiously. *Damn it!*

"What's the matter?" Manning asked.

"I can't get the seat belt unbuckled. The release mechanism feels like it's jammed."

Manning glanced down at the seat belt. His eyes seemed clearer, more focused. "Cut it. There's a Swiss Army knife in the glove box."

Abigale searched beneath the deflated air bag for the latch and popped open the door to the glove compartment. She fumbled through loose papers and some CD cases, until her fingers closed around the cold steel of the knife. She flipped open the blade and held it against the shoulder-harness portion of the seat belt near the buckle, angled away from Manning.

"Ready?" Abigale asked.

Manning's eyes leveled at her. She saw beads of sweat on his upper lip. He nodded.

The blade sliced through the webbing with a whoosh, and Abigale jerked the blade back as the belt released its hold on Manning. He dropped down, thudding against the door frame near the ceiling. Abigale held her breath as the car shuddered beneath her. Metal screeched as the roof scraped along the tree trunk, and Abigale felt strong hands yank her away.

"No!" she screamed, grabbing at the door as they pulled her from the car.

Doug wrapped his arms around her and jerked her away from the car as it broke free from the tree and smashed onto its roof.

"Oh, my God. *Do something!*" Abigale shrieked as the BMW shot down the bank. It plunged into the creek like the log plume ride at an amusement park. She thrashed against Doug's grasp. "Let me go! We have to get him out of the car."

Doug tightened his hold on her. "We'll never reach the car in time. It would be suicide to go after him."

Mallory swung the searchlight at the water, and Abigale's body went numb as she watched the swift current suck the car toward the center of the creek. It seemed to happen in slow motion, yet it couldn't have taken more than a matter of seconds before the car was swept downstream, its rear wheels bobbing in the swirling water.

"I'm sorry," Doug murmured, letting her slip out of his arms.

Abigale clutched her arms to her chest, hot tears pouring down her rain-streaked cheeks. Her vision tunneled around the BMW until it vanished from sight and Mallory pulled the light away. She felt paralyzed for a moment, trapped in her own skin. The drum of rain on soggy earth, the wind whistling through naked trees, was suddenly hushed, as if someone had lowered the volume. She half stumbled, half slid down the bank to the water's edge.

"Abigale!" Doug shouted.

She ignored him, crouching down on a rock outcropping that jutted into the creek. Waves splashed across the jagged stone and lapped at her feet. A powerful force seemed to tug her toward the restless water—to beckon her into the dark abyss. It would be so easy to slip into the current, let it carry her away. *Take her to Manning.* Abigale heard branches snap as someone tramped down the bank behind her. Probably Doug. She didn't turn around.

Mallory's searchlight sliced through the lashing rain, casting long shadows that danced across the water's surface. Tree limbs and debris tumbled past her, caught up in the unforgiving current. Her eyes followed a gnarly branch twirling dizzily downstream until it disappeared beyond the reach of the searchlight, only to be replaced by another dark shape that bobbed in the water. She watched, mesmerized, waiting for it, too, to vanish from sight. But it didn't. In fact, it appeared to be moving sideways. Toward the bank.

"Shine the light over there!" she shouted, jumping to her feet.

Mallory directed the light toward where she was pointing. *Where did it go?* Abigale held her breath as she squinted at the water.

"There!" she cried.

Her heart felt as though it would jump out of her chest as she saw Manning's head skim the surface. He gulped in a mouthful of air as his arm sliced through the water, pulling him toward the bank.

Abigale's boots skidded across wet rock as she leapt from the outcropping into the thicket along the bank. Swampy mud sucked at her feet, and she swore as she dropped to one knee, arms flailing for purchase among the slippery foliage.

Doug gripped her hand, hauling her to her feet. Together they shoved through brambles along the edge of Goose Creek, dodging trees now rooted underwater. The spotlight skittered erratically around Manning as Mallory plowed down the bank after them, and fear jolted through Abigale each time Manning disappeared from the beam's reach.

Time fell away as Abigale plunged into the creek beside Doug, vaguely aware of the bone-numbing cold, the current grabbing at her legs. Water slapped her face, blinding her, and she lost sight of Manning. She groped for him in the swirling water, hope slipping through her fingers as swiftly as the tide. Panic mushroomed in her chest as she pawed the inky depths . . . and then—a wisp of fabric brushed her hand, powerful legs churned the water beside her. Manning's head shot up above the water's surface and joy burst through Abigale as his eyes shone at her in the spotlight. Manning seemed to almost manage a smile as she and Doug each grabbed him under one of his arms and the three of them kicked toward shore.

EPILOGUE

*M*anning groaned with frustration as his arm got hung up in the sleeve of his scarlet coat. "Goddamned cast."

"Uh-uh-uh, don't go getting any ideas," Abigale said, helping him ease the sleeve over the cast. "You promised you'd keep this one on until the *doctor* takes it off." She buttoned the front of his coat and straightened the knot on his stock tie, smiling as she rose on her tiptoes and pressed her lips to his. "You look very nice this morning, Master."

Manning wrapped his arms around her. "Say that again."

"You look very nice this morning?"

He grinned. "No. *Master.* I love to hear you call me that."

Abigale pushed playfully at his chest. "Forget I said anything." She slipped out of his embrace and climbed through the people door at the front of the two-horse trailer. Braveheart regarded her with big, gentle eyes as he grabbed another mouthful of hay from the hay net. "Hi, buddy. Ready to go hunting?" she said, unclipping the trailer tie from his halter. He snorted softly, rubbing his head against her shoulder. Abigale sucked in a lungful of air, savoring the fresh scent of hay and shavings. She stood and watched the big gray for a moment. Was there a more peaceful sound in the world than that of a horse munching hay? Any place she'd rather be?

She thought of the unopened FedEx envelope from Max, her editor at Reuters, on Manning's kitchen counter. Part of her wanted to rip it open, see where her next assignment would be. But she had held back, despite Manning's urging. Whether she was more afraid that she'd want to go or that she wouldn't, she wasn't sure. For today, she'd let it sit. Max had said he'd give her time.

Abigale heard Manning talking to Dario outside the trailer, explaining that the hunt would last about three hours, that Dario could relax in the truck until the riders returned. There had really been no need for Dario to accompany them to the hunt—Manning would rather drive the rig and take care of his own horse than have a groom do it—but Manning thought seeing what happened at a hunt would help Dario adapt to his new job. Dario was a quick learner and even Michael seemed pleased with his performance so far, with none of the complaining he'd had with Larry.

Poor Larry. No one had given him much credit in the brains department, yet he'd been the first person to figure out who'd tampered with Uncle Richard's saddle. Tragically, it had cost him his life. Margaret and Manning had established a college scholarship in Larry's name at his former high school, so at least his memory would live on. Larry's mother wanted the scholarship to be based on character—courage—rather than academics, and was already working with the guidance department to identify potential recipients.

A shudder ran through Abigale as she thought of Thompson, rashly killing anyone who got in his way. All for what, money? There was no question Thompson had been in serious financial trouble. They'd found out he'd been fired from Knightly & Knightly for engaging in illicit online gambling using the firm's computer. Yet for over two months Thompson had kept up a charade among his foxhunting friends—pretending to go to work each day, even going so far as to complain at various times about being swamped at the office and unable to go hunting.

They'd learned Thompson owed almost ten thousand dollars to the firm for unauthorized dining and entertainment expenditures he'd run through his boss's expense account. After Thompson had been fired, his boss—Donald, the man she'd spoken to on the phone—had discovered the scam and threatened to press charges. But Thompson had fabricated a story about his ailing mother's mounting medical bills, and Donald had agreed not to blow the whistle if Thompson paid the firm back. Donald had been outraged to hear they'd tracked down Thompson's mother—who was in robust health— in Ohio, and discovered she hadn't had contact with Thompson since she'd cut him off financially three years ago because he refused to get help for his cocaine habit.

It turned out Thompson wasn't a partner at Knightly & Knightly, as he'd claimed to be; he was Donald's administrative assistant. And the trip to Iraq had been a boondoggle on which Donald had let Thompson tag along.

Donald told them in hindsight he realized he should have seen a red flag at that time, that Thompson had been inexplicably fascinated by the various ways a company could cook its books.

"Hey, are you just going to stand there and watch Braveheart eat, or are you going to put his bridle on?" Manning asked, stepping through the door on the opposite side of the trailer.

She smiled, picking a piece of hay out of Braveheart's forelock. "I guess we'll go hunting."

Manning bridled Henry and backed him off the trailer, then released the butt bar so she could unload Braveheart. He looped Henry's reins over his arm and gave her a leg up on Braveheart, checked her girth, and adjusted her foot in the stirrup. "You're good to go," he said, patting her knee.

"Here comes your mother," Abigale said as Manning swung into the saddle. She nodded toward Margaret, who jabbed the ground with her walking stick as she picked her way across the field toward them.

"Good morning, Mother."

"It'd be a lot better morning if I could get rid of this goddamned thing," Margaret said, waving the stick in the air.

Manning smiled. "It won't be long."

Margaret grumbled something unintelligible, then reached up and patted Henry on the neck. "I've been roped into hauling around some city-folk friends of Doug's who want to hilltop by car. Any help you can give me on which direction you'll be hunting today?"

"What do you think? Should we draw toward Hickory Vale or Chadwick Hall?" Manning asked.

"It's up to you," Margaret said.

Manning said, "I know, but I'd like your advice."

"Well, then, I'd probably say cast hounds toward Chadwick Hall. It might still be a little boggy down in the bottom of Hickory Vale."

"That was my thinking as well," Manning replied, nodding.

Margaret turned away, but Abigale caught the pleased look in her eye.

"What about you, Abigale, are you whipping today?" Margaret asked.

"Yes. Fingers crossed I don't get lost," Abigale said with a smile.

"I don't think there's much chance of that. If you do, you can always ask for help on the walkie-talkie, although I still don't agree with us using those." Margaret shook her head, her lips pressed together with displeasure. "I know Smitty says we need the radios in case hounds run toward the road, but if you ask me, we just need to work a little harder to keep the hounds under control. Folks are losing all their hunting knowledge, that's what's happening. Half the whips out there these days don't even bother to think anymore, they just wait for the huntsman to tell them where hounds are running. I hope you won't fall into those lazy ways, Abigale."

"I'll try my hardest not to."

"I know you will. You learned how to hunt from the best, and I know you'll make Richard proud." The lines around Margaret's mouth softened into a smile as she looked at Manning. "You both will."

GLOSSARY

BILLET STRAPS: Leather straps underneath a saddle to which the girth is buckled.

BUCKLE GUARD: Leather flap that protects the underside of the saddle from being worn away by the buckles of the girth.

BUTT BAR: Restraining device at the rear of a trailer stall that prevents a horse from backing out.

CANTLE: Raised rear part of a saddle.

CHECK: Interruption of the chase during a foxhunt.

COLIC: Abdominal pain characterized by pawing, looking at the flank, and rolling. Mild colic can often be resolved with nonsurgical veterinary treatment, but acute colic can be life-threatening and often requires surgery, as in the case of a colon torsion—twisted gut—whereby a portion of the intestine twists, causing a blockage.

COLORS: Distinctive color or colors—unique to a particular hunt—typically worn on the collar of a hunt coat. Wearing colors is a privilege awarded at the master's sole discretion, generally to members who have hunted regularly for several years, shown exemplary skill and sportsmanship, and contributed to the success of hunt activities.

COOP: Wood panel jump, fashioned after a chicken coop.

COVERT: Area of woods or brush where a fox might be found. Pronounced "cover."

CUBBING: Informal foxhunting in early fall, used for training and conditioning young hounds and horses. Cubbing attire—"ratcatcher"— is less formal than foxhunting: tweed or wool coat in a muted color, earth-tone breeches, brown or black leather boots, light-colored shirt and stock tie or man's tie, black riding helmet, and brown leather or string gloves.

DRAW: Search for a fox in a certain area.

FIELD: Group of people foxhunting, excluding the master and hunt staff.

FOXHUNT: Hunt with hounds, followed by riders on horseback, after a fox. Hunting attire is formal: black wool melton coat, buff or rust breeches, black leather boots, white shirt, canary or tattersall vest, white stock tie secured with a horizontal gold stock pin, black riding helmet, and brown leather or string gloves. Male hunt members who have earned colors, and lady masters/hunt staff, may wear a scarlet coat, white breeches, and black leather boots with brown tops.

FULL CRY: Sound of a pack of hounds in hot pursuit.

GONE AWAY: Call on the horn when the fox has left the covert and the hunt is on.

GIRTH: Strap fastened around a horse's belly to hold the saddle in place.

HACK: Leisurely ride, usually cross-country.

HAND: Measurement of a horse, from the ground to the highest point of the horse's withers. One hand equals four inches.

HILLTOPPERS: Group of foxhunters who generally go at a slower pace than the rest of the field and usually do not jump. Also referred to as the "second field."

HOUNDS: Foxhounds. They are never called dogs.

HUNT BREAKFAST: Meal served after the hunt. Usually hosted by the property owner where the hunt meet is held.

HUNTSMAN: Person who controls the hounds.

LONGE: To work a horse in a large circle at the end of a long line.

MASTER: MFH (Master of Foxhounds)—the person in command of the hunt.

MEET: Assembling of a foxhunt at a certain place.

NATIONAL FENCES: Portable hurdle fences that are moved from one racecourse to another.

OUTRIDER: Mounted official charged with catching loose horses and maintaining order on the racecourse.

OXER: Spread jump with at least two sets of jump standards.

RUN: Period during which the hounds are actively chasing the fox.

POINT-TO-POINT/STEEPLECHASE: Cross-country horse event consisting of races over hurdles, timber, and on the flat. Sanctioned steeplechase races often offer substantial purse money, but point-to-point races are referred to as the "pots and pans" circuit—very little money is offered; the prizes awarded are mostly silver trophies.

POMMEL: Raised front part of a saddle.

SCARLET: Red coat worn by certain select members of the hunt. Also referred to as a "pink" coat, after the British tailor, Mr. Pinque, who designed it.

SCARLET IF CONVENIENT: Phrase used on formal invitations indicating it is proper for gentlemen who have earned their hunt colors to wear scarlet tails/white tie to a black-tie event.

SCENT: Smell of the fox.

STIRRUP CUP: Drink served to mounted riders before the hunt.

STOCK TIE: Hunting necktie—white for formal foxhunting, plain or colored for cubbing—tied in a square knot or four fold, secured with a plain gold safety pin fastened horizontally.

TACK: Equipment used on a horse.

TALLYHO: Hunting cry when the fox is sighted.

TRI-COLOR: Horse show championship ribbon consisting of three colors— champion combines blue, red, and yellow streamers; reserve champion features red, yellow, and white.

VIEW: To see the fox.

WHIP: Short for "whipper-in." Person who helps the huntsman control the hounds.